DISPOSAL

DAVID EVANS

ABOUT THE AUTHOR

Born and brought up in and around Edinburgh, David Evans graduated from Manchester University and had a successful career as a professional in the construction industry before turning to crime … fiction that is and writing thereof.

In 2013, his novel, *TORMENT*, was shortlisted for the CWA Debut Dagger Award. His Internationally Best Selling Wakefield Series was published in 2016, consisting of *TROPHIES, TORMENT* and *TALISMAN*, so far. A fourth in the series will follow.

DISPOSAL is the first of a planned series set in the Tendring area of North Essex. A second book is also underway.

Find out more by visiting David's website at
www.davidevanswriter.co.uk
or follow him on Facebook at
www.facebook.com/davidevanswriter
and Twitter @DavidEwriter

ACKNOWLEDGMENTS

I have been privileged to meet some amazing people, without whose help, encouragement, support and above all friendship got me through some occasions when it would have been easier to walk away and do something else with my time.

First and foremost, I have to say a huge thank-you to Sally Spedding who was the first in the publishing industry to take my writing seriously. I owe her a great debt for all her continued support and encouragement.

I am fortunate to have a great little band of writing friends and I would like to thank Sarah Wagstaff, Jan Beresford, Julie-Ann Corrigan, Manda Hughes, Lorraine Cannell, Glynis Smy and Peter Best, all of whom are talented writers in their own right and have made some significant contributions.

I am also fortunate to have the input of Colin Steele, ex-Detective Superintendent of the Essex Murder Squad, Tom Harper, ex-Principal Crime Scene Coordinator for the Kent & Essex Serious Crime Directorate and Steve Eastwood, ex-DCI of the City of London Police. All have given their time and guidance generously. Any residual errors here, are all mine.

IN MEMORY OF
·D. E. L. EVANS
1915 - 1971

DISPOSAL

To MADGE

Thanks for your support!

Enjoy

Dave Evans

x

David Evans

DAVID EVANS

1

05:50hrs. on a fine August morning. It promised to be another blistering sticky day. This was the longest, hottest, driest spell in living memory and the weather forecast was extremely favourable for a trip that had been carried out several times before. All pre-flight checks had been performed; the delivery had been placed in the passenger seat and everything was good to go. Switches were moved, lights came on and a hand reached out and turned the key to start the aircraft's single engine.

At walking pace, the plane pulled forward onto the grass runway, turned and made its way to the far end. It stopped for a moment as the pilot checked the cargo in the seat beside him. This was definitely the last time, he'd made up his mind on that. The aircraft then turned through 180 degrees, and the full length of the flat scorched airstrip lay ahead.

The sun was making its appearance over the North Sea horizon as the engine was given full throttle. Brakes released then the acceleration kicked in. Down the grass the plane picked up speed bouncing along the baked dry ground, the pilot wincing at the vibrations shuddering through him. As it got to the recognised point, the control was pulled back and the aircraft lifted off. This was always the exhilarating part.

Seconds later, the engine noise suddenly changed. Coughs and splutters as it misfired. The pilot frantically switched his attention from one instrument to another. Stomach churning, he desperately adjusted various controls. Struggling to gain any height, the plane faltered.

* * *

"So how long have you got to go now, Skip?" PC Sam Woodbridge poured out the last of the tea from the flask into his sergeant's cup.

"I'll probably go at the end of the year." Cyril Claydon took his drink and dunked a Rich Tea biscuit; a fine art, just long enough for it to go soft without disintegrating. He ate it then rubbed the crumbs from his thin moustache.

Woodbridge gazed out of the car window and off across the sea wall. The dawning sun cast its first fingers of the new day's light over the calm sea. "I can't imagine being in the job that long," he said. "Twenty-five years. It's a lifetime."

"It is for you, you're only twenty-five." Cyril took out his pipe and began to fill it with his favourite tobacco. Now he'd said it out loud, approaching fifty, retirement wasn't a prospect he was particularly looking forward to.

The arrest of a burglar attempting to break in to a bungalow in Holland-on-Sea was the sum total of the night's action. That was five hours ago. Woodbridge, at over six feet tall and Cyril at five feet ten, were now sitting incongruously in their Austin Mini panda car in shirt sleeves, their night shift on patrol in Clacton on the Essex coast nearly over.

"How long d'you reckon this'll go on for?" Woodbridge mused, wiping his sweating brow with a handkerchief.

"I don't ever remember a hot spell like this. It's been nearly three months."

"Must be over seventy now and it's only ..." Woodbridge turned his wrist to look at his watch, "... ten to six."

"Probably go down in history," Cyril said. "The long hot summer of '76."

They fell silent for a short while.

"I don't know if I'll be able to sleep in this." Woodbridge had his eyes shut, head back. "I'm looking forward to the full English Mum'll have for me though."

"Young ones today," Cyril responded, "you don't know you're born." A smile on his face, he wound down the window of the car and lit his pipe. Smoke belched out into the humid morning air. When his shift finished, he'd take Charlie out for a walk. The old Labrador wasn't as lively these days. Then he'd probably sleep in the chair for an hour or two before popping down to his allotment. As he puffed he thought how this combination of the heat and hosepipe bans had made it difficult to keep his crops healthy. He'd have to use buckets and watering cans again.

His thought pattern was suddenly disturbed by the noise of an aircraft engine firing up. Both men automatically turned to look inland. There was nothing to be seen. The airstrip lay on a slight rise behind the hedgerow next to their parked car.

It was Cyril's turn to glance at his watch. "Seems a bit early," he muttered to himself and puffed another ball of smoke through the window.

He could hear the revs maximise and grow louder as the small plane approached. The sounds helped him imagine lift off several hundred yards beyond the hedge. War-time memories came flooding back. A mechanic on the squadron's ground crew, faces flickered through his mind; most long gone, many never returning from bombing missions over Germany.

Moments before the plane appeared over the top of the scrub behind the hedge, the engine tone changed. Cyril looked sharply at his colleague. One thing he could recognise was an engine in trouble; and this one was struggling. It spluttered and spat, fighting to fire properly. By the time it cleared the hedge it was only about ten feet above the road and some fifty yards in front of them. He could see the pilot wrestling with the controls as more height was lost. The wheels were ripped from the fuselage by the concrete sea wall and it disappeared from view. A moment later, a plume of water rose up then, almost in slow motion, fell back down like some ornamental fountain.

Cyril reacted first, opening his door. "Radio in, Sam," he said, "Tell 'em we have a major incident down here. We'll need the Fire Brigade as well as an ambulance."

As his constable did as asked, Cyril ran over the road and jumped up onto the wall. He paused for a second and took in the scene. A lone furrow had been ploughed through the sand to the water's edge about fifty yards away. The sea, at almost full tide, was disturbingly calm, the waves lapping gently onto the shore. Some thirty yards beyond, in about three feet of water, the single engine light aircraft stood, looking fairly intact, the right way up, steam rising from the engine.

Jumping down the six foot drop off the wall, Cyril rolled onto the sand as if he'd just been parachuted. Old training still holding him in good stead. Scrambling quickly to his feet, he ran into the water and waded out to the wreckage. As he got to the pilot's side, a yell from the beach made him turn round. Sam had followed him but looked as though he'd turned his ankle jumping down. He limped towards him.

Wrenching open the door, Cyril pulled the pilot back off the windscreen. His face was bloodied, eyes open but sightless.

"Sam! Here, quick, this side," Cyril called to his colleague as he struggled to free the pilot from his seat. He had the body half out when Woodbridge joined in the effort.

"Is he dead?" Woodbridge asked.

Cyril ignored the question. "Let's get him onto the sand first."

With Sam's hands under the armpits and Cyril holding onto the legs, they made their way slowly back to the shoreline. Clear of the tide they placed the man on the sand on his back. Cyril knelt down and felt at the neck for a pulse. Unnecessary, he thought as the open eyes told him all he needed to know. He shook his head at Sam and swept his hand over the pilot's face to close his eyes.

"Stay with him," he instructed, rising to his feet. "I'm just going back to look in there."

"But …" Sam looked puzzled but said no more as he watched his sergeant walk back into the sea on the other side of the craft.

Cyril waded around the wing and approached the passenger side. Something had caught his eye when he'd hauled the pilot out and he wanted another look. He opened the door and saw the large upright bundle, wrapped in black plastic, which had obviously been thrust forward off the seat on impact and was now leaning against the cockpit windscreen, half in the footwell. Standing in the doorway, he tugged the package backwards. The bottom was caught under the seat. As he tried to pull it free, his hand slipped and caught some of the wrapping, ripping it open a touch. He paused then looked closer at what had been exposed. The unmistakeable look and colour of dead flesh, part of an ankle possibly. He pulled away more of the plastic then was sure.

Definitely a human foot.

He stepped down into the water and looked over to where his constable was standing next to the pilot's body. "Sam!" he shouted. "Get on the radio and tell CID to get down here. We've got something for them!"

2

The noise was like a peal of church bells. He thought his head had only touched the pillow, but DI John, "Dick" for obvious reasons, Barton had been comatose for about four hours. He grunted and pulled the sheet over his head. The noise persisted and he turned towards the bedside cabinet. Eyes glued shut, his hand flailed around for the telephone. Knocking the handset from its cradle, it fell to the floor. Some remote voice spoke to him from down there. Finally, he rolled over to the side of the bed, picked up the phone and held it to his ear.

Freeing his tongue from the roof of his mouth, he spoke. "Barton."

"Dick, you need to get down to the seafront now." His Detective Chief Inspector's voice barked from the earpiece.

He struggled to force his eyelids open. "What bloody time is it?"

"Just gone six. The section by the airstrip. Meet Cyril Claydon down there. Might be an interesting one for you."

"Cyril? Winco? Why?" Barton was sitting up on the edge of the bed now. "Has someone given Danny a call; he'll love this almost as much as I do." Danny referred to DS Danny Flynn, Barton's bag man.

"You don't know?"

"Know what?"

"Danny's in hospital. Smashed his car up on the way home last night."

"But I thought …"

"I know," his boss interrupted, *"but they got called away."*

"Shit. How is he?"

6

"Haven't got the full details yet but it sounds serious. Now get your arse out there and I'll join you as soon as I can."

Barton wanted to ask more but the line had gone dead.

He looked down to see he was wearing yesterday's underpants ... and socks. They'd do for the time being. Scanning the bedroom he spotted trousers on the floor and a shirt thrown over the back of a chair. He couldn't remember how he'd got back in the early hours. The last thing he could recall was a disjointed conversation with a DI from Colchester as he was about to leave the pub. Rubbing his face, he stood. For a second, dizziness swam over him. He steadied himself and made his way to the bathroom.

Leaning over the toilet, arms on the wall, he peed. Turning to the sink, splashing water on his face, he paused to study himself in the mirror. He looked like shit, tousled brown hair, puffy eyes and stubble growing from a jowly jaw. Thirty-six years old and one divorce already. He didn't miss her. Well he missed the sex; but there again, he'd had a few good sessions since. A couple of bad encounters too but he was enjoying his return to bachelorhood. Or was he? A rented scruffy one-bedroomed flat in the middle of town, visits to the launderette, when he could be arsed. He splashed his face again, dried himself off and padded back to the bedroom to retrieve his trousers.

Opening the wardrobe, he took his last clean shirt off the hanger. Supposedly drip-dry eliminating the need for ironing, it looked creased. Still, with a loose tie and his jacket on, nobody would notice. And what do they expect on his salary?

On the ten minute drive along the seafront, windows down, Barton took it steady. He was sure he'd still be over the drink-drive limit. No sense in pushing things. Besides, what was so important? Probably some pissed up dosser washed up on the beach with the incoming tide.

Behind him, sirens grew louder as he passed the entrance to the Butlin's Holiday Camp. A few seconds later, his rear-view mirror was filled momentarily with the front end of a fire engine before it swept past him. Were they bound for the same incident? Five minutes later, he had the answer, drawing to a halt behind the vehicle. It was the second engine there and along with the ambulance and marked patrol cars, the flashing blue lights did nothing to ease his throbbing head.

* * *

Within ten minutes of the alert, an ambulance was on the scene. Cyril had returned to the pilot whilst Sam was securing the site with blue and white plastic police tape. One of the ambulance crew confirmed Cyril's opinion that there was nothing more to be done for the pilot but a doctor would have to certify death. A blanket from the patrol car gave some dignity to the deceased. The other body in the wreckage would have to wait for the Forensic team to arrive.

The first fire appliance appeared a few minutes later but the Station Officer who'd come with the crew quickly established the plane was stable and in no danger of catching fire. An oil tank would be sent to pump out the fuel tanks later.

Shortly afterwards, two cars with uniformed constables from the day shift arrived to take over, the sergeant instructing Cyril and Sam to return to the station, make their reports and go off duty. Just before they did, the Rover 2000 of DI Barton arrived behind the second fire engine.

He strutted over towards Cyril. "What have we got then?" he asked, pulling out a cigarette and lighting up.

Cyril gave his account, pointed to the pilot's body on the sand and told of the other remains wrapped in plastic in the passenger seat.

The news seemed to surprise the DI. "Do we know any identities?"

"Not yet," Cyril responded. About to lead the way onto the sea wall, he paused as another car pulled up.

DCI Martin Sanderson stepped out and buttoned up the jacket of his suit. Taller and slimmer than Barton at six feet three, with a full head of hair, sprinkled now with grey, he always seemed immaculately dressed.

Approaching the pair, he chuckled, "Christ, you look rough, Dick. Best not ask you to blow in a bag." Turning to Cyril he offered his hand which was shaken warmly. "Cyril, you witnessed this I gather?"

"That's correct, Sir. Saw him fly over the hedge about six feet off the ground, clip the wall and dive into the sea."

"Let's take a closer look."

Cyril guided them fifty yards along the sea wall to where some concrete steps made for an easier descent to the beach.

As they reached the pilot's body, Barton stood beside Cyril and repeated Sanderson's request. "Let's have a look then."

Cyril lifted the blanket and held it up, allowing both CID officers to see the face. He couldn't be absolutely sure, but he thought a glimmer of recognition passed over Barton's face. "Know him?" he asked.

Barton slowly shook his head. "Can't say I do." He looked to Sanderson. "You, boss?"

The DCI shook his head then turned to the wreckage in the sea. "What about out there?"

"Appears to be a corpse wrapped in black plastic. Forensics are on their way." Cyril waved a hand towards the body at their feet. "And the duty doctor should be here any time to certify death for this one."

"Sounds like everything is in place down here," Sanderson said to Barton. "Best get yourself up to the airfield and find out what you can about this."

Barton took a deep drag on his cigarette. "What about you, boss?"

"I've got a meet with the Super at eight." He pointed a thumb in the direction of the wreckage. "God knows how we absorb this now. We're up to our armpits as it is."

"What about Danny? How long is he going to be out the frame?"

"Not too sure yet, but I think we best forget about him returning for a while. In the meantime, see if you can get a clue as to who the pilot might be from up there." He nodded inland.

Barton said nothing, appearing deep in thought. He trod his cigarette butt into the sand and walked off.

"Looks like the duty doctor's here," Sanderson said, glancing over Cyril's shoulder. A man in a short-sleeved shirt carrying a medical bag made his way towards them over the sand. The DCI then looked down at Cyril's trousers. "Best get changed into some dry clothes. It's going to be a hot day again but we can't afford another officer off sick. Don't forget to write up your report before you knock off. I'll catch up with you later," Sanderson concluded.

Cyril shivered; not from his damp trousers, but with other, chilling images swimming through his mind. He rubbed his face to clear them, turned and walked away.

3

"Silly bastard was pissed as a fart though, wasn't he?"

"I dunno. Wasn't Traffic supposed to keep an eye on them? They usually do."

"Got a shout. Drunk driver on the A120, apparently."

"Some bastards never learn, do they? So what time did this happen?"

"About two this morning."

As he walked up the stairs at Clacton Police Station just after one that afternoon, Cyril could hear the conversation through the open door to the CID office. All available windows were open in a vain attempt to generate some through draft to keep the place cool. It also helped to clear the fug of stale cigarette smoke that permanently engulfed the offices.

DC Bill Walker looked up from his desk as Cyril entered. "Hello, Sarge, what brings you in here?" He loosened off the large knot to his wide tie even more. His shirt sleeves were already rolled above the elbow.

Subconsciously, Cyril moved a hand to his tie, making sure it was central. He'd been home, shaved and changed into a suit with a crisp white shirt and a dark blue tie. He always took a pride in his appearance, especially if he was representing the police force; another trait instilled from his war-time years. "DCI Sanderson's asked me to come in," he said. "You're struggling for staff, apparently."

"Always." DC Ben Miller stubbed out his cigarette in the overflowing ashtray. "Things not been helped by what happened to Danny last night."

"I heard." Cyril approached Miller's desk. "What news on his condition?"

"Broken pelvis and collapsed lung the most serious I heard," Miller responded.

"Did the Super say what you were going to help with?" Walker wondered.

"He wants me to report to DI Barton and work on the plane crash investigation."

Cyril caught the two of them exchange glances.

"Don't worry, I know what he's like." Cyril indicated the DI's office. "Not back yet, then?"

"Not seen him since last night's bash," Walker replied.

Cyril walked over to a window and looked down on the car parking area. "His car's there, though." He turned, leaned against the sill and folded his arms. "So where were you all?"

"The Ferry Boat Inn out at Point Clear."

Cyril shook his head. "Not changed in the last ten years."

"Same landlord, same décor, yeah."

"I meant you lot. Still getting pissed up and expecting Traffic to see you home safely."

Miller smiled. "Perk of the job, Sarge."

Outside on the staircase, footsteps sounded.

"You need a bag man, Dick," DCI Sanderson could be heard saying.

"But Winco? Come on," Barton replied.

Because of his wartime RAF history, some officers called Cyril 'Winco' behind his back, but never to his face. Walker and Miller looked down to their desks as Sanderson and Barton appeared in the doorway.

"Ah, Cyril, you're here already," Sanderson said.

"Sir."

Barton appeared behind without a hint of embarrassment, said nothing and strode past towards his office.

"I've got to call the Chief Super," Sanderson said, then added in a loud voice, "Now you two play nice." The DCI turned and left.

Cyril followed Barton into his office and shut the door.

"Can I just say," Cyril said, looking straight at the DI, "I'd rather you didn't make references like that about me. I find it disrespectful of those who served."

Barton took out a cigarette from the packet on his desk, sat down and lit up. "Look, Cyril." He blew smoke out emphatically. "Nothing personal, but sometimes you need to lighten up. Look at me, they christened me Dick, but I don't get upset with that. It's part of life."

"I'd just prefer it if you didn't. Okay?"

Barton leaned forward on his desk. "The alternative for me is to temporarily make up one of those two, Bill and Ben the Flowerpot Men out there, so I haven't got a lot of choice. Besides, you're qualified. You were in CID when I joined. So let's just make the most of this arrangement, shall we." He leaned back and gave a thin smile. "Sit down a minute."

The blood still pounded through Cyril's veins, but slowly he eased himself into the chair.

"Okay," Barton began, "what I found out when I visited the airfield this morning was that the pilot is believed to be a Jeremy Fletcher, Jem they called him."

Cyril frowned.

"Name mean anything to you?"

"I remember a little runt called Jem Fletcher. We nailed him for nicking cars a long while back. Maybe when I first joined CID. Must have been late 50s 1960, '61 perhaps?"

"Before my time." Barton conceded. "Apparently he does some mechanical work now; servicing, that sort of thing. Or did, I should say."

A knock on the door interrupted their conversation and Barton beckoned Bill Walker in.

"The Fingerprint Bureau just came back, guv," Walker said. "Confirmed fingerprints of the pilot are a match for a Jeremy Fletcher."

"Record for car crime about fifteen, twenty years ago." Barton stated.

Walker looked surprised. "How did …"

Barton nodded to Cyril.

"Well anyway," Walker continued, handing over a slip of paper. "Got an address for him in Great Bentley."

13

Barton took it as Walker left, almost colliding with DCI Sanderson.

Barton looked up. "We've got an ID on the pilot, Sir."

"Good." Sanderson closed the door and sat down in the spare chair. "Because you'll be leading this investigation. I've got to get more involved with those armed robberies with Colchester, and we're stretched to buggery here." He looked to Cyril. "You two okay working together then?"

"We'll be fine," Barton said.

"You said that without moving your lips, Cyril," Sanderson quipped. "But that's okay, because we don't have a choice." He rubbed his face with his hand. "You can have Walker and Miller out there too, but they'll also have to carry on working the cases they've already got, so just bear that in mind." His attention focused on Cyril again. "And find yourself a spare desk out there for now. Use DS Flynn's if you have to; just tidy his paperwork to one side first."

A shocked expression appeared on Barton's face and he was about to speak when Sanderson stopped him.

"Danny's not going to be back for a while, Cyril needs somewhere to base himself and it makes sense."

Cyril glanced at the DCI and thought the man appeared tired.

As Sanderson stood to leave, he added, "God, let's hope this doesn't grow into something more significant because we just don't have the resources."

"We'll try and wrap it up quickly," Barton said.

Sanderson opened the door then paused. "Excellent. In the meantime, call a briefing for six and I'll join you for that." He looked to Cyril. "And there's some paperwork with Cathy, one of the secretaries downstairs. Give it a bit and check she's finished what I asked her to do. If you need some admin backup I've told her to prioritise this enquiry." The door closed and he was gone.

"We don't need bloody secretaries," Barton said quietly to himself, "we need detectives."

"Fletcher?" Cyril thought out loud. "Surely it wasn't his plane? I can't imagine he'd be able to afford one."

"No, it belongs to Walter Yardley from Frinton."

"Has anybody spoken to him?"

Barton looked put out. "Spoke to him on the phone this morning. Seemed a bit shocked."

"He'll need to give a statement."

Barton held up a hand. "I'll deal with that. Apparently, he's a good friend of the Chief Super, so we won't want to bother him any more than we have to."

"Mr Viney, you mean?"

Barton nodded.

Cyril changed tack. "What about the CAA?"

Barton relaxed once more into his chair. "Eventually got hold of them this morning," he said. "Lazy buggers don't answer until after nine. They passed me on to their accident investigation bods. Somebody's supposed to be on their way down. We can't move the plane until they've seen it in situ. Apparently, they'd want to take it down to Farnborough but I told them bollocks, it's our case and it stays here until we've finished with it." The DI took another cigarette from the packet on his desk, lit up, took a deep draw and exhaled loudly. "Reminds me," he continued, "I need to get a garage organised to store the bloody thing for now." He picked up the telephone. "All right, check if uniform have found anything interesting and I'll see you downstairs in fifteen minutes. We can have a trip out into the country." Another drag. "You can drive," he said in dismissal, before speaking into the phone, "Hello …"

Cyril closed the DI's office door behind him and paused. Bill Walker was away from his desk and Ben Miller, cigarette in hand was engrossed, typing with one finger. He shook his head and wondered if they really knew their DI's opinion of them.

4

Great Bentley had the distinction of having one of the largest village greens in the country. Plenty of room for several football pitches and the local cricket club to fulfil their fixtures and a whole lot more area besides. But now, the green wasn't living up to its name. Various shades of yellows and browns betrayed the months of dry weather.

It took Cyril fifteen minutes to cover the distance from Clacton Police Station. The address they sought was in a side street near the railway station. The two-storey mid-terraced cottage had a section of scaffolding outside and a deeply tanned man, wearing only a pair of shorts, was at first floor level painting the front a pastel yellow.

Cyril drew the Rover to a halt and Barton stepped out. The man on the scaffold eyed them suspiciously. Cyril joined the DI by the gate.

"Can I help you ... officers?" the man said pointedly.

"This is the address of Jeremy Fletcher?" Barton asked.

"What of it?"

"And you are?"

"Adam Fletcher, Jem's brother. What are you trying to stitch him up with now?"

"Can you come down please?" Cyril joined in

Fletcher squinted at Cyril. "I know you, don't I? Didn't you stick Jem away last time?"

"A long time ago Mr Fletcher. And you and I have had words in the past too, but you were a youth then."

"Come down, we'd like a word." Barton instructed

"I've got this to finish."

Barton shook one of the uprights.

"Hey! You'll spill the bloody paint!"

"Just get your arse down here. We haven't got all bloody day." Barton sounded exasperated.

Cyril put a hand on Barton's arm as he was about to rattle the scaffolding again. "Please Mr Fletcher, this is important," he said.

Fletcher sighed, put his brush in a bucket of water and swiftly jumped down off the boards. "This had better be good," he said, opening the front door.

Five minutes later, Adam Fletcher's world collapsed. He sat on the settee nursing the mug of tea Cyril had made for him.

"But I don't understand," he said through tears. "He was so careful. He'd check everything before he got in a plane."

"We won't know any more until the aircraft investigation experts have examined it," Barton explained. "In the meantime, is there anyone else we need to inform?"

Fletcher put down his drink and wiped the back of his hands over his eyes. "Vicky, there's Vicky. Oh God, this'll kill her. I need to …"

"And Vicky is Mrs Fletcher?"

"Er, no. There is … I mean there was … Jem is divorced. She pissed off three years ago. Living up north somewhere, I think. No, Vicky's his partner. This is their house. I'm just giving them a hand; doing a few jobs for them."

"So where is she at the moment?"

"Colchester. She works for an insurance company." Fletcher stood. "I'll have to …"

Cyril looked to Barton then back to Fletcher. "Mr Fletcher … Adam," he said calmly, "what we need to do is have Jem officially identified."

"Of course. I'm forgetting … I'll do that. But … is he … I mean …?"

An image of the pilot's body on the beach flashed through Cyril's mind; only a few hours ago. "No," he said, "He's not in a bad way."

"Only ..." Fletcher considered, "I'm not sure if Vicky would ..."

"Do you want us to call on her?" Cyril offered, aware that an unannounced 'agony visit', as it's known, by uniformed officers would be more upsetting.

"If you want, I can take you into Colchester," Barton added. "Pick her up and, if she wants to come too, I can organise things; with the mortuary."

"Let me call her first. I think it best if it comes from me," Fletcher decided.

*   *   *

"Thanks, Sam, I appreciate it."

"You mean he just drove off and left you to make your own way back?" Sam Woodbridge was chuckling as he drove his beloved ten-year-old blue VW Beetle. "I knew he had a reputation as ... well, difficult, but you're one of our own."

Cyril was in the passenger seat, staring out of the window. "Well, it made sense. Driving Adam Fletcher into Colchester after organising the identification with the hospital." He'd called Sam at home from The Plough in the village. His mother said he couldn't sleep.

"You could have gone with him."

Cyril knew Sam was right but he wasn't going to criticise a superior. "He did suggest I get the Great Bentley village bobby to take me back, or the train." He turned to Sam and smiled. "But I thought you'd be better company."

"Thanks."

"And he wants me to check on the uniform team down on the beach."

"I think there's only a couple of lads left down there now, the rest are all back on normal duties," Sam said.

Cyril glanced over at Sam who still had a smile on his face at the latest Barton episode.

"Did you have time to get Charlie out for his walk before the call from the DCI?" Sam asked.

"Yes. He's next door with Doris now. I think she loves him almost as much as I do."

"Doris?"

"She's seventy-six and a widow. She loves the company; reckons she feels secure with him." Cyril looked over at Sam once again. "She tells people she looks after a police dog." It was his turn to smile. "He's more likely to lick someone to death than savage them.

"By the way, did you enjoy your fry-up?" Cyril continued.

Sam's expression turned serious. "I wasn't hungry."

"How's the ankle?"

"Walked it off. Just a bit of a sprain."

They were quiet for a minute.

"Are you okay?" Cyril asked.

"Yeah, I'm fine. Just didn't sleep very well, that's all."

"Bit of a shock for you this morning."

They drove on in silence for a few more minutes before Sam finally broke it. "You know that was the first time I've ever seen anyone die?"

Cyril studied Sam. "I didn't. But you have been called to other deaths before though, haven't you?"

"Four, I think. But they'd all been old. They'd had their lives. But that pilot, he'd be, what, forty-ish?"

"Thirty-seven. A couple of years younger than his brother, Adam."

"Married? Kids?"

"Divorced I'm told. Living with another woman now, no mention of children," Cyril said. "But listen, Sam, this is life. People have accidents all the time. We can't do anything to stop that. All we can do is pick up the pieces, so to speak. But we're not social workers."

"I know, I know." Sam screwed up his face. "Still doesn't make it easy."

"No," Cyril said quietly, resuming his view from the window.

Sam glanced at him. "Anyway, listen to me going on. What you lived through in the war, you must have seen far worse than this morning?"

19

Cyril blew out his cheeks. Sam was right, he had seen some awful things, things a seventeen-year-old boy, because that's what he was, shouldn't have seen. An image of that Lancaster coming in to land on one engine, two others out of action and the fourth ablaze flashed into his mind. The pilot was younger than Sam was now and he'd done a brilliant job to bring it back over the channel. But it hadn't been enough.

A car going the other way beeped its horn at someone, bringing Cyril back to the present. Finally, he replied, "Yes, well ... I have but ... just like you, it doesn't make it any easier. You just learn to cope."

5

Cyril had the windows down on the Ford Escort he had booked out from the car pool. He'd removed his jacket but resisted the temptation to loosen his tie and undo the top button of his shirt. Clacton thronged with holidaymakers, many having booked into the Butlin's Holiday Camp he passed on his way west. Even if Sam hadn't told him, he didn't need to check on 'his uniform colleagues'. And he didn't need Barton to patronise him either. No, he decided to visit the airstrip.

Parking on the spare bit of land that doubled as car parking, he made his way to the timber cabins that housed the offices of Clacton Aero Club.

"Hello there," the short stocky woman behind a reception desk greeted. "Can I help you at all?"

"I need to speak to someone in charge," Cyril said, holding up his warrant card.

"Ah, you'd best talk to Jimmy," she replied. "Jimmy Gibson is one of our senior pilots. I'll just give him a shout."

A minute later, returning from a rear office, she encouraged him to go through.

The man sitting behind the desk looked a youthful fifty-something, brylcreemed dark hair and a thin moustache, not dissimilar to Cyril's own. He stood up and offered a hand. Cyril noted he wore a RAF tie on a starched white shirt, a tweed sports jacket was slung over the back of his chair.

"Jimmy Gibson," he announced in a slight Scots accent, "How can I help?"

"I see you served," Cyril said, indicating the tie.

"600 Squadron for the most part, North Africa, Malta, Italy."

"Great reputation on night fighters."

Gibson nodded modestly. "Well … You?"

"I joined up in '42 when I was 16," Cyril responded. "Managed to join the ground crew with 604 Squadron. Mostly based around England but a couple of spells in France."

"Ah, 604 were night fighters too. And weren't they involved in airborne radar systems?"

"That's right, but that was before I joined."

There was a pause before Cyril refocussed the conversation. "What I'm here about, as you can probably guess," he said, "is the incident this morning,"

"Yes, of course. Dreadful business. But I spoke earlier to your Inspector Barton, was it?"

"Just checking on a few details, Mr Gibson, if that's okay."

"Not surprised he missed some of what I told him," Gibson said quietly.

"Oh?"

"Sorry, I shouldn't be critical. Not of senior officers, eh? But he did seem to be suffering the effects of the night before, if you know what I mean."

Cyril took out his notebook and pencil. "If you could confirm for me the aircraft's owner, that would be a great start."

Gibson opened a drawer in his desk and pulled out a file. "It was a single engine craft owned by Walter Yardley. These are his details." Gibson spun the file around so Cyril could see. "He owns his own electrical manufacturing company in Colchester."

Cyril leaned forward and noted Yardley's address. It was on one of the avenues in Frinton, inside the gates, as it was known; an affluent area. "We understand that Mr Yardley wasn't flying the plane this morning." he said, sitting back in his seat once more.

"He wasn't. I reckon it was Jem." Gibson closed the folder. "Jeremy Fletcher is one of the mechanics some of the owners regularly use to service their planes." Gibson sighed as he returned the file to his drawer. "I told all this to DI Barton. Has he not told you?"

"We do know that, sir, and we are following that up." Cyril looked to his notes before continuing. "Is it usual for flights to take off at 05:50, Mr Gibson?"

The pilot looked embarrassed. "Well, no. We don't usually begin operations until 09:00hrs."

"So have you any idea why Mr Fletcher would be flying so early this morning?" Cyril stroked his moustache. "I mean, would it be usual for a mechanic to take a plane up on a test flight before your normal hours of operation?"

Gibson considered for a moment. "It might, I suppose, if Walter would have wanted to fly today, but he didn't. I spoke to him on the phone this morning after I found out what had happened. He'd need to contact his insurers. But maybe Jem just wanted to check something out. In any event, we have no one here until half past eight at the earliest."

"And the keys for the aircraft, where are they kept?"

"Those craft we, the flying club, own, have their keys in the cabinet behind the reception desk. Those owners who want to can place them there as well. Most would have a spare set they keep themselves, or one or two might lock them in the maintenance hangers over on the other side of the airfield."

"And in Mr Yardley's case ...?" Cyril persisted.

"Apart from a set he kept himself, I think Walter kept a spare set over in the hanger."

"And Mr Fletcher would have access to the hanger?"

Gibson nodded. "A couple of local mechanics we use would."

"Do you mind if I have a look over in the hangers?"

"Be my guest. Just be a bit careful ..." he paused, "... well, no need to tell you about the dangers of an airfield."

Cyril gave a wan smile. "Just one last thing, do you have a list of those owners Jeremy Fletcher has worked for recently?"

Again, Gibson opened his desk drawer, pulled out another list and began to write on a slip of paper. "I think

23

these have used Jem in the past," he said, passing the piece of paper over.

Cyril stood, thanked him for his help and made his way outside.

Seagulls screeched overhead as Cyril looked across the grass runway towards the small hangers at the far end. Around a dozen or so planes were parked nearby. There appeared to be at least one person moving around the area. Keeping close by the fence at the bottom end, he turned and made his way up the other side towards the buildings. As he reached the first hanger, a small man of around forty appeared by the side of one of the planes.

Closing an engine cover, he caught sight of Cyril. "Are you from the investigation unit?" the man asked.

"Clacton Police," Cyril announced, holding up his warrant card. "DS Claydon."

The man wiped his hands on a rag and walked towards Cyril. "Alan Massey. This is my plane." The man indicated the aircraft he'd just been attending. "Shocking business," he added.

"Did you know Mr Fletcher?" Cyril asked.

"I've seen him up here quite often. Spoken to him a few times but I can't really say I knew him." Massey returned to the side of his plane and began to tidy tools into a box.

Cyril followed. "So he never did any maintenance work for you, Mr Massey?"

The man looked up and smiled. "Do all my own. It's half the fun."

Cyril nodded. "I can appreciate that." He looked to the building. "Do you all share these facilities?"

"Mostly. Some members do their own work in there, not many. And some use outside mechanics who can share them too."

"Do you know Mr Yardley? I believe it was his craft that crashed."

"Yeah, I know Walter. He's been a member here for years. He doesn't fly that much these days. Won't be

24

doing any for a while now either with no plane," Massey added with a smile. "Sorry, I shouldn't make light of it."

"Did Mr Yardley use Fletcher regularly?"

"I wouldn't know." The man nodded towards a white Ford Transit van parked behind the hanger. "But that's Fletcher's van over there. It'll need to be moved soon, it's blocking access."

Cyril walked over to the van and peered in through the driver's window. It appeared reasonably tidy for the cab of a working vehicle. A plastic folder lay on the passenger seat with what looked like a manual alongside. He took a handkerchief from his pocket and tried the door. Locked. He walked around to the passenger side and repeated his action with a similar result. The double rear doors were the same but he held a hand to one of the windows and squinted inside. Tools lined the van's sides, neatly hung on hooks whilst the bulkhead behind the cab had a range of cupboards fitted. The van floor seemed clear.

Cyril turned and made his way to the front of the hanger and stepped through the open doorway. A twin-engined plane sat on the concrete floor, wheels chocked. The once familiar scents of engine oils mingled with a hint of aviation fuel greeted his nostrils. A cabinet on one wall caught his attention. The metal door was open. Several sets of keys hung on hooks inside.

Massey appeared in the doorway, carrying his heavy tool-box.

Cyril turned towards him. "Are these keys always this accessible?"

The man dumped the box against the rear wall before responding. "The cabinet is usually locked. I'm about to return my set, and then I'll lock it up. The door is locked too but most owners will have a key to the hanger and the cabinet, if they choose to keep their keys there."

"Okay, thanks," Cyril said, making for the door.

"I don't suppose ..." Massey began to say, "... there's any news on what went wrong?"

Cyril paused. "That'll be for the Air Accident boys to determine. Unless you have any theories?"

Massey shook his head. "Just wondered, that's all. But losing power on take-off … it would have to be electrical or fuel."

Cyril said nothing and walked away. Pulling his pipe from his pocket, he filled it and lit up as he made his way back to the car. Looking to the sky, there wasn't a cloud. Straight in front of him the sun sparkled off the sea. Puffing on his pipe he thought about what he'd witnessed this morning. But the events of a similar morning, some thirty-three years ago now, forced their way into his mind. Early morning sunshine bathed the airfield when the Lancaster limped out of the sky, barely holding altitude of a thousand feet. They could see the smoke trail from the damaged engine. Every man on station willed the craft to make it and was ready to act. The pilot somehow managed to bring it round to line up with the grass airstrip. It was at that point they could see the full extent of the damage to the fuselage. Bullet holes had ripped through the metal. The rear gun turret had been virtually shot away.

A seagull swooped down screaming loudly, disturbing his memory. A puff on his pipe and he focused on current events.

He and Sam Woodbridge had been instructed to say nothing about the plane's 'cargo'. As far as Gibson and Massey were concerned, the news blackout seemed to be holding. But it was only a matter of time before a revelation like that became known. Nothing like a police station for leaking like a sieve. But who was the victim? That would determine the next steps. For the time being, Cyril was enjoying yet another hot summer's day and wondered when this heat wave would end.

6

It was just gone five when Cyril returned to the station. He'd called by the crash site and spoken to the sergeant organising the search for debris. Engineers from the Air Accident Investigation Branch had arrived mid-afternoon and conducted an initial survey of the plane. The fuel had been pumped from the tanks in the wings and a crane and low-loader had arrived. The wreckage was in the process of being taken to a warehouse in Colchester. So Barton had got his way, Cyril thought.

Parking up outside the station, Cyril stepped out and walked to the main doors. He almost collided with Cathy Rogers, the civilian secretary Sanderson had mentioned. She was just leaving, bag on one arm and coat over the other.

"It's Sergeant Claydon isn't it?" she asked. Her face lit up with a warm smile.

"Cyril, call me Cyril," he responded, holding the door open. "And you're Cathy, right?"

"That's me," she said. There was an awkward pause as they looked at one another. "I've left some notes with DC Walker upstairs." Cathy gestured inside. "DCI Sanderson asked me to type them up. And he wanted you to take a look at a file from records. I've put that on your desk. I'm assuming you're sitting at DS Flynn's."

"Okay, thanks."

Before the conversation could continue, DI Barton barged his way through the doors. "You done those notes yet?" he barked at Cathy as he drew on his cigarette.

"Upstairs with DC Walker," she repeated.

With an expulsion of smoke and a grunt for a response, he disappeared into the building.

Cyril saw the look of disgust on the secretary's face.

"Obnoxious man," she said quietly.

"Sorry about that," Cyril said. "We're not all as rude as DI Barton."

"I'm sure you're not." She smiled at him again. "Well, have a good night."

"You too."

Cyril turned and watched her walk away. He'd put her mid-forties at most. A shapely figure in a floral summer dress. Lovely smile too.

Surprised by his thoughts, he shook his head as if clearing those images from his brain. It had been years since he'd paid any attention to a woman. More to the point, it was probably years since a woman had paid any attention to him. Not since his beloved Maureen succumbed to cancer three years ago. It was a pain that had started to ease through the summer months, but he still felt guilty for it.

Up the stairs, he walked through open doors and into the haze of cigarette smoke that had descended on the CID office once more. With not a breath of wind outside, the open windows did nothing to help. Several detectives were involved in conversations or sitting at their desks. A couple of them he knew glanced up at him. "Cyril," they greeted.

"Gents," he acknowledged, checked his desk and picked up the file Cathy had left there. Making his way to Barton's office, he knocked on the door and waited a second for the DI to beckon him in.

Barton was leaning back in his chair behind the desk. "You'll be glad to know we've got the right body. Adam Fletcher confirmed it was his brother, Jem. His partner Vicky insisted on coming too, but she got herself into a bit of a state." He began to shuffle through various files and bits of paper on his desk. "Now I did leave a message for that dozy secretary to dig out Fletcher's file but she doesn't seem to have done it."

Cyril held out the manila folder he'd collected from his desk. "It's here. She left it on my desk."

Barton flashed a disapproving look as he took the file from him.

"DCI Sanderson asked her to leave it with me," he said by way of explanation.

Barton gave another grunt, flicked open the file and scanned it quickly before closing. "So what have you got to tell me then?" he asked.

Cyril recounted what he'd learned from his visits to the airfield and the crash site. "So uniform were just clearing away when I left, but nothing of any significance has been found," he concluded.

Barton glanced at his watch. "Right, ten minutes until the DCI's briefing. I've got a phone call to make so I suggest you get your notes together on today's events and we'll be ready for six."

"Okay gentlemen, listen up," DCI Sanderson announced.

A hush descended on the gathered group as he glanced around, mentally taking a roll call.

"John, give us the lowdown as far as you know, will you?" he instructed.

DI Barton stepped forward and turned to face the detectives.

"At five fifty this morning a light aircraft belonging to Walter Yardley crashed on take-off from Clacton airfield," Barton began. "Confirmed dead was the pilot, a mechanic from Great Bentley, Jeremy Fletcher. Alongside him in the passenger seat was a body, as yet still unidentified, wrapped in plastic."

"Has Fletcher been officially identified?" Sanderson interrupted.

"I accompanied his brother and girlfriend this afternoon," Barton responded. "The PM is scheduled for nine tomorrow morning. Me and DS Claydon will attend."

Cyril was surprised. Not wanted for the formal identification this afternoon, he deigns to have me hold his hand at the gory bits, he thought.

"With regards to our other stiff," Barton continued, "the forensics lads will be with the pathologist tomorrow for the

29

PM on that. Until that happens, we won't know any more. They'll also be recovering Fletcher's van from the airfield and searching that for anything to connect it with the body."

"But until we get an ID on the body, we can't really progress things," Sanderson said. "Ideas anyone?"

"I'm just thinking, Sir," Cyril said, "if Fletcher's van gives no forensic evidence to show that the other body was ever in it, and it seemed pretty clean to me when I looked in it this afternoon, then it must have been transported to the airfield in another vehicle."

Sanderson began to pace. "Look, this is all ifs and buts for the moment. We need to find out what the PM on matey comes up with first."

"But what I was thinking, Sir," Cyril persisted, "was that the body was probably brought to the airfield in the early hours of this morning. That being the case, why don't we carry out a check tomorrow morning? People travel to work for early morning shifts. Let's see if anyone was around this morning and saw anything suspicious near the locked gates to the track leading up to the hanger?"

"Good point, Cyril," Sanderson said. "Even if it turned out that Fletcher brought the body himself, it would still be useful if we had a witness to confirm what time he arrived."

A uniformed constable knocked at the doorway and nervously approached the group. "Sorry," he said, looking at Barton. "Message for you, Sir." He handed the DI a folded slip of paper.

As Barton read, the colour visibly drained from his cheeks. He glanced at Sanderson then walked back to his office.

"Okay gents, carry on with what you're all doing," Sanderson said, followed Barton to the office and closed the door.

7

The evening was still warm when Cyril returned home; the house he'd shared with Maureen all their married life. Stepping in through the front door, he picked up the free paper that had been delivered that afternoon and walked through to the kitchen. From the window, he could see Doris sitting in a chair in her back garden enjoying the evening sun and reading the paper. Charlie was at her feet.

He stood for a moment, lost in thought. When he and Maureen had moved in, twenty-six years ago now, they thought it would be the perfect place to raise a family. After years of trying, Maureen was devastated to learn she couldn't have any children. Cyril didn't think she ever got over it fully. And then the cancer came. She fought it well but finally, three years back, she succumbed. Forty-two. No age at all really.

He looked around the room, searching out the evidence that she had once lived here. The tea cosy on the teapot he never used because he preferred a tea bag in a mug; the two egg cups on a stand she'd bought for them on holiday in North Wales – he only used the left-hand one – he never used the other, that was hers. He listened. The silence of an empty house.

Looking down the hallway, he spotted the photo frame that shared the small table with the telephone. He walked to it and picked it up. Maureen and he were sitting at a restaurant table. The picture had been taken by a waiter who had fussed around them. Italy, ten years ago, their only holiday abroad. She looked gorgeous; deep brown eyes and a tan that accentuated her lovely high cheek bones. Dark chestnut hair framed her face and tumbled to her shoulders. That was before the illness ravaged her. It was as he would always remember her.

A tear began to make its escape and he felt pulled once more. But he didn't want to go there. Not today, there'd been enough tragedy already. Snapping himself out of his mood, he opened the back door, walked out onto the path, through the low gate and into the next door garden.

Doris looked up, removing her reading glasses.

"Evening Cyril," she greeted.

Charlie gave a low bark and struggled to his feet. Tail wagging, he approached his master.

"Are you alright, Doris?" he responded then made a fuss of Charlie. "Has he behaved himself?"

"You know I love the big soft mutt. We even had a walk down to the park this afternoon but it got a bit hot for him."

Doris had lived next door when they'd first moved in. A thoughtful neighbour, she would do anything for you. But she was getting on a bit now.

"Is it not a bit hot for you too?"

"Take the weight off your feet," she said. "My friend Betty's only just gone home. We've been sitting out here for an hour or two. I love it a bit warm. Does my arthritis a power of good."

Cyril sat in the other garden chair, Charlie settling down on the grass between them.

"I keep thinking this has got to end soon," she went on, "but the forecasters say it'll be a while yet."

"We should just enjoy it while we can."

"Been a busy day for you." She folded up the newspaper. "With that plane crash and all."

"And it's going to get a whole lot busier," he replied.

They sat in silence for a while, both leaning back, eyes closed, absorbing the warmth.

"You've been widowed a long time, Doris," he finally said.

"Over thirty years."

"You would still have been a young woman then."

"Forty-five."

Again a short silence.

"Did you never think you'd meet someone else?" He could feel her turn to look at him.

"Different times then," she said. "It was just as the War ended. Besides, I never met anyone to compare with my Howard."

Cyril opened his eyes to see Doris studying him.

"What's prompted this?" she asked. "You're thinking of retiring soon, aren't you?"

"Well I could take the police pension at the end of the year."

"Second thoughts?"

"I've got my allotment and I might look at doing a bit of travelling."

"You are, aren't you?"

Cyril had to smile. He liked her, she was easy to talk to and very perceptive.

"I'd best get off and make some dinner." He stood to go.

"But if you're not ready, you know …"

"See you Doris."

"Just make sure you look after yourself. And is my friend staying with me tomorrow?"

They both looked at Charlie who was back on his feet.

"If you're okay with that?"

"Course I am. Night, Cyril."

She's great, Cyril thought. Just like my mum.

Back inside, he wondered what he could eat for dinner then remembered the Vesta Chow Mein he had in the cupboard.

While that was heating through he began to turn over the day's events in his mind. Ten to six this morning seemed a long way off now. So, they'd identified the pilot and the owner of the plane. But had anyone taken a formal statement from Walter Yardley? Barton had spoken to him this morning, but had he followed that up? Either way, there was no mention at the briefing. And that was a bit of a farce. But at least he'd found out the subject of the note the constable had handed to the DI that caused the meeting to break up so suddenly. He'd tackle Barton about that tomorrow.

8
Wednesday 1ˢᵗ September

The group had dispersed the previous evening with no real plan to the investigation. But Cyril had taken the initiative and spoken to the sergeant who was covering the night shift to see if they could do a check on early morning traffic past the airfield. There was no mistaking the look that had passed between DI Barton and DCI Sanderson. Cyril knew the information on the piece of paper the constable had passed to Barton was significant. So significant in fact, it had brought the briefing to a swift and premature close.

For today, all Cyril knew was to turn up early and report to Barton. And now, they were on their way to the County Hospital in Colchester to witness the post-mortems on Jeremy Fletcher and the other body, Cyril driving them in the DI's Rover.

After ten minutes of silence, Cyril decided to broach the subject. "So, the disappearance of Jimmy Morgan is important?" He glanced across at Barton.

Barton screwed up his face. "How did …"

One of the most important things Cyril had taken from his previous days in CID was to try and ask questions to which he already knew the answers. Not always achievable but, in this case, a word with the desk sergeant yesterday evening revealed the subject of the message.

"I don't know yet."

"Reported missing by his girlfriend, I understand?"

Barton looked at Cyril. "You seem to know as much as me."

"So who is he?"

Barton wound his window down a bit more before he answered. "Small time crook from East London originally. Rumoured to have connections with some of the faces up there."

"Like the Krays you mean?"

"Towards the end of their reign, yeah. Was just a runner for them. Did a little bit of thievin' himself. Couple of spells in prison in the late sixties, early seventies."

"And now?"

Barton pulled out a packet of cigarettes from his trouser pocket, drew one out and lit it before answering. "Now runs with the Robinsons."

"The Robinsons?"

"Yeah." He took a deep draw and exhaled. "They've filled the void left by some of the old-timers. Running the three P's; protection, prostitution and porn up in The Smoke."

"And he's obviously got connections here."

"You know what it's like, a lot of East-Enders come to Clacton for breaks. Some have bought static caravans on the parks. Even Reggie and Ronnie have one they brought their mum to."

Cyril slowed to negotiate a roundabout. "So Morgan has a caravan down here?"

"No. Him and his slapper rent a grotty bungalow in Jaywick."

Cyril let the conversation lie for a minute then added, "And you think our body could be Morgan?"

Barton took one last drag, flicked the butt from the window and looked at his watch. "Just get us there on time, will you?"

* * *

Essex County Hospital was a Victorian brick built structure on the west side of Colchester town centre. Cyril managed to find a space in the car park and they made their way inside. As is customary, the mortuary was located in the basement, along a dingy corridor. In contrast to the outside world, the place was refreshingly cool, albeit impregnated with the scents and aromas of various chemicals.

In the office, the pathologist, Dr George Maguire, was chatting to a couple of lab technicians and a forensics officer who was there to bag and note any evidence.

"Morning everybody," Barton greeted. "Can we get started?"

The pathologist made a point of checking his watch. "DI Barton, a pleasure as always."

"And you Dr Maguire."

"In fact we were just waiting for you, so let's go."

Barton followed the pathologist back out to the corridor and into a room on the left. A body was ready on the stainless steel slab.

"You have a confirmed identity for the pilot, I believe?" Dr Maguire stated.

"We do, yes. Identified by his brother."

"Well let's get started then, shall we."

Jem Fletcher's post-mortem revealed no surprises. Cause of death was an intra-cranial bleed caused by his head impacting the plane's screen. He was a fit and healthy male for his age and there were no signs of any illness or disease. A toxicology test would be conducted but that was not expected to show any evidence of alcohol or drugs. His personal effects, however, did throw up an interesting discovery. His wallet contained a hundred pounds in ten pound notes. Bagged by the forensics officer, Barton asked for them to be checked for prints. Some were new and the serial numbers would also be reviewed to see where and when they were issued.

By ten-thirty, the most interesting part of the morning was about to commence. The unknown body on the second slab was carefully unwrapped from the clear plastic sheeting the forensics team had sealed it in before transporting it to the mortuary.

"Can we get fingerprints from the black plastic?" Barton asked.

"Should do if there are any," the forensics officer replied.

"Well let's be careful cutting that off," the DI said.

Cyril caught the momentary expression on the officer's face. No doubt he'd had dealings with Barton before.

"But can we start with the head."

The pathologist looked up. "If all you're going to do is teach us to suck eggs DI Barton, then I suggest you find something useful to do."

Cyril glanced at his superior and struggled to stop the smile that so desperately wanted to form on his face.

Barton moved in closer as the scissors cut through the wrapping to reveal the discoloured face of a man who could be in his forties or fifties.

"Shit," Barton said quietly.

One of the assistants began to take a series of photographs.

"Not a pretty sight, I agree," Dr Maguire declared.

"Is it who you thought?" Cyril asked.

The pathologist glanced up. "You know him?"

Barton nodded. "Reported missing by his girlfriend yesterday." He looked to the forensics man. "Can you take his prints and get them compared to Jimmy Morgan. He has a record. Details for him should be on file in Chelmsford."

"This gets more interesting," the pathologist said, crouching down to study the side of the head nearest him. "A gun shot entry wound here." He moved aside to allow more photos to be taken.

"So we're looking at murder then," Barton mumbled.

"There is one other possibility," Dr Maguire said, a faint smile playing on his lips. "It could be suicide. He could have organised others to wrap him up in plastic and arrange for his burial at sea."

Barton looked up. "Are you taking the piss?"

"Just checking your sense of humour hasn't been surgically removed, Dick," the pathologist responded, exchanging looks with the photographer.

* * *

Outside once again, Barton pulled out a cigarette and lit up. Cyril decided to follow suit with his pipe. He thought it might help overcome the back taste he had in his mouth from being in the mortuary environment for the last few hours. Leaning against the wall, they were silent for a while, watching patients, medical staff in white coats and nurses come and go.

Finally, Cyril spoke. "Interesting assessment from Dr Maguire that Morgan had been dead for at least two days, possibly longer."

He puffed on his pipe and glanced across at the DI who'd said nothing in response. "So he's fully clothed but no possessions on him," Cyril thought out loud. "Only that Yale key inside the lining of his jacket pocket. Now why would you think that was? Had whoever killed him missed it? Well obviously. But had Morgan deliberately hidden it? Or had it just got caught in there? It'll be interesting to see if there's any fingerprints on it."

Again, Cyril glanced across and saw no reaction from Barton; he just continued smoking his cigarette.

"So the Met will want to know about Morgan's demise then?" Cyril continued.

"I would think so." At last a response.

After a couple of minutes, Cyril pressed on. "And they'll have some interesting info for you as well, no doubt?"

Barton drew on his cigarette once more. "How long have you been in the police service, Cyril?" he asked.

"Joined in '51."

"And you had a spell in CID before, right?"

"Yes." Again Cyril looked at the DI, puzzled at the change of direction in the conversation. "Had ten years as a DC after I'd passed my detectives exam. '56 to '66."

"So how come you're back in uniform?"

"Passed my sergeants exam but nothing came up in CID. Then a uniform position did, so I took it. Where's this going?"

Barton took one last drag on his cigarette, dropped it on the pavement and trod on it, blowing smoke into the air as he did so. "So you're old school, right?"

Cyril didn't respond to that but felt the DI was holding back. "But there's more, isn't there?" he asked

Barton folded his arms and took a deep breath. Cyril thought he was about to open up, but he only pushed himself off the wall and began to walk to the car. "Did you organise that checkpoint on the coastal road with uniform?"

Cyril knocked his pipe out, put it back in his pocket and followed him. "Yes. Some of the night shift were putting that in place from four this morning, provided there were no major incidents."

Barton stopped after a couple of steps. "But you've not heard anything?"

"Didn't see anyone before I left the station, but I'll chase that up when we get back."

"Yeah, do that will you?" Barton said. "Now while I'm here, I suppose I'd better kill two birds with one stone, so to speak." He turned and headed back into the hospital.

Cyril was puzzled. "Where are you …?"

"I'll be back in a bit."

Cyril watched him disappear along a corridor. At least this time, he can't leave me to make my own way back, he thought, feeling for the reassuring outline of the car keys in his pocket.

* * *

Barton pushed open the door to the Intensive Care Unit.

The Sister looked up from her desk as he walked in. "Can I help you?" she asked.

"My colleague, Danny Flynn?" He held up his warrant card.

"His wife's with him now." She indicated one of the rooms. "Number five. But he's sedated and needs to stay calm."

Barton nodded, hesitated for a second then walked over and opened the door. Helen Flynn was sitting by Danny's bedside.

She flared up when she saw her husband's boss. "You've got a nerve showing up here," she hissed.

He held up both hands in surrender.

She gave him a disgusted look and stood up, "How could you let this happen. 'We look after our own,' that's what Danny used to tell me." The tears were welling in her eyes. She looked over to the man in the bed, wired up to machines that beeped and displayed green lines on monitors. "Well you certainly did."

Barton saw the tears run down her anguished face. "I'm so sorry," was all he could think to say.

She took a step towards him. "Sorry? Sorry? You're pathetic. I don't want you here. Go."

"Look …"

She virtually bundled him back out through the open door. "Go!"

The Sister came out from behind her desk. "I told you Mr Flynn needs rest and to stay calm. I'm not having you disturb my ward."

"That's all right Sister, the gentleman …" Helen Flynn looked him up and down. "… was just leaving."

Barton held her stare for a moment, looked back at Danny in the bed then walked away.

* * *

When Barton returned to the front doors, he merely grunted what sounded like, "Let's go," as he strode past.

Cyril strolled after him and by the time he got to the car, the DI was impatient to be on his way.

Despite a couple of attempts by Cyril to start a conversation, the return journey to Clacton was conducted in silence, the DI preferring to be alone with his thoughts. The atmosphere was tense.

Back at the station, Barton disappeared into his office and closed the door.

The note on Cyril's desk was from Sam. He'd worked the checkpoint this morning and had come up with a possible sighting of suspicious behaviour the previous morning. Cyril didn't need to disturb Sam at home, there was enough information for him to follow up so, in the absence of any involvement from Barton, he put his jacket back on and made his way outside.

About to put the key in the lock of the Escort, a greeting from behind stopped him.

"Off out again, Cyril?"

He turned to see the smiling face of Cathy Rogers.

"Oh, hello Cathy. Busy times," he responded.

"Did you get that file I left on your desk yesterday?" She took a step closer.

"Yes I did, thanks, although Inspector Barton was expecting it apparently."

"Was he now," she said, raising an eyebrow. "Well I hope he wasn't disappointed."

Suddenly, Cyril felt awkward. Was she flirting with him? It had been years since anyone had. She was certainly an attractive woman. He looked down to his hands. "I'd best get on," he said, fumbling with the car key.

"Oh, yes, me too," she said. "I'm due back from lunch three minutes ago. See you."

As he sat in the driver's seat, he watched her walk over to the front doors, admiring her shapely legs, accentuated by the wedge sandals she was wearing. With a smile on his face, he started up the engine. "I'm getting too old for this," he told himself, and drove off.

9

The personnel manager at Butlin's reluctantly provided Cyril with Jack Finnegan's home address. "What's he been up to now?" he'd asked. Cyril told him that, as far as he knew, Jack hadn't been up to anything but was a possible witness to an incident. He did, however, make a note to search for a criminal record on the man.

Finnegan's home turned out to be a semi-detached bungalow on a side road off Golf Green Road on the way in to Jaywick. The next door garden was well-tended, despite the drought conditions and Cyril could imagine the neighbour's irritation with the state of Finnegan's front garden. The privet hedge looked as though it hadn't been trimmed all summer and the centre section had been an obvious target for passing school children 'bombing' it, the large compressed sections evidence of that.

Cyril walked up the path past the dead-looking overgrown area that had once been a lawn and rang the bell to the half-glazed door at the side of the property. A dog began to bark loudly. Instinctively, he stepped back. Some shouting and slamming of a door preceded the appearance of a figure approaching, visible through the rippled glass. The door was opened by a woman dressed in a blouse and skirt and wearing glasses. He took her to be in her fifties.

She eyed him warily, "Yes?"

"I'd like to speak with Jack Finnegan?" Cyril said, holding out his warrant card.

She folded her arms, a stern expression forming. "He's having a rest. He's on early shifts."

"I realise that er, Mrs Finnegan? But it is important. He spoke to a constable this morning. I understand he could have vital information for us."

"Wait there," she said and closed the door.

Moments later a short stocky man with a bald pate opened the door again. He was in bare feet and dressed in a vest and trousers with braces hanging by his sides.

"Sorry about that," he said, "She thinks I work too hard. Come in a minute."

He held the door wide and Cyril stepped into a neat kitchen with a small table and three chairs to the side.

"Sit down," the man invited, swiftly moving both braces over his shoulders. "I'm assuming this is about yesterday morning?"

"You are Jack Finnegan?" Cyril asked as he sat at one end of the table.

Finnegan took a seat opposite. "Yes, yes of course."

Cyril flipped open his notebook. "I'm DS Claydon from Clacton Police. I understand you spoke to one of my colleagues this morning on your way to work?"

"That's right. He was asking about yesterday morning, when that plane crashed." He stood again. "Sorry, did you want a drink? Tea? Or a cold one, there's some squash?"

Cyril held up a hand. "No thanks Mr Finnegan, I'm fine. Now if you could just take me through what you saw yesterday, that would be great."

The man resumed his seat, rather nervously. "Well, I set off from here about four-thirty. I work in the kitchens at Butlin's and I start at five, breakfasts and that. I bike it down so I suppose I passed the lane end to the airstrip about …" He screwed up his face in concentration. "… a quarter to five."

Cyril, writing down notes, paused and looked up. "So it was still dark."

"Sort of. I mean with this weather, the nights aren't so dark anyway. But yes the street lights were on."

"And what exactly did you see?"

"Well I thought it was a bit odd. I mean that time of the morning there's nothing much on the road anyway. But this car was pulled up to the gate at the end of the lane."

"What sort of car, could you tell?"

"Oh, it was one of these big old Jags. You know the sort the villains always seem to smash up on that new TV show that's on, *The Sweeney*." A broad grin came on his face. "Margaret and me, we love that programme."

"Sounds like the old mark 2," Cyril mused.

"I'm not up on cars but if that's what they use, yes."

"I don't suppose you got anything of the registration?"

"I think it was D which is, what, 1966?"

Cyril nodded. "Any indication of colour?"

"It was dark."

Cyril looked up once more as Finnegan hesitated, before adding, "I mean the car was dark coloured. Could have been grey or black."

"Could you see the driver?"

"There was two of them, just sitting there. The engine was running, fumes coming from the exhausts …"

"Twin exhausts?"

"One either side, yes. Is that important?"

"Maybe. Sorry, you were saying."

"Yeah, and the lights were on. I mean the headlights, not the inside lights."

"And there were two people inside the car? Any idea what they looked like?"

"No. I was just cycling past and saw the car there. They were in the front facing the gate. It was two blokes, though, but all I saw was the backs of their heads, silhouette like."

"I know this is difficult, Mr Finnegan, but sometimes just the smallest detail could be important. I mean was either of them wearing a hat, or bald, or anything distinguishing?"

Finnegan looked down at the table and appeared to be thinking hard. Slowly he shook his head. "I can't think of anything. I don't think they were wearing hats, but I couldn't be one hundred per cent. Oh, but one was bigger than the other; the passenger I mean. The driver was a smaller bloke."

Cyril closed his notebook. "Okay, Mr Finnegan, that's been a great help. Thanks for that and I'm sorry if I disturbed your rest." He stood to leave. "Obviously, if there is anything else that springs to mind, can you let me know at Clacton Police Station?"

Finnegan also got to his feet. "Sure, no problem." He opened the door.

As he stepped outside, Cyril stopped and turned. "Oh, I've got to ask Mr Finnegan ... what sort of dog do you have?"

The man smiled. "That's Sabre. She's an Alsatian."

"Certainly sounds big."

"Soft as anything really but she makes a noise."

*   *   *

Back at the station, Cyril climbed the stairs to CID only to be met by Barton coming down.

"Where have you been?" he grunted. "I've been looking for you."

Cyril stopped. "You asked me to check what progress with the checkpoint this morning, so I followed up on that."

"Have you seen this?" Barton thrust a copy of the Evening Gazette at him.

"No," he replied, taking the paper and opening it out on the front page. The headline pondered, *Mystery Object Recovered From Crashed Plane*. "Do they come up with an answer?" he asked.

"So far they don't know what we found, only witness reports of a large object wrapped in plastic taken away in a van."

"Only a matter of time, I suppose."

Barton continued down the stairs. "Never mind that for now, tell me what news on this morning's checkpoint on the way."

"Where are we going?" Cyril followed in Barton's wake.

"To see the delightful Beryl Boynton."

"Who the Hell's ..."

10

This time Barton drove the Rover 2000 down to Jaywick as Cyril recounted his conversation with the witness.

Jaywick was a total enigma, the area having grown up around the holiday chalets that had been built for holiday makers, mostly from London, back in the thirties. After the war, it was a target for people looking for cheap accommodation with the result that many of the properties, originally intended for holiday use only and totally unfit for year round living, began to deteriorate. And tragedy struck with the deaths of thirty-five people in 1953 when the North Sea suffered a surge tide and swamped the place.

Driving down Jaywick Lane, the standard of property visibly reduced the further progress they made.

"Beryl Boynton," Barton explained, "live-in partner of the late Jimmy Morgan. Although I don't know what she'll be able to tell us. Her sort won't want to tell us anything, even if Morgan did talk to her about what he was up to."

"So where exactly are we headed?" Cyril asked.

"Brooklands."

"I might have known."

That area was the worst in the village. All the roads named after cars from the thirties, forties and fifties. Names like Riley, Humber and Alvis. After five minutes, Barton turned the Rover into its namesake Avenue. The property he drew to a halt outside resembled a garden shed.

"Incredible that people still live like this," Cyril said.

"You should see my flat," Barton responded before quickly getting out of the car.

His knock on the door was greeted by a dog barking inside.

"Looks to be a 'must have' accessory," Cyril quipped.

Before Barton could ask what he meant, the door was opened by a woman of around fifty with bleach blonde hair in ringlets, dressed in a V-necked top which showed a generous cleavage and a skirt that Cyril thought too short for a woman of her age. At her feet, a brown and black Yorkshire Terrier circled.

"Miss Boynton?" Barton enquired, holding up his warrant card.

"Mrs, yes, but just call me Beryl," she said, bending down to pick up the dog. "Have you found Jimmy?"

"Detective Inspector Barton and this is Detective Sergeant Claydon. Do you mind if we come in a minute?"

A worried expression came over the woman's face as she turned back into the house and led them inside. The door opened straight into a small but comfortably furnished living room. Cyril could hardly describe the interior as 'grotty' which is how Barton had thought of it. A small two-seater settee and two matching easy chairs took up most of the floor area.

Cyril shut the door behind him. When he turned back round, Beryl was closing the door to the kitchen, having deposited the dog inside. She sat in one of the chairs and nervously pulled a cigarette from a packet that rested on the arm.

"What's he done," she asked after the first puff. "It must be something serious for a DI to turn up at the door."

Cyril looked to Barton who, in turn looked briefly to the floor before he spoke. "I'm afraid I have some bad news," he said.

Ten minutes later, Beryl was cupping a mug of coffee in both hands. She'd grabbed some toilet roll to use as tissue and had finally regained control after the first wave of tears.

"How did he die?" she struggled to ask.

"I'm afraid we believe his death to be suspicious," Barton said.

Cyril was incredulous. You can't get more suspicious than being shot in the head, wrapped in plastic and on your way out over the North Sea for a last swim, he thought.

"You mean murdered." Beryl stated firmly.

Barton nodded. "It looks that way, yes."

The woman shook her head and began to cry again.

Cyril looked to Barton who seemed uneasy with the situation. He caught his eye and Barton nodded approval.

"Beryl," Cyril said gently, "I get the impression you're not exactly surprised to hear this."

Through sobs, she shook her head once more. "I told him to stay away."

"Away? Away from where?"

"He was mixing with … well it doesn't matter anymore." She looked up at Cyril. "Can I see him?"

"We will need someone to make a formal identification …" Barton began.

But Cyril interrupted. "We'll see what we can arrange, Beryl. But who were you worried about him mixing with?"

She wiped her eyes and nose then straightened up. "You know as well as I do the sort of company he was keeping. I don't know their names but he was mixed up with some London men."

Cyril decided to change tack. "So when was the last time you saw Jimmy?"

"Four days ago now. He said he was off to meet someone. See a man about a dog, he said. But I knew what that meant. He'd got some racket going on."

"What time was that?"

"About nine he left here. At night."

"And you've no idea who he was going to see?"

Another shake of the head.

Cyril was aware of Barton's restlessness. "Did he have any visitors in the days before?" he continued.

"No. No one."

"Did he go out much in the days leading up to his disappearance?"

Before she could respond, Barton finally exploded. "For Christ's sake, Mrs Boynton, if we're going to get to the bottom of this, you're going to have to tell us what you know!"

That outburst prompted another round of sobs and tissue dabbing. Cyril looked sharply at the DI. He was beginning to wonder how he ever got results with his attitude. It might work for some minor criminal who could be intimidated by an angry and threatening demeanour but not in this case.

"Just take your time, Beryl," Cyril said. "Try and think of what Jimmy was doing, who he might have mentioned, in the days leading up to his disappearance."

Slowly, Beryl settled down and appeared to give the question some thought. Finally, she seemed to remember something. "The only thing I can think of is that he mentioned having to see someone called Victor."

"Victor?" Barton queried. "Did he mention another name?"

"No, just a Victor."

"And when was this?" Cyril followed up.

"Last week, maybe Monday, no Tuesday. He went out on his own early in the evening. He was back about eleven."

Barton took a deep breath and exhaled, as if in frustration, then stood. "Okay, Mrs Boynton, we'll leave it there for now. But, as I said, we will need someone to make a formal identification. Would you be willing to do that?"

Beryl also got to her feet. "Of course," she said sharply.

On the way out, Cyril paused. "If there's anything you remember, no matter how insignificant you might think," he said, "give me a call at Clacton." He gave her a grim smile. "And someone will be in touch shortly regarding the process we'll need to go through."

Barton was already by the car.

"Thank you," she said.

"Oh, by the way, I notice you don't have a Yale lock on here." Cyril glanced at the front door.

Beryl looked puzzled. "No. Is it important?"

"No," he said. "Not at all."

* * *

"You're a bit of a smarmy git on the quiet, aren't you, Cyril?"

Barton was driving them back to the station, windows down, the warm wind whistling through the car.

"Did you fancy her or something?" he went on.

Cyril took a breath, determined to keep some self-control. Maybe that's what Barton wanted.

"I suppose you would have held her up against the wall and given her a few slaps," he responded. "Beat a confession out of her."

Barton laughed, surprising him.

After a few seconds, Cyril asked, "Any ideas on someone called Victor?"

"Notice it was Victor, not Vic or any other shortened version," Barton said. "That makes me think of only one person."

"Any chance of sharing that?"

Barton looked across at Cyril, a broad smile on his face. "Victor Robinson, son of gangland boss, Frank," he said.

"So, we're back to the Robinsons."

"Fancy a pint, Cyril?" Barton didn't wait for an answer, he pulled in to the side of the road outside the aptly-named Never Say Die public house, switched off the engine and wound up his window. "I'm buying."

Cyril sat on the sea wall at the rear of the pub, looking out over the beach. He puffed on his pipe, waiting for Barton to come out with his pint of bitter. The irony of Jaywick was that although a lot of the housing stock was dilapidated, it had one huge attraction. The beach was one of the best on this coast. The golden sands were peppered with family groups laying down, soaking up the sun, children playing football, toddlers running around starkers on long term missions back and forth to the calm sea fetching buckets of water to fill the moats of their sandcastles. Others were busy using spades to bury their dads in the sand. It was times like these he missed not having any children with Maureen.

"Here you go," Barton said, holding out the glass to him, dispelling any more regretful memories.

"Cheers," Cyril responded, taking a sip then wiping the froth from his moustache.

Barton sat on the wall beside him and loosened his tie a fraction more. "You got any kids, Cyril?" he asked.

A puff on his pipe gave him a chance to consider his response. "No," was all he decided to say. He certainly wasn't going to discuss the fact that, unfortunately Maureen couldn't have any.

"And your wife died, didn't she?"

"Three years ago now."

"I'm sorry." Barton took a drink of his lager. "You still miss her."

"Every day." Another puff of the pipe. "Anyway, what about you?"

Barton lit up a cigarette. "Divorced about eighteen months ago."

"Sorry to hear that too."

"No, it was my fault." He turned to look at Cyril. "Did you ever fancy anyone else when you were married?"

Cyril shook his head. "No, we were happy together. Soul mates really."

"Maybe that's where I went wrong. Married a great pair of tits but I wanted to test drive other models." Barton gave a snigger.

"But where are you now?"

"I know. Some shitty one-bed rented flat in town. Still … handy for taking a bird back for a shag. Plenty of them in Clacton, especially in the holiday season like now."

Cyril turned away to view the beach once more. Barton's comments made him feel ill. After a few seconds, he turned back to face the DI. "But are you happy?"

Barton took a drag. "Oh I don't know …"

"I don't think that you are, John."

Whether it was Cyril's first use of Barton's Christian name since working with him or he had hit a nerve, the DI quickly changed the subject. "So what do we think about this case then? What's your take?"

Cyril took a large swig of his drink. "Well, I don't think there's any doubt that Jem Fletcher intended to fly out over there," he indicated the sea, "maybe ten or so miles and dispose of Morgan where he hoped he'd never surface. But I don't believe Fletcher was a murderer. This has all the hallmarks of a gangland assassination. But how Fletcher got caught up in all this, I don't know. The one hundred pounds in his pocket would be a pretty big inducement. But is Morgan the first? How many times has he successfully disposed of a corpse? You're going to say that the Robinsons are in pole position for this, especially with what Beryl's just told us but …"

"But you're not entirely convinced?"

"No, it's not that, it's just I think we have a lot more to find out yet." Cyril used his pipe to make a point. "I mean, what did Yardley say about his plane and Fletcher?"

Barton rolled his eyes. "Oh shit, I forgot to get over and take a statement."

"Was that the first time Fletcher had taken his plane up without asking? Had he done that with anybody else's craft? I got a list of other owners who sometimes used his talents."

Barton broke into a broad grin. "You know, Cyril," he said, "I knew it was a good idea bringing you back into CID."

Like hell you did. Cyril knew full well it had been Sanderson's decision.

11

The Three Jays pub sat on a crossroads part way down Jaywick Lane to the west of Clacton. A big property, brightly lit with large windows meant that the people inside could be seen after dark without them being aware.

Cyril parked up by the nearby parade of shops and strolled past. He spotted his target sitting on a bar stool nursing a pint and chatting to three other men. Crossing the road, Cyril opened the door to the public phone box, lifted the receiver and dialled a number.

"Yeah?" a voice answered as the tones to insert coins interrupted. Cyril pushed them in.

"Is Lennie in tonight?" Cyril asked.

"Lennie?"

"Lennie King yes."

"I'll have to check. Who wants to know?"

"Tell him it's Dirty Harry."

There was a muffling noise as the barman attempted to cover the mouthpiece, not very effectively. *"Lennie,"* he could hear the man say, *"It's some fucking joker, says it's Dirty Harry for you."*

Another load of shuffling and muffling and then, *"Hello?"*

"Lennie, it's Cyril. How are you?"

"How did you know I was here?"

"Call it an educated guess. Now, I need a word."

There was a pause before Lennie responded. *"Well I'm not sure I can get them for you, Harry. It'll take time."*

"Stop messing about Lennie and meet me outside. Walk down the street and I'll pick you up." Cyril put the phone down and made his way back to his car. Passing the pub once more, he could see Lennie draining his pint and walking towards the toilets.

Back in the car, Cyril watched as Lennie appeared a few minutes later, looked up and down the street then made his way down Jaywick Lane.

Passenger window down, Cyril pulled alongside him. "Get in Lennie," he instructed.

The man leaned in through the window. "Look, this is a bit awkward for me, Mr Claydon. If anybody sees ..."

"Relax. Nobody knows you're talking to me."

Lennie King was a character Cyril had had dealings with many times over the years. In his early fifties now, he'd lived a life on the line between honesty and criminality, veering towards the wrong side from time to time. But overall, Cyril found him to be an honest criminal, if there could ever be such a thing. And, he had his ear to the ground.

He got in and they drove down the street, turning sharp right at the bottom to run parallel with the shore. As they passed the Never Say Die pub where he'd shared a drink with Barton only a few hours before, Cyril spoke, "Thought that was your regular watering hole."

"Clientele are a bit rough for my liking," Lennie retorted.

Finally pulling up on some waste ground by the side of the amusement arcade, Cyril switched off the engine and turned to face Lennie. "Jimmy Morgan," he said, "what's the story?"

A bewildered expression appeared on Lennie's face. "Jimmy Morgan? What's he done now?"

"Just tell me about him."

"Can I smoke?" Lennie asked.

"Be my guest."

The man pulled a cigarette packet and a lighter from his pocket, tapped one out and lit up. "Jimmy keeps himself to himself these days. You know he has a small bungalow down here?" He indicated the streets beyond the arcade.

Cyril nodded. "So I believe."

"Shacked up with some divorced bird. Dresses a bit tarty but I think they're solid."

Cyril smiled. "But what's the word, Lennie? You know what I'm asking."

He took a deep draw and exhaled loudly. "He thinks he's close to some big people. Talks a good game but I would think he doesn't know half of what he reckons he does. I can't see anyone letting him in on anything big. Just a bit of a gofor."

"So when was the last time you saw him?"

Lennie screwed up his face. "That must have been ... ooh, about five days ago. He was in the shop buying some cigs."

"Did you speak to him?"

"Exchanged a nod, that's all. Like I say, he tends to keep a distance and, to be honest, I don't want to get too involved."

Cyril studied him for a few seconds. "But no word on the street as to what he's been up to, specifically?"

Lennie puffed on his cigarette once again. "Not heard anything involving him, Mr Claydon. But you've obviously got him in the frame for something." He looked pleadingly for some morsel of information from the sergeant.

Cyril was amazed word still hadn't leaked out about Morgan's demise, and he certainly didn't want to be responsible for that revelation hitting the streets. "Okay Lennie, thanks for that."

The man looked disappointed, pulled a last drag on his cigarette, flicked it out of the window and opened the door.

"Careful you don't start a grass fire," Cyril quipped, about to start the engine.

Before he closed the door, Lennie popped his head back in. "Very droll Mr Claydon. Grass fire. But you do know he's a grass, don't you?"

Cyril froze and looked to the man. "What do you mean? Morgan? Who for?"

"Word is, one of your lot in Clacton." A smirk appeared on Lennie's face. "See you Mr Claydon."

DISPOSAL

The passenger door closed and Cyril watched him make his way across the rough ground to the road before disappearing around the front of the arcade.

12
Thursday 2nd September

Cyril had called Yardley Electrical and made an appointment for eleven that morning to take a formal statement from Walter Yardley. Barton had told him to arrange that when they were on their way back to the station yesterday afternoon.

"I'm sure if there's anything significant in what he has to say, you'll find it," he'd said. "But don't upset him, he has connections." With that, Barton had raised his eyes skywards. "Oh, and take Walker with you. It might be interesting for him."

DC Bill Walker was twenty-four and in his first year in CID. He looked enthusiastic when Cyril told him what was planned for later that day. DC Miller, sitting one-fingered typing on the ancient Remington manual machine that sat on his desk, gave a grumble and lit another cigarette. He was the older of the two, thirty-two, overweight and had probably reached the highest rank he'd achieve, whereas Walker appeared to have some ambition about him. That was Cyril's opinion but he'd be surprised if Barton didn't share it.

Cyril had also done a lot of thinking since talking to Lennie King last night. In his head, he replayed some scenes he'd witnessed since becoming involved in the investigation. The sharp close to the briefing on that first night; the look on Barton's face when he received the note; Sanderson's reaction. And then Barton's behaviour when they spoke to Beryl Boynton. It just made him wonder … but how best to handle it, that was his dilemma.

After walking Charlie and dropping him off early next door with Doris, he hadn't had time to eat anything before coming in. So by half-past nine, Cyril was beginning to feel peckish. Still, there'd be something interesting for him in the canteen.

About to put the first forkful of bacon, toast and beans into his mouth, a familiar voice interrupted.

"Hello, Skip, mind if I join you?"

Skip, short for Skipper, was the favoured term most uniformed constables used to refer to their sergeants.

Cyril looked up into the smiling face of Sam Woodbridge.

"Sit yourself down," Cyril invited.

Sam plonked his cup of tea onto the table and took a seat. "How's progress with the air crash investigation?" he asked.

Cyril looked around then, keeping his voice low, said, "You know we've identified the other body now too?"

"I heard rumours you had but not who."

Cyril decided to keep that information to himself. "That was a good witness you uncovered yesterday morning, Sam. The chef spotted a big Jag waiting at the lane entrance, and from what he told me I think I could narrow it down."

"Glad to be of service." Sam took a drink of his tea. "By the way, I heard something else you might be interested in."

Cyril wiped his moustache with a paper napkin. "Really?"

Sam leant in close across the table. "You know the pilot, Jem Fletcher ..."

"Yes."

"He has an older brother, Adam ... of course you do, I was forgetting, he identified Jem's body."

"Go on."

"Well, from what I hear Adam Fletcher owes money to some fairly unsavoury outfit. Not really the sort you would want to cross."

Cyril widened his eyes. "How much?"

"Didn't hear specific amounts but rumoured to be fairly serious."

"And the 'unsavoury' banking outfit?"

Sam looked disappointed. "I didn't hear who, but I got the impression it was someone with London connections."

"Well that's certainly interesting, I'll look into that." Cyril prepared another forkful as Sam drained his tea.

"Must get off," the young constable said. "Supposed to be out on patrol ..." he paused to glance at his watch. "... about now."

"Take care, Sam," Cyril said. "And if you pick up any more tit bits, let me know."

Sam nodded as he left, taking his empty cup and saucer with him.

As Cyril followed Sam's progress, he spotted Cathy Rogers enter the canteen and study the menu. Up on tiptoe momentarily to look at something, he found himself admiring her legs once again. Surprised by his interest, he looked down at his plate and continued to eat.

After a few minutes, he looked up again to find her looking across at him, breaking into a smile. She walked over with a tray containing a cup of tea and a sandwich.

"Hello again," she said. "Do you mind if I join you?"

He coughed on his last mouthful and indicated the seat opposite him. "Sorry about that," he said, wiping his mouth with the paper napkin. "Went down the wrong way."

"And here's me thinking I'd caused it," she quipped, taking her cup, saucer and plate off the tray.

Cyril felt himself colour.

"I always seem to get hungry this time of the morning," she went on. "Don't eat at lunch-time but ..."

"Actually," he interrupted, "I'm glad I saw you." He wondered if she might be talking nervously. "Could you could get hold of a file for me?"

"Sure. Just let me know." She took a bite of her sandwich.

"Can you get hold of Adam Fletcher's record? He's the older brother of Jeremy, the file you tracked down the other day."

She swallowed. "Mmm. I'll pop it up to you a bit later."

"Thanks, Cathy." He began to tidy his knife, fork and plate then noticed Bill Walker enter and look around.

Spotting Cyril, Walker walked towards them.

"I've got to go," Cyril said, standing up. "Speak to you later."

"Bye then." Cathy gave him that smile again.

As they left the canteen, Cyril was sure Walker wanted to say something but daren't risk it.

13

The premises of Yardley Electrical Manufacturers Ltd were located in The Hythe district at about the limit of shipping up the River Colne. Colchester, renowned for being Britain's oldest recorded town, to the surprise of many was also a port. Presumably that was one of the reasons the Romans settled the area.

Cyril pulled to a halt in one of three visitor's parking spaces outside the Victorian brick built offices and killed the engine. As he swung the car in, another vehicle caught his eye. He and Walker stepped out and he locked the car. Strolling over to the bay marked 'Chairman', he took note of the dark grey Daimler V8 Mark 2 which sat there. The Daimler was a variant of the Jaguar with exhausts either side. Interestingly though, this was 'G' registered, 1969.

After a wait of a few minutes, the young receptionist guided them through to the Chairman's office. Walter Yardley stood to greet them, holding out a hand. He was a tall well-built man in his sixties with thinning grey hair.

"DS Claydon," he said, "Good to meet you."

"And you, Mr Yardley," Cyril responded. "And this is DC Walker."

Yardley indicated the two chairs in front of his desk.

"Please," he said, before sitting down himself. "Shocking business," he went on.

Walker flipped open his notebook whilst Cyril pulled out a statement form from the folder he'd brought with him. "I'm sorry to bother you, Mr Yardley, you're obviously a busy man but we just need to go through the formality of obtaining a statement from you."

Yardley held up a hand. "Of course, I understand. And if there's anything I can do for Mr Fletcher's family …"

"I'll pass your sentiments on."

"Sorry gentlemen, can I get you some refreshments? Tea, coffee, or something stronger, eh?"

"We're fine, sir, thank you," Cyril said. "Now if I can just go through some of the facts? How long have you owned the plane?"

Yardley leaned back in the old comfortable-looking winged back leather chair and clasped his hands together. "Well, that one I've had for about four years. It's the second model I've had. I sold the previous one to fund this one. I've always had the flying bug since a pal took me up in a Spitfire at the end of the war. Probably wouldn't be allowed to have that sort of treat nowadays, but back then, things were a bit different." Cyril nodded agreement as he began to write. "And once this place took off ..." he gestured around him with both hands. "I began to realise I might have the money to indulge myself."

"So the business is doing well?"

"Despite the government's best efforts to cock things up, yes." He grinned at his own comments.

"So how do you handle maintenance on the plane?"

"When I first had one, I used to do a lot myself, but I was younger then. Also, I seemed to have more time. But as the business grew, I realised it was more effective to have external mechanics carry out the routine maintenance. First of all there was old George who was one of the stalwarts of the flying club. He'd been a top engineer in the Castle Bromwich factory that produced Spitfires and Lancasters in the war and retired down here. But then he died." Yardley shook his head. "A sad loss. What he didn't know about an aircraft engine wasn't worth knowing."

Walker began to fidget but Cyril was happy to let Yardley carry on reminiscing. Although it might take a little longer, he knew he'd get more and better information if he just let the man tell it in his own time.

Yardley leaned forward. "And that's when someone recommended a couple of the mechanics the others use,

Barry Hill and Jem Fletcher. So I gave Barry a try about … ooh, two years ago now, and he keeps the machine airborne."

Cyril looked up from the statement pad. "So your regular mechanic was this Barry Hill?"

Yardley looked a bit flustered. "Yes, he was supposed to be doing some servicing for me last week but I've also used Fletcher too."

"But did you know Fletcher was going to take the plane up on the morning he did?"

Yardley coughed. "Well er … not exactly. But he did have permission to fly it," he added quickly.

"Mr Yardley, I'm not concerned with any insurance issues you may have here, I'm only interested in establishing the facts. Now, if Jeremy Fletcher took your plane up without your specific knowledge but had blanket permission to do so, that's of interest to us. What about Barry Hill? Was he subject to a similar arrangement?"

"Well, yes. They both were."

"Do you have contact details for Mr Hill?"

Yardley opened up a desk diary and flicked through some pages before making some notes on a piece of paper. "This is where Barry's based," he said, handing the paper to Cyril.

"Thanks." Putting the note in the folder, Cyril resumed his questioning. "Knowing what we know now, that Fletcher was attempting to fly the plane, can you think of any other occasion when you might have suspected that he'd done this without telling you?"

Yardley furrowed his brows for a second. "I can't think of anything. But, it's not beyond the realms of possibility."

"So when was the last time you actually flew the plane yourself?

Again, he referred to his diary. "Let me see, it must have been …" He flicked back a few pages. "Ah yes, here we are. Three weeks ago on the Saturday. I took a client up to Cromer for a day out. Had lunch at a lovely hotel up there, overlooking the pier, then headed back."

"And since then it's been parked at Clacton?"

"Why, yes."

"Oh, one last thing … do you know a Jimmy Morgan?"

Yardley screwed up his face. "No. No, can't say I do. Why? Is it important?"

"No, it's just another name that's come up in a different line of enquiry. Okay, Mr Yardley, you've been most helpful." Cyril completed his last note then stood. "If I could just ask you to read through what I've written and if there's anything you're not happy with, please amend in your own hand and initial it. And when you're satisfied, if you could just sign at the bottom where it's indicated."

Yardley took the statement and read it through thoroughly. Cyril expected nothing less, after all the man had been in business for decades. Finally, with a flourish of a signature, he said, "Well, that seems to be pretty much what I've told you."

"That's great. In which case we won't take up any more of your time." Cyril removed the carbon copy and gave that to Yardley, who stood and offered him a hand.

As they were about to leave the office, Cyril turned and asked, "By the way, is that your Daimler in the parking bay?"

"Yes that's mine," Yardley answered.

"Lovely piece of machinery," Cyril commented.

"Drives like a dream. I've had it from new, so it's what … seven years old now. But I don't think I could get anything as comfortable to replace it."

"Well, thanks again for your time, Mr Yardley."

14

"Where to now, Sarge?" Walker asked, once back in the car.

"I think we should have a word with Barry Hill." Cyril handed the piece of paper with the address Yardley had noted down to the young DC. "Give me directions to here."

Half an hour later, Cyril pulled up on the forecourt of a vehicle garage on an industrial estate on the outskirts of Clacton. Hill's Motor & Aeronautical Engineers looked closed and locked up. A white Ford Escort van with the company name on the side was parked in front of the roller shutter door. To the right, a single door had a sign in its glass pane announcing *Reception*.

"Looks deserted," Walker muttered.

Cyril studied the premises for a second or two. "Maybe not," he said quietly. "We're here now, so let's have a look anyway."

They both got out of the car and Cyril led the way to the single door, put his hand on the glass and pushed. It opened. Glancing towards Walker he saw him raise his eyebrows. The door led into a small reception area with a counter. An array of spare parts was arranged on shelves behind. To the left they could see part of the workshop bays through an open door.

"Hello," Cyril shouted.

All seemed quiet. "Anyone there?"

"We're closed," came a voice from the back of the workshop area.

"Mr Hill?" Cyril persisted, "Barry Hill?"

Footsteps began to sound closer, then a bald-headed man in his fifties appeared, dressed in overalls. "I'm sorry, we're closed this week," he said, a surly expression on his face.

His demeanour changed when he saw Cyril holding up his warrant card.

"Sorry to trouble you, but if you're Barry Hill, we'd like a word," he said.

The man's shoulders slumped. "Oh God," he uttered. "I'm sorry. I'm so sorry."

The two detectives exchanged puzzled looks.

"Mr Hill, is there something wrong?" Cyril asked.

"You've come about the plane crash, haven't you? I knew you would." The man visibly paled.

"We would like to talk to you about that, yes."

"Will you charge me?"

"And why would we want to do that, Mr Hill?"

He looked at Cyril, eyes glassy. "Because I caused it."

*　*　*

In the interview room at Clacton Police Station, Hill sat hunched over the rickety table opposite Cyril and Walker.

"So, Mr Hill," Cyril said, "you began to tell us about your involvement at Clacton Air Strip earlier but I'd like you to tell me about your specific connection to Mr Yardley's aircraft, the one that crashed two days ago."

Walker had his notebook open and Cyril was poised with pen over a Statement Form.

Nervously, Hill began his account. "Mr Yardley asked me to check his plane over and do some servicing work on it last week. He told me there was no particular rush as he wasn't planning to use it until after the Bank Holiday weekend." He paused and rubbed his eye with his hand. "I'd completed most of the work, changed whatever parts were required and then I got interrupted."

"And this was when, exactly?"

"Last Friday, about half past three."

"Go on."

"Colin, the young lad who helps me at the garage, he arrived to tell me one of my regular car clients was having trouble with his car. He needed it the next day because he was planning to go to Scotland. Like I say, he was a good client. So I left what I was doing, closed the engine cover and tidied my tools away and went to attend to his car."

Cyril thought he knew where this account was going. "So what state was the plane in when you left it?"

Hill looked down at his hands. "I'd changed a couple of fuel lines." He looked up at Cyril. "The old ones were okay but I just like to be safe. They can perish if they're left too long." Head down once more. "But I'd only loosely tightened the glands. I should have tightened them with a spanner."

"And you think they may have come loose when it took off?"

He looked up again, this time with tears in his eyes. "What else could it be? When I heard it had happened ... and how it had happened, it could only have been when the fuel lines came apart. But I didn't mean to leave it. I was distracted. Mr Yardley said he wasn't going to fly the plane. I remembered on Monday morning and I intended to call in on Tuesday afternoon except ..."

Cyril sighed. "Except, it had crashed that morning."

Hill turned away, both hands covering his face, body shaking in sobs.

Cyril looked to Walker who had stopped writing. "Go fetch Mr Hill a cup of tea, would you?"

The detective constable stood and left the room.

"Mr Hill, you will need to speak to the Air Accident Investigation officers. What you say seems very relevant to their enquiry but only they can assess the significance of what you've told us."

"But I'm responsible for that man's death," Hill struggled to say, tears running down his face and spittle around his mouth. "How can I live with that?"

"But it wasn't deliberate. You couldn't have known someone else would attempt to fly the plane."

"But I should have left a sign on it."

* * *

"Where the Hell have you been?" Barton was coming down the stairs as Cyril left the interview room.

"I think I might have discovered why the plane crashed," Cyril said.

The DI walked over to him. "Smart arse," he said.

"Obviously, the Air Accident boys will have to talk to him." Cyril indicated the interview room.

"So who have you got in there?"

Cyril told him and began to relate the morning's events.

Barton stopped him. "Hold it for a minute. Let's go upstairs." Once again, he climbed up to the first floor and led the way to his office.

By the time Cyril had recounted everything from that morning, Barton was leaning back in his chair and on his second cigarette.

"So how did Walter Yardley seem?" he asked.

Cyril, sitting opposite, was puzzled. "Fine. Apart from just having had his plane wrecked. Why wouldn't he be?"

Barton shrugged but said nothing.

"Why are you so concerned that we don't upset this man?" Cyril continued.

"It's just … well you know how these things work … friends in high places and all that."

"Is he somehow involved in this?" Cyril leaned forward. "Are there things you're not telling me?"

"No, don't be so bloody soft. Of course there's not."

But Cyril could see the worry on the man's face. "You know he drives a Daimler?"

Again a shrug. "So?"

"Dark grey, like the one spotted at the airstrip lane gate."

It was Barton's turn to lean forward, eyes narrowing. "Are you saying you think he was involved in the crashing of his own plane?"

"Not that particularly, maybe in Jimmy Morgan's demise though?"

Barton slowly shook his head. "No," he said.

But Cyril wasn't convinced. "You suspect something too?"

"Bollocks!" Barton stubbed out his cigarette with some force.

There was a moment's silence. Cyril weighed up his next question. "Is it you?" he finally asked.

Now Barton looked puzzled. "Is it me what?"

"Is … was Morgan your snout?"

"Who told you that?" Barton's default setting was denial, Cyril knew, but the flush in his face told him he was on the right track.

"Just some information I received," he said, calmly.

"Well it's bollocks." He picked up his cigarette packet, shook it then realised it was empty. ""Fuck!" He stood and made for the door. "Get on with something useful DS Claydon," he said, snatching the door open.

As he strode across the CID room, he bundled past Cathy Rogers, knocking a file from her hand. With no word of apology, he disappeared out into the corridor.

Cyril rushed over to the flustered secretary.

"Here, let me help you," he said.

She was kneeling down slotting some loose sheets of paper into a manila file. "This is for you anyway."

They both stood up and faced each other. Another awkward pause arose. "Looks like I've been *Bartoned*," she said with one of those smiles.

Cyril chuckled. "I think we all have at one time or another," he responded. "And thanks for this." He took the file from her hands and sat down at his desk.

She hesitated then turned and walked away.

Ben Miller looked up from the adjacent desk and waited for Cathy to disappear. "She's got the hots for you, Sarge."

"Don't be stupid. It's just what you get when you treat people with a bit of respect," Cyril replied.

"If you say so." Miller resumed reading his paperwork, a smirk on his face.

*   *   *

An hour later, Barton returned. "Right, gather round team," he said.

Team was a bit of a misnomer, Cyril thought. There was only Miller, Walker and himself in the room and from what he'd said previously, Barton didn't have too high an opinion of the DCs. From the heated discussion Cyril had had with him before he left, he doubted he was considered part of this team either.

"So where are we now with our enquiries on this plane crash? Sanderson's biting my arse. Cyril, give us all a quick summary."

It was as if the previous discussion between the two had never taken place. Cyril took a breath then succinctly summarised the state of the enquiry, as far as he was aware. The pilot and the corpse identities had been established; Yardley owned the plane but had never intended to fly it in the near future; Barry Hill was certain he had inadvertently caused the plane to come down; two Air Accident investigators were interviewing him downstairs right now; and a witness had spotted two men in an old 'Jag with twin exhausts' by the airstrip lane at four forty-five on the morning of the crash. "I also think we need to speak to Adam Fletcher again," Cyril concluded.

Barton, with both hands in his trouser pockets leaning against an empty desk asked, "Specifically because …?"

"Information received that he owed money. Maybe nothing to do with anything, but if he needed cash quickly, perhaps he persuaded his brother to carry Morgan's body and dump it. We do think that was the intention, don't we?"

"Okay, follow up on that." Barton pressed on, "Now we also know that Jem Fletcher had a hundred pounds in cash on him." He turned to Miller. "Ben, you were trying to track down where those new notes might have been issued?"

Miller blew out smoke then answered, "I tried the Bank of England who print and distribute banknotes but they're not helpful at all. At the moment, I'm working my way through the local banks to see if they match any batches they've had recently."

Barton started to pace. "So, we have what appears to be an accident ... and, if it hadn't happened, we'd have been none the wiser on the murder of Jimmy Morgan. He'd have just been another missing scrote who would have been forgotten about. Maybe some of his mates would have suspected he was propping up a new motorway bridge somewhere."

"We need to try and establish a motive, Sir," Walker piped up.

"Very good, I'd never have thought of that," Barton responded.

Back to his sarcastic self, Cyril thought. In his opinion, Bill Walker was a smart lad who would benefit from a bit of encouragement, not ridicule.

"Bill's absolutely right, of course," Cyril said. "The motive will be found amongst his associates, and that's what we need to concentrate on."

"My money's on the Robinsons," Barton said. "What do we know about their activities down here on the Essex coast, or do they confine themselves to London?"

"You yourself said they have a static caravan on one of the parks."

"I didn't actually say that. What I said was, a lot of the East London gangs come down here for breaks and some have bought or rented them." Barton wagged a finger as if in thought. "Look, you have another word with the delightful Beryl. See if you can squeeze something else from her. I'm sure you'll manage it with your charm. Take Bill with you, she might be able to teach him a few things." A broad grin appeared on his face. "In the meantime, I'll see what I can find out about the Robinsons' local presence." He set off for his office. "Right, that's it. Chop chop," he said over his shoulder before closing the office door.

15

Beryl opened the door to Cyril and Bill Walker. "Not brought the Rottweiler with you, then?" she asked, stroking the Yorkshire Terrier she held in her arms.

"We've left him back in the kennels." Cyril couldn't help but smile. "Can we have another word, Beryl?"

This time, more soberly dressed in dark trousers and a white blouse, she stood aside to let them in. "That's good, because Pinky didn't like him."

"Pinky?"

She nodded to the dog. "Pinky"

"This is DC Walker." Cyril indicated his colleague.

"Sit yourselves down. Would you like a cup of tea or coffee?" She put the dog down and began playing nervously with her hands. "Or a cold drink?"

"We're fine, honestly." Cyril and Walker sat on the edge of the settee then waited until she was sitting in the armchair opposite. Pinky settled down on the floor in front of her. "I understand you've now officially identified Jimmy," he said.

She nodded, her eyes immediately turning moist.

"Please Beryl, I don't want to make this any more difficult for you but thanks for that. I know how difficult it can be."

She looked across at him. "I believe you do, Sergeant Claydon."

Cyril paused. He felt as though she could see inside his soul. "I wondered if you could tell me a bit about Jimmy? How you met for instance? What you liked to do?"

She dabbed her eyes then smiled at her memories. "We met in Clacton about two years ago at one of the clubs. I was with a friend. She'd gone off with another bloke, I was left on my own and Jimmy came up and started chatting. Nothing heavy, just a nice guy. He was kind to me." She stood up. "Are you sure you don't want a drink? I'm going to make myself a cuppa."

Cyril considered for a moment. "Go on then, I'll have a tea, milk, no sugar."

"Not for me thanks," Walker said.

While she made their drinks, Cyril wandered around the small sitting room taking in some details. On a unit by the side of the television, he picked up a framed photo of Beryl and Jimmy smiling at the camera, sitting at a bar table with drinks in front of them. Putting it down, he picked up another of a much younger Beryl holding two small children, a boy and a girl.

"That's Christine and William." Beryl came back into the room with two mugs. Handing one to Cyril, she went on, "Christine's twenty-five now and working in London, William's twenty-three. He's a mechanic in the Ford garage in Chelmsford."

"You must be proud of them."

She smiled, the first time Cyril had seen her do so. "Yes, they've done well considering ..." Her expression changed and the smile was gone.

Cyril raised his eyebrows and gave her the photo back.

"Their father left just after this picture was taken."

"So you brought them up on your own?"

She nodded, studying the photograph. "Bastard's never paid a penny. But I wouldn't want it. It was hard, yes, but we managed." She put the picture back on the unit.

Cyril resumed his seat on the settee. "You were telling me about Jimmy."

She took a sip of her tea and sat down on the armchair again. "I knew he was a bit of a rogue," she began. "I've learned to tell the bad ones, but Jimmy was good to me. Never imposed or took me for granted. I suppose our relationship grew slowly. After their dad," she indicated the framed picture by the TV once more, "I wasn't too keen to get taken for a ride again. I mean, don't get me wrong, I've had a few men friends since … after all, a woman has needs." She glanced at Walker, a smile playing on her lips.

"So you'd been together for about two years?" Cyril asked.

"I met him two years ago, as I said, but he didn't move in with me until about a year ago."

"I wondered if you've thought about the days leading up to Jimmy's disappearance …"

"I've thought of nothing else."

"I mean whether anything stands out as unusual? Did he go out on his own and not tell you where he'd been? Was he secretive about anything?"

"He always had secrets. But I did trust him. He looked after me."

Cyril took a drink of his tea and allowed a pause. He thought it best to try a different angle. "So what did Jimmy do for a living?"

Beryl looked a bit defensive. "We got by. I do a couple of shifts in a pub and Jimmy did some odd driving jobs for people."

"Who specifically, can you remember?"

She looked down to the mug of tea in her hands. "Just a couple of people he knew."

Cyril glanced at Walker then shifted forwards on the settee. "Look Beryl, I can understand you being defensive when Jimmy was still here. I'm sorry he isn't for you, but the best way you can help him now is by being open with me."

She shook her head and put the mug down on the hearth. "I can't," she said, pulling a tissue from her blouse sleeve.

Cyril pressed on. "Are you frightened of someone?"

She wiped her eyes and seemed to recover. "He didn't tell me everything, but he did do some delivery work for Yardley Electrical in Colchester on occasions."

Cyril looked to Walker then back to Beryl. "But you said '*some* people'. Who else gave him some casual driving work?"

Again a look of alarm spread over Beryl's face.

"Please," Cyril said. "We need to know." He could see her weighing up her options.

Finally she replied, so quietly, Cyril asked her to repeat it.

"The Holland Flower Company."

Cyril had never heard of them. "Are they some florist in Holland-on-Sea?"

"No, nothing like that." She bent down and picked up her drink. "Apparently they import flowers from Holland on the continent. Jimmy would take a van over on the ferry from Harwich and come back later with a load."

"Do you know where they're based?"

Beryl shook her head. "No idea."

"So how often did he do the Dutch run?"

With both hands around her mug, she took another sip. "I don't know … maybe three or four times?"

"And was he due to do that again soon?"

She put the mug down again and wiped her eyes with her hand. "I think so," she said.

Cyril took a deep breath. "And was this why he went out …" He made a point of studying his notebook. "… last Tuesday, the 24th? To meet Victor?"

Again, a look of alarm appeared on her face.

Cyril clarified. "Victor Robinson?"

16

They left Beryl Boynton shaken. She knew more about what Jimmy Morgan was involved with than she was willing to say. But for now, Cyril had enough to make some progress on the case. He could understand her reticence; after all, the Robinsons had a reputation for punishing those who betrayed them. Had that been Jimmy's fate? Had he spoken out of turn to the Clacton CID officer that Cyril suspected was Barton?

If anything, the day was even hotter. With no wind to take the edge off, it was unbearable. Back in the stuffy CID room, Barton was studying some files when Cyril and Walker returned. He beckoned Cyril into his office. A strong aroma of BO attacked Cyril's nostrils.

"Take the weight off," Barton said, indicating the chair in front of his desk. "I've been doing a bit of digging ..."

In a swamp, Cyril thought as he sat and watched Barton lean back in his seat, hands above his head revealing damp patches on his shirt under the armpits.

"... the Robinson's own a static caravan on the Seawick site." Seawick lies on the coast to the west of Jaywick, but was accessed by road through the village of St Osyth.

"Odd you should say that," Cyril replied, "because Bill and I have had an interesting conversation with Beryl."

Barton leaned forward and grinned. "I'll bet she frightened him to death."

"Well, apart from that, Jimmy had been doing some driving work, delivery vans. And guess who for?"

Barton looked serious. "Victor Robinson," he said slowly.

Cyril smiled. "Apparently he was taking a van over on the ferry from Harwich. It was labelled up as belonging to The Holland Flower Company."

"Really?"

"I've asked Bill to check it out, but I'll bet the firm doesn't exist."

Barton nodded approvingly.

"But not just the Robinson's," Cyril continued.

"Go on, surprise me. You've got that smug look on your face."

"Our old friend, Walter Yardley. Seems he was delivering for Yardley Electrical as well."

DCI Sanderson wafted in on a cloud of cologne. "Christ Dick, it smells like an abattoir in here," he commented.

Barton smelt his pits. "Well it is bloody hot."

"Anyway, what's that you're saying about Walter Yardley?"

Barton repeated what Cyril had just recounted.

"Forget about Yardley for now," Sanderson said. "I can't see him being involved in this."

"He did deny knowing Jimmy Morgan when I took his formal statement though, Sir." Cyril said.

"But if it was just a casual arrangement, he probably wouldn't involve himself with that. Probably arranged through his factory manager or whoever."

"What I was thinking, Sir," Barton jumped in, "was arranging for a warrant to search the Robinson's static … just to see what that throws up."

"Okay, Dick, it's probably worth upsetting them," Sanderson said. "You never know what you might find."

He took a step towards the door then paused. "Might also be worth investing in some air freshener," he quipped, then was gone.

"Tosser," Barton said under his breath. "Anyway, Cyril, he's right, we need some fresh air. You reckoned Adam Fletcher had money problems … let's rattle his cage."

* * *

One result of the weeks of hot weather was that when people were at home, windows would often be opened, and in some cases doors, to let what breeze there was flow through. That played to Barton's advantage as he and Cyril approached Adam Fletcher's neat council-owned semi. As they walked up the path to the front door standing ajar, the row was reaching its climax.

"... and all because of you," a shrill female voice was saying. "You saw how the kids reacted. How can you look at them again when they ask about Uncle Jem? Answer me that!"

"Look, we can get through this," Adam Fletcher said.

"Don't touch me."

"Come on, I can sort it."

"How? How are you going to fix it? You're in over your head."

There were a few seconds of silence before the woman spoke again. "Come on then, you're the one with all the smart ideas. How are you getting out of this? And I mean 'you'. You're not dragging me down."

"Fuck's sake, Carol!" Fletcher finally shouted, slammed a door inside then strutted out through the front door.

"Bit of a temper you've got there, Adam," Barton said, leaning against the wall on one side of the doorway; Cyril was on the other.

Fletcher stopped in his tracks, turned slowly round, saw the two detectives and rolled his eyes. "That's all I fucking need," he said. "What do you want?"

Barton looked across at Cyril. "That's no way to talk to officers of the law, is it, DS Claydon?"

"We'd like a word," Cyril said.

"Aren't you going to invite us in?" Barton pressed on, a grin spreading over his face.

"Piss off."

Barton pushed himself off the wall and took a step closer to Fletcher. "Well, we could go inside and have a chat with ... Carol, is it? Or we might just arrest you here, outside in the street. But let's face it, this seems a nice little neighbourhood. I'm sure you wouldn't want to have the curtains twitching."

"Or," Cyril joined in, "we could just have a little drive and a chat."

Barton looked across at Cyril. "That's a good idea, DS Claydon. A compromise. Always a good idea, a compromise."

Fletcher looked from Cyril to Barton then over his shoulder to Barton's Rover parked kerbside. "Come on then," he said, shoulders slumped in surrender.

With Barton and Adam Fletcher sitting in the back and all the windows open, Cyril drove, keeping the speed down.

Barton pulled out a packet of cigarettes. "As we said, Adam, we'd just like a little chat." He offered a cigarette to Fletcher who took it. "Now, if at any time we don't think you're taking this seriously or if you're telling us a load of Billy Bollocks, then DS Claydon here can simply drive us down the nick and we can make things more official." Barton looked straight at Fletcher. "You get my drift?"

Fletcher nodded and Barton lit both their cigarettes.

Cyril had adjusted the mirror so he could keep glancing at Fletcher's reactions. The man certainly seemed less cocky than when they'd all stood on his path a few minutes ago.

"I hear you have some problems, Adam?" Barton began.

A flash of anger appeared on his face. "Like my younger brother's just died."

"That's not what I'm particularly talking about. You had other problems before that."

A shrug of the shoulders. "No more than anybody," Fletcher responded.

"Specifically money."

"Like I said. We've all got rent to pay, food to buy, clothes for the kids."

"Adam, I was hoping for a full and frank discussion here but ..."

Fletcher stiffened. "So I owe some money. Big deal."

By now, they were slowly driving along the seafront, heading east towards Holland-on-Sea. Families were picnicking and playing on the greensward and beyond, where the paths dropped down to the promenade, the sea reflected the depth of the late afternoon sun. There were a few parking spaces so Cyril pulled the car to a halt facing the sea. Switching off the engine, he half-turned in his seat to face the two men in the back.

"I think it might be a big deal, though," Barton continued.

Again, another shrug.

"That would depend on who he owes money to," Cyril joined in.

Barton nodded theatrically. "Very true."

Fletcher took a last draw of his cigarette and flicked it out of the window. "I got into a bit of trouble." He blew out smoke and looked down at his hands. "At school, we used to play cards. Only for coppers, but I was good at it, you know. I'd not really played since but … earlier this year I got involved with a card school." He looked to Barton. "Don't ask, because I won't tell you but … to cut a long story short, it turns out I wasn't as good as I thought I was."

Barton shifted in the seat. "How much?"

Fletcher hesitated. "Two," he finally said.

"Hundred?" Cyril asked.

"No. Grand."

"Bloody Hell, Adam, that's serious money."

"I know."

"And your job is …?"

"I'm a postman. So with my hours, that's why I could afford some time to help … well, do a bit of decorating for …"

Cyril rubbed his hand over his face. "That's got to be a year's salary," he wondered aloud.

Fletcher slowly nodded his head.

"So how are you repaying that?" Barton asked.

This time Fletcher shook his head, still looking down onto his lap. "Slowly."

"They must be quite understanding ... these people."

Fletcher was silent.

"So who do you owe?"

"I can't."

"Adam!"

Fletcher looked to Barton then Cyril, sheer terror in his eyes. "I can't. They'll kill me."

"Look ..." Barton began angrily, before Cyril put up a hand.

"You said you lost money in this card school," Cyril said in quiet measured tones.

"That's right."

"How much have you managed to pay back?"

Fletcher's eyes were watery. He looked away across the greensward to the shape of Clacton pier. "About half," he finally responded.

"So how have you managed that?"

He wiped his face with his hand and sniffed. "Odd jobs."

"Who for?"

Another shrug. "Different people."

Barton finally snapped and grabbed hold of him roughly by his tee shirt. "When we ask you a question," he snarled, "we expect a fucking answer!"

Adam Fletcher cowered as Cyril placed a hand on Barton's arm.

"A word," Cyril said, opening the door and stepping out.

Reluctantly, Barton released his grip. "Stay there," he barked then got out of the car to join Cyril by the boot, a dark expression on his face.

"He's scared," Cyril said in hushed tones.

"He fucking well ought to be. I'll take him down the station and give him a ..."

No," Cyril interrupted. "Whatever he's gotten himself into, he fears them more than us. We need to try a different tack to squeeze that out."

Barton seemed to calm slightly, leaning against the back of the car. "Go on then genius, what do you suggest?"

"I think Mrs Fletcher might be the way in."

"And you think he's told her what he's been up to?"

Cyril put both hands in his pockets. "Think back to the argument we overheard. What was it she said? *'How are you going to fix it? You're in over your head.'* She knows. Certainly more than he's saying." Cyril pointed towards the rear window.

"So how do you suggest we play this? Take him back and interview the wife with him present?"

For the first time, Cyril thought Barton was taking him seriously. "She'd probably clam up," he said. He slowly walked in a circle, considering what to do. "He's a postie. We can try and talk to her on her own tomorrow morning. She'll either be at home or, if she works, we can engineer something."

Barton finally nodded. "Okay, let's work on that. Although I'd still rather have five minutes on my own with him in an interview room."

17

The Gateway supermarket was quiet in the evening. This was Cyril's preferred time for an activity he hated. Shopping for food didn't interest him these days. Although it was a necessary function, he couldn't get excited about it. But a quick check through his cupboards after he'd returned home, revealed a lot of empty space. He'd asked Doris if she needed anything and she'd given him a small list which he'd gladly added to his. After all her help since Maureen had passed on, especially with looking after Charlie, it was the least he could do.

Wandering around the aisles, he reflected on what progress had been made that day. Adam Fletcher had been dropped off at the end of his road and they had learned that, while his wife worked some evenings, she was around in the day, apart from picking up her two boys from school in the afternoon. Cyril and a female uniformed constable would call round the following morning.

It also sounded like the reason for the plane's failure was down to Barry Hill, albeit inadvertently. The engineers had confirmed the cause and Hill would suffer for a long time. He obviously had a conscience.

Beryl had given them links between Morgan and both Walter Yardley and the Robinsons. Cyril had an uncomfortable feeling about Yardley. That car; there couldn't be too many models like that. Denial of knowing Morgan could be true but he'd like an opportunity to probe further. Every time Yardley's name was raised, the defences seemed to rise; both Barton and Sanderson were guilty there. And then there was the rumour of Morgan being a snout for a CID officer. Despite the denial, Cyril was in no doubt that Barton was the one.

Barton said he was arranging for a warrant to search the Robinsons' static but had said no more to him since. For some undisclosed reason, was he keeping Cyril in the dark? That thought unnerved him too.

Steering his trolley around the end of the tinned vegetables aisle, Cyril collided with another. He looked up and saw the shocked expression on Cathy Rogers' face turn into a smile.

"Sorry about that … Oh, it's you," he said.

"Yes, it's me." She swept a hand through her shoulder-length dark curly hair.

"I was on auto-pilot."

They looked at one another for what seemed like ages but must only have been a split second.

"Is this your regular shopping venue?" Cathy asked.

"Er, no. I don't have one. But Doris likes the bread in here."

Cathy raised her eyebrows. "Doris?"

"Yes. She's my next-door neighbour. She's seventy-six and looks after Charlie."

"Her husband?"

"No, my Labrador."

She laughed infectiously and Cyril joined in.

"That sounded like one of those comic sketches on TV," she said.

"I suppose it did." An awkward pause. "So is this your local?"

"Supermarket? Yes. I only live a few streets away."

Another uncomfortable silence. "Well, I'll let you get on," Cyril said, and began to manoeuvre his trolley to the side.

"Actually," she said, nervously, "I was just wondering …"

He stopped. "Yes?"

"No, it doesn't matter," she flustered.

"Go on."

"No. You'll think I'm … well."

"What is it Cathy?"

She took a breath before blurting out quickly, "Well, some friends of mine have asked me if I'd like to join them on Saturday night as part of their quiz team. They go regularly and they're two men down this week, well a man and a woman down because their other friends Jim and Sandra are away for the next two weeks and ..."

"Slow down," Cyril said, amused by the fact that Cathy seemed not to take a breath.

"Stupid idea, I know," she went on, "but I just wondered if you'd like to come with me? I'm sure you're very knowledgeable on all sorts of subjects ..."

"Okay," he said, surprising himself.

"... having been in the RAF and the ... You would?" A surprised look appeared on her face.

"Obviously dependant on how this investigation goes but, yes, I like quizzes."

She beamed one of her big smiles. "That's great."

"Just let me know where and the time. I'll look forward to it." Cyril returned her smile and set off for the checkout.

It was only when he got back to the car that he realised he'd forgotten half a dozen items from his list. Still, all of Doris's were there, so he decided to pick up the remainder from a different shop on the way home. As he drove, he grinned to himself. He couldn't remember having ever been propositioned by a woman before – never mind in a supermarket.

18
Friday 3rd September

The sun was just about up, emerging from the sea and sliding into another clear blue sky when Barton pulled into the Seawick Holiday Park. He drew his car to a halt alongside one of the static caravans, a row away from the one owned by Frank Robinson. He knew Robinson senior wasn't there but the information he had was that his two sons, Victor and David, were. Another two marked police vehicles with six male and two female uniformed officers had drawn up close by, one to the rear and the other a row behind their target. At precisely six am Barton, with DCs Ben Miller and Bill Walker alongside, gave the call for the raid to begin.

With a loud rap on the caravan door and shouts of, "Police! Open up!" the eight uniformed officers circled the van. Inside, curtains moved. Just before a particularly burly member of the Clacton force swung the battering ram into the door, it opened.

A bleary-eyed man stood in the doorway with a towel around his waist.

Barton stepped forward to face him.

"Fuck d'you want?" the man said.

"Mr Robinson? Victor Robinson?"

"It's David actually." Five foot eight with dark wavy hair, he scratched the stubble on his cheek, an insolent smile appearing on his face.

"DI Barton from Clacton police. We have a warrant to search these premises." Barton held up the piece of paper he'd brought with him and attempted to bundle his way past.

Robinson put up his hand. "Just a minute, let's have a look at that," he said, taking the warrant from him.

"What's going on?" Another man appeared behind the first. He was taller with fair hair, and in the act of tying the cord of a silk dressing gown around him.

David smirked, handing the paperwork back to Barton. "The police here think we've got something to hide Vic," he said to the other man.

"Only a couple of sexy birds," the fair-haired man said.

Both men stood aside to let Barton, Miller and Walker enter.

Barton looked around and took in the plush furnishings of the interior. Static caravans could be well finished but this one was at the top end. He could feel the thick pile carpet below his shoes and noted some of the other details; the lounge area with a television in the corner and two white leather sofas, the breakfast bar fitted out with optic measures, whisky, gin, brandy and other spirits bottles standing around. Behind the bar, he could see the well-appointed kitchen with fridge and freezer and a four-ring gas hob and oven. On one of the sofas in front of the breakfast bar, a dark-haired woman seemed comatose below a blanket.

Barton turned to the brothers and smirked. "Very cosy."

The taller man spoke. "A couple of friends stayed over." He held out a hand. "Victor Robinson, by the way … just so's you know who you're dealing with."

Barton ignored the handshake offer. "Is she alright?" He nodded to the prone figure on the sofa.

"She's just a bit tired," David answered.

Through the open door to the main bedroom at the rear, a blonde woman shrieked, "What the fuck …?" Pulling a sheet up around her neck, she got to her feet. "'Ere, wha's goin' on, Vic?" she continued, in a thick London accent.

"Get some fuckin' clothes on, Sandra. We don't want this lot to get too excited," Victor responded.

Barton's gaze lingered for a moment before he turned and shouted out to the female uniforms to come and join them indoors.

"Supervise the delightful Sandra getting dressed," he instructed the first to appear. "And get this one sorted as well," he said to the second female officer as she stepped inside, indicating the woman on the sofa.

Meanwhile a nod to Miller and Walker was the sign to begin the search of the caravan.

David and Victor Robinson seemed relaxed at the early morning intrusion, too relaxed Barton thought. As Miller and Walker worked their way systematically through the cupboards and fitted units in the lounge, Barton searched the sofas, bedding and discarded clothes on the floor. Nothing of any significance was found.

Outside, the uniforms were searching the various external storage bins and the underside of the van itself.

"Can I get you some refreshment, DI Barton?" David Robinson asked, the same smirk on his face that Barton would love to wipe off.

"Not on duty," the DI responded.

By the time Miller and Walker had progressed to the kitchen area, searching the food cupboards as well as below the sink unit, Barton was rifling through the cabinets in the bathroom. David Robinson was watching from the doorway.

"What are these?" Barton held up a tube of pills.

"Victor's," he responded. "He has a little embarrassing problem. Don't worry, they're on prescription."

The dark-haired woman was now on her feet, a pink dressing gown wrapped around her, standing behind David Robinson. She giggled drunkenly. "Has he been a naughty boy?"

Barton ignored the comment and continued searching the bathroom, even lifting the toilet seat. Finally, he made to leave the small room "Excuse me," he said, squeezing past Robinson. As he did so, the woman leaned into him. "Sorry, am I in your way," she whispered into his ear.

One of the uniformed officers put his head in through the van door and caught the DI's attention. A gentle shake of the head told Barton that the external search had turned up nothing. He suspected inside would follow suit. The cocky attitude of both brothers, the attempts by both women to cause embarrassment led him to believe they had known this visit was coming.

Another ten minutes and they had completed the search of the two bedrooms, bedclothes removed, wardrobes explored, all to no avail. Finally, Barton led the way back to the lounge area and watched as his officers left.

In one final act of irreverence the brothers dropped their towel and robe to the floor. "Don't you want to search us too, Inspector?" David Robinson said.

Barton felt the colour rising in his face; not through any embarrassment, but pure anger. "We'll see ourselves out," he said, striding from the caravan.

"Let's get out of here," he said quietly to his DCs.

The door to the caravan was thrown shut and a burst of raucous laughter came from inside.

Back to his Rover, Barton climbed into the driver's seat and slammed the door. Miller joined him in the front with Walker in the back. There was an awkward silence as Barton fumed. Finally, he pulled a cigarette from his packet and lit it. Miller watched him before deciding he wasn't going to be offered one, so produced his own packet.

"Did either of you two tell anyone about this raid?" Barton asked.

"How could we, guv?" Miller responded, "You didn't tell us what this was all about, only to get our arses in early this morning."

"No whispers at the nick?"

"No." Walker wound down his rear door window to give the smoke from the cigarettes more room to escape.

"They fucking knew." Barton insisted.

Miller had a smile on his face as he turned to his boss. "Still, those two birds looked like goers. I bet they're in there shaggin' the ..."

"Fuck's sake, Miller."

"I'm only sayin'."

"Well don't!"

"Anyway, what about Winco, Sir," Miller persisted.

"What about him?"

"Well, did he know about this morning? Could he have let it slip?"

Although Cyril knew a search warrant for the Robinson caravan was being pursued, he was the one officer Barton felt could be trusted implicitly. The fact that Miller questioned that fell nicely into what he had planned.

"Where is he, by the way?" Miller went on.

"Win-, look, he's on another line of enquiry," the DI responded. "And, do me a favour, show a bit of respect, Miller; don't call him *Winco.*"

Miller turned in his seat to exchange looks with Walker.

Barton started the engine. "Let's get back to the nick."

19

"Where to now, Skip?" WPC Annie Cauldwell asked. Originally from Newcastle, her Geordie accent had been softened by the twenty-odd years she'd spent in Essex. In her early fifties, married with two teenage boys, she was a very experienced officer and Cyril felt she was the ideal person to accompany him on his visits.

"Let's see if we can have a word with Vicky, the late Jem's partner," he said as they walked away from Adam Fletcher's house down the path to the car.

On the way to Great Bentley, Cyril and Annie discussed the half hour they'd just spent with Carol Fletcher. They'd gleaned very little from Adam's wife. She'd remained fairly tight-lipped giving non-committal one word answers for the most part as Cyril tried to delve into Adam's financial state. The house seemed comfortably furnished, no signs of any tight budgets but, there again, who knew what went on below the surface.

No, so far as she knew there was no pressure over money. His job paid well enough to cover their outgoings and yes, he sometimes went out for the evening on his own. So what? Most men like to have a couple of pints with their friends, she'd argued.

"She did seem genuinely upset over Jem's death though," Annie concluded.

"Only to be expected," Cyril said, drawing to a halt outside Jem Fletcher's mid-terraced house for the second time in a few days. He looked up at the scaffolding and wasn't surprised to see the painting operation exactly as it was when he and Barton had first called. "Don't suppose she'll be here but we'll try it first," he said and got out of the car.

His knock on the door was answered a minute later by an attractive woman in her early thirties with blonde hair tied back in a ponytail and wearing jeans and a tee shirt. Her eyes looked puffy.

"Vicky, is it?" Cyril asked.

She nodded.

"DS Claydon. And this is PC Cauldwell from Clacton police." He held up his identification.

"Come in," she said, standing aside to let them pass. "Excuse the mess, we're …" she caught a breath. "We were getting this place sorted but … well now …"

"I understand." Cyril stepped directly into the living room. "Look, I know it's a difficult time for you but, if you feel up to it, I'd like to ask you a few questions if that's alright?"

"Sure. Can I get you anything to drink, I'm sure there's tea and coffee, not sure about any cold drinks though?"

"We're fine, thank you."

Vicky fussed around clearing newspapers off the velour settee. "Sit down a minute," she said.

Cyril and Annie sat down as Vicky sat on the arm of the matching chair opposite.

"I'm not sure if anyone's said anything to you," Cyril began, "but it looks like Jem's death was a tragic accident. There was a fault with the plane's engine."

Tears pricked at the woman's eyes and she drew a paper tissue from her pocket to dab her cheeks.

He carried on, "Did you know Jem was taking a plane up that day?"

Vicky wiped her nose and put the tissue away. "Not especially. But that was his business, a mechanic, I mean."

"Did he ever talk to you about his job? Who his customers were? The sort of things he had to sort out?"

"I probably wouldn't understand if he did." Vicky began to look puzzled. "Is there something you're not telling me?"

"We're just trying to get a picture of Jem and what happened leading up to the accident," Cyril replied.

"But that's just it. You said it was an accident. A fault with the engine. What more could there be to it?"

Cyril stood and walked over to the fireplace. "It's just we need to make the report as complete as we can." He picked up a photo of Jem and his brother smiling at the camera in front of a light aircraft. "They look pretty close," he commented.

"I suppose they are … I mean were. Jem looked up to Adam. But Adam liked to look after Jem too. That's why he was giving us a hand here." She stared off into an unseen distance, "Now, I'm not sure I can stay here."

Cyril glanced to Annie and she joined in the conversation. "Well, I wouldn't make any hasty decisions," she said. "Give it time and see how you feel."

Vicky looked sharply across at Annie. "How I feel? I'll feel the same as I do now. Jem's gone and this was his place really. I don't think I want to stay here."

Cyril quickly interceded. "You say Jem and Adam were pretty close. Did they do many things together? I mean, did they have nights out? Do favours for each other? I know Adam was helping out here."

"Recently, they seemed to have been closer …" Again a puzzled expression came over Vicky's face. "But why all this interest in Jem and Adam?"

Cyril sat back down on the settee. "Oh, don't worry about me. I'm just nosy that's all." He opened his notebook. "The morning of the accident, can you tell me what time he left?"

Vicky relaxed slightly. "It was early. I mean it was still dark, so it must have been around five."

"Was that usual?"

"Well …" She seemed to give the question some thought. "He had been out at that time on a few occasions recently."

Cyril looked up from his notes. "Recently? So this was a bit unusual?"

"I think he'd gone out a couple of times before like that. Said a customer wanted him to check out the plane as he wanted to use it later the same day. So he thought he'd give himself time to do a proper ... check." She paused and looked at Cyril as if realising something. "But if he'd done a proper check, he wouldn't have crashed, would he?"

"Like I said, we believe it to have been an accident and it may have been something he wasn't likely to spot. But if I can just focus on what you said, can you remember when he was out that early before?"

She furrowed her brow then replied, "Maybe about four or five weeks ago and then about a week later."

"So three times in the last month or so?"

"Yes."

Cyril made some notes in his book. "And you say Jem and Adam seemed closer recently?"

"I suppose they have."

"Say ... in the past month or so?"

Vicky frowned as her suspicions appeared to surface once more. "Are you linking that to the early morning departures?"

"We just don't know. It may not be connected, just an avenue we're exploring before we conclude our enquiries."

"So what's Adam saying?" she asked.

"Well ..." Cyril paused, "... not a lot actually, that's why we wanted to chat to you."

The conversation finished a few minutes later with nothing further of any use. The period they could keep the existence of another corpse in the plane at the time of the accident a secret must be running out but Cyril didn't want to be the one to tell Vicky.

20

When Cyril returned to the CID room from his morning's activities talking to Carol Fletcher and Vicky, the two DCs were at their desks. Walker was quietly studying some files. Miller, a smouldering cigarette in his ashtray was typing something on the old typewriter on his desk. Both were silent and neither looked up when he entered.

"Everything okay?" he asked.

A mumble and a shrug of the shoulders were all that his question elicited. The door to Barton's office was shut and he could see the DI sitting at his desk poring over some paperwork. Something had happened. He walked up and knocked on the door.

"Yes," came the grumpy response.

Cyril walked in and closed the door behind him.

"Something gone down?" Cyril wondered.

"Just the bloody opposite." Barton indicated for Cyril to take a seat. "Sweet Fanny Adams in fact."

Cyril sat down, puzzled.

"The Robinsons' static," Barton began to explain. "They were expecting us, I'm sure of it. Cocky bastards."

"I knew you were applying for a warrant but I didn't know you were going to raid them this morning? How come I didn't …?"

Barton held up a hand to stop him. "That was deliberate," he said.

Now Cyril was confused. "Deliberate? You mean you kept me out of the loop on purpose?" He could feel his anger rise. The incident where he was left to make his own way back from Great Bentley, Barton's disappearances without telling him what he was up to. And now this.

Cyril got to his feet. "So is this all window dressing then?" he went on. "Following through with a raid that you knew would give you nothing? Because you'd already tipped them off." Somehow, he stopped himself from telling him to find some other mug to keep in the dark.

Barton also stood. "Look, I know you think I'm an arrogant obnoxious twat. God knows I've seen it in your face often enough, **but I am not bent**." He walked round the desk. "I came into this job to put the bastards away, not line my own pockets or protect them." He was face to face with Cyril, hands on hips. "Now, you either believe that and help me find out just who is keeping those bastards one step ahead ..." He indicated with his thumb. "...or you can fuck off back to uniform."

The silence was heavy. The two men held each other's gaze, only about a foot apart. Barton seemed wound tight as a coiled spring. Cyril weighed him up; the lack of respect, his bluntness and poor manners, but was he 'bent', as he put it? No, Cyril's instincts told him he wasn't, he only hoped they didn't let him down.

"Okay," Cyril finally said, "Any ideas?"

Barton visibly relaxed. "Thank you." He breathed out deeply, walked back around the desk and sat down. "I've been thinking ..." he continued slowly, "... it has to be someone above me." He jabbed a finger in the direction of the CID office. "I can't think any of them has the connections ... or the balls."

They both glanced through the glazed door to the CID room where Miller and Walker had heard their raised voices. Once they became aware that the argument had stopped and they were being watched, they dropped their heads, attention focussed on their desks.

Cyril resumed his seat. "Well let's just keep an open mind on that for now."

Barton's eyes narrowed. "You suspect one of them?"

"No, but I just think we rule nothing out at the moment." Cyril rubbed his moustache with thumb and forefinger. "So, up the line, what are your feelings?"

"I hate to think of the possibilities."

Cyril sat back in his seat, confident for the first time since re-joining CID that he had Barton's full support. "So what was the story with Jimmy Morgan?"

Barton began playing with a pen then took a breath, as if still considering how much to tell. "Okay," he finally said, "this is strictly confidential …"

"Of course."

"I admit, Morgan was my informant. Not very often but, from time to time, he brought me some interesting snippets."

"So what snippet did he bring you last week? Specifically just a few days before the crash."

"No, that wasn't me when Beryl said he'd gone to see a man about a dog. I've no idea who that was. I met him a few days before then. But he didn't tell me anything about the Robinsons."

"So what was it?"

"Yardley."

"Walter Yardley?"

"Yes. He told me that Yardley was organising the smuggling of diamonds from Holland."

Cyril raised his eyebrows. "But why would Yardley get involved in something like that? He's got a successful business."

"But is it?" Barton argued. "That's what I asked. Apparently not everything in the Yardley Electrical garden is rosy, at least not according to Morgan. Since he told me, I've been trying to make some discreet enquiries to substantiate what he hinted at. But it's difficult when you don't want certain parties to find out you're digging around."

"Chief Superintendent Viney, you mean?"

"For one. But I did discover they have some cash-flow problems. One of their biggest customers went belly up just after Easter and they've been struggling since."

Cyril turned this over in his mind. There didn't seem to be any panic or atmosphere of unease when he interviewed Yardley the other day. After a few seconds of consideration, he said, "But do you think Yardley might have had anything to do with Morgan's demise?"

Barton puffed out his cheeks then reached for the packet of Peter Stuyvesant on his desk. "I don't know." He pulled a cigarette free and lit it. Blowing out smoke, he added, "Perhaps not him personally, but someone who worked for him."

"And he does own a grey Daimler V8 like the one spotted parked up by the track entrance to the hangers the morning of the accident. I know his is a 'G' reg and our witness reckoned it was 'D', but in the dark, riding past on a bike, it would look similar."

"Ah," Barton said, as if just remembering something. "I forgot to say, parked up by the Robinson's static this morning was a dark grey 'D' reg Daimler."

Cyril took a hand through his hair. "So that doesn't really get us much further forward. We've got Morgan with connections to both the Robinsons and Yardley and they both have vehicles similar to one spotted on the morning of the crash."

Barton nodded and exhaled smoke. "Plus, Yardley Electrical bank with Williams & Glynn's in Colchester, the same branch who issued the new ten pound notes we found on Fletcher. Miller found that out this morning. I mean, there's no way they can confirm who they issued the notes to, could have been anybody over the period of a week leading up to the accident."

Cyril took his pipe from his pocket. He didn't intend to light it, it just helped him think. "Okay," he said, pointing with the stem. "Let's look at it another way, who else knew Morgan was your informant?"

"Hmm, that's the thing ..." Barton drew on his cigarette. "The only one I told was Martin."

"DCI Sanderson?"

Barton nodded. "No one else. I only told him because of the close friendship Yardley supposedly has with the higher ups."

"I thought you were going to say that." Cyril rattled his teeth with the pipe stem as he considered for a moment. "And definitely nobody else?"

"No."

"And of course the DCI knew you were planning to raid the Robinsons' caravan this morning."

Again Barton nodded affirmation.

"No," Cyril said. "I can't believe Sanderson is on anyone's payroll."

Barton took a last draw and stubbed out his cigarette. "I must admit, I can't either but ... I think we need to play things carefully from now on. And that's why I said it was deliberate on my part to keep you in the dark about this morning's raid."

"Go on."

"I have a little plan. It may not work but, if you're prepared to give it a chance ..."

Cyril put his pipe back in his trouser pocket and leaned forward on to Barton's desk to hear what his DI had in mind.

21

About six miles off shore from the Seawick Holiday Park, the skipper of the small fishing vessel, *Margaret B*, was looking forward to another fruitful morning. He was accompanied as usual by his best mate from schooldays. They'd both sunk their savings into the boat about ten years ago. It had been a profitable decision on the whole. A small but regular clientele, including hotels and a couple of holiday parks had been built up over time, helping them to see through even the dark days of the three day week a couple of years ago.

Also on board once again was the skipper's fifteen-year-old son. The boy had been with them several times during the summer and loved the sense of freedom out at sea, as well as the great summer weather they'd enjoyed this year. What he wasn't particularly looking forward to was the return to school next week, so he was making the most of these opportunities to be with his dad.

The net had been reeled out from the boat and, as they slowly dragged it behind, the skipper and his mate chatted about the latest TV news reports of the drought. Apparently, some rivers had actually run dry, there were standpipes in the streets of Yorkshire, and the water level in a Lake District reservoir had dipped so low that parts of a village had become visible once again after years submerged.

Finally, it was time to pull the net back in. This was when they began to get excited about what size of catch they would make. With the skipper at the wheel and his partner operating the winch, the young lad watched the net slowly break the surface. After a few seconds, the lad cried out, "Dad! Dad, look at this!"

The winch was stopped immediately and the engine set to idle as all three peered over the side. Firmly entangled in the net was a large shape wrapped in black plastic. They stood for a few seconds studying what was bobbing around in front of them. The skipper and his mate exchanged concerned looks.

"What the Hell is ...," the skipper said, "It's certainly not an old wartime mine."

"Let's have a closer look then," the mate responded.

The three of them struggled to draw the net in closer. Each grabbed a piece of net as they pulled the package alongside. Twice they tried to heave the net on board and twice one of them almost fell overboard.

"Hold on," the skipper said. "We're going to have to be careful here. Let's see if we can use the winch to help us."

The mate stepped over to the controls. "When you're ready," he shouted.

The skipper gave the signal and his mate gently urged the winch forward as he and his son wrestled with the bundle. Slowly, they dragged it up to the bulwark. With one last effort, the mystery object, still entangled in the net fell over onto the deck.

The winch was stopped and all three crowded round.

"Get this out of here first," the skipper said, pulling at the netting. His son joined in but came to a dramatic halt as his fingers caught a taped joint in the plastic.

A mushy substance oozed from the tear and his father stood up.

The young lad threw up over the side.

"Christ! What the ..." He stopped mid-sentence. With his hand covering his nose and mouth, he knelt back down and began to feel the shape contained within the plastic. He looked up at his mate.

"Is that what I think it is?" his friend asked.

"Radio in," the skipper instructed. "Tell them we're bringing a body back to shore. We'll need the police."

22

Brightlingsea has a strong historical foundation, being one of the Cinque Port limbs. It was a limb of Sandwich, one of the Kent and Sussex ports formed for military and trade purposes. Its recent industries have been fishing, specifically connected with oysters, and boatbuilding. With one road in and out, it was along this that Barton was driving his Rover 2000 with Cyril sitting alongside.

Barton had been discussing his plan for Cyril's weekend when the telephone call interrupted. Cyril had watched the expression on Barton's face grow serious as he listened to the voice on the end of the line. When the call was ended, Barton grabbed his jacket from the back of his chair and simply uttered a 'Come on' to Cyril. On the fifteen minute drive to the harbour, Barton explained what he'd been told about the fishermen's find.

The sun was beating down once more as the Rover paused by the uniformed constable at the end of the road, keeping unauthorised persons at a distance. Cyril could see a couple of Escort vans further along the quayside, recognising the unmarked white vehicles used by forensics officers.

Barton drew the car to a halt and stepped out. Cyril followed. As they approached the circle of activity surrounding a small fishing vessel tied up against the quay, a gap opened up allowing them to see for the first time the black plastic covered shape lying on the concrete. The two forensics attendants wore face masks and the two uniformed officers held handkerchiefs to their mouths and noses. Barton and Cyril followed suit. Sitting on a nearby bollard, Cyril saw a youth being comforted by an older man whilst another man dressed similarly in all-weather fishing gear looked on.

"The crew of the *Margaret B*, Sir," one of the uniforms confided in Barton. "The two men own the boat and today, one of them had his son on board. They dragged this up in their nets about six miles out."

Barton nodded. Then to one of the forensics men, "Is this what it seems like? A human body?"

"Certainly is, Sir," the man confirmed. "Looks like it's been in the sea for at least four weeks, I'd say. We'll know more when we get it back to the morgue."

Barton gave orders for the uniforms to get statements from the crew then turned away and walked back down the quayside, grateful to put some distance between himself and the corpse.

"Christ, Cyril," he said, "Is this the start of a fucking epidemic?"

"Well that's two," Cyril responded. "If what Vicky told me is correct, there's still one more out there."

"Shit!" Barton quickened his pace back to the car.

On the way back, Barton resumed the conversation about his proposals for Cyril. "Well there's nothing we can do until we get matey there back on the slab and I'm not looking forward to that," he said. "In the meantime, any thoughts on how you're going to play things?"

"I've got an idea," Cyril said.

A grin spread over Barton's face. "So you've discounted the delightful Annie Cauldwell then?"

"I think her husband might have some objections to that, don't you?"

"Maybe you're right. I wouldn't like to get the wrong side of that big Geordie bugger." Barton thought for a second. "Mind you, there is always the lovely Cathy Rogers ..."

"Oh, damn," Cyril reacted. "Sorry, didn't mean to ... It's just ..." he shook his head, remembering the invite from Cathy to join her in her pub quiz team on Saturday night. "It doesn't matter. But no, that's not an option either." He knew Barton was trying to wind him up, but he was becoming adept at ignoring that strategy. "I have another idea but I need to do a bit of work on that when I get home. I'll let you know later today," he concluded.

Barton resumed a serious expression. "Okay, but let me know what's happening. And don't forget, this is purely between you and me. I don't want this leaking out … not yet anyway."

23

"Cup of tea for you, Doris." Cyril walked out into the back garden. His neighbour was sitting in her garden chair, Charlie in his favoured position by her side. The old dog struggled to his feet as he walked over to the pair of them.

"Careful, Charlie," he said, placing two cups and saucers on the table by his neighbour's side.

"You're a treasure," she responded. "Just what I need."

Cyril sat down beside her in the other chair. "Has he been good?" he asked, making a fuss of the big Labrador.

"My best friend." She took a drink of her tea. "You're home early today. Have you solved the riddle?"

"Riddle?"

"Crashed plane, mystery object."

"Ah, the Gazette. No, not yet." After a few seconds, he spoke again. "Doris, I wanted to ask you something."

She turned and using a hand to shield her eyes from the bright sunshine, looked at him. "Of course you can, Cyril."

"When was the last time you had a holiday?"

"Ooh, it must have been …" She thought for a second or two. "… last July. Yes. Me and Betty took a coach holiday to Torquay for a week. Why do you ask?"

"So you're really overdue one now?"

A broad grin broke on her face. "Cyril, you're not propositioning me are you? Not at my age?"

He snorted. "No, Doris but I thought we might be able to do each other a favour."

"I'm intrigued."

Over the course of the next few minutes, Cyril outlined the scheme he and Barton had come up with.

*　*　*

"Is Cyril not with you, Sir?" DC Walker asked as Barton strode through the CID room towards his office.

Barton turned round and made an exaggerated point of looking all round him. "No, I don't believe he is." He continued on his way.

"It's just …"

Barton paused again. "Yes, Walker."

"He asked me to have another word with the chef from Butlin's."

Barton scoffed. "That's two words I thought I'd never hear together. Since when did Butlin's employ chefs?"

"Anyway," Walker ignored his boss's sarcasm. "Jack Finnegan, the bloke that spotted the car idling by the track end on the morning of the crash …"

"What about him?"

"When I spoke to him this afternoon, he was wearing glasses. When I asked him if he always wore them, he said he didn't really like to, but he had to when he was working."

Barton sighed. "What's the point of this, Walker?"

"The point is that when he was cycling to work that morning, in the dark, he couldn't really tell if the car was D registered or G. He just thought it might be a D."

Barton looked to the ceiling. "God give me strength. Okay lad, thanks."

As he approached his office door his phone began to ring.

"Barton," he growled into the receiver, listened for a minute then added a 'thanks' and replaced the handset.

Back out into the CID room, he pointed at Walker, the only officer present.

"With me, Walker," he said, striding out and leaving the DC to grab his jacket and hurry after him.

This time Barton was not so lucky to find a parking space at the Essex County Hospital. He cursed his luck driving around the small car park. Finally, one car began to back out but was turning towards them. Another car was behind ready to take the space.

"Make sure we get that," Barton instructed Walker who was sitting beside him.

The DC jumped out and ran to the spot. He held up a hand to the other hopeful driver and produced his warrant card. Some shouting erupted from the car but Walker stood firm. Barton eventually drove into the vacant spot.

"Hell d'you think you are!" the middle-aged man shouted, getting out of his car.

Barton jumped out to join his colleague. "This is police business," he said. "If I were you I'd get back in your car and find another space."

The man studied the two officers, each holding out their identification, then turned away, muttering under his breath.

Barton locked the Rover and led the way through the main doors and up the stairs to the Intensive Care Unit. They were directed to the room adjacent to where Danny Flynn had been looked after. Thankfully, Danny was now on a general ward for recovery.

The Sister in charge of ICU told them Adam Fletcher was still unconscious, his wife was at his bedside and they wouldn't be able to speak to him any time soon. Barton assured her he wouldn't disturb the patient but he did need to speak to Mrs Fletcher.

He peered through the vision panel, knocked on the door and slowly entered. Walker remained outside.

"How is he?" Barton asked, taking in the figure lying on the bed, tubes appearing to enter every orifice and an oxygen mask covering most of his battered and bruised face.

He could see her eyes red and puffy as she turned to look at him. "Not good," she said quietly.

"I wondered if I could have a word?" He nodded towards the corridor.

She slowly picked her handbag up off the floor and followed the detective from the room. Outside in the waiting area, she sat down on a padded chair, Barton on one side of her and Walker on the other.

"Mrs Fletcher, I wondered if you could tell me what happened to Adam?" Barton asked.

She stiffened. "I was hoping you could tell me."

"If you could … just as much as you know."

The woman relaxed. "Sorry, it's just … it's such a … Look, all I know is that he was found by his van, near the end of his round in St Osyth just after one. Two blokes found him lying on the pavement."

Walker was taking notes as Barton paused. "He's certainly been given a good going over. Have you any idea who might want to do this?"

She looked down into her lap and a couple of tears dropped from her face before she could stop them with a paper handkerchief. "I'm not … not really." She wiped her nose.

Barton sighed and leaned back in his seat, head against the wall. After a second he bent forward once more. "Walker, get Mrs Fletcher a coffee would you?"

She looked up and gave Walker a thin smile. "Two sugars please."

They watched the DC leave then Barton turned to the woman. "Look, I'm not interested in any petty activities Adam might have been involved in but this is serious business. Nothing from his mail bags was taken, as far as we can tell, so this was personal. Now I know you gave my colleague DS Claydon short shrift earlier on but we're looking into some serious crimes ourselves." He watched as she seemed to consider her options, although he would be surprised if she actually had any. He pressed on. "So what can you tell me?"

She looked up to a point where the wall met the ceiling in front of her. "Adam owed money," she said. "He got involved with a card school back in February. One of his mates introduced him." She gave an ironic chuckle. "Reckoned he'd been good at school. But that was only for pennies. This got serious."

"How serious?"

"A couple of grand, apparently."

At least that tied in with what Adam had told them earlier and it demonstrated he'd been honest with her. "So how is he paying that sort of money back?"

She looked at Barton. "That's the thing. I think he roped Jem into helping him."

"And how would Jem be in a position to pay back that sort of money?"

"The two of them have been spending a bit of time together recently. I think Jem was using his access to the planes to ... to do favours for whoever Adam owed money to."

"Do you know what sort of favours?"

"I didn't ask. I can only imagine. I mean you're the detective. How long would it take to fly over the sea to Holland or Belgium or somewhere and bring something back?"

"Drugs, you mean?"

"Like I say, you're the detective."

That was a new angle. Somehow, Barton didn't think the Fletchers were involved in drug smuggling. No, disposing of *'awkward material'* would still be his guess.

"Any idea who Adam owed this money to?"

She looked down and shook her head. "He wouldn't tell me. Only that they weren't pleasant people to deal with." She snorted. "Huh, he can say that again." She turned to look at Barton. "Is Adam in trouble? With you lot, I mean. Has he committed some crime?"

"We don't know yet, Mrs Fletcher. There's a lot we've still to find out."

* * *

Cyril rang the station from home. First of all, he tried to speak to Cathy. The desk sergeant told him she'd already gone home, it was Friday after all.

"Has she left a message for me?" Cyril asked, then added quickly, "She was looking out some information."

"Not with me, Cyril," the sergeant responded. *"You could ask upstairs. Want me to put you through?"*

"Is DI Barton in?"

"Came back about ten minutes ago with young Walker in tow. Like a bulldog chewing a wasp as usual," the sergeant laughed.

"I can picture it," Cyril said. "I do need to speak to him though."

"Hold on."

After a few seconds, Barton came on the line. *"You'll never believe where I've just been,"* he said.

"Surprise me."

Barton then related the details of his visit to Adam Fletcher's bedside earlier that afternoon.

"But that doesn't make any sense," Cyril thought out loud.

"How do you mean?"

"It just seems a bit counter-productive. I mean if someone owes you a grand, the last thing you'd want to do is give them such a hiding that they can't repay the money. That way you won't get anything back for a while, if at all if you've gone too far."

"I see what you mean but the other motive doesn't seem to stack up either because there's nothing to suggest there was anything missing from his mail."

"How do you know that?"

"Whoever it was attacked him near the end of his round in St Osyth. According to the postal guy who came out, the mail for all the addresses he still had to deliver was still on the van."

"Hmm, I wonder …"

"Anyway, have you sorted whatever it was you had in mind for this weekend?"

"Oh yes. I thought I'd give my elderly neighbour a little treat."

He could hear Barton sniggering on the other end. *"Oh, yes. How elderly?"*

"Enough to be my mother," Cyril retorted. "And by the way, have you thought Fletcher might have held back some valuable mail from earlier in his round to pass on to whoever attacked him? They probably overdid it. Meant it to look like a robbery and Fletcher would have already given them what he thought they could use. Pay down his debt. I'll leave those thoughts with you."

24
Saturday 4th September

"Well this is lovely," Doris remarked, looking around the lounge area of the static caravan. "And we've got it all weekend?"

"We have," Cyril confirmed, standing with her small case in his hand.

Charlie waddled up the steps and into the van behind him.

"Come and choose which bedroom you want," Cyril said, then looked down at the dog and smiled. "Not you," he added quietly.

Ten minutes later, with Doris comfortably settled in the main bedroom, he took in the view from the large bay window to the front of the lounge. They could see the sea through a big gap between the next row of vans. The Robinsons' static was to the left and just in front of the van that had been organised for Cyril. If Barton was to be believed, the park's manager owed him a favour and had made this van available for the weekend. All Cyril had to do was to appear to be on a weekend break and try and find out what he could from the next door van. He now appreciated what Barton had meant when he said he was deliberately left out of the raid on the Robinsons' van. He could slip into the undercover role Barton suspected he might have to employ. Barton had also explained the set up he'd found the day before; David and Victor Robinson plus, as he put it, a couple of bimbos. His assumption was that the women were staying there for a while and not just a couple of cheap pick-ups.

Cyril put the kettle on for some tea but when he checked the fridge there was no milk.

"I'll go," Doris offered. "I can take Charlie with me to the site shop."

While she was gone, Cyril began to study the details of the Robinsons' static. The main entrance door was on the other side but on the side nearest him, there appeared to be a bedroom window, one for the bathroom and a larger window towards the front that served the lounge. This time of day, they were all closed. Hopefully, as the temperature rose, that would change. What Barton hoped Cyril would find out, he wasn't sure.

After ten minutes, Doris came rushing back, Charlie struggling to keep up.

"Cyril, Cyril," she called as she got to the door.

"What's up?"

"Have you seen this?" She waved a copy of the Clacton Gazette in her hand, a plastic carrier bag with milk and fresh bread in the other.

Cyril took the paper and opened it out to reveal the headline, *'SECOND BODY DISCOVERED OFF BRIGHTLINGSEA'*. He read on.

'The discovery of a body wrapped in plastic sheeting dredged up by a fishing vessel from Brightlingsea is being connected to a similar find in a plane that crashed on Clacton beach on Monday.'

"It's out there then," he commented.

"Is this what we're working on?" A mixture of concern and excitement on her face.

"Don't worry about anything, Doris. I'm just here to have a look around. You just relax and enjoy the change of scene." He put his hands on her shoulders. "Now, let's have a cup of tea and some breakfast."

25

The sunlight streamed into the bedroom through thin curtains. Barton put a hand over his eyes before opening them. But he realised it wasn't the light on his face that had woken him. Snoring sounds from somewhere at his back had done that. He struggled to make sense of it for a moment. Slowly, he turned to see a strange head covered in long curly hair of a dirty blonde colour on the pillow. Lifting the sheet, he saw his own bare form next to a naked arse, female, thankfully.

Who the Hell was this? He struggled to remember much beyond ten o'clock last night. He could recall the pub. After that, he had a vague recollection of visiting a club. Pulling the sheet off him he swung his legs round and sat on the edge of the bed. Everything looked normal. This was definitely his bedroom. The phone was on the bedside table along with his alarm, a packet of Rothmans and a creased copy of *The Valley Of The Dolls*. He'd been attracted by the cover but could never get on with it.

He stood and walked round the foot of the bed. His bare feet kicked one of a pair of red slingbacks. Whoever it was, was still fast asleep. A red dress hung on the floor. That rang a distant bell. A black bra draped itself over the top of his chest of drawers. Picking it up, he sought the label. 38D, promising, he thought. Finally, on the opposite side of the bed was a matching pair of lacy black knickers. All the signs were that he'd had a good night; just a pity he couldn't remember any of it.

The female stirred, the snoring had stopped. As she turned over, her face became visible. Horror struck him; and then depressing thoughts. She looked old enough to be his mother; well at least fifty. 'Christ, I've hit a new low.'

She opened her eyes, mascara stains down her cheeks. "Hello, Johnny boy." She smiled at him, revealing deep wrinkles around her mouth. "You enjoyed yourself last night."

He hoped his expression had recovered and his shock wasn't reflected on his face. "Er, yeah ... about that," he stuttered.

"You can't remember, can you? Why don't you get back in and I can remind you." She sat up and giggled like a girl, her saggy breasts in full view.

Instinctively he covered himself with both hands.

"Aw, don't be shy. You weren't earlier on." She looked him up and down. Finally, her expression changed to one of disappointment. "Well at least get me a drink. Tea or coffee, I don't mind."

"Look, I'm sorry, it's just ... Of course. I'll put the kettle on." He turned away, glad of something to distract him. Opening a drawer, he pulled out some underpants before putting them on and walking through to the kitchen.

As the kettle boiled some images began to run through his mind from last night. There were two of them he thought; a shorter, dark-haired girl and her taller, older, blonde mate. It was the dark haired one he'd fancied. Some of it was coming back to him. What happened to her?

The kettle clicked off and he poured water onto tea bags in two mugs.

There was another bloke ... a bit later. Did the younger bird piss off with him?

He could hear the woman next door shuffling around; no doubt getting herself back into her clothes.

In the fridge there was just enough milk for the teas. Removing the bags, he added the last of the milk. About to shout out about sugar, she clacked her way into the room in her heels.

"It's Sharon, by the way. I can see you're struggling," she said.

"I'm starting to remember." He held up the sugar bowl. Shaking her head, she went on, "Good memories?"

"I ... I think so." She filled her dress out very well; looking a bit sexy after all. "I seemed to remember you were with a mate." He handed her a mug.

"Karyn, yeah. She pulled. Went off with some smarmy git. You got a fag?"

"Bedside table."

He watched her walk through to the bedroom. The heels definitely improved the look; lovely legs, he thought.

He followed behind with his own mug.

Back in the bedroom, sitting on the bed, she offered him one of his own cigarettes. He nodded and she lit both of them, handing one to him. The way she did that began to stir his feelings.

"So Sharon," he said, "Did we ever get to the part where I asked you what you do?"

She giggled again. "Oh come on John, no point dancing around that one. I'll drink my tea, finish this ..." She looked at her cigarette. "... and let you get back to your life."

"Look ..." The telephone interrupted him.

"Saved by the bell." She stood up, leaned over and kissed his cheek. "I'll see myself out," she said, heading for the door.

"But ..."

"You better get that. See you around."

He watched her go. The sound of the flat's door closing brought him back to the insistent ringing of the phone.

"Barton," he snapped.

26

By mid-morning signs of life began to appear in the next door van. The bathroom window opened a touch, followed a few minutes later by the bedroom one to the rear.

Cyril and Doris were sitting on the veranda to the front of their unit, empty tea cups in front of them. Cyril had read as much as he wanted in the paper and Doris, glasses on, was busy reading the reports from the magistrates' court.

"So wot the bleedin' 'ell are we supposed to do for the afternoon, then?" a shrill female voice was asking in the Robinson bedroom. Barton's assessment of who was there was probably right, Cyril thought.

"I don't know. Go for a swim, take a bus into town and do some shopping," the male voice replied. *"I thought that's what you women liked to do."*

"Fine," the woman snapped.

Doris put the paper down, leaned forward and, in a quiet voice said, "She's not best pleased, is she?"

Cyril smiled. "Probably the gangster's moll," he whispered.

She looked surprised. "Is that what she is, do you think?"

"I'm only joking."

"But it's them we're here to keep an eye on though." Her eyes flickered in the direction of the voices.

Someone opened the Robinsons' lounge window. *"Smells like a bloody armpit in 'ere,"* a man's voice declared.

"You are only here to relax, Mum." Cyril stood and picked up their tea cups. "I'll do us another drink."

Doris put her paper down and got to her feet. "You sit down, Son," she said, joining in the act. "I'll go." She took the cups from him and added quietly in his ear, "You need to listen in."

He laughed to himself and looked down at Charlie, dozing gently at his feet. "She's loving this," he said quietly. "But you need to earn your keep too."

The big dog raised his head off his paws and looked up at Cyril as if he understood every word.

"Here you are." A tennis ball was pulled from his pocket.

Charlie scrambled to his feet, suddenly interested.

"Fetch." Cyril threw the ball onto the grass in front of their caravan by the side of the Robinson one.

Charlie trotted off after it, picked the ball up in his mouth then slumped onto the grass, as Cyril knew he would. He'd always happily chase a ball but very rarely returned with it.

"Good boy, Charlie," he said, got to his feet and wandered over to the dog.

Charlie's tail thumped the ground as his master approached. Cyril got to his knees and made a fuss of him ... just below the Robinsons' open lounge window.

"What time's he supposed to be here?" one man asked.

A slight delay before the second man answered, *"Any time now."*

Cyril was about to settle himself in for an earwigging when he spotted a familiar form making its way from the park entrance. He got to his feet and encouraged Charlie to follow him. He was back in the van watching from the lounge window when the figure walked past the spot on the grass where he'd just been lying moments before.

Lennie King strode purposefully around the front of the Robinsons' static.

"I thought we were having another cup of tea outside?" Doris stood looking puzzled, holding two tea cups in her hands.

"Sorry." Cyril indicated the Robinson abode. "Developments."

He took a cup from her and sat down on a chair.

"Do we need to get closer to listen in?" she asked, her eyes twinkling.

"They have a visitor and he knows who I am."

"Soon sort that," she said, putting her cup down and rising to her feet.

"Where are you …?"

"Come on, Charlie," she said. "Let's have a short walk."

"No, wait …"

Charlie followed her out of the van and Cyril watched them make their way slowly up the side of the next door static before she stopped a short way from their lounge window and bent down over the dog.

After ten minutes, Doris and Charlie strolled back to the van. Just as she got to the door, Cyril saw Lennie King walk off in the direction of the main entrance.

"Interesting," she said stepping up into the lounge.

"I don't know, Doris." He shook his head. "What am I going to do with you?"

"Listen, you don't get to my age without knowing how to eavesdrop and pick up gossip." A big smile appeared on her face. "Now, make us a fresh pot of tea and I'll tell you as much as I could get."

Settled back in the comfortable lounge seats, Doris gave her account.

When she'd finished, Cyril put his empty cup back down on its saucer. "So basically, they have a job for Lennie on Monday, but we don't know what," he summarised.

"If 'Lennie' was the visitor they had, then yes. I'm sorry I didn't hear any of the details for you."

Cyril put his hand on hers. "You did well, Doris." I couldn't have risked Lennie spotting me. It would have made all this a waste of time."

"I did find out something else too."

"Go on."

"The four of them are going to the entertainment evening in the site club tonight. Apparently, the women want to see this 'glam rock' band that's appearing."

Cyril gave her a dubious look. "Glam rock?"

"Yes, you know, like Slade and Sweet."

"Who?"

"Oh, Cyril, you need to get with it. They're two of the biggest bands around."

"How do you know all this?"

"Oh, I keep my finger on the pulse; that and listening to Radio Two." She laughed at her own comments. "Anyway, it'll be good for you to get out for a change. You never know, you might meet someone nice."

His expression grew serious. Cathy, he remembered. He hadn't been able to tell her he couldn't join her at the pub quiz tonight. He hoped she wouldn't be angry with him. That in itself surprised him; the fact that he thought about her and that he'd be letting her down.

Doris snapped him out of it. "Come on, you've got a lot going for you, you know. You're still young, you're a good looking man with a good job, your own house, got all your own teeth and hair ...Ooh d'you know if I was thirty years younger, Cyril Claydon ..."

"Doris, if I thought for one minute ..." His face cracked into a big smile.

"How long have we known one another? Twenty-five years? More?"

"Twenty-six actually."

"And I can't talk to you openly and honestly after all that time?" She shook her head in mock admonishment. "I was heartbroken after Howard went. I should have shaken myself after it but, like you, I found it difficult to let go. After all, you don't share your life with someone for all that time and can just forget about them. But maybe I should have moved on sooner. After all, as you made me realise the other day, I was still only forty-five." She leaned forward and looked at him earnestly. "Now I've never told you this but Maureen and I used to have long conversations. You were on shifts. She just needed someone to talk to after … well, you know, after they'd told her. She said to me near the end, 'keep an eye on Cyril for me. And don't let him go all maudlin' on you.'"

Cyril chuckled. "I could hear her saying that."

"But she also said that when the time was right, and I think it is now, to tell you, 'I wouldn't mind if he found someone else. In fact,' she said, 'I'd love it. I couldn't bear to see him unhappy because of me.'"

His mouth opened but it was a moment before he replied, "She actually said …?"

He stood and walked slowly to the door.

"Where are you going?" she asked. "Have I upset you?"

"No. No, you haven't. Keep an eye on Charlie for me. I'm just going for a walk."

27

"And you're sure there was nothing missing?" Barton was in the depot manager's office at the main Post Office Sorting Centre in Clacton.

"Not so far as we can tell, and we've spoken to most of the deliveries he would have made on his round." The short balding man nudged his glasses up the bridge of his nose, clearly irritated at having his Saturday morning disrupted.

The detective was silent for a second. This wasn't what he wanted to hear. It was Cyril who had posed that possibility to him as regards a motive for the attack on Adam Fletcher. And the more he thought about it, the more likely it had seemed. Still, it gave him an idea. "Well thanks for your help anyway," he said and followed the man as he was escorted from the building.

It took him ten minutes to drive to the station. He wanted to check on a few things and make a couple of phone calls. Dashing in through the entrance, he was surprised to pass Cathy Rogers.

"Ah Sir, is DS Claydon in today?" she asked.

He paused by the second set of doors. "No. Why? Anything I can help you with?" he leered.

Her expression change to one of disgust.

"No. I'll catch up with him another time." She turned and strode off.

Definitely, he thought. Old Cyril's pulled. He took the stairs to his office, struggling to keep his face straight.

He hardly had time for his buttocks to touch the seat before his office phone rang. Answering, he listened for a few seconds then said, "What now? Today?" A pause, then, "On my way."

This was one duty Barton dreaded. The call was from Dr George Maguire who informed him he was about to begin the post-mortem shortly. Barton walked down the familiar basement corridor of the Essex County Hospital towards the pathologist's office. As before, Maguire's familiar figure was readying himself for the task in hand. Whoever it was the crew of the *Margaret B* had dragged from the depths of the North Sea, they were about to give up their secrets.

"Christ, you don't half bring me some cases, Dick." Maguire looked put out.

"I try my best. At least it keeps you off the streets."

The doctor frowned. "Come on then," he said leading the way to the same room where the PM on the first body had been carried out.

Joining them was a mortuary attendant and a forensics officer to collect and bag any evidence. The shape, still wrapped in plastic, lay on the stainless steel slab.

Dr Maguire slipped on surgical gloves and covered his face with a mask. "Right," he said with feeling, "To work."

To begin with, he walked around the gurney. "Evidence of some marine activity here." He indicated some rips in the plastic where two hands could be seen. Kneeling down, he examined it closely, looking with particular interest at the digits.

"Unfortunately for you, Inspector, we have no skin left for fingerprint identification purposes."

Continuing around the shape, he commented at various points. "Looks like the plastic sheet has been snagged by something, rocks maybe. The feet are also exposed here and again, our little marine friends have had a nibble."

Back at the top end, scissors in hand, he began to cut through the plastic. After a few seconds, he paused. "Ah."

"What do you mean, 'Ah'?" Barton asked.

"I mean there isn't much left up here, and I'm not talking about little fishes … or big ones come to that." He looked up at Barton. "Whoever this is, they were blasted by a shotgun I'd suggest. The head is a mess."

"Oh Christ! You mean dental records will be no good?"

Maguire shook his head. "Not much of anything here, let alone teeth." He covered the mess over with the plastic once more and stood back. "If we're to gather as much evidence as possible for you, Dick, we'll need to carry out X-ray examinations first." Giving a nod to the attendant, he walked to the door.

The assistant prepared to slide the body back into a fridge.

"So when do we do that?" Barton looked perplexed.

The pathologist removed his gloves. "Probably tomorrow now."

"Can't it be done now?"

Maguire turned at the door. "I don't think it's a good idea to wheel matey there past live patients sitting waiting to have their own X-rays done, do you?"

"I didn't think they worked Saturdays."

"Well they are today. Bit of a backlog to catch up. They've been working Saturdays for the past two weeks." A smirk appeared on his face. "Anyway, he's not going anywhere. I think we'll reconvene on Monday morning."

Barton was left looking at the disappearing green surgical gown.

"Nine am sharp," Maguire added from further down the corridor.

Before he set off to return to Clacton, Barton climbed the stairs to the Intensive Care Unit. He felt as though he'd spent more time here in the past few days than back at the nick. A different Sister was sitting at the nurse station when he walked in.

She looked up from paperwork. "Can I help you?"

Barton pulled his warrant card from his trouser pocket and tried one of his best smiles. "Adam Fletcher. I need a quick word."

She frowned. "Not today you won't."

Okay, so the smile hadn't worked. Strange, he thought, because it did last night. "But it won't take a minute."

She stood and walked round the desk towards him. "Did you not understand? Mr Fletcher is still unconscious, so he can't talk to anyone."

Barton sighed then held up his hands in surrender. "Sorry, Sister," he offered. "Do you have any idea when I might be able to ...?"

"Hard to say. He's had a severe beating and his body will take time to recover. The doctors are thinking maybe another forty-eight hours."

28

The function room was crowded but Cyril and Doris found a table towards the side which offered a good view of the stage. Doris sat down whilst Cyril went to the bar for some drinks. She'd taken some pride in her appearance, he thought. Her hair looked freshly coiffured, she wore a sparkly dress and had even applied subtle make-up. For his part, he was wearing smart flannels, shirt, his RAF tie and a sports jacket.

When he returned, the compere was beginning his first routine; a bit of comedy, a few gags, before introducing the warm up act.

"It's not bad, this, you know," Doris said. "Chicken or scampi and chips in the basket and entertainment too. All for £3.50."

"We haven't seen the entertainment yet."

"Now don't put a downer on it, Cyril. I'm looking forward to the band."

"Of course. Your, what is it now, Glam Rock act?"

"You can mock. But I quite like some of this modern stuff."

Any further conversation was curtailed by the opening act appearing on stage. A male and female duo, he on the guitar and backing vocals, she on lead vocals. They weren't bad at all, Cyril thought. A pleasant collection of favourites from the sixties and a few standards.

As they finished, Doris made a detailed sweep of the room. "Can't see your friends from next door," she said.

"About to make an entrance." He indicated the main doors. The Robinson brothers, together with two women, a blonde and a brunette, were being shown to a prime table near the front of the stage by the entertainments manager.

Doris leaned in towards him. "Who says it doesn't pay," she said.

The compere was back with the mic. "So we'll have a little interval while your food is served and we'll be back with the main act of the night," he announced then left the stage.

The hubbub of a multitude of conversations took over as a dozen or so waiters and waitresses appeared and began to distribute the meals. The Robinsons were served quickly, Cyril noticed.

"A nice summer job for these boys and girls," Doris remarked. The waiting staff all looked sixteen or seventeen. A few minutes later, a girl with short dark hair and acne placed two plastic baskets with chicken dinners in front of them.

Cyril opened two of the Ketchup sachets and squeezed the contents onto his chips.

"Are you okay?" Doris sprinkled some salt on her meal. "With what I told you earlier, I mean. You worried me when you went off."

Cyril had returned to the caravan mid-afternoon after a long walk along the sea shore. A pipe-full of tobacco had helped him sort out his thoughts. He was glad Doris hadn't questioned him then. She left the matter alone, until now. He felt she understood him better than anyone at the moment and he respected her quiet concern.

Putting down his fork, he hesitated for a moment then spoke. "I suppose it was a bit of a surprise, not the fact that Maureen said what she said to you but, I don't know, perhaps that she even thought it in the first place. When we found out she couldn't have children, she actually asked me if I wanted to find someone else." He felt tears prick. "I mean, that's how unselfish she was. Of course I didn't want to leave her. I love her … loved her. And I shouldn't be surprised that even after she's gone, she's still thinking of me, not herself. You know, Doris, Maureen was the most unselfish person I've ever met."

She leaned over and put her hand on his. "I'm glad I told you. I think the time is right." She took her hand away. "Now, eat your food before it goes cold."

He studied his neighbour, watching her tuck into her meal. Finally, he picked up his cutlery and began to eat.

For Cyril, the band just seemed a noise. He was more appreciative of the music of the forties and fifties. Big bands were his favourite. For a split second, Glenn Miller popped into his head. No one had ever discovered what had happened to him on his last flight, back in December 1944. It was the main topic of conversation on the base for weeks. He'd no doubt he was somewhere in the English Channel, lost forever, like so many others. He did a quick calculation; Miller would have only been seventy-two now, younger than Doris.

His reverie was interrupted as Doris stood up. "Won't be a minute," she said.

He watched her make her way towards the toilets. That's when he saw the two women from the Robinson table heading in the same direction. What was Doris up to, he wondered?

Ten minutes later he found out.

"You weren't just going to the toilet, were you?" he asked.

She made herself comfortable at the table before answering. "The thing is, nobody pays much attention to a little old lady like me." That twinkle was back in her eyes.

"Let me guess, you've been listening in again."

"Why do women these days feel they have to go to the toilet with a friend? I've seen some that actually squeeze into the one cubicle."

He was amused by her observations but knew she'd tell him what she'd found out once she'd built up her part. "And were those two cubicle sharers?"

Her expression changed to one of mock surprise. "Oh, you mean the blonde and the brunette?"

"What did you find out?"

"Well ... I could really do with another gin and bitter lemon, if you don't mind."

A short while later, he returned with her drink and a half of Watney's Red Barrel for himself; not his favourite beer but it was all they sold on draught.

"So, come on," he prompted.

She took a sip before beginning her account. "Well, it seems the men are going to be busy on Monday."

He nodded. "That ties in with what you heard earlier. It's involving Lennie, that character who turned up today."

"Whatever it is, they're going to some warehouse in Colchester. Those two are off shopping there while the men do whatever business they have to do."

Elbows on the table, he clasped his hands together, thumbs under his chin. "Did they say where exactly ... or time?"

A smile played over her face. "It's down by The Hythe. Early afternoon, I think. Oh, and what was it now ..." She looked as though she was thinking hard, trying to recall something else. "... that was it, they mentioned it was at the back of Yardley's."

29

1944 and the war is going well. It's a bright sunny morning, little cloud and a light breeze from the west. The smoking shape slowly appears out of the southern horizon. Every available man from the base is outside, willing the stricken craft to make it back. Brian Richardson is performing heroics at the controls.

Cyril likes Brian. He's twenty-four, only six years older than Cyril. This is Brian's second mission. The radio operator alerted the base as to what befell the Lancaster on its way back from Germany. Attacked and strafed with fire from two Messerschmitt fighters, the crew are in trouble. The rear gunner hasn't made it and from what they can gather, two others on board are dead. By Cyril's reckoning, that leaves four men to make it home.

He watches as the bomber turns first one way then slowly manoeuvres in the opposite direction to line itself up with the grass runway. Members of the fire crew nervously wait in their vehicles, ready to chase the plane down once it lands. One engine is on fire and he can see the stilled propellers of two more. Brian struggles to control the craft with the one engine still working.

The plane is barely a hundred feet off the ground as it clears the hedge between the corn field and the base. Now he can see the damage to the undercarriage. Handling is almost impossible, minor corrections difficult to make. About to touch down, the Lancaster lurches and a wingtip touches the ground with catastrophic effects.

The wing and propellers of number four engine catch the grass and slew the plane in a sideways motion. Brian is clearly visible through the Perspex cockpit. It looks as if everything is happening in slow motion. The wing is ripped from the fuselage as the main body of the plane slides sideways down the grass, debris flying in all directions. The fire crew are in pursuit. Finally, after what seems an eternity, it comes to a halt. One crewman has been thrown from the plane and is lying on the grass some distance from where it has come to rest. A few men run to help him, the rest are running towards the wreckage, Cyril included. Before they get there, fire takes hold.

There is shouting of orders and people scurrying around. He is running too. He can see his friend still in the cockpit. He's close enough to see the panic in his eyes. Brian can't release the Perspex covering. They all know the Lancaster is difficult to evacuate. Someone pulls Cyril back. Shouts of 'Stand clear!' and 'She's about to blow' resonate. Cyril struggles to break free. He must help Brian. Brian who's helped him.

And then the explosion. Men are blown off their feet. Cyril is thrown backwards several yards. He gets back on his feet as fire envelopes the craft. And Brian is still sitting there. Cyril can feel the heat. Why isn't someone trying to get them out? Tears are streaming down his cheeks now. Someone is holding him back. He tries to break free again.

He looks round; and it's Maureen. She tugs at his arm. "Wait, Cyril. Wait!"

He can't understand. What's she doing here?

He turns back to the wreckage. The water spraying from the fire tenders is totally inadequate.

He turns once more to see who's stopping him running to help his friend. This time it's Cathy. "Wait, Cyril. Wait," she says.

He screws his eyes shut, struggling to wriggle loose. "Let me go, Cathy!"

"Wake up, Cyril. Wake up!"

He opened his eyes to find a bright light shining from the ceiling. Blinking, he looked into Doris' concerned face.

"Cyril, are you alright?" She released his arm that she'd been shaking.

He was back in the bedroom of the caravan. Drenched in sweat, the bedclothes were in a heap at the bottom of the bed.

He studied her for a second, quilted pink dressing gown and a hair net. "Doris? What …?"

"It's okay. It was a nightmare you were having." She smiled at him. "I don't know about you but you were frightening me … shouting out, thrashing about. And who was Brian?"

He lay back on the bed and wiped his face with his hands. "I'm sorry, Doris. I didn't mean to …"

"It's okay. I was just concerned." She took a step towards the bedroom door. "I'll make us a cup of tea."

In his mind since that day thirty-two years before, he'd seen the crash played out hundreds of times. And every time, he felt guilt. Guilt that he couldn't help Brian. But that was the first time Maureen had appeared. But why had Cathy been there as well? Slowly, his heart rate returned to normal.

Doris had switched on the kettle and was moving cups around. He got up and went to the bathroom, dried himself down with a towel and changed into fresh pyjamas. When he came out, she was sitting at the dining table with the teas.

"Maureen told me about the nightmares," she said. "She used to be worried for you."

"I told her once." He sat down opposite her. "She needed to know. After all she was living with the consequences just as much as me."

"The war did terrible things." She stared off into an unseen distance. "My Howard was in North Africa. He didn't tell me anything about it. But I could tell, just from his face. Poor soul didn't live long enough to say anything about it either." Focussing back on Cyril, she added, "If you ever need to talk about anything … I'm a good listener."

"Thanks, Doris. But you best get back off to bed. I've disturbed you enough for one night."

She got up and headed for her bedroom then paused. "But who's Cathy?" She didn't wait for an answer.

30
Monday 6th September

Doris had enjoyed their adventure on the holiday park. She'd really come into her own as Clacton's answer to Miss Marple. They'd discovered quite a bit of useful information about the Robinsons and their operations. It looked like there might be a direct connection between them and Walter Yardley. It certainly sounded coincidental that their Colchester base was next door to Yardley Electrical. And Cyril didn't believe in coincidences.

On a personal level, he was given a lot to mull over after what she had told him about her conversations with Maureen. But he was disappointed he'd disturbed her with his nightmare. That was the first time he'd suffered one for a good few months. There again, he wasn't surprised after witnessing the plane crash. He tried to make sense of Maureen appearing in the dream, and was really struggling to understand Cathy's involvement. Doris hadn't pushed for an explanation of who she was, for which he was grateful. But he did suspect she had an inkling there might be someone else making an impression on him.

He took the stairs two at a time to the first floor CID office on Monday morning. He wanted to check his desk for messages before anyone saw anything that looked suspicious to them. The last thing he wanted was for Cathy or him to be the butt of any mickey taking. The office was empty when he walked in with no sign of Barton in his room either. Checking his desk, he found what he was looking for. Tucked under a couple of files was a handwritten note. *'Robin Hood 7pm.'*

Sod it, he thought. The Robin Hood pub was a lovely old establishment on London Road heading out of town. He'd pop down and see Cathy later when she came in. He'd apologise and try and repair any damage. Hold on, what did he mean damage? It wasn't as though it was a definite arrangement anyway. His confused thought pattern was interrupted with the arrival of Ben Miller, jacket draped over his shoulder with his thumb through the loop.

"Morning, Ben," Cyril greeted.

"Sarge," was all that Miller replied before hanging his jacket over the back of his seat.

Cyril thought the DC's manner cool. "Is the DI expected in this morning?" he asked.

"Dunno."

One thing Cyril hated was people being moody for the want of being honest. Deciding to flush things out, he pulled a spare seat from nearby and sat opposite Miller. "Come on, I'm sensing some hostility here. What's eating you?"

Miller shrugged then decided to speak. "How come you weren't with us on that caravan raid on Friday?"

Cyril leaned back. "So you suspect it might have been me who tipped the Robinsons off, is that it?"

Miller coloured. "It does look suspicious."

"Okay. Well, there are three things." He counted on the fingers of one hand. "First, I was conducting interviews with Adam Fletcher's wife and Jem Fletcher's girlfriend on Friday morning. Second, DI Barton knew where I was and hadn't told me about the raid. And third, if you think the DI suspects I had anything to do with it and I'm still here, then you don't really know him as well as you might think."

"Sorry, Sarge. That's good enough for me."

He stood up. "So, any idea where he is?"

"I've a feeling he might be at the County. That second body's PM."

"Thanks." Leaving the CID room, Cyril paused when he saw DC Walker coming in. "Bill," he said.

"Morning, Sarge."

Turning, he indicated Miller sitting at his desk. "I'll let Ben reassure you."

As he left, he saw the puzzled expression on Walker's face.

* * *

"These are the X-ray images here." Dr Maguire slipped the plastic sheets up into the clips and switched on the lamp. "You can see there, the black spots, they're the shot."

He and Barton were in his office in the basement of the County Hospital once more. The pathologist was giving the detective the edited highlights of his findings following the post-mortem.

"So, definitely a shotgun." Barton stated.

Maguire slowly nodded, his eyes never leaving the viewer. "Probably both barrels by the number of pieces of lead I've removed. No wonder there wasn't much left of the head."

Barton sat down in the chair next to the desk. "I can see this one being a bugger to identify."

Maguire turned, a thin smile playing on his lips. "All might not be lost, Dick," he said.

"Go on then, pull some rabbits out of your hat."

The doctor sat down on his side of the desk and opened a manila file. "What I can tell you is that the body is that of a male, somewhere between the ages of forty-five and fifty-five, five feet nine or ten inches tall. I reckon he would be around fourteen and a half stones in weight, so probably slightly overweight."

"Great, so we've got Joe Average out there. That'll narrow it down." Barton produced a packet of cigarettes from his jacket pocket and was about to pull one free then changed his mind with the withering look Maguire gave him. He put the packet away again.

"From the state of his liver and kidneys, he was a drinker, and from his lungs, a smoker." The pathologist looked directly at Barton, as if making a point. "His heart showed early signs of the arteries furring up," he went on.

"All right, I get the picture. He wasn't an Olympic athlete. Any clothing?"

"Shirt and trousers, no possessions in the pockets," Maguire confirmed. "I can tell you he'd been married. He was used to wearing a wedding ring but that's missing. There were marks on the ring finger where it would normally be."

"Whoever was responsible seems to have gone to a lot of trouble to stop us identifying the victim."

"But ..." Maguire held up a finger. "... there is something that might help you."

Barton leaned forward onto the desk. "What's that?"

"Our friend broke his left leg, quite badly, possibly in his twenties, in adulthood anyway."

Barton sighed. "So we've got to trawl medical records going back maybe thirty years?"

"You might be interested in one other aspect. The break was bad enough for it to be plated. I took the initiative of removing it to see what information it would yield."

"And?"

Maguire pulled a sheet of paper from the file. "And there's a manufacturer's reference number on it. So all you need to do is to match that to an operation."

"How easy is that going to be?"

"Won't know until you start trying to trace it. But if you think of the number of hospitals that would have done those sorts of operations over the past three decades, quite a task. Then add in any places overseas ... and you can see what you'll be up against."

"Great." Barton stood up. "I need that cigarette now."

*   *   *

It was just gone ten o'clock when Cyril spotted Cathy. He was sitting in the canteen just finishing a bacon butty and a cup of tea. Walker and Miller had been quiet all morning so he was sitting alone. Standing at the counter for her coffee, she glanced over at him then quickly looked away. He was beginning to feel like a pariah. He watched her walk down the line to the till, pay, then walk out without looking in his direction again.

He stood, took his crockery to the trolleys and quickly followed her out. He checked the typists' office first, but she wasn't there. Stepping through the main doors, he saw her sitting on the low wall, enjoying the sun.

"Mind if I join you?"

She shrugged and he sat down next to her.

"Look, I didn't get your message until this morning," he said.

She didn't respond, just took a drink of her coffee.

"I did try and call you here on Friday, but you'd gone home. I'd got no way of making contact." He looked away. "How did the quiz night go?"

"All right, I suppose."

"Look, Cathy, I did want to come with you but I had to work. It's this case they brought me in to help out on."

Finally, she looked at him. "All weekend?"

"Friday afternoon through to yesterday afternoon, yes."

Another sip of her coffee … and then the smile. "Did you really try to get hold of me?"

"Of course. I really wanted to go. I told you I enjoy quizzes. So how did you get on?"

"We came second. We were a man down but Jim, you know, Jim and Sandra, they were the ones who'd asked me, well, Jim knew a bloke at the bar who joined us to make four. But he was useless." Probably aware she was rambling on, she laughed.

"I am really sorry about that," Cyril offered once more.

"Well, if you want to make it up to me, you can take me out for a drink tonight."

A broad grin spread over his face. "How about Dedham?" he suggested.

"Ooh. One of my favourite places. I love the church and down by the river."

139

"That's settled then."

She stood up and smoothed her skirt. "Pick me up at seven," she said before giving him an address in Little Clacton.

As she strode back towards the main doors, Cyril was left admiring her legs, again.

"What are you looking so pleased with yourself about, Skip?"

He looked across at the source of the interruption to see Sam Woodbridge walking along the pavement towards him.

"Ah, just enjoying the weather, Sam," Cyril answered. "Are you on a day off?" Cyril studied the constable's attire; cheesecloth shirt, jeans and trainers. "Or under cover?"

"Ha! Very good. No I'm back on an early tomorrow."

A thought struck Cyril. "Are you doing anything special at the moment?"

Sam thrust both hands in his pockets. "No, not especially."

"You don't fancy helping me, do you?"

"Official business, like?"

Cyril shrugged. "Sort of."

"What's up with your CID colleagues?"

"Let's just say, this might be better with people I can trust."

"So when you mentioned 'under cover' …?"

"Don't get excited, Sam."

31

Having smoked a cigarette whilst considering what Dr Maguire had told him, Barton wondered what he was up against in trying to identify the latest victim lying in the morgue's fridge. If ever there was any doubt over the body recovered from the plane, he was in no doubt that the one dragged up by the fishing boat was a professional gangland hit. With both wrapped in the same black plastic sheeting, they were most definitely connected. The only significant difference, was the murder weapon; a .45 calibre revolver in the first case and a 12-bore shotgun in this latest.

But while he was here, he decided it was time to see if Adam Fletcher had returned to the land of the living.

A different Sister was the gatekeeper to the Intensive Care Unit. In response to his enquiry, yes, Mr Fletcher had regained consciousness but was in need of rest as his body was still recovering, she told him. "His wife went off about an hour ago, but she should be back shortly," she added.

Assuring her he wouldn't agitate the patient, only some basic questions that needed answers, he walked over to Fletcher's room and looked through the vision panel in the door. The patient was propped up in bed with fewer tubes than before connecting him with various machines and monitors by the side.

Cautiously, he entered the room. As he walked to the chair by the side of the bed, Fletcher's eyes flickered open.

"Oh, it's you," he said through a bruised and battered jaw.

A cut over his left eye and one down his right cheek had been stitched. Elsewhere, the bruising gave his face some autumnal hues of yellows and browns with some reds clinging on.

"How're you doing?" Barton asked.

"Never better," Fletcher said, through gritted teeth.

Barton smiled. "Have they said how long you'll be in?"

"Another day or so here, then down to the ward. But I should be out by next weekend."

Barton leaned in closer. "So, Adam ... have you had any thoughts on who was responsible for this?"

Fletcher clenched his eyes shut for a second.

"You must have seen something," Barton persisted.

"They jumped me from behind."

"They? So there was more than one?"

Despite the state of his facial injuries, his expression gave a hint of annoyance. Barton knew he was making progress.

"Must have been. Came at me from behind."

"Why do you think you were attacked, Adam?"

He tried to give a shrug. "I don't know. Probably after the mail."

"Is there usually something of value in that?"

"Sometimes."

Barton theatrically pulled out his notebook from his jacket pocket. "But according to the Royal Mail blokes that came out to collect your van and complete the round..." He flicked through some pages. "...they don't reckon there was anything missing."

"Well that's good."

"So there must have been another motive."

"Suppose."

"Come on, Adam, you know what this is all about. Why don't you tell me?"

All Barton got in response was a slight shake of the head.

The detective leaned back on the chair and flicked through his notebook once again. "But then I asked your Depot Manager at the Clacton Sorting Office to check through the deliveries that you'd already made on the round ..."

"So?"

"And he tells me there were some items missing from some customers, businesses and the like, who reckon they were expecting cheques, postal orders, cheque books even, which didn't turn up." Barton paused for effect. "Now, that tells me you could have held those items back. After all, you've been a postman now for, what … fifteen years? You know what these envelopes look like. You know your customers well; you'd be able to identify who was likely to have these valuable items delivered." Despite the damage, Barton could see the alarm sweep across Fletcher's face. Glancing at one of the monitors, he recognised Fletcher's pulse spike from the 82 or so it had indicated constantly since he'd entered the room to the mid-nineties it read now. He pressed on, "And if you had held them back because … oh, I don't know, let's say you have some outstanding debts … you could have given them to your *'attackers'*. They give you a bit of a going over, just to make it look good, and bang, there's another chunk of your debt paid off."

"No, no!"

"And when they checked your van, all your post yet to be delivered would appear to be untouched. How am I doing?"

"No! It wasn't like that."

Barton pulled the chair up nearer to the bed and leaned in close to Fletcher. "Well how about you start telling me what it **was** like," he snarled.

Fletcher closed his eyes for a few seconds. "Look, you don't understand."

"Well help me out here."

A tear escaped from his eye. At last, he spoke. "I'm trying to protect my family; Carol and the kids. And because of my stupidity, Jem's dead."

Barton adopted a softer tone. "Adam, if you tell me, I can help. We can protect Carol and your family. But you need to help me to help you."

"Promise me you will?" Fletcher pleaded.

Barton nodded and Fletcher began.

"The card school was organised by a hard nut, Scottish guy by the name of Dougie Chalmers." Fletcher wiped his cheek. "I realised afterwards that the game was bent. But by that time I was in deep."

"And this game was when, exactly?"

"February."

"And since February you've managed to reduce your debt by half. That's what you told me last week, right?"

Fletcher nodded. "Yeah."

"How have you done that? Forget all this bollocks you told me earlier about doing odd jobs. You got Jem involved, didn't you?"

Again he clenched his eyes shut before tears began to flow. "He was my brother. He said he wanted to help."

"Disposing of bodies in the North Sea?"

"Yes."

"And it was this Chalmers character's idea?"

"No. I was contacted back in July by someone else. Don't ask me who, they never said. Only that Chalmers' debts now fell to them and I'd have to repay."

"Contacted? How?"

"Telephone call. At home. They never said who they were. But they knew all about me, my family … and Jem too. They knew he was a mechanic and had access to planes."

"Are you telling me that someone else had taken over Chalmers debts and were forcing you to carry out favours for them?"

"Yes."

"And it was their suggestion to coerce Jem into disposing of the bodies?"

"Yes, but we didn't know what they wanted us to dump at first. All they said was that they had a package which needed to be got rid of and Jem could offer the best solution. In return, my debt would be reduced by £300."

"So how were these 'packages' delivered for disposal?"

"We were given times, all early mornings, when delivery would be made. All Jem had to do was to supervise where they needed to be in the plane."

"Who delivered them?"

"I don't know. I was never there."

"And how many did Jem do?"

"Three. One at the end of July, another a week later and then … well, this last one."

"And this was all that they ever asked you to do? Get Jem to dump bodies out at sea?"

"Yes."

"No drugs runs to Holland or anything?"

Fletcher's eyes opened as wide as he could manage. "Never. We'd never get involved in that."

"Only, your wife thinks that maybe that was what you were involved with."

"Oh, Christ, no. Neither wonder she was so upset with everything. Her younger brother died about ten years ago with a drugs overdose."

"I think you need to come clean with her."

"This is all such a fucking mess."

"So who did attack you?"

"I don't know, honest. Just a couple of thugs. They said that since Jem had 'messed up' as they put it, I should remember I still owed a grand."

"Have you any idea why Jem would have one hundred pounds in cash on him when he died?"

Fletcher looked puzzled initially, then realised something. "That was probably for me. He was going to pay me that for the painting work and other stuff at the house. I'd bought a load of materials."

32

"Just remind me again, Skip, what exactly are we doing here?" Sam Woodbridge was sitting in the passenger seat of the Ford Escort Cyril had once again signed out of the car pool.

They had pulled to a halt on some waste ground opposite a three-storey brick-built building. Faded paintwork proclaimed it had once been a seed warehouse. Windows were boarded up giving it an abandoned air. But the closed double doors to the street, secured with a hasp and staple and new padlock, looked as though they were regularly maintained. The building adjoined the rear of premises belonging to the *Yardley Electrical Manufacturing Company*.

"I just want to check out this property, Sam." Cyril switched off the ignition, eyes scanning the building as he stroked his moustache.

"Part of the Yardley empire?"

"That's one thing I want to try and find out." Cyril was still studying the building. This area of The Hythe was undergoing some redevelopment, buildings either side had been demolished so, with no other probable contenders, he figured this had to be the one the Robinsons were using.

Leaving his jacket on the back seat, Cyril got out of the car. "I'll have a look around the side and check if there's any way I can see inside. Wait here a minute," he instructed his companion.

"Take this." Sam held a torch out through the open window.

"Thanks." Cyril took it and headed over the road.

As he crossed to the other side, Cyril looked up and down the street. The last thing he wanted was to be surprised by the Robinsons' big grey Daimler. The passing traffic was mostly commercial; several lorries, vans and a bus. He approached the main double doors and tried the pedestrian access door that was incorporated into one of them. That was secured by a Yale lock. A Yale? Was it possible that the key that was found in Jimmy Morgan's pocket would fit it? He made a mental note to check that out. Next he tried around the left hand side of the building. The plywood security hoarding to the desolate site next door stood about two feet away from the brickwork giving him just enough room to squeeze down the side. There appeared to be only a couple of small windows at high level on this elevation and no visible access to them. At the far end, a brick wall blocked any chance of checking out the rear of the warehouse. He guessed that enclosed the compound to Yardley Electrical.

Back to the front, a quick glance across to the Escort saw Sam shrug through the windscreen at him. Cyril walked to the right hand side where some wire mesh fencing blocked his path. He bent down and saw that it wasn't fixed at the bottom. Lifting it up, he got to his knees and crawled through. Dusting himself off, he walked slowly down that side of the warehouse. To his right, a chain link fence separated the property from another cleared site. The sun streamed onto this elevation reflecting heat off the brickwork. Above, there were several windows at first floor level populated by half a dozen seagulls perched on the sills. Even they looked exhausted by the weather. A couple of long narrow windows that looked as though they could be toilets at ground level, plus a wooden door completed the details of this side of the building. He tried the door first. Secured fast. At the end of the space between the wall and the fencing several discarded wooden pallets lay on the ground. He dragged one of them over to below one of the ground floor windows and propped it up. Standing on the pallet, he could reach the decayed plywood covering the old window. It was fixed by some screws to the frame itself. Fingers behind the ply, he managed to pull the board free, the screws long since holding something solid. The wood at the bottom of the window frame had rotted near the catch. Jiggling it, the wood disintegrated into dust. The glass had been smashed years ago, leaving only a few shards which were easily removed. Carefully he opened what was left of the window.

Shining a torch inside the room, it was, as he suspected, a toilet. The missing entrance door enabled him to see through to the main open warehouse area. Light streamed in from some openings at the rear of the building. Parked on the concrete floor was a small box van. On the side was a colourful logo announcing *'The Holland Flower Co.'*

Bingo, this is definitely the Robinson warehouse.

Stepping down off the pallet, he made his way back to the road. Another glance up and down, then he waved to Sam sitting in the car. A hand with a thumbs up appeared in the windscreen. He beckoned him over.

Sam got out of the car and crossed the road to the fence. "What's up?"

"I need you to give me a lift up so I can get in through the window."

"You're going in? I thought you only wanted a look."

"This is definitely the warehouse. The Robinson van is in there, the one Jimmy Morgan's girlfriend reckoned he drove." Cyril looked up and down the street nervously once more. Bending down, he lifted up the mesh fence.

Sam looked distastefully at the gap.

"Come on then," Cyril said, indicating the space he had to crawl through.

"I like this shirt," Sam said by way of explanation, "and these jeans."

"Don't be soft, I'll hold it clear for you."

Reluctantly, Sam ducked down and carefully crept below the fence. Once clear, he dusted off his trousers and smoothed down his shirt.

Cyril looked him up and down, shook his head then led the way to the open window.

Sam clasped both hands together at knee height with his back to the wall. Cyril put a foot on Sam's hands and, on the count of three, launched himself upwards and over the opening. Stomach on the sill, Cyril struggled to turn and get one leg inside. After a couple of attempts and with Sam helping, he finally managed to turn and drop inside.

"Alright, Sam, you go back to the car and keep an eye out," Cyril said. "The Robinsons' car is one of those big old grey Daimlers. I should be able to climb back out from in here. There's plenty old boxes and crates I can use."

"If you're sure, Skip?"

"Go on. I'm not sure when they're due but it will be this afternoon some time."

Cyril heard Sam walk away. He imagined him dreading trying to make his way under the fence without someone to hold it out of the way for him.

Inside the warehouse, Cyril walked towards the van. Around the side of the open area, a few tea chests and empty cardboard boxes littered the place along with old newspapers, The Sun and News of The World mostly.

He approached the van, 'H' registered; six years old. He tried the driver's door. Surprisingly, it opened.

Inside, it was clean and smelt of air freshener. An AA map of northern Europe was in the driver's door pocket but nothing else. Closing the door, he walked round to the other side and opened the passenger door. Nothing in the side pocket. The glovebox held only the service manual and when he opened the ashtray, some sweet wrappers tried to make their escape.

He walked to the back and tried the rear doors. Again, they were unlocked. The aluminium floor and the sides with plywood linings and metal brackets all looked clean. Closing the doors, he decided to explore the rest of the building

At the back, a fire escape door he reckoned should lead to Yardley's premises was locked. Nearby, a solid timber staircase led up. Carefully, he began to climb. Up onto the first floor, he had to admire the workmanship that had gone into the Victorian construction. Heavy section beams supported on cast iron columns allowed a vast open area for storage on this level. The floor was empty save for what appeared to be a workbench and some shapes to one side. He walked towards them, his footsteps echoing off the walls and the underside of the floor above. How long since this had been a hive of activity with men hauling sacks of seed and other merchandise, he wondered?

As he walked across the floor, it was clear that someone had been here recently. Footprints and scuff marks led from the stairs towards whatever was at the side. A thick layer of dust and dirt covered the rest of the floor. Close up, he could see dark stains on the top surface of the workbench. Walking round the rear of it, he halted. Lying flat on the floor was a roll of industrial black plastic. He turned and looked more closely at the bench top. He was sure the stains were dried blood. Was this the location where the bodies were wrapped prior to disposal? A sudden thought hit him. According to Dr Maguire, Jimmy Morgan had been dead for at least two days, maybe three before he was discovered in the crashed plane. And yet, when he'd found it, the body hadn't begun to smell. In this hot weather that was incongruous. Therefore, it had to have been stored in a refrigerated environment. And ... he rushed back to the stairs and down to the ground floor.

Before him was a strong contender for the answer. The flower van was fitted with refrigeration equipment over the top of the cab. At the rear, he opened up the doors for the second time. Stepping up inside, he looked closely at the floor and the sides. He was near the front when he heard the sounds of a car drawing to a halt outside in the street. He paused and listened. Before he could make his way to the back doors and jump down, the access door had opened and a voice he recognised as Victor Robinson spoke.

33

Sam had his eyes closed with the radio on in the Escort, listening to Radio One. They were playing a 'Golden Oldie' and he was back in the *Summer of Love*, 1967 with Scott McKenzie and *San Francisco*. He was sixteen again and listening to Radio Caroline anchored just off the Essex coast near Frinton. His thoughts drifted to the gorgeous Stephanie Crossland in his class; he remembered watching her walking past a garden and picking one of those big daisy flowers and pushing it behind her ear. His first love; unrequited. The last he heard, she'd gone to London, modelling someone had told him.

The big grey Daimler drew to a halt near to the warehouse doors. Sam opened his eyes and sat up straight. Shit, he thought. Two men got out, one taller with fair hair, maybe around six feet, the other shorter by about three inches with dark wavy hair. From Cyril's descriptions, these had to be Victor and David Robinson. Sam glanced to the right hand side, willing Cyril to appear. Nothing, not even a seagull.

The two men stood chatting for a while. The shorter man checked his watch and looked nervously up the road towards the railway station. The taller man appeared to placate him.

Sam switched off the radio. Still no sign of Cyril

From the direction of the station, a slim man probably in his fifties, dressed in a tee shirt and jeans and carrying a holdall came walking towards the two men. No handshakes, just a nod of recognition. The tall man produced a key and opened the pedestrian access door and the three of them disappeared inside.

Sam felt his stomach heave; the first signs of his inner panic. He'd give it five minutes then he'd have to try and find out what was happening over there; and more importantly, where Cyril was.

* * *

Lennie King picked up his holdall and left the train, slamming the door behind him. This was Hythe station and it was a three minute trot to the warehouse. A check of the watch confirmed the train was on time and he had five minutes to the rendezvous. Good. One thing he didn't want to do was upset the Robinsons on this his first job.

Lennie looked up at the clear blue sky and hurried off the platform. Dressed in tee shirt and jeans, his favourite leather jacket, sweater and a change of clothes were in his holdall. Last night's TV news items spun through his mind and he'd begun to wonder if it would ever rain again. From the train, he'd seen the River Colne meandering its way to the sea. Exaggerated by the low tide, there seemed an even wider expanse of mud flats either side of the narrow channel that trickled towards the coast. Could this dry up completely, like some rivers in other parts of the country he'd seen news footage of?

With these thoughts, he walked away from the station. As he turned a corner, he saw two figures he recognised standing by a big grey car. He picked up his pace towards them.

"On time, Lennie," Victor Robinson greeted, before turning to his brother. "Told you he wouldn't let us down, Dave."

David Robinson remained silent as Victor unlocked the door. Lennie followed him inside with David bringing up the rear, closing the door behind him.

Victor turned to face Lennie. "Right, you know what's expected. I explained all the details on Saturday."

"Yep. And this is the van?" Lennie said.

"Got your passport?"

"In the holdall."

"What else is in there?" David asked.

"Change of clothes, a jacket, jumper and a book."

"Let's see."

"Christ's sake, Dave, relax. Stop being so paranoid. Lennie here'll be fine," Victor addressed his brother. "Because if he isn't …" he turned to Lennie. "… he knows what'll happen."

"I won't let you down."

"Good to hear it." Victor held out an envelope. "Here." Lennie took it and looked inside.

"Tickets and some Dutch Guilders, and the first payment as agreed," Victor went on. "The address of the café is in there and the phone number. You know what to do."

"Yes."

"So you get back here on Wednesday morning, ten o'clock and we're all happy, right?"

"Right, Mr Robinson."

"Good man. There should be a full tank," Victor assured him. "Get yourself settled in the cab and we'll open the doors for you."

Lennie began to walk around the vehicle. "Just want to check everything's okay first. Wouldn't want to get stopped by some over-zealous traffic police."

Victor walked to the back of the van with him, immediately spotting the doors were unsecured. "I thought you closed these up when we left it last time, Dave?" he asked his brother.

David was standing at the front of the van. "I did, I'm sure," he shouted back.

Victor swung open one of the doors and looked inside at the empty space before shutting it and moving the catches over to close it securely.

Lennie, satisfied all was well, climbed into the cab, threw his holdall into the passenger footwell and adjusted the mirrors. Two minutes later, he drove the van out into bright sunshine. A last glance in his wing mirror saw the Robinsons closing the warehouse doors. And now he was on his way.

34

Now Sam was really panicking. Why did he allow himself to get involved in this? He liked Cyril, he was a great mentor. But this was career suicide. Taking himself off on a venture when he wasn't even supposed to be on duty.

A glance at his watch. Six minutes they'd been inside and still no sign of Cyril having climbed back out. He'd give it another four minutes then he'd have to do something. But what?

Just then, the access door opened and the dark haired Robinson came out, unlocked the padlock on the main doors and swung them open. The other brother joined him as the van nosed its way forward. Finally, it appeared into the daylight, paused for a break in the traffic then pulled away, the man who'd joined them with the holdall driving. Immediately the doors were closed again and the padlock put back in place. After a short conversation on the street, both men got back into the Daimler and the fair haired man drove them away towards town.

Sam got out of the car and locked it. After a break in the traffic, he crossed the road. Satisfied the Daimler had disappeared, he pulled up the mesh fencing and scrambled underneath. Standing on the pallet, he peered inside. All seemed quiet.

"Cyril. Skip! Cyril!" he yelled.

No answer.

Louder, "Skip!"

Still no answer.

Deciding there was nothing for it, he grabbed the sill and pulled upwards, at the same time springing off the pallet and launching himself towards the window. Stomach on the sill, he managed to turn himself around and drop feet first into the room. His shirt was a mess but he quickly put that out of his mind.

Walking into the open ground floor area where the van had been parked, he stopped and listened. The only sounds were of wind noise higher up the building and some seagulls screeching.

"Cyril. Skip!" he called out again.

Once more there was no answer.

Had they discovered him? Was he lying injured somewhere in here? He walked around the ground floor, looking behind some old tea chests and cardboard boxes, but there was no sign. He paused by the door to the rear of the building and tried that. Locked. The staircase led up beside him and he began to climb.

"Skip. Cyril," he called out once more.

Stepping out onto the first floor, he stopped and listened. As before, just wind noise and seagulls. Over on the other side was a bench. It was the only thing on this level that could conceal someone. He walked towards it.

"Skip!"

The bench itself was empty and behind that, only an old roll of plastic sheeting lay on the floor.

This was serious. If Cyril wasn't in the building, he could only be in the van. And if he was in the van, what state was he in? Was the driver aware?

This was way over anything he could deal with. He needed help. He'd probably get the biggest bollocking of his life, but he had to tell Barton.

Rushing back down the stairs, he had one last look around the ground floor then made his way back to the toilet. Gathering a couple of old boxes, he placed them below the window and climbed up. Outside, he scrambled below the mesh fencing.

"Shit," he said to himself, as in his rush to get out, the fence snagged his shirt. He kept moving then heard and felt the rip. Standing up he scanned the street. About a hundred yards away, he spotted two telephone boxes and ran towards them.

Fortunately, when he picked up the handset, the dialling tone told him it was working. He checked his pockets and pulled out a couple of two pence pieces. Dialling the Clacton Police Station number, he only hoped Barton was in.

* * *

With sweat marks showing under the armpits of his shirt, Barton swept into the CID room.

Walker looked up from his desk. "Sir," he greeted.

The DI paused on his way to his office. "Where is everybody? Miller? Cyril?"

"Ben's dealing with a couple of shoplifters in the interview room."

"And Cyril?"

"Not seen him since this morning."

Barton thought for a moment. "Right, well I've got something interesting for you, Bill."

Walker perked up. "Yes, Sir."

Barton pulled out the slip of paper that Dr Maguire given him with the details of the metal plate recovered from the latest body. He placed it on Walker's desk then stood behind him.

"Bit of a needle in a haystack but I need you to stick with this."

Walker looked up at his boss, puzzled.

"These are the reference details of a plate that was surgically implanted into our latest victim's left leg possibly twenty to thirty years ago."

"Thirty years?"

"That's what I said. So, what I need you to do is try and trace that operation and hence the identity of our victim."

Walker looked bemused. "But how …?"

"Start with the hospitals in this area, then maybe London and work your way out." Barton paused as if considering something else. "Christ if it wasn't even used

156

in this country then you could be going till next Christmas."

Walker visibly sagged.

"Come on then," Barton said. "Quicker you get started …"

He turned and walked into his office, a grin on his face, just as DCI Martin Sanderson appeared.

"Amused are we, Dick?" he said, closing the door behind him and settling into the chair opposite Barton's desk.

"Just given something for young Walker to get his teeth into, Sir," Barton responded.

"Right, well I need you to give me an update on our friends wrapped in plastic." Sanderson stood up and walked over to the window. "You really need to get some air through here," he said and pulled up the bottom casement.

Ten minutes later, Barton had told his DCI everything he knew on the background of Jimmy Morgan and the difficulties they could have in identifying the second victim.

"And what about the attack on Adam Fletcher?" Sanderson asked.

Barton settled back in his chair, playing with a pencil. "Ever come across a big Scottish twat by the name of Dougie Chalmers, Sir?"

Sanderson screwed up his face in concentration. "Came down here about … ooh … ten years ago? Used to get involved in some rough stuff in the pubs, mostly with other members of his tartan army."

"That's him," Barton agreed. "Well, apparently he was the one that Fletcher owed money to."

Sanderson nodded sagely. "He's certainly tough enough and daft enough to have given him a good pasting."

Barton bent forward onto his desk. "But he doesn't own the debt now, so he wasn't involved. I don't think so anyway."

"So who exactly *does* Fletcher owe money to?"

"He doesn't exactly know."

"Or he's not saying," Sanderson added.

"No matter what, we need to speak to Chalmers."

Before the conversation could continue, the phone rang.

The DI picked up the receiver. "Barton," he said gruffly. After a pause, "Who? ... Okay put him through ... Yes constable."

Barton listened for a few minutes, interspersed with, "He's done *what*?" and "Where is he now?" followed by, "Are you sure?" Then, "And the registration number?" He scribbled on a pad on his desk. Finally, he said, "Just get your arse back to the station as soon as."

"What's all that about?" Sanderson asked.

"Bloody Win... I mean Cyril. God give me strength." Barton leaned far back in his chair, both hands covering his face.

Sanderson waited until Barton began to tell the story that Sam Woodbridge had just related.

"So he thinks he's in the back of that van." Sanderson said. "What did you say it was, the Holland Flower Company?"

Barton nodded. "That was the van Jimmy Morgan's old bird told us he'd driven. The one we suspect Victor Robinson is using to bring porn in from Holland." Barton felt his heart rate increase. "Shit." He looked steadily at the DCI.

"You thinking what I'm thinking?" Sanderson asked.

Barton picked up the phone again and made a call. When he'd spoken to the person on the other end, he felt numb.

"We've got to get to Harwich," he said, grabbing his jacket from the chair back. "The next ferry to Hook of Holland is due to leave shortly."

Sanderson stood also. "I'm coming with you," he said.

As they left the office, Ben Miller was returning to his desk.

Barton paused. "Oh, Ben, I need you to try and track down the whereabouts of Dougie Chalmers for me." He and Sanderson resumed their rush for the stairs. "And if that big streak of piss Sam Woodbridge turns up, tell him I want to see him tomorrow first thing."

"Where are you off to now, guv?" Miller wondered.

"Harwich ... Parkeston Quay to be precise."

35

Cyril heard the voices as the men entered the warehouse. There was no time to jump down from the van. He could probably do it quietly but the route from the van to the toilets was exposed; he'd never make it. He pulled the second door to and walked as silently as he could to the front of the van. The voices were clearer now and he heard David Robinson quizzing Lennie about what was in his holdall, for he was in no doubt that Lennie King had turned up,. David sounded suspicious. And then Victor told him to relax and stop being paranoid. All the while, Cyril was studying the front wall of the van section.

That was when he spotted it; the well-concealed line of a doorway in the middle. Thinking about things, it did seem as though inside the van was shorter than it should have been from outside. A false front. One of the metal brackets was disguised as a handle. He turned it and the door was silently released. A small section about two feet long, the whole width of the body was revealed. He had no doubt this would be where the illegal material would be stored for the return journey. He stepped inside and pulled the door to, feeling for a handle on the inside before closing it.

Outside, he heard Victor tell Lennie that he expected him back on Wednesday. Two sets of footsteps walked to the rear. Victor shouted to his brother that he must have left the door open. A pause, then the clang of metal as the rear door closed and a lever moved to lock it in position. Seconds later, the van rocked as someone climbed into the cab.

Bloody Hell, Cyril thought to himself as the engine fired up. He felt for the handle on the inside of the secret compartment and let himself out into the main open body.

As he stepped out, the van slewed, catching him off balance and knocking him to the floor. A bracket caught his head and total blackness descended.

Slowly, light gradually fights its way through the pitch black. A warm early summer's morning has witnessed the disaster of the Lancaster breaking up and catching fire on the grass runway. Cyril is in an agitated state, desperately trying to break free from the arms that are holding him back from going to the aid of his friend. The image of Brian, flying helmet already removed, struggling to release the covers to his position in the fuselage comes into sharp focus. Men are pulling at the hatches of the stricken craft when the explosion occurs. Cyril is thrown backwards.

Pain and more blackness.

And then Brian is talking. "Don't worry, Cyril. There was nothing you could have done. I'll be okay, honestly."

"But Brian, I couldn't get to you. They wouldn't let me," Cyril says.

"I know. If they had, you would be here with me. But I'm fine now. You have a life. Don't waste it. And when we do see each other again, I want you to tell me everything you've done."

"But Brian ..." Cyril hesitates. His friend is gradually being enveloped by white smoke. Finally, he is gone.

And then another voice speaks, "Cyril? Cyril, darling. You must be strong."

Strange, Cyril thinks. Sounds like ... "Maureen? Maureen, what are you doing here?"

"I've come to take care of you," she says. "Just like you took care of me. You know I couldn't have gotten through it without you."

"But I don't understand."

"You'll be fine. I just need to be with you for a little while."

"But ..."

The fuzzy feeling in his head begins to clear and he is aware of calm.

36

"Christ's sakes, John, we need to get there in one piece, otherwise we're no good to anybody."

Barton had just overtaken an articulated lorry on its way to the Harwich freight terminal. He'd pulled in sharply in front of it just before another lorry coming the other way took them out. Both drivers had blared horns and flashed lights at them. Barton immediately realised how close they'd come to oblivion and tried to calm himself. The use of his proper first name, John, by Sanderson sitting alongside him in the passenger seat of his Rover, only emphasised his reckless driving.

"Sorry, guv," he said. "It's just we don't have much time before that ferry's due to sail."

They were still a few miles from the Parkeston Quay turning for the passenger terminal. For the next few minutes, an anxious silence descended in the car. Finally, Sanderson spoke. "What's getting at you, Dick?" He turned to look at Barton.

"I'm just nervous about Cyril. If anything happens, there'll be an enquiry and it'll be my bollocks on the line."

"But it's more than that," Sanderson persisted. "You've been … distracted, deep in thought, however you want to describe it, for a few days now."

Barton held his breath for a few seconds then exhaled. He wasn't sure how to handle this, whether the time was right or even if he could analyse whatever answer he got. "Look," he said at last, "Is there anything about the events of the past few weeks you want to tell me?"

Sanderson seemed puzzled. "What are you talking about?"

Again Barton hesitated. "How long have we worked together? Four, five years?"

"I chose you as my DS when I was a DI nearly five years ago," Sanderson replied. "And I recommended you for promotion eighteen months ago. You know I've always supported you, Dick. Where's this going?"

"Oh, I don't know. It's just with Jimmy Morgan turning up dead just after he gave me information on Yardley then this Robinson involvement. They always seem to be one step ahead."

"And you think I might be connected in some way?"

"I didn't say that."

"But it's what you're asking."

Barton let his silence do the talking.

"You told me what Morgan said and I reported that up the line," Sanderson explained. "When you were applying for the search warrant for the Robinson static, I did the same. I'd got no reason to keep that information from the Chief Super."

"So does Mr Viney have connections with …?"

"I just don't know, Dick." Sanderson sighed. "I can see why you think someone is keeping the Robinsons in the know but it is not me," he said slowly and deliberately. "You have to trust me on that. Whoever it is, and that's if there is someone on the inside, it's above my head."

Barton didn't respond. Finally, he steered the car left onto the passenger terminal approach road. The big ship was still at its berth. Drawing the car to a halt, both men jumped out, Barton only pausing to lock it up.

Through the entrance doors, past the check-in desks and on to security, Barton and Sanderson hurried through with warrant cards displayed. At the immigration desk, they were met by an official who introduced himself as DI George Crimond from Special Branch. The man looked to be around forty and spoke with a slight Highland lilt. Although situated in Essex, responsibility for policing at the port fell to the Branch.

"DCI Martin Sanderson and this is DI John Barton," Sanderson began. "We've not got much time. We believe one of our officers is trapped in a vehicle on board this ferry." He nodded towards the quay.

"Are you sure? Do you have the vehicle details?" Crimond asked.

"We believe so," Sanderson responded.

"A Leyland three and half ton van labelled up as belonging to *The Holland Flower Company*." Barton pulled out a scrap of paper from his pocket. "This is the registration number."

"Right, follow me." DI Crimond led the way along a corridor and up several flights of stairs to an office where a group of men in casual clothes were sitting around a large desk, filling out paperwork.

"Okay gents, listen up," Crimond announced, "Can you drop what you're doing a minute and check whether we have this vehicle on board." The DI dropped the piece of paper Barton had handed to him in the centre of the desk.

"These are members of our team," Crimond said, by way of explanation.

Barton leaned from one foot to another, looking at Sanderson. He shared the concern he could see etched on his DCI's face.

Within a few minutes, one of the men confirmed that the flower van was indeed on board.

"Right," Crimond said, "Let's get you guys out there."

"But Sir," the same man interrupted. "They've just cast off." He stood and looked out of the window; Sanderson and Barton following his gaze.

"Shit!" Barton exclaimed, agitated. "What do we do now?"

"All is not lost," Crimond assured him. "Frank, with me," he said to his colleague who'd attracted their attention to the ship's departure. "Let's go, gents."

Barton and Sanderson followed in the wake of Crimond and the officer introduced to them on the way as Detective Sergeant Frank Gray.

They made their way down to the quayside, the huge bulk of the ferry about a quarter of a mile away already.

"Fuck. What the Hell are we going to do now?" Barton whispered to Sanderson.

Crimond was speaking into a hand-held radio. Barton couldn't hear what he said but a few minutes later a small black and white craft came alongside the jetty; PILOTS in large letters down the side.

"Right, I've spoken to Trinity House and these guys will get you on board. They're collecting the pilot off the ferry and taking him out to a freighter on its way in. I've contacted the ferry captain and he'll keep the speed down before they make the open sea and you're safely on board," Crimond explained.

"I could go with them, Sir," Gray said, "Make sure everything goes well."

"Good idea, Frank. Then come back with them on the return sailing."

Sanderson looked at Barton. "You go, Dick, I'd best stay here. We can't have two senior officers away from the station for the rest of the day and the night."

Barton looked exasperated as he realised the truth of the situation. He would have to go and wait until the ferry came back tomorrow morning.

"Go on," Sanderson urged. "At least it looks like you'll get a calm crossing."

"Here," Barton held out his car keys. "You best look after these until I get back."

The DCI took hold of them and nodded. "Give me an update as soon as you can."

"I can arrange a call from the ship's telephone," Gray offered.

"DCI Sanderson will be with me in my office until we hear," Crimond said. "Now go!"

Gray led the way down some metal steps onto the tender. Barton followed suit, more nervously. He didn't like being on water at the best of times. He hoped he'd be okay when he got onto the ferry but he wasn't looking forward to the ride on this small craft to catch it up.

The boat cast off and accelerated away into the channel in pursuit of the vessel.

"We just shadow it until we get out beyond the breakwaters then pull alongside and bring the pilot off," the skipper of the tender explained.

*   *   *

Cyril opened his eyes and struggled to make sense of where he was. Putting his hand to the side of his head, he winced. Rubbing his fingers together, the dampness told him his blood had been spilt. Then it all came back to him; the visit to the warehouse in Colchester, the flower van and the Robinsons turning up. And then there was Lennie King. What the Hell was …? Of course Lennie King had arrived. Cyril had found that out when he was on the holiday park.

He felt cold, so cold. He couldn't work it out at first. The van was now stationary but there was a throbbing noise coming from the front of the vehicle. Suddenly it stopped. Now he could feel a heavy drumming vibration. Yes the van was at a stop, but was that movement Cyril detected? Of course, they were on the ferry. But it was cold. Here he was in only shirt sleeves. Suddenly, the throbbing noise started up again and Cyril knew immediately what it was. The chiller had been switched on and the temperature was dropping. He had to get out before they reached Holland. He put his hand to his head again; this would have to get some attention.

Holding onto a bracket on the side of the van, he slowly pulled himself to his feet. His head spun and he closed his eyes for a moment. He stretched but caught himself as a sharp pain stabbed through his back. He rubbed the spot with his hand and flinched. He'd obviously clattered himself when he'd stumbled and he could imagine the bruising spreading.

Opening his eyes, he remembered Sam. Where was he? Had they spotted him sitting in the car over the road? No, they wouldn't have. So where was he now? Does he realise what's happened? Has he reported in? Christ,

166

that's going to be one massive bollocking for the pair of them.

Thoughts of Sam reminded him he'd had hold of the torch that he'd been given. Sweeping a foot around the floor, he eventually kicked against it. Bending down, he picked it up and switched it on. Still groggy, he shuffled towards the back doors but couldn't see any way of releasing them from the inside. On top of that, the batteries in the torch seemed to be failing. He switched it off for a minute to try and preserve what little power they had left.

The chiller had stopped once more; obviously down to temperature. He banged on the doors, shouted then listened. The only sound was the steady humming of the ship's engines. Of course, he thought, once under way, the vehicle deck access doors would be locked and nobody would be allowed to wander through.

Feeling his way around the sides, he arrived at the front bulkhead and groped for the release bracket to the hidden section. Maybe there was a small door to the outside from in there? His head was pounding when he eventually turned the handle to the disguised door. The space was pitch black. This didn't bode well. If there was another way into this compartment, he would expect some chink of light to show.

Another spell of yelling and banging on the walls before listening. Again, no response. He decided to preserve his strength. When they reached port and activity began prior to arrival, he'd have another go. In the meantime, he sat down on the floor and leaned against one side. He wrapped his arms around himself and closed his eyes.

* * *

It took around fifteen minutes before the small boat drew alongside the big ferry, preparations being made for the personnel transfer. Barton watched members of the ferry's crew swing a galvanised metal ladder down from a doorway on the side, about twenty feet above the water. Nervous as he was, he had to admire the skill of the pilot boat's skipper in manoeuvring the craft alongside, another man picking up the rope dangling from the steps and holding on firmly.

"Come on," Gray said, tottering over to the side and grabbing the handrail of the steps.

Barton was feeling decidedly queasy, the small boat moving up and down on the slight swell. Timing was everything. He hesitated a couple of times before grabbing the handrail and pulling himself up onto one of the steps. Immediately, he felt much better, the ferry very stable compared to the pilot boat. Don't look down, he told himself. He took a breath before slowly climbing up to the door on the ferry's side. There, he was met by the grinning face of a Sealink staff member.

"First time you've done that?" he asked.

Barton just nodded and stepped clear, DS Gray right behind him.

The crewman ushered the two of them to one side leaving his colleagues to complete the pilot's transfer, pull up the ladder and make the door secure.

"You're looking to find a van?" the crewman asked.

"DS Gray and DI Barton. Yes, as quick as you can."

"Follow me." The man in the Sealink jumper led the way down the corridor to a doorway opening onto some steps. "Your boss has spoken to the captain," the man explained as they walked. "Normally, they wouldn't allow anyone onto the vehicle decks once they've cast off but I've been asked to accompany you down there and open the doors for you. It could be dangerous, especially if the sea's a bit rough, but we should be okay today." He grinned again at Barton. "Plus, they'll keep the speed down for a little bit to keep it as safe as possible."

One flight down, they came to the locked door to B deck. The crewman unlocked it and opened the door. Immediately in front of them was a coach.

Barton looked up and down the row; heavy goods vehicles, buses and a few cars stretched as far as he could see. "Any idea where this van might be?" he asked.

Gray looked blank.

"Which van are you looking for?" the crewman asked.

Barton described it.

The man thought for a few seconds then turned to the left. "I think I remember that. Quite late boarding so it should be down this end," he said, striding along the narrow lane between the vehicles and the sidewall.

"Let's just hope you haven't pulled another lorry up so close behind it that we can't get the doors open," Barton stated.

Along the line of buses and lorries they went to the very end where the bow doors had closed. Barton strained to look over the vast array of cars, buses and wagons, but it was impossible. So many large vehicles blocked his vision. Plus they were parked in a slight curve down the length of the boat.

"We'll split up," Barton said to Gray and the crewman. "Take one row each and we'll meet at the other end. You both know what we're looking for. If you find it, big shout. Okay?"

The other two nodded and they set off down the rows as quickly as the space would allow. Five minutes later, they were at the other end of the deck. Barton glanced at his watch. "It's got to be here," he said. "Are you sure you saw it?" he asked the crewman.

"Positive. This next sweep should cover most of the deck."

The three set off once more. Barton had made it about three-quarters of the way to the opposite end when he heard a loud shout from DS Gray.

"Here! Over here!"

*   *   *

"I'm sorry I couldn't give you children." Maureen's familiar voice drifts through Cyril's head once more.

"Don't," Cyril was saying. "You've got nothing to apologise for. You were the best friend, wife, lover … everything I could have wanted."

Softly, Maureen says, "I know."

Cyril rubs his hands up and down his sides. It's getting colder. "Are you happy?" he asks.

"I'm at peace. I would have liked a few more years with you but … it wasn't to be."

"I miss you Maureen," Cyril says, unsure whether aloud or in his head.

There is silence for a while then Maureen speaks again. "I know Doris told you."

"Told me what?"

"I want you to be happy, Cyril. I want you to let go. If there's anyone else that comes into your life, don't think I'll be upset."

"There isn't … I mean …" Cyril hesitates.

"I know there might be someone who likes you." Maureen takes a breath. "I'd be glad if there was. I don't want you to mope around. You're still young."

"I'm so cold, Mo. Am I joining you?"

"You've still got things to do, Cyril. It's not time. You need to stay warm."

Cyril opens his eyes. "Maureen? Where are you?" He can see nothing in the pitch darkness. The temperature has dropped and he is shaking uncontrollably. He's tired, so tired. Stay awake, he tells himself but he feels his eyes closing. I'll just have a little doze, he thinks.

From somewhere in the distance, an unfamiliar voice shouts, "Here! Over here!"

37

"Okay, thanks. If you could as soon as you can," Walker said, ending the call.

"Who was that?" Miller flicked ash from his cigarette into the overflowing ashtray on his desk; he'd brought it into custody for its own protection after a session in the pub next door earlier in the year.

"Ipswich." Walker responded. "So that's Colchester, Chelmsford and now Ipswich, all saying the same thing; they'll have to get someone to trawl through their archives and get back to me."

Miller blew out smoke. "How long's that going to take?"

"Could be bloody weeks. Barton asked me to go back thirty years."

Miller laughed. "You might get a result by Christmas."

"That's what the boss said."

Miller's phone rang. He stubbed out his cigarette and answered.

Walker leaned back, stretched and cracked his back. He'd been on the phone for the best part of an hour since Barton and Sanderson had left, trying to track down someone, anyone who could give him some help on tracing operations using the metal plate.

Miller scribbled something on a pad, thanked whoever was on the other end and put the receiver down. "Come on, Bill." He stood up, tucked his shirt back into his trousers and grabbed his jacket. "Let's get some fresh air."

"Where are we going?" Walker asked.

"Track down Robert the Bruce."

The address Miller had been given from records was a run-down large Edwardian house not far from the police station. It would have been impressive when it was first built and Clacton was a resort of choice for Londoners but now, it had been split into flats and single rooms. The main door was open. Music was playing from somewhere on the upper floors. A smell of stale food wafted out.

A battered table sat in the hallway with a pile of post waiting for someone to collect. Miller flicked through it, pulled out several envelopes and studied the address. "Flat 5," he said to Walker and led the way up the creaky staircase. Doors with numbers 3, 4, 5 and 6 were on the first floor. Miller approached number 5, put his ear to the door and listened. After a few seconds, he knocked. No response.

"Mr Chalmers, we'd like a word," Miller said.

Still no response.

The door and frame looked battered and worn. Miller took out a plastic card from his wallet and slid it into a gap around the Yale lock. It opened.

"We'll need to send the crime prevention officer round," Miller said, a smile on his face.

"I didn't think we could ..." Walker began.

"I think there may danger to life if we don't check this out," Miller interrupted. "Wouldn't you agree, DC Walker?" He pushed the door open and called out Chalmers name. The only sounds were of traffic from outside and the booming base line of a stereo system from the floor above. Miller's other senses were attacked with the smell of rotten food and the sight of the room being a complete tip.

"Christ my Mum would go spare if she walked in here," Walker offered.

"You'd be surprised how many sad bastards live like this, Bill."

Miller took a few steps inside. It appeared to be a bedsit. The one room was dark, the curtains pulled roughly together at the window with gaps at the top where they didn't quite meet. To one side, a double bed looked as though the occupant had got out and left it in a hurry. On the floor, the empty metal cartons of takeaway food lay scattered. A chest of drawers stood opposite the end of the bed, a couple of drawers not quite shut. Miller picked his way carefully across the floor towards it and opened the top drawer. Socks and underpants lay inside. The next drawer down contained a couple of shirts. Next to this, a wardrobe stood, its doors open. Amongst the empty hangers, a couple of jackets and a pair of trousers were hung up. A pair of almost new trainers sat forlornly at the bottom.

Miller flicked through the four or five envelopes he'd brought with him from downstairs and studied the postmarks. "They go back over the past five or six weeks," he said.

Suddenly footsteps were heard from the hallway and a woman who looked to be in her forties but could have been younger appeared at the door. "Fuck you doin' in Dougie's room?" Her aggressive tone sounded more to do with the can of strong lager she had in her hand than any real concern.

Miller flicked open his warrant card. "And you are?"

"None o' your business," she responded in a strong Glaswegian accent and drew on the cigarette she held in the opposite hand.

"You know Mr Chalmers then?" Miller took a step towards the doorway.

"Used to. Why? What d'you want wi' him noo?"

"Just a chat, that's all. Have you seen him?"

She looked the DC up and down considering her answer. "No' for weeks," she finally said. "I thought he'd pissed off." She turned and walked down the corridor and up the stairs to the second floor.

"Shall we get her back?" Walker wondered.

"Don't see the point," Miller considered. "She's just another piss head who won't be able to tell us any more. Looks like our Mr Chalmers has moved on."

"Bit strange for him to leave some of his stuff though, don't you think?"

Miller shook his head. "Probably moved on to create havoc in another unsuspecting seaside resort. Let's go." He led the way out of the room and closed the door, the lock snapping shut behind them.

38

Barton squeezed himself between the front end of an articulated lorry and the rear of a tour bus, wishing he were a stone or two lighter. On the other side he saw DS Gray by the side of the van he'd been seeking.

He scurried towards the DS. "Let's get the back doors open," he said.

The Sealink crewman reached the van at the same time.

"Cyril! Cyril, are you in there?" Barton shouted.

At the back of the van, another van had been drawn up within three feet. Gray was already pulling on the door levers. "Could be a bit tight," he said.

A faint shout and a muffled bang came from the van.

Barton ducked under the door that Gray had just managed to open a foot or so. Inside, he saw the bloodied face of Cyril Claydon, blinking.

"Cyril, how are you doing? Are you okay?" Barton asked before realising how stupid that sounded. "We'll get you out. Can you move? Can you get over here?"

"Bloody free …zing but I'm alright," Cyril said between yawning and the involuntary shudders sweeping through his body. "This probably … isn't as bad as it … looks."

Cyril slowly shuffled himself towards the open door, turned and swung his legs down. The narrow gap the door could only open made it difficult for him to squash through but with Gray and Barton's help, he finally made it. They helped him to the narrow corridor between the rows of vehicles. He bent over, hands on his knees, backside against the side of the van and took in some deep breaths.

"How did … How did you know where I was?" he struggled to ask.

"Never mind that for now, let's get you checked over," Barton replied.

He began to shiver violently.

Barton took off his jacket and placed it around Cyril's shoulders. "You look pale, man," he said as Cyril yawned again.

"I'm just a bit tired, that's all," he said.

The Sealink crew member looked concerned. "I think he's suffering from the initial effects of hypothermia," he suggested. "I've seen it before. It can be a danger for us, especially on the winter crossings." He looked to DS Gray. "Best get him up to the Medical Bay. We've got a doctor on board who can take a look at him. This is the quickest way," he said, indicating a bulkhead door nearby.

* * *

Lennie King had checked in with his paperwork, no problems with the tickets that Victor Robinson had provided and he'd been through the Immigration checks. It was cooler on the vehicle deck where he'd been guided by the ferry's crew.

It was about ten minutes before sailing when he locked the driver's door on the van and made his way up the stairs to the passenger decks. First off, he'd buy a newspaper, catch up on the sport and find the bar. Seven hours was a long time to kill on the sailing. At least it looked as though it should be a calm crossing; nothing worse than being tossed around on the North Sea for hours on end.

He pulled his leather jacket from the holdall and put it on. Despite the warm weather, it would be breezy on board plus he liked the comfort of a pocket to keep the envelope safe that Robinson had given him. He checked it again before taking a ten pound note from his first instalment to use on the journey. He'd keep the Dutch Guilders for when he got to Holland.

He found the kiosk and bought a Daily Express. The bar wouldn't open until they were on their way, so he sat in a comfortable chair in one of the passenger lounges. Although the weather was summer-like, the kids had gone back to school so the boat wasn't particularly busy. He settled down and opened the paper. Drought measures were causing concerns, mostly in the north of England. Prime Minister, Jim Callaghan had created a Minister for Drought, Denis Howell, who Lennie had always thought was a bit of a waste of space. Turning to the back pages, he was surprised to read of rumours of Third Division Portsmouth being on the brink of going bust. He tried to remember the last football league club to go out of business; Accrington Stanley, maybe?

He turned to an inside page and quickly scanned the cricket news. It had been a poor summer for an England supporter. The West Indies cricketers were touring and had stuffed the visitors three nil in the tests with the same results in the one day internationals. The match up in Scarborough looked like going the same way.

Folding up the paper, he looked out of the window and saw that they were on the move, the big vessel cruising along the channel towards the open sea between Harwich and Felixstowe. Time for a drink, he thought, and made his way to the bar.

* * *

"Mild hypothermia," the ship's doctor announced. "Should be okay in a few hours." He'd cleaned up the gash to Cyril's head, put in a couple of stitches and covered it over. "You'll have a bit of a headache," the doctor had told him before turning to Barton. "He needs some rest. We'll keep an eye on him. A hot drink is fine but no alcohol," he said, looking at the DI who had suggested a small Scotch would do him wonders.

The doctor then departed, leaving Barton alone with the patient.

"Christ, Cyril, what the Hell were you thinking? Going off on your own?" Barton sat on a chair by the side of Cyril's bed.

"I wasn't on my own. Was it Sam? Did he alert you?"

Barton nodded. "Just wait till I see him."

"He's a good lad. I talked him in to coming with me," Cyril pleaded. "And if he hadn't been there, I'd still be on my way to Holland."

"No you're quite right DS Claydon. I need to see you in my office first thing." A slight smile belied the stern tone Barton had adopted.

DS Gray came in with a hot drink and handed it to Cyril.

"Thanks." Cyril pulled the blanket tighter around his shoulders.

Barton introduced Frank Gray as Cyril sipped the drink.

"Did you want to make that call now?" Gray asked of Barton.

Barton nodded. "Just going to speak to the DCI," he said to Cyril. "I'll be back in a bit to see how you're doing." He followed Gray outside.

39

Cyril cupped his hands around the mug and sipped the tea that DS Gray had brought him. He appreciated just how lucky he was. He could have been in that van all the way to the suppliers in Holland. With the chiller operational, he was struggling to stay awake. Chances were that when Lennie King came back to the vehicle, Cyril would have been unconscious and incapable of raising the alarm. That wasn't a prospect he wanted to dwell on. He owed Sam a beer or two, that was certain. And he would do all he could to ensure the lad wasn't disciplined over the incident.

He was bemused by the thoughts that had swum through his head when he'd been in the back of the van. That was the second time in recent days he seemed to have been in contact with Maureen. He didn't believe in all that spiritualism nonsense but he was confused. Possibly it was his own internal thoughts combined with memories of his late wife that somehow became entwined when he was struggling to remain conscious.

He put his hand gently to his head wound. The doctor had done a neat job with the dressing. It felt tender and he knew it would be for some time but he felt more or less back to normal. He hadn't had a chance to tell Barton what he'd found in the Colchester warehouse. That was a priority; that and finding Lennie King. He had to be on board and he needed to speak to him too.

Shrugging the blanket from around his shoulders, he stood up. He felt okay; no wooziness, although he thought the gentle throb of his headache would linger for a while. Hesitating for a few seconds, he listened. There were no voices and the only thing he could feel was the steady vibrations of the ship's engines as the vessel ploughed its way towards Holland. He walked over to the door and looked out. The corridor was empty. Where had Barton disappeared to? He walked carefully along towards some stairs. The sign told him the next deck down was the passenger deck, so he headed that way.

On the large landing area, the foreign exchange office had opened and a few travellers were waiting to change pounds into guilders. Cyril instinctively felt his trouser pocket for his wallet. He remembered he had two five pound notes and a couple of pound notes in there and maybe another pound in loose change in his other pocket. Fortunately, he also had his warrant card in his wallet too. But he cursed as he remembered his jacket was still in the Escort he'd driven to Colchester in; and in one of the pockets was his pipe and tobacco.

On either side of the open area, doors led into the passenger lounges. He walked towards one of them and began to look around at those sitting there. It didn't appear to be too crowded and he casually walked down the central corridor trying to spot Lennie King's head. There were a few families with small children below school age, quite a few students with rucksacks on the floor in front of them, no doubt enjoying a late summer break before university started again next month. Although there were a number of men sitting on their own, reading newspapers or dozing in the seats, Lennie wasn't among them.

At the far end, the lounge opened out into another large lobby area. From this, doors led out on either side to the promenade decks. A man and a woman of around forty came in from one of them, the man holding the door open thinking Cyril was heading outside. After a moment's hesitation, Cyril stepped through and out into the fresh air. Here about a dozen passengers were leaning against the rail or strolling around, all with coats or jackets on; none of them Lennie. He felt cool so he turned around and went back inside.

Opposite, the cafeteria area was busy. Again, no sign of his target. Turning through another set of doors, he walked into a second passenger lounge, this time with a bar at the far end. Another scan of faces and heads finally picked up a familiar profile. Of course, Cyril thought, if Lennie would be anywhere it would be in the bar.

Carefully picking his way through the tables and chairs, he circled his prey, approaching him from the rear and sitting down in a vacant seat immediately behind him. Lennie took a sip of his beer and opened out his newspaper.

Cyril turned in the chair and leaned over to speak quietly to him. "Hello, Lennie. Fancy seeing you here."

*   *   *

"I'm in DI Crimond's office but he's not here at the moment," DCI Sanderson was explaining.

"I'm with DS Gray now Sir." Barton warned.

"Well not a word, Dick. Keep what I've told you under your hat."

"Absolutely," Barton replied.

"Just get yourself and Cyril back here safely on the return sailing."

Barton ended the call. They'd just spoken to the Harwich station where Crimond and Gray were based. "Thanks, Frank," Barton said. "I'll just go and see how my officer is getting along."

"Sure," Gray replied, "If you need me, I'll probably be in the officer's mess."

Barton left the Communications Room and made his way back to the medical bay, deep in thought. On route, he took in one of the promenades and breathed in some ozone. What Sanderson had told him had given him plenty to think about. After a minute or two, he decided he'd had enough fresh air and needed a smoke. Back inside, he lit up and wandered through the gift shop, wondering just how much business it actually did with their prices. The thought also struck him that he might get some duty free cigarettes to take back on the return journey. Couldn't waste an opportunity. After a few more minutes browsing, he began to make his way back up to the medical bay.

When he looked inside the room where he had left Cyril, it was empty. The doctor was in an office further down the corridor. The door was open and he was reading a magazine.

"What's happened to my colleague?" Barton asked him

The doctor looked up. "I was going to ask you the same question. I went to check on him ten minutes ago and he'd gone. I thought he was with you."

Barton breathed out heavily and walked away. Shit, he hoped Cyril hadn't gone wandering off looking for King. That could bugger everything up.

Back down to the passenger deck, Barton scanned the faces. First he did a circuit of the promenades. Towards the bow, he thought he saw a man who looked like Cyril, puffing on a pipe but on closer inspection, he was much older. Once more back inside, he walked through the lounge area. Still no sign of Cyril. At the far end he followed the signs for the bar. Finally, in a corner, he saw him.

"Shit," he mumbled to himself then made his way towards him.

40

Lennie King jumped and turned around to see Cyril grinning at him.

"Jesus, Mr Claydon," he said, clutching his chest, "You nearly gave me a heart attack there."

"Off on a foreign trip?" Cyril asked.

"Er ... just a little business trip to Holland." Lennie squinted, looking at Cyril. "Are you all right Mr Claydon? Have you had an accident?"

"You could say that, Lennie. Mind if I join you?"

"Well ..."

"Thanks." Cyril stood and walked round to a spare seat next to him. "So, how are things going?"

King looked nervously around before answering, "Not too bad."

"I didn't realise you and Victor Robinson were so close."

King looked sharply at Cyril. "Who told you that? What are you on about?"

"All that nonsense you gave me the other week when I was asking about Jimmy Morgan and you telling me, what was it now," Cyril made a show of trying to recall the exact words, "that was it, he thinks he's close to some big people; talks a good game but he doesn't know half of what he reckons he does." He looked at King. "A bit of a gofor, was how you described him. So what are you, Lennie? Just a gofor, or are you much closer?"

"How the ..."

"Cyril, a word." The voice of DI Barton interrupted the conversation.

"Oh hello," Cyril said. "Look who I've just bumped into."

"Cyril," Barton repeated sharply, taking a couple of steps away from the table where Cyril was sitting with King.

Taking the hint, Cyril stood and joined his DI. "I'm just asking him about Victor Robinson." He glanced over to King still sitting at the table.

Barton leaned in close to Cyril, his voice low. "There's something you need to know."

Cyril moved his head nearer to hear.

"King is a participating informant for the Met."

"Good God!"

"Exactly. So we need to let him carry on with this operation," Barton responded.

"But we need to talk to him about his relationship with Robinson and Jimmy Morgan," Cyril persisted. "He gave me a load of old Horlicks the last time I spoke to him."

"Look, we can't tread on the Met's toes here." Barton whispered, "They've got something much bigger ..."

"Everything alright?" Frank Gray had appeared.

"I was just ..." Cyril began.

Barton jumped in. "I found DS Claydon getting his bearings. You were bored up in the sick bay, weren't you?"

"Er, yes. Bored."

"As long as you're okay," Gray responded. "I'm just trying to organise a cabin in the crew's quarters for you. Might be more comfortable, seeing as you'll be spending a good bit of time on board."

"That's great. Thanks Frank."

"And I need to speak with the KMar; let them know the situation." Gray then spoke of the good working relationship the Branch had with the Dutch authorities on the ferries. "I'll come back and find you," he concluded, before striding off towards the opposite end of the lounge.

"What was all that about?" Cyril puzzled.

"Tell you later. In the meantime ..." Barton turned to the table where King had been sitting. It was empty.

"Where's he gone?" Barton asked.

"There." Cyril pointed to the quickly disappearing back of Lennie King.

"You go after him, and I'll cut round this way," Barton said, dashing off around a column and down the opposite side of the lounge.

Cyril set off in pursuit of King forming a route through the tables and chairs and other passengers and out into the lobby area. King was nowhere to be seen.

Barton appeared from the other side. "I'll take the outside decks, you make your way through the other lounge and meet back here," he said then shot out through the door to the side.

Cyril decided it wasn't going to be worth dashing around the ship. It wasn't as if King could disappear anywhere. Besides, Cyril was supposed to be resting after all. He made his way into the toilets. All this tea he'd been drinking was having an effect.

A man on his way out held the door open as Cyril entered. All the cubicles seemed empty, apart from one at the far end with the door closed and the red bar showing. A young man with long hair, dressed in flared trousers was standing at one of the urinals. Cyril did the same and prepared to relieve himself.

The young man quickly finished and left; the toilets now quiet. Cyril zipped himself up, washed his hands and dried them on some paper towels. Walking towards the exit, he paused. Opening the door, he stood where he was and let it close. Standing quiet, he listened. He could just detect someone breathing in that engaged cubicle. He waited. A man coughed. He thought he recognised the sound. He remained motionless and as quiet as he could.

The bolt slid across and the door slowly creaked open. Then a head peered out.

"Come on, Lennie," Cyril said. "Let's have a chat."

The man visibly sagged.

"There's nowhere else to go," Cyril went on. "We may as well have a drink and sit down somewhere private and you can tell me all about it."

With hot drinks in front of them, Cyril, Barton and King were seated around a table in a quiet corner of one of the lounges.

"So Mr King," Barton began, "Tell me about your involvement with Victor Robinson."

"Sorry," Cyril interrupted, "before you do, can you tell us about your relationship with Jimmy Morgan?"

Barton looked puzzled but Cyril kept his focus on King.

King looked down into the mug on the table in front of him. "Jimmy was my mate," he said. "We went back a long way. I met him during the war. We were in Italy together."

"So when we spoke last week, you led me to believe you only knew *of* him but you kept your distance."

"I was just being protective of a mate. Christ, I didn't know he'd been murdered then."

"But you told me he was a grass," Cyril persisted.

"I just thought I had to say something. Besides, I thought you knew that anyway. I didn't think it would be news to you."

Barton leaned forward in his chair. "If we can just focus on what you're doing for Victor Robinson, Mr King," he said.

King looked to Barton. "You know what I'm doing. I'm driving his van to Holland, picking up a load of fresh flowers and taking them back to Covent Garden."

Barton snorted. "Since when have the Robinsons been interested in flowers?"

"I don't know. It's what it says on the van."

"What about the porn?"

King looked down. "Well, there is that too, but ..."

"Look Lennie," Barton went on in a softer tone, "we know about DCI Holt from the Met. We've been told about your 'participating informant' status."

King leaned back in his seat. "Well, there you go then. You know all about it."

"A bit dangerous isn't it?"

King shrugged.

Cyril took up the conversation again. "Lennie, how long have we known one another?"

"Too long, Mr Claydon."

"Must be nigh on twenty years." Cyril took a drink from his mug. "It isn't like you to put your neck on the line. I know you've been a bit naughty in the past, but this is something else."

The use of the word 'naughty' drew a smirk from Barton.

King responded, ignoring Cyril's boss. "When we were in Italy … me and Jimmy … we were in a unit attacking a German gun position." King drained his tea, avoiding eye contact. "I'd crawled ahead and nearly got to it when I got shot. Here." He placed his hand on the top of his left thigh. "The rest of the boys began firing … keeping them pinned down like. The next thing, Jimmy runs up, dodging some bullets and lies flat beside me. When the time was right, he gets me up and somehow drags me back to safety." He looked directly at Cyril. "I owed him, Mr Claydon. You were in the war. You must have had some incidents like that? You understand, don't you?"

Instantly, Cyril thought of Brian. Clear images of him trapped in the burning Lancaster flashed in front of him. He nodded and closed his eyes for a second.

King continued, "I wanted to find out what happened to Jimmy. I thought if Robinson had topped him, I'd want to find a way of making him pay."

"And do you think Robinson did for Jimmy?"

King shook his head. "No, I don't think so."

"So who do you think did?" Cyril encouraged.

"Not until I'm sure."

"Very commendable," Barton snorted. "But listen …" He looked from Cyril to King and back again. "Before DS Gray spots us, there's something else you should know …"

41

"What do you think?" Barton asked.

Cyril was lying down on a bunk bed, Barton lounging in a chair by its side in the cabin Gray had managed to obtain for them.

"On the face of it, it could make sense." Cyril pulled himself upright. "But that's a hell of a leap. Are you sure?"

Barton rubbed his face. "I'm not sure of anything at the moment. But until we know more, we keep as much of what I've told you between ourselves."

After a pause, Cyril spoke again, "I haven't had a chance to tell you what I found in the warehouse in Colchester."

"Go on."

He proceeded to describe what he'd discovered on the first floor; the workbench with stains he thought were blood and the roll of industrial plastic sheet similar to that wrapped around both bodies.

"At the very least it looks like the corpses were prepared there ready for disposal. And remember when I found Morgan's body, there was no smell? The PM suggested he'd been dead for a number of days, and that tied in with Beryl's statement that she'd last seen him three days before we found him. In this weather especially, he would have begun to smell. Now, when you think about it, where better to keep a body and stop it stinking than in the back of a refrigerated van."

Barton was nodding. "I'll organise forensics to get in there when we get back."

Cyril swung his legs off the bed and faced Barton. "So why don't we let this run a bit? If we let Lennie come back with the load, we can catch the Robinsons red-handed."

Barton was thoughtful.

Cyril pushed on, "I reckon I should go with Lennie on the run to the suppliers in Holland and stay with him on the return leg," Cyril said.

Barton stood up. "No way. For a start, whoever he's meeting will only be expecting King on his own. And neither of us have a passport or tickets."

"But you heard DS Gray," Cyril interrupted, "he could organise one of the open passes they keep on board for something like this. They've got a good working relationship with the Marechaussee …"

Barton stopped him. "I don't care what sort of relationship they have with the Dutch Gendarmerie, the KMar, or whatever the hell they call themselves, I'm not sanctioning you heading off into the wild blue yonder of a foreign country with Lennie King, and that's final."

Barton held Cyril's stare for a second. "Besides," he continued, "have you forgotten what I've just told you?"

Cyril realised further protest was futile. "Okay," he said. "But tell me this, what exactly did Morgan tell you when you saw him last?"

Barton sat back down. "He said the word was that Yardley's were in trouble."

"That's what you said earlier."

"But Morgan also had information that Walter Yardley himself was planning to make some runs to Amsterdam. Something about old war-time connections." Barton pulled out a cigarette and lit up.

Cyril looked at him, reminded that his pipe and tobacco were still in the Escort.

Barton blew out smoke and continued. "Yardley's idea was to buy some cheap stones through his contacts, bring them back to England and sell them on at a profit."

"All to keep the company afloat?"

"I wonder …" Barton looked as if deep in thought. "Is it possible that the Robinsons had nothing to do with Morgan's death? It was all the actions of Walter Yardley?"

"You heard Lennie say he didn't think the Robinsons were responsible, although he's not saying who he thinks was. And then we come back to the second body? Who is that? And, we think there might be a third based on what we know of Jem Fletcher's excursions."

"We need more information, Cyril." Barton stubbed out his cigarette. "When we get back, see what you can find out about Yardley Electrical's financial state. I told you one of their biggest customers had gone bust last Easter?"

Cyril nodded. "Do we know if Yardley himself has made any trips abroad yet?"

"Dunno, Jimmy was never able to tell me before he disappeared."

"And who exactly knew that Morgan had told you about Yardley's plans?"

"Only the DCI."

"Sanderson?"

"That's right."

Cyril shook his head. "But he must have passed that on, either directly or in conversation." He paused, looked directly at Barton then continued, "If you're still convinced he's not the leak."

"I'll speak to him again when we get back, but I'm positive Sanderson is sound. But according to the Met, that might not be our only problem."

Cyril was thoughtful for a second then gave it one last shot. "I still think I should ride shotgun with Lennie."

Barton gave him a withering look.

42

Sam Woodbridge replaced the receiver and walked from the call box back to the car. Barton had sounded … well, like Barton. But what else could he do? If he hadn't come with him, Cyril would have gone on his own, he knew that. The result would have been the same, except that no-one would have known anything about him being trapped in the back of that van.

Sam unlocked the car and opened the door, letting some of the heat out before he got in. Let's face it, he wasn't in a hurry to drive back to Clacton, not with Barton in a mood. He looked down and saw Cyril's jacket lying on one of the rear seats. Picking it up, he felt the weight and shape of his pipe and tobacco pouch in the pocket. Old Cyril will be missing those, he thought to himself. He folded it up and placed it on the passenger seat so he wouldn't forget it.

Finally, Sam sat in the driver's seat and started the engine. Fortunately, Cyril had left the keys with him, otherwise that would have been another awkward situation to explain, not to mention him having to leave the car there and get the train back.

Sam locked up the Escort in the police station car park and, carrying Cyril's jacket over his arm, walked in through the main doors.

"Hello Sam," the desk sergeant greeted. "What are you doing here on your days off? Can't keep away?"

"Something like that, Skip. Is anyone in upstairs?" Sam asked, referring to CID.

"Don't think so. Dick Barton and the DCI took off a couple of hours ago as if there was free beer somewhere.

Miller and Walker went out about an hour after that and they're not back. Anything I can do for you?"

"No thanks, I'll just drop this off for Cyril," Sam said, indicating the jacket over his arm.

Up the stairs to the CID office, Sam didn't feel so bad knowing Barton wouldn't be there. At least his bollocking would be put off until tomorrow.

As the desk sergeant had said, the room was deserted. Barton's office door was ajar as if he'd left in a hurry, which he had. He walked over to Cyril's desk and hung his jacket on the back of the chair before taking the car keys from his pocket and placing them on his desk.

Footsteps and voices could be heard on the stairs so Sam hurried to the door. Coming up were Bill Walker and Ben Miller.

"Looking for anyone?" Miller asked.

"The DI," Sam said, nervously.

"He's gone out," Miller said, walking into the office.

"You don't know when he'll be back, do you?" Sam went on.

"No idea, mate," Walker responded. "He dashed off to the ferry terminal with DCI Sanderson."

Sam's eyes widened. His stare darted around the office before settling on the floor. That must be where the van was going, with Cyril inside. Would they have got there before it sailed? God, he only hoped Cyril was okay. He could feel himself pale.

"He did say he wanted to see you first thing tomorrow," Miller added, slouching down at his desk. "I won't tell you exactly what he said, though." A smirk on his face.

"Are you alright?" Walker asked.

Sam looked up. "Fine, yeah. I'm okay." But as he left and walked back down the stairs, he knew he wasn't.

* * *

Cathy Rogers picked up a manila file and made her way to the stairs. A glance at her watch told her it was nearly four-thirty and she hadn't heard anything further from Cyril. Up the stairs and into the CID room, Ben Miller and Bill Walker were sitting at their desks.

"Look, I know it's going back a long time but ..." Walker was saying into the telephone. "If you could," he added. "As soon as you can."

Walker put the phone down, groaned loudly and leaned back on his chair.

Cathy walked over to Cyril's desk and noticed car keys on the desk and his jacket hung over the back of his seat. "Is DS Claydon not around?" she asked the two detectives.

"Not seen him since this morning. Anything I can do?" Miller asked, with a leer.

"He just wanted a file, that's all," Cathy responded. "It can wait till tomorrow."

Miller turned round to Walker. "Fancy a pint then, Bill? I'm bloody parched."

"In a bit," Walker responded. "I'll just try one more before we go," he said, picking the handset up once again.

Cathy walked out of the room, still clutching the file. She afforded herself a slight smile as she remembered one of the other secretaries referring to the pair as Tweedledum and Tweedledee.

Cathy stood in front of the bathroom mirror applying the final touches; mascara and lipstick. Nervously glancing at her watch, she noted it was five to seven. Cyril must have returned to the station, she was sure, despite those two saying they hadn't seen him. His jacket was there along with a set of car keys. And he was wearing that jacket this morning when he'd asked her out. She smiled to herself at the thought that, more accurately, she'd propositioned him. But he did seem keen. A final check and, plumping her hair with both hands, she walked into her bedroom and looked out of the window. No sign of a car.

Simon, her fourteen-year-old son was riding up and down the street on his bike with his mate, Kevin, from around the corner. She'd arranged with Kevin's mum for him to stay with them until she got back to pick him up. She knew he would be safe, she'd reciprocated for Kevin's mum a few times in the past.

Another check of the watch. Seven dead on now and still no Cyril. God, if he lets me down again, she thought, well … She caught sight of herself in the wardrobe mirror. A floral dress she'd had for a couple of years, just on the knee, and white slingbacks with a medium heel. I'll do, she thought, picking her white cardigan off the bed; just in case the evening drew in. Despite the hot sunny days, the nights could be cool. And sooner or later, this incredible dry spell would have to break.

Downstairs in the living room, she automatically switched on the television. Crossroads, she never liked that, so she switched over to the BBC. Damn, she'd missed Nationwide and she did enjoy that. Some game show had just started so she left it on for background noise and looked through the window again. Nothing.

By twenty-five past seven, disappointment had evaporated to be replaced by anger. Finally, she went into the kitchen, made herself a cup of tea and returned to the lounge. One last look from the window before changing TV channels to watch Coronation Street.

* * *

About two miles from Cathy's house, Doris was wondering what to do with Charlie. The big old boy had again been her companion for the day but normally Cyril would have appeared by now and taken him back. She checked her watch; half-past seven.

"I'll bet you're hungry, old lad," she said to the dog.

He just thumped his tail twice on the grass.

"Come on then, let's sort you out."

Ever since Maureen had become ill, Doris had a key to Cyril's house. He had one for hers in case of emergencies. Unlocking the door, she let herself in, Charlie lumbering close behind. She hadn't been in the house for some time but it struck her that nothing had changed since Maureen's passing. Items in the kitchen were where they had always been.

She opened the door to the cupboard where she knew Cyril kept Charlie's biscuits. A tin of dogfood was already on the worktop next to the fridge. First she refilled his water bowl and put it back on the floor. He wasn't interested in that; he was waiting for his supper.

With Charlie noisily munching his biscuits and meat, Doris wandered from the kitchen and into the hallway. Some post lay on the mat behind the front door, so she picked it up. In the lounge, the same dralon three-piece suite sat around the focal point of the fireplace with a gas fire. A small television was in the corner on a unit.

She didn't feel she was being nosy, it was just something for her to fill the time while the dog ate. On the fireplace she recognised the distinctive shape of a Spitfire. It was cast in bronze with a moving propeller. Maureen had told her someone in Cyril's squadron had made it for him as a reminder of their war-time days. That brought her thoughts back to Cyril's nightmare. Whatever he experienced during those dark days still haunted him now. Maureen had told her he sometimes woke in a cold sweat, jabbering something incoherent, but he never spoke of it. That frustrated Maureen because she thought that if he talked to her, she could help him through it. Sadly, she died before she could persuade her husband. Doris enjoyed her conversations with Maureen. She missed her as a neighbour and she only hoped she'd helped her in her last days.

She was brought out of her reverie by the sounds of Charlie slobbering some water from his bowl and burping, signifying he'd enjoyed his meal.

Back in the kitchen, she wondered about calling the station to see what Cyril was up to but dismissed it. She was sure he would be involved in something important and wouldn't welcome his neighbour pestering him. No, Charlie could come back with her. It had been some time since she'd had his company for the evening.

43

"Oh, sod it!" Cyril was studying his watch.

"What's up?" Barton asked. They were still sitting in their cabin.

Cyril rubbed his face with both hands. "I've just remembered I should be somewhere else right now."

"Shouldn't we all."

They were quiet for a few seconds, Cyril lying flat on the bed, Barton slouched in a chair, eyes closed.

"I'm starving," Cyril finally said. "Shall we get something to eat?"

"Don't think you can book it on expenses." Barton still had his eyes closed.

Cyril got up. "Come on then."

They found the self-service restaurant and chose their meals before settling into a table near a window. There was nothing to be seen outside but the wide grey expanse of the North Sea.

Cyril took a couple of mouthfuls of his shepherd's pie, chips and beans before looking up to speak to Barton. "You haven't told me what the PM came up with ... that second body."

"Mmm, interesting," Barton said, chewing his food and waving his fork at the same time. "The one thing I can tell you is that whoever he was, he wasn't killed with the same weapon." He took a forkful of his chili-con-carne before elaborating. "This poor sod was blasted by a shotgun."

"Head?"

Barton nodded.

"Doesn't mean he wasn't dispatched by the same perpetrator though," Cyril argued.

"I know. But there was one thing that might lead us to finding out who he was." In between eating, Barton outlined the discovery of the plate in the victim's leg.

"I'll bet you're Bill Walker's favourite at the moment," Cyril said, referring to the DC's task of contacting hospitals all over the country.

"It's the only bloody thing we've got to work on." Barton scooped another forkful of food into his mouth. "No possessions on him to give us a clue."

"Whereas we did find something in Jimmy Morgan's pocket lining," Cyril said slowly.

"A key."

"A Yale to be precise." Cyril paused while he ate. "Well, I think I know where it might fit."

"Go on then." Barton was impatient.

"We can check it out when we get back but I'll bet it'll unlock the pedestrian access in the double doors to the Colchester warehouse."

Barton was still chewing. After a pause, he spoke again, a grin on his face. "I'm assuming it was worth your while spending a couple of days on the holiday park?"

"That's how I found out about the warehouse. Lennie turned up on Saturday morning for a meet." Cyril placed his knife and fork on his empty plate and took a sip from the mug of tea in front of him. "But what about Adam Fletcher? What news on him?"

"Ah, well …" More chewing from Barton. "He was back in the land of the living this morning."

"You've been to see him?"

"Yup." Barton then related his tactic of a double-bluff to get Fletcher to talk.

When he'd finished, Cyril shook his head disbelievingly.

"Anyway, what do you know of a character by the name of Dougie Chalmers?" Barton asked.

Cyril was puzzled by the change of tack. "Big Glaswegian nutter."

"That's the boy. Turns out he was the one that Adam Fletcher owed money to at first."

"At first?"

"The debt was taken over by someone else, we don't know who." Barton pushed his empty plate away. "Got Miller trying to track Chalmers down to see what he can tell us."

"Good luck with that. The guy gave us all sorts of grief in uniform. Always at the heart of one disturbance or another; and all involving drink."

The conversation was suddenly halted by activity in the nearby passenger lounge. Several people were running towards an area half way down. Barton spotted the ship's doctor rush past.

Cyril stood to look. "What's going on there?" he wondered aloud.

"Let's check it out," Barton said.

Just then, they overheard someone coming out of the lounge mention something about somebody having a heart attack.

Barton, with Cyril in his wake, struggled to push his way through other passengers trying to get a better view of what was happening. A group were on their knees surrounding someone he couldn't yet see. One of them, Barton recognised was the familiar form of Frank Gray. On the other side the doctor was performing CPR. Finally, Barton manoeuvred himself to be able to see the patient. He froze. The man was Lennie King.

44

In the sick bay where Cyril had rested after his rescue, Lennie King now lay on the bed, pillows under his head and an oxygen mask covering his face. He'd survived the attack, pointing the doctor in the direction of his jacket pocket where he had pills to put under his tongue. His angina and the stress of the day's events had obviously led to his situation.

The doctor thought it was a mild attack but he'd radioed ahead for an ambulance to meet the ship and take the patient to hospital.

Cyril sat in the chair by the side of the bed. "I never knew you had heart problems, Lennie," he said.

King pulled the mask clear of his face for a few seconds. "It's not something I tend to broadcast, Mr Claydon."

"Is there anyone we can contact for you?"

"Not really, I live on my own now." A few gasps of oxygen before he continued, "But listen, can your DI get in touch with DCI Holt from here?"

Cyril was puzzled. "Possibly, I'm not sure."

"If he can, can he tell him 'Code seven'?"

"What are you on about, Lennie?"

"Please Mr Claydon, just ask him to pass it on. It's important."

Cyril held up both hands. "Okay, I'll ask him."

"Thanks. Now what about the van and the Robinsons?"

"Leave that with me for the moment. I'll have a word with the DI and see how best to play this. You just rest. I'll be back to see you later." Cyril stood, gave a thumbs up sign and left the room.

Back in their temporary cabin in the crew's quarters, Barton and Frank Gray were discussing events when Cyril joined them.

Gray looked up. "How is he?"

"Lucky, I think," Cyril responded. "According to the doc, it was only an attack of angina but he's off to hospital to get checked out as soon as we dock." He sat down on a spare seat. "But what do we do about the operation now?"

"Do?" Barton appeared surprised. "Nothing. It's all come to an end. If King can't carry on, then the whole exercise has to be abandoned."

"But everything's in place. This was to be Lennie's first run for Robinson."

Barton frowned. "In the light of what's happened, I've brought Frank up to speed with King's status."

Cyril was surprised. "Oh, okay."

"But I was wondering, how do we know he wasn't in this for his own benefit? He could be double-crossing this DCI … Holt, is it?"

Gray nodded. "That's right."

"He's not the most upright citizen," Barton continued. "Plus he lives in Clacton."

Cyril decided to ignore the last jibe. "Look, Lennie's not doing this for the money. You've heard how he served with Jimmy Morgan in the war. Bonds like that are not easily broken, believe me. No, he's doing this to find out what happened to Jimmy. Now I know you think Lennie's a bit dodgy but I've known him for years. He might sail close to the wind now and again but he's basically straight."

"Let's say you're right, Cyril," Barton considered, "King can hardly carry on now, so how can we?"

"Me."

"You? What do you mean, you?" Realisation dawned on Barton face. "No fucking way. You might be happy putting yourself at risk but there's no way my arse is going on the line."

"But just think about it for a second. I'm roughly the same build as Lennie. He's a few years older, admittedly, but I'd pass for his age."

"You are a bit shorter than him, though," Barton interrupted. "Plus that head wound might look suspicious."

"But whoever he's supposed to be liaising with has never met him before. As I said, this is his first run. So what can go wrong?"

"You want me to make a list?"

"It might work," Gray put in.

"But you've no documentation; no tickets, no passport," Barton argued.

"Lennie's got the tickets and ..." Cyril turned to Gray, "You said you've got a couple of passes on board for emergencies and you have a good working relationship with the KMar."

Barton stood up. "Fuck, this is what you wanted all along."

"At least let Frank here make some enquiries."

Barton was silent for a few seconds, staring through the porthole at the last of the daylight. "Shit." He turned and looked at Gray. "Okay, make the call and see what your superiors say."

Gray left the room as Barton pulled out a cigarette.

"At the very least, we need to consider it," Cyril said. "But look ..." Cyril leaned forward and lowered his voice before telling him what Lennie King had just asked him to do.

Barton lit up and took a deep drag. "Code seven? It'll have to be passed on through Sanderson. And how the hell am I going to sell this daft idea of yours to him anyway?"

"But in the light of what you said earlier, you need to hear what Gray has to say. In fact, I'd get up to the Comms Room now, if I were you. Listen to the conversation first hand," Cyril suggested.

"You're right." Barton made for the door.

"In the meantime, I'll learn as much as I can from Lennie."

"How are you doing now, Lennie?" Cyril sat down on the chair by the side of the sick-bay bed. King was dozing, the oxygen mask hanging by his neck.

He opened his eyes. "Just a bit tired," he responded. "What time is it?"

Cyril checked his watch. "Just gone half nine, or half ten Dutch time."

"Not long before we dock, then."

"About our little problem," Cyril began. "I think I've got a solution."

King gave a chuckle. "Somehow I thought you would."

"Do you mind if I look through your things?"

"Help yourself," King said, "I've got nothing to hide. What you need is in the envelope in my jacket pocket; tickets, address in Amsterdam."

Cyril felt the pocket of King's jacket hanging up by the side of the bed then pulled out the envelope.

"What's your idea?" King asked.

Cyril spread the envelope's contents on the bed cover. "For the next day or two, I'll be Lennie King."

King wriggled to sit up a bit more. "You may as well have the Guilders, then," he said.

"You might need them … when you get to hospital, I mean. My boss can sort something out for me." The offer from King reinforced Cyril's gut instinct that he was being straight with him. "So what are the arrangements?" Cyril asked.

King explained what he was to do when he drove away from the ferry terminal. "And you can see from the ticket, you need to be on tomorrow night's sailing, back in Harwich on Wednesday morning. Robinson will be expecting me at the warehouse with the shipment by 11.00am," King concluded.

Barton walked in at that point. "Got everything you need?" he asked Cyril.

"I think so."

"Good, because Sanderson has given me the green light. He's been coordinating with your DCI Holt at the Met and I've asked him to pass on your message." Barton then explained to Cyril that Sanderson thought it best that he substitute for King.

"You?" Cyril couldn't hide his disappointment.

"Me," Barton repeated then looked over to the man in the bed. "I just hope to Christ you're not setting me up."

"Look, Mr Barton, I want to see the bastards who did for Jimmy as much as anyone. I'd have loved to follow this through but how was I to know this was going to happen But listen, maybe on the way back I could resume my duties?"

"Leave it to us, Lennie," Cyril replied.

"Just one more thing," Barton wondered, "you said you thought you knew who murdered Jimmy Morgan, but you never told us."

"No, you're right. I didn't."

Barton exhaled, exasperated.

"But could I have a word, Mr Barton … in private, like?" King leaned up on an elbow and looked over at a puzzled Cyril.

Pausing for a second, Cyril finally relented. "Okay," he said to Barton, "I'll see you outside."

45

"So this is your documentation for the Dutch immigration and customs." DS Gray handed over an envelope to Barton. "We've spoken to the KMar and you should have no problems. Anything else, like being pulled over by traffic police, give them this contact." Gray pointed to a number he'd written on the back of the envelope.

"Thanks." Barton folded the package and put it in his trouser pocket.

"And good luck." Gray looked from Barton to Cyril then left.

They were back in the borrowed cabin, about twenty minutes away from docking. Barton watched Gray go before placing both hands on his colleague's shoulders. "Now listen, Cyril, trust me on this. I've managed to speak to Sanderson again and Holt recognised King's message."

"What did it mean?"

"It's best if you don't know." Barton saw the expression on Cyril's face. "No, don't be like that. It's safer for you not to know."

"Thanks," was Cyril's withering reply.

"Anyway, how do I look?" Barton posed in the leather jacket that Lennie King had loaned him. "I've always fancied one of these. Might keep it. Handy me being much the same size as him."

Cyril shook his head. "You'll give it back, we promised Lennie."

"Lennie'll be alright. He's got a jumper in his bag."

Cyril hesitated for a second. "You did that on purpose, didn't you?"

"What? The jacket?"

"No, not the ruddy jacket," he snapped. "Sanderson. You told him you'd carry out this mission. I'll bet you never even mentioned my going."

Barton smiled. Cyril's mention of a 'mission' made it sound like something from World War Two. "He just agreed with me that it would be better for a DI to go. You'd be better placed to follow up on what you discovered in the warehouse."

They were preparing to leave the cabin, the ferry had slowed and announcements were being made on the tannoy for drivers and passengers to return to their vehicles.

"But listen," Barton's expression became serious. "Keep your eyes and ears open on the return journey. You know what I'm saying?"

"Of course." Cyril's anger had subsided. "But I still don't like this."

"Aw, I didn't know you cared."

Cyril pulled his shoulders back. "You're meeting God knows who, in a foreign country with no back-up and all you can do is make jokes."

"Look, it'll be fine."

"I know Lennie's told us as much as he knows and I believe him on that." Cyril stroked his moustache. "But let's just hope no one's leaking information about this."

"I know. But we need to flush that out." Barton looked straight at him. "I'm sure Sanderson is sound. We had that conversation. There is only him and me as far as Essex is concerned. What I don't know is what these buggers in the Met or Special Branch are up to exactly. I mean, do the Robinsons have influence there?" Barton walked around to the other side of the table. "I know what you're thinking Cyril, if they find out that their driver has been substituted … well, it's my bollocks on the line."

"We can always check on Lennie for the return," Cyril suggested.

Barton looked away. "Well he might not be fit enough to drive the van back."

"No, maybe not, but he might be okay to drive the last, say quarter of a mile. That way the Robinsons couldn't possibly suspect anything." Cyril studied the DI. "Is there something you're not telling me?"

"No, everything's fine."

Cyril didn't believe him. "Anyway, what's your thinking on this? Are we just going to let the shipment come in and be transferred up to London?"

"That's what the Met want us to do. They're looking to uncover the full process and catch the Robinsons red-handed."

"But we could do that in Colchester."

"I know."

"In any event, if you drive the van back and not Lennie, you'll have to hit them there anyway." Cyril argued. "Also, that way would reduce any risk of a leak."

Barton nodded, deep in thought.

"Plus it would give you some Brownie points."

Barton hesitated before his serious expression eased. "Listen Cyril, you didn't really like me at first, did you?"

"What makes you think I do now?"

Barton grinned.

The tannoy announcements began once again.

"Oh, have you got the keys?" Cyril asked.

Barton tapped his pocket.

"Well, it's time you got down to the vehicle deck." And as an afterthought, "Oh, and John …"

Barton paused at the door, surprised Cyril had used his first name.

"Look after yourself," he said.

Barton nodded and was gone.

46

By ten-thirty, Barton was approaching the Amsterdam district of Haarlem where the address Lennie had given him was located. A smile had come to his face as he thought of the area in New York, home to the famous basketball team, the Globetrotters.

He'd negotiated customs at the port, with an officer having a cursory glance in the back of the van. The documentation DS Gray had produced allowed him to be waved through immigration checks. The journey had taken him just over an hour and a half, the traffic light at that time of the evening.

Turning off a dual carriageway, he looked for the street names and followed the directions he'd been given. One final left turn and he was on the street he wanted. Slowly he drove, keeping an eye out for *Gert's Bar* which is where he was to be contacted. Finally, on the right, he saw it, sandwiched between a fruit and vegetable shop and a tobacconist's. About thirty yards beyond, outside a pharmacist's there was a space big enough to accommodate the van.

He parked up, got out and looked up and down the street before locking the cab door. It was mostly residential with a few shops on either side. No one appeared to be around but the lights had been on in the bar when he'd driven past.

He approached *Gert's* and walked in through the door, pausing for a second to gain his bearings. The room was about thirty feet long and twenty feet front to back with the bar opposite the door. The barman, sitting behind, looked up from his newspaper and gave a brief nod. Barton approached the counter, glancing at the couple sitting at a table to his right and noticing two men standing chatting behind the vestibule.

"Heineken, please," Barton said.

"Bottle or draught?" the barman replied in perfect English.

"Draught."

"Large or small?"

Barton smiled. "Large. It's been a long day."

His lager was poured with no further conversation and he sat down at a spare table. The first swig tasted good. Wiping the froth from his top lip, he had a quick check of his watch. This was certainly a change from some of the rough pubs in Clacton he sometimes frequented. When he woke that morning, he never for one minute thought he'd be sitting in a small bar on the outskirts of Amsterdam enjoying a lager. Looking back, it seemed a lot more than just over twelve hours ago since he was in Dr Maguire's office at Colchester County Hospital looking at X-rays of some unidentified bloke's head, blasted into oblivion by a shotgun. Just who the Hell was he? He smiled to himself at the thought of Bill Walker trawling through hospital records for a match on the surgical plate discovered in the victim's leg.

Leaning back in the seat, Barton focussed his thoughts on the job in hand. So Jimmy Morgan had been working as an informant for the Met, a participating one at that. But what had he gotten himself into? Had he been stitched up by some double dealing? Did the Robinsons find out what he was up to? And why did he persist in feeding information to him, albeit concerning Yardley? Did he really buy King's story? He supposed he did. But if Morgan had been set up, maybe King was about to be. And for Lennie King, read DI John Barton. No, he had to discount that idea. And then there was what Sanderson had told him from DCI Holt of the Met. Was that reliable?

The two men who had stood behind the vestibule drained their glasses and left. The middle-aged couple sitting at their table, the barman and himself were now the only ones left.

Just then, the door opened and a man of around thirty dressed in a denim shirt, jeans and trainers entered. He had long fair hair and a full beard. He nodded to the barman then walked over to Barton's table.

"Mr King?" he asked.

"Who wants to know?" Barton responded guardedly.

The man smiled briefly and sat down in a chair opposite. "You're here to pick up a delivery for Mr Robinson?" he continued with only a hint of a Dutch accent.

"You're Freddie?" Barton asked.

"That's right." The man turned towards the door then back again. "I see the van outside. Do you have the keys?"

Barton nodded.

The man held out his hand. "Well can I have them? It was explained to you before you left, yes?"

"Partly. What happens now?"

"You come back here tomorrow night at nine o'clock and we give you back the keys. Simple as that."

Barton reached into his trouser pocket and produced the keys to the van.

The man took them and gave him a card. "Just around the corner. Hotel Ostade will put you up for the night at a reasonable rate. Tomorrow, enjoy yourself in our wonderful city." The man grinned. "You like the ladies? There are plenty to choose from. We cater for every taste."

Barton didn't react.

Freddie shrugged. "Or if you like some culture, we have museums, including Anne Frank's House. You will like."

The man stood and, with another gesture to the barman, walked to the door and was gone.

Barton studied the card Freddie had left him then looked at his watch again. Quickly he finished his lager, deciding not to leave it any later to find this hotel. On his way out, he showed the barman the card. He was directed to turn left out of the door and take the first street on the left. The hotel was small but comfortable, the barman added. Barton thanked him and departed.

209

Outside on the street, there was a space where he'd parked the van. So far, so good, he hoped.

47

Cyril had watched the van disembark and slowly make its way through official checks before joining the exit road from the terminal.

"He'll be alright," Gray commented.

Cyril looked across at the man then back to the quayside. "I hope to God you're right."

He had several hours to kill before the ferry set sail on the return journey to Harwich. Gray led him up to the crew's mess where they could have a couple of beers and relax.

"Have you done this many times before, Frank?" Cyril asked.

"Having to do the crossing on business, you mean?"

Cyril nodded and took a mouthful of beer.

"Not too many. Sometimes we shadow a suspect and, like I say, we work closely with the KMar." Gray pulled out a packet of cigarettes and offered one to Cyril.

He shook his head. "I'm a pipe man myself," he said. "But I've left it back in the car."

Gray smiled. "Somehow I thought you might have been."

Cyril wiped the beer froth from his moustache. "So what do you know of this DCI Holt?" As Gray was now aware of the Met officer's involvement, he thought he might be able to flush out an interesting response.

Gray blew out smoke and nervously flicked the ash from the end of his cigarette. "Not a lot really. Heard his name once or twice, but never had any direct dealings with him myself."

"He's Vice, isn't he?"

Gray drank some of his beer. "So I understand."

Cyril turned his glass on its mat. "Got a bit of a reputation, haven't they?"

Gray looked guarded. "What way?"

He lifted his glass to his mouth and paused. "You know, on the take, free samples, if you follow, evidence going missing." He took a swig.

The DS grinned. "It's Holt not Regan. You've been watching too many episodes of *The Sweeney*."

Cyril shrugged.

"Anyway, I'm off to get my head down. I had a late night last night too." Gray stubbed out his cigarette and drained his glass. "I'll see you in the morning before we dock no doubt." Gray stood and made his way out through the door.

"No doubt," Cyril said quietly to himself then drained his own glass. He felt uneasy about the situation. Nothing he could put his finger on but something didn't feel right. Barton knew more than he'd been prepared to tell Cyril, and that rankled once again. And Gray seemed guarded.

It had been a long day. He could get some shuteye back in the cabin but his mind was buzzing. But no more beer though, he thought.

A couple of hours later, the ferry had set sail. It was late but Cyril wanted to try and make contact with DCI Sanderson. Apart from catching up on what developments, if any, had taken place back in Essex, he wanted to try and assess Barton's opinion of him. As he approached the Comms Room, he could hear Gray's familiar voice. The door was ajar.

"No, the local plod have got involved now," Gray was saying. "One of their blokes has driven the van to the rendezvous."

Cyril stopped and listened.

"There wasn't a lot I could do. How were we to know he had a dicky ticker," Gray continued.

Cyril quickly glanced up and down the corridor. No one appeared to be around at this time of night.

"Yeah, he's gone off to hospital in Rotterdam. The doc doesn't reckon it's too serious." A pause. "I know but it's still fucked things up."

Cyril didn't like the sound of the conversation. He could only catch one side of it but just who was Gray talking to? His boss, Crimond? Holt? Or someone else?

"Right well, I'll check back in before we hit Parkeston." Another pause. "What? No, I left him drinking in the mess." Gray gave a laugh which rose Cyril's hackles. "Not really. We'll speak later."

The phone was put down and Cyril ducked up the corridor and into a toilet just before Gray came out and walked away in the opposite direction. His unease grew. Was Barton in danger? Was Lennie in the firing line before that? He did feel that Lennie was genuine, despite Barton's innate distrust of everyone, especially outside the job. What was he saying - he wasn't even sure about some within the job? And Sanderson, what did he feel about the DCI? In any event, he had to speak to him.

In the Comms room, he asked the operator if he could make a ship to shore call and gave him Sanderson's home number, which Barton had given him. After a minute or two with unfamiliar beeps and tones, he finally heard the DCI mumble an answer.

"Apologies for the late call Sir," Cyril began, "I'm back on the return journey, due to dock at 08:30."

"Everything go okay with John?" Sanderson asked.

"As far as I know. He cleared Customs and Immigration and was on his way to Amsterdam."

"How are you getting along with DS Gray?"

Cyril looked round to see what the radio operator was up to but seemed satisfied he was busy with his own duties and not paying any attention to the conversation. He still lowered his voice. "I'm just a bit … What's your take on Gray, Crimond and this DCI Holt?"

"Well Holt is typical Met. Dick related my conversation with him earlier, didn't he?"

"He did."

"Are you sensing something, Cyril?"

213

"As DI Barton asked, just keeping my ears open. Will you be picking me up when we dock?"

"Of course, but you're making me feel uneasy now. Be careful and I'll see you in the morning."

Cyril ended the call. Still not thinking he could sleep, he wandered down to the passenger deck and through the lounge to the bar. A cup of tea would help.

Before he went to the cafeteria, Cyril had a stroll round the duty-free shop on board and bought himself some of his favourite pipe tobacco. No point in passing up this opportunity he thought. He entered the cafe, bought a tea and, feeling hungry despite the hour, decided on a bacon roll. He sat down at a table and took a bite of his snack. There had been no sign of Gray since he saw him leave the Comms room, and that was nearly an hour ago.

He took a sip of his tea and began to discretely look round at the few passengers who were sitting at the other tables. Most were in the lounge areas, heads back, sleeping in some uncomfortable positions. The back of one passenger's head caught his attention. He was sitting in one of the lounge chairs, visible through the glazed screen that separated the bar area. He was alone and seemed to be nervously looking around. Someone with a secret?

Cyril finished his tea and glanced over once again to the man who had attracted his attention. He stood and sauntered to the exit, determined to walk past him. As he approached, he thought the back of his profile was familiar. From how he was sitting, the man looked to be reasonably tall and quite well-built. His grey hair was thinning and Cyril thought he might be in his mid-sixties. As he passed, he could see a holdall on the man's lap, protectively covered with his hands. Cyril walked to the far end of the lounge then turned, casting a brief glance back towards the man. Of course, that's who it is.

48

The Hotel Ostade looked like just another house in the row, built of Flemish brick with some steps leading to the half-glazed front door. Barton stepped up and could see inside a wide hallway with a lit lamp sharing a table with some flowers in a vase. He tried the door handle and it opened. To his right, there was a small reception desk with a shut leather-bound register, telephone and a brass hand bell. Before he could ring it, a tall woman of around forty appeared from a room to the side.

"Good evening, sir," she greeted.

Am I that obvious, Barton thought? An Englishman abroad.

"Does everyone here speak perfect English?" he asked, a broad smile on his face.

"It is the second language taught in schools." She returned his smile. "So how can I help?"

He showed her the card Freddie had given him and explained that his new Dutch friend had recommended the establishment.

"How long will you be staying?"

"Just the one night."

"That's fine. If you would sign the register for me." She opened the book and turned it towards him, offering him a pen at the same time. "And your passport," she continued.

Barton felt the colour rise in his cheeks. "Ah, well … you see, I don't actually have it on me."

She raised her eyebrows.

"Does that matter at the moment?"

"Well, we are supposed to see it." She studied him closely.

Barton felt self-conscious but patted the pockets of the leather jacket he'd borrowed from Lennie King, as if to make some attempt to find it.

The woman persisted. "But your passport?"

"It's … I left it in my van." He hesitated as he thought of what to say.

She nodded. "And Freddie is dealing with the … consignment."

He was puzzled. How much did she know?

"It's okay," she went on, indicating the register. "If you could just sign in with a name and address." She offered the pen once again.

'A name and address', Barton thought; not 'your name and address'? He took the pen and just managed to stop himself from beginning to write a J in the register. Instead he spelt out *'Leonard King',* signed a version of the name and gave a false address in Jaywick, Essex. He handed the pen back to her.

With a quick look at the entry, she closed the book.

"No luggage?"

"It was a last minute thing. Travelling light," he quipped.

"Well, Mr King, if you'd follow me, I'll show you to your room." She led the way through a door to a staircase behind.

He couldn't help but study her legs as she climbed the stairs.

The room was on the first floor and contained a comfortable looking double bed, wardrobe and chest of drawers.

"Breakfast will be from 7:30 until 9:00," she explained. "Are you an early riser?"

"I'll be down for 8:00, if that's okay."

"That's fine," she said. "Towels are there and the bathroom is at the end of the hall. Enjoy your stay."

Barton gave her a thanks and she closed the door leaving him to his situation. He walked over to the window, nudged a curtain and looked out. The street below was deserted.

He sat on the bed and shook his head. What a day, he thought. Bloody Cyril. Just what was he doing pursuing his own investigation into the warehouse. Why hadn't he told him about it? A bloody good job that young PC was with him. Woodbridge, was it? He shuddered. If he hadn't been with him, Cyril would probably have been a corpse in the back of that van. Another one. As it was there were two of them already; Morgan and some other poor sod. In fact there might even be another body waiting to surface if Fletcher's flights were any indication.

Slowly, sleep overcame him as he lay on top of the bed. It was going to be another warm and sticky night in this never-ending summer.

49
Tuesday 7th September

The dawning sun streamed in through the porthole acting as nature's alarm clock for Cyril. A steady throb penetrated his senses. It took a second or two before he realised he was on the ferry. A deep dreamless sleep had engulfed him. His thoughts immediately returned to the character he'd seen in the lounge, nervously guarding the holdall on his lap.

He glanced at his watch; 6:30. The ferry was due to dock in another two hours. He turned and swung his legs over the side of the bed just as a knock sounded on the door.

"DS Claydon?" the voice of Frank Gray enquired.

"Hello."

"Fancy some breakfast?"

Cyril stood and opened the door. "Morning," he greeted.

Gray cracked a smile. "Are you hungry?"

"Give me ten minutes."

"Crew's mess," Gray announced. "See you up there."

Face freshly splashed but still wearing yesterday's clothes, Cyril sat down at a table with his fried breakfast, opposite Gray.

"Get some rest?" the Special Branch DS enquired.

"Stilted."

"Should be in on time." Gray checked his watch. "Did you get hold of your colleague and organise a lift?"

"Managed to speak to my DCI last night, yes." He didn't particularly want to engage the man any more than he had to and shovelled some food into his mouth.

"No sign of this heatwave ending," Gray said, although Cyril had the impression it was to no one in particular.

After a minute or so's silence, Cyril spoke. "So, did you get all you wanted done?"

"How d'you mean?"

Cyril kept eating. "You know, speak to everyone you needed to speak to?"

There was a pause before Gray answered. "I managed to catch everybody I needed to last night before we met up for a drink."

Cyril looked up and caught the hint of a puzzled expression on Gray's face. He nodded. "Good. That's good." Then resumed eating.

"Right, well, I'll just go and call into base. I said I would before we docked. Let them know everything is okay." Gray stood and took his plate back to the counter.

"That's right," Cyril said quietly to himself, "you said you would." He mopped his plate with the last half slice of bread and watched the DS leave.

Cyril's warrant card eased his passage through Immigration and Customs and he stepped out into the fresh air of another warm early morning. Looking around the area in front of the terminal building, he couldn't see a car he recognised. He was sure Sanderson had grasped the arrival time. Maybe he decided he'd be longer passing through the formalities.

He leaned against a wall, closed his eyes and enjoyed the morning sun as he waited. He wondered what Barton would do to amuse himself today. He imagined he could get himself into an awful lot of trouble in a city like Amsterdam. Cyril had visited the place himself once before and imagined the DI strolling down the streets full of windows. Worse, there were the clubs; all sorts of unsavoury activities taking place in them. But just how much money did Barton have with him? However much, he could imagine him coming home penniless.

His thoughts were interrupted by the arrival of a big grey Daimler in the waiting area. The Robinsons had one similar. Was that them? He squinted to see the driver but the sun glinting on the windscreen prevented him. But why would they be meeting the ferry, he wondered?

The familiar outline of Barton's Rover 2000 then trundled up the road. He could see DCI Sanderson in the driver's seat. The car swung round and pulled up in front of the Daimler. Cyril pushed himself off the wall and walked towards the passenger door. Opening it, he climbed inside.

"What happened to your head?" Sanderson asked.

"Ah, just a bit of a bump in the back of the van," Cyril said dismissively.

"You might need to get that looked at. The police doctor can dress that for you when we get back."

Before Sanderson could put the car in gear, Cyril put his hand on the gearstick.

"Just give it a minute, Sir," he said.

Sanderson hesitated. "Everything alright, Cyril?"

"Just curious." Before Sanderson could answer, Cyril put his hand up to the internal mirror and adjusted it so he had a clear view of the car behind. "I just want to check something."

"Something up?"

"That car behind …"

"The grey Daimler?"

"Yeah. Victor Robinson drives one."

Sanderson turned his head slightly to look in the wing mirror. "You think that might be his?"

"Maybe."

"Not too many of those on the road," Sanderson commented.

"But I thought I spotted someone I recognised on the ferry last night."

"Looks like a woman in the driver's seat."

"Ah. Now who do you think that is?" Cyril nodded towards the mirror. He watched the man he'd spotted in the lounge the night before approach the Daimler.

The man opened the passenger door and, before he got in, cast a nervous look around.

"Well, bugger me," Sanderson quietly said.

"It is him, isn't it?"

"Walter Yardley, yes."

"Thought I recognised him," Cyril said. "Looks a bit on edge, don't you think?"

The big grey car set off and swept past them down the approach road.

"Made it through customs then. The question is, was that him doing a 'dummy run' or was it the real thing?" Sanderson pondered. "In the meantime, let's get back to the station."

Sanderson fired up the Rover and set off.

Cyril loosened off his tie and undid the top button of his shirt. "Actually, do you think I can nip back to the house? I need a change of clothes. I wasn't expecting to be out all night. And I want to make sure my neighbour is okay. She's been looking after my dog."

"Sure."

"And then I can tell you what I overheard last night."

50

Back at the station, Cyril collected his jacket from the back of the chair where Sam had left it. He picked up the car keys and quickly made for the car park. He owed Doris a huge apology.

When he pulled up in his driveway, he heard Charlie give a bark before he appeared through the gateway to the back garden. The big dog waddled up to him as he got out of the car, his whole body rocking from side to side, not just his tail.

"Hello, old lad," Cyril greeted as Doris appeared from the back garden, his lead in her hand.

"What can I say?" Cyril held his arms wide. "You won't believe the last twenty-four hours. I'm sorry I couldn't get word to you."

"We thought you must be involved in something," Doris said. "But what's happened to your head?"

Automatically, Cyril put his hand to the dressing. "Oh, nothing, just a little bump that's all. It was my own fault."

Doris's expression told him she was sceptical. "Don't worry, we were just fine, weren't we, Charlie?" She rubbed the dog's head.

"But I don't like putting on you, Doris."

She looked him up and down. "And you'll want me to keep hold of him today too."

"Do you mind?"

"Go get yourself sorted," she said. "You've been up all night, haven't you?"

"Thanks. I don't know what I'd do without you."

While Charlie and Doris went off for a walk, Cyril had a shower over the bath and dried himself off. He sorted out some fresh clothes and began to shave in front of the bathroom mirror. As he lathered up, he thought about

Lennie King and his relationship with Jimmy Morgan. He had no doubt that Lennie would want to find out what had really happened to Jimmy. After all, if he owed him his life, he would be determined to right the wrong he saw. But who was Lennie talking about when he said he had a good idea who was responsible and that it wasn't the Robinsons? He needed to get back into that warehouse for a better look round but he wouldn't be able to conduct a proper search until Barton returned, otherwise suspects would be scared off. His thoughts started to bounce around like a pinball machine. That song spun through his brain; *Pinball Wizard*. It was one of those groups; who was it who sung that? He couldn't remember but Doris would, he was sure. Barton also wanted him to track down Dougie Chalmers. Then there was the identity of the other corpse. Oh, and don't forget Cathy. He would have some making up to do there. So much going on.

Walking in through the main doors of Clacton Police Station, he paused by the desk sergeant.

"I don't suppose DI Barton has been in touch this morning, has he?" Cyril asked.

The sergeant looked up. "What's happened to you, Cyril?"

"Oh nothing. Anyway, has the DI made contact?"

"Not seen him since yesterday morning," the sergeant answered.

"Well if he calls in, can you let me know?"

"Sure."

Cyril paused as he thought of something else. "Oh, is Sam Woodbridge on duty this morning?"

"Yes, he's on refs at the moment. Should be in the canteen."

Along the corridor, he saw Cathy Rogers coming in the opposite direction. She kept her head down, determined to ignore him.

"Cathy, look, I know you'll be angry with me but ..."

She swept past him, not even glancing up.

"Cathy ..."

223

She continued on her way to the secretarial office, the door closing behind her.

Looks like I've got a *lot* of making up to do, he thought. There again, they'd only ever exchanged a few words and hadn't even met up socially. But he did like her and he was embarrassed by how things had worked out. He didn't like rudeness, and that's what he thought he had been. He'd have to think of something. But he quickly shifted it from his mind and strode out for the canteen.

Pausing by the canteen doors, he looked round for Sam Woodbridge, finally spotting him sitting at a table in conversation with two other PCs and a sergeant. He caught Woodbridge's eye and mouthed, 'Upstairs when you've finished.'

A big smile appeared on Sam's face and he gave a thumbs up.

Cyril climbed the stairs to the CID office. The place was almost deserted; only DC Walker was at his desk, talking on the phone. Cyril waved a hand in greeting, walked to his desk and sat down. There were no new messages. He leaned back in his chair and rubbed his eyes. Sam Woodbridge interrupted him.

"Skip, good to see you back," Sam said. "But what's happened to your head?"

Cyril stood and put a finger to his lips, motioning for them to use Barton's office. Walker was still engrossed on the phone.

Once inside and with the door closed, Cyril offered the young PC his hand.

"Sam, I owe you," he said.

Sam blushed, looked down and shook it. "No … well … it was only …"

"No, it wasn't," Cyril interrupted. "If you hadn't called it in and if this man …" he indicated Barton's empty chair with his thumb, "… well, I wouldn't be here now. So, thank you."

"Just glad you're back in one piece, Skip … apart from …" Sam had recovered his composure and was looking at Cyril's dressed head wound.

"That's nothing. Just a graze."

"So where is the DI now?"

Cyril glanced at his watch. "In Amsterdam, but what he might be getting up to, I dread to think."

"Amsterdam?" Woodbridge looked puzzled.

"We ended up on the Hook of Holland ferry. DI Barton is currently involved in something confidential. So we don't want any talk in the canteen about where he is and what he's up to. Have you spoken to anyone about yesterday's events?"

"Not really, no. To be honest, I was expecting a bollocking from the DI this morning. When I rang in to tell him about you yesterday, he sounded pretty pissed off. He wanted me to, how was it he phrased it, 'get my arse back to the station,' but he'd gone out when I turned up."

"A great turn of phrase, the DI." Cyril grinned. "Well, play it down if anyone asks, at least until he gets back. Anyway, don't worry about it, Sam. He's got more important things on his mind right now." He opened the office door. "Best get back to your duties."

Sam smiled. "Thanks."

Cyril watched him make his way out of the CID office towards the stairs, DCI Sanderson passing him on the way in.

Sanderson indicated for Cyril to stay in Barton's office as he walked over to join him. "Heard anything?" he asked, as he entered and closed the door. "From the DI?"

"Not a thing as yet, Sir."

"I'm sure we will. If he can find a way to let us know what's happening, he will."

Sanderson walked round the desk and sat in Barton's chair. "Sit down a minute, Cyril," he said. "While DI Barton's away, I think we need to progress other enquires."

"I know we're still looking for Dougie Chalmers and the DI told me he'd got young Walker on the case trying to identify the surgical plate from the second corpse."

Sanderson nodded then looked through the glazed partition. "Walker's off the phone now. Ask him to come in."

Cyril rose from his chair and opened the door. "Bill," he called, "In here a minute."

Walker came in.

"Any news on that surgical plate you're investigating?" Sanderson asked.

"Nothing yet, Sir. I've spoken to all the hospitals in East Anglia and most of the London ones, but they all say they need time to check records going that far back."

"How far back are we going?"

"Thirty years," Walker responded.

"Just need to be persistent," Sanderson said. "Where's Miller this morning, by the way?"

"In court, I believe."

"Did he chase up on Chalmers, do you know?"

"Yes, Sir. We called round to his last known address but there was no one in. Clothes and things there but no sign of him."

"The door was unlocked?"

Walker coloured. "Well … not exactly."

"Miller?"

Walker nodded.

"But you secured the door behind you?"

"Yes, Sir."

Sanderson checked his watch. Just gone eleven. "Just gone midday over there," he said to Cyril.

"We need to try and locate Chalmers. Only he can tell us who might be pressurising Fletcher."

Sanderson stood and lowered his voice. "You go. I'll wait for any call."

Cyril considered for a second. "Come on then, Bill," he said. "You can take me back to Chalmers place."

226

For the second time in two days, Walker walked into the hallway of the old house. Music was still playing loudly from somewhere above. "He's in Room 5, Sarge. Upstairs," he said.

Cyril followed him as they made their way up to the first floor. By the door, Walker stood to one side. Cyril approached and put his ear to it. All was quiet inside. He knocked loudly but there was no response.

"Just like yesterday," Walker told him.

Cyril tried the handle. It opened. "I thought you said you'd made this secure?"

Walker looked puzzled. "We did."

Slowly, the door swung open.

"Sarge," Walker put up his hand. "When we left yesterday, the curtains were closed."

Now, the sun streamed in through the window that looked out onto the street.

Cyril stepped inside. The wardrobe doors were wide open and the drawers from the chest opposite the end of the bed were upturned on the bed itself.

"Someone's definitely been in here," Walker said as he stepped towards the wardrobe, scattering the discarded takeaway cartons that had been lying around on the floor the day before.

Cyril picked up one of the drawers from the bed and turned it over. Below were some envelopes. He picked them up and flicked through them.

"Ben put them on the bed yesterday when we left," Walker said looking at the bills. He turned around, arms wide. "But this has been cleared out. There were clothes in the drawers and in the wardrobe. Now there's nothing."

Outside, footsteps could be heard coming down the stairs from the second floor. Cyril moved quickly to the door and watched a man and a woman turn at the bottom step. The woman hesitated when she saw him, before aiming to walk past, the man close behind.

"Just a minute," Cyril said, "I'd like a word."

"Fuck are you?" she said, then quickly added, "As if ah didnae ken."

"That's no way to greet an old friend, Morag. You know perfectly well who I am. I've lifted you often enough."

"We need tae get on. He's got an appointment." She indicated her companion.

"The pair of you," Cyril continued pointedly. "Hughie." He smiled at the man. "You two getting along okay now?" He turned to Walker who had appeared at his side. "Morag and Hughie here often have a few heated disagreements."

"We're a' fine noo, Mr Claydon," Hughie said.

"Have you seen Mr Chalmers recently?" Cyril asked.

She looked disparagingly at Walker. "You were here yesterday. I told you then we hadnae seen him for weeks. I think he's cleared off."

Walker cast a glance down at the man's feet then panned up his body to face him. "So when was the last time you were in Mr Chalmers' room?"

Hughie looked nervously towards Morag. "I've never been in."

"Sure about that? Not even for a wee bevvy," Walker dropped into a mock Scottish accent.

Hughie stiffened. "You tryin' tae take the pish?"

Cyril was bemused with Walker's questioning but decided to let him carry on.

"How about you?" Walker turned his attention to Morag.

Again she avoided eye contact. "As if you think I would go intae his room."

Walker looked to Cyril. "I think we should carry on this conversation down at the station."

That was the cue for Hughie to bound down the stairs.

Walker was ready for it and was quickly after him. Years of drinking cans of strong lager and God knows what else had an adverse effect on him and Walker brought him down in the hallway before cuffing his hands behind his back.

"Looks like he might miss his appointment," Cyril commented before cuffing Morag too.

51

Barton had spent a restless night. The room was too warm for him to gain much sleep. Opening the window around midnight improved matters until early morning deliveries to the various shops roused him from his light doze. He squinted to look at his watch. Five past seven, or was it five past six? No, seven, he remembered changing the time before he left the ferry.

After a quick shower in the bathroom, he dressed in the same clothes from yesterday. He'd have to try and find some new underwear and a shirt, some deodorant too, otherwise he'd be arrested for a breach of the peace when he stepped back onto the ferry.

Downstairs in the small dining room, there was no sign of the woman from the night before. A tall man in his fifties, probably her husband, served a basic breakfast. Although there were two other tables set with cutlery, no other guests appeared. He wondered if he were the only one staying that night.

After checking out and paying his bill, he wandered down the street and bought some underarm deodorant from a chemist. At least that would cover odours for now. He checked his wallet to see how many Guilders he had left from the amount DS Gray had given him. He wondered how easy it would be to justify all this when he made it back to Clacton. He imagined having to fill in reams of forms and have everyone from the DCI up to Deputy Chief Constable sign the bloody things.

Thoughts of Sanderson brought to mind the fact that he'd have to find some way to make a telephone call to Clacton to let them know where he was in the scheme of things; and find out what was happening back in Essex. He pulled out the piece of paper Lennie King had given him after sending Cyril from the sick bay. On it was written a Dutch name and reference to the main police station by Amsterdam train station. This should be his best bet.

He walked to Haarlem railway station and boarded a train to Amsterdam. Ten minutes later, he walked through the main concourse of the train station and spotted the Politiebureau. At least one existed where King said it was.

An awkward conversation with the officer on the front desk began. But with the help of his warrant card, the documentation Gray had given him and the name he'd been given, he was invited upstairs by a plain clothes detective who looked as if he could have been a lead singer in a rock band. Shirt sleeves rolled up and jeans, his long curly fair hair reminded him of Roger Daltrey.

The Dutchman introduced himself. "Inspecteur Lars Hendriks," he said. "You wish to call your force in UK?"

"If you wouldn't mind," Barton answered.

The Dutch detective grinned. "This is a bit unusual," he said. "You're on a secret mission we know nothing about."

"I had to substitute at the last minute for an informant who took ill," Barton explained. "Look, I really need to speak with my boss back in England."

"How you say over there, I pull your leg." The Inspecteur lifted the telephone and spoke to the switchboard. After a few seconds, he handed the receiver to Barton. "I'll get you a drink," he said, stood and left the room.

52

With Hughie and Morag in separate interview rooms, Cyril had a chance to ask about Bill Walker's line of questioning.

"The fact is, Sarge," Walker said, "those trainers the bloke's wearing are brand new. I noticed there was a pair exactly like that in the bottom of Chalmers' wardrobe when we looked round yesterday."

He was impressed with Walker's observational skills.

"And another thing, I'm pretty certain there was a suede jacket in there too, just like the one he's wearing now."

Cyril grinned. "Let battle commence then, Bill. We'll take Hughie first."

He knew Hugh McKinley well, having arrested him several times over the past few years. Mostly drunk and disorderly and a couple of assault charges, he was a nightmare for the uniforms sent to deal with the disturbances. Morag Watson, his common-law wife, wasn't much better. She had a sharp temper on her, mostly fuelled by drink. The pair of them had migrated south to London from their native Kilmarnock initially, like so many of their fellow countrymen in recent times, then east to Clacton.

Hugh was sitting on a wooden chair at a metal table in the dingy interview room when Cyril and Bill Walker entered.

"What's this all aboot?" Hughie asked.

Cyril flipped open a notebook. "First of all, Mr McKinley, if we can just take a few personal details."

Hughie shrugged.

"You are Hugh McKinley, are you not?"

A nod of the head. "You know bloody well I am, aye."

231

"Currently living at the address where you've just been detained?"

"Detained? What have you detained me for?"

Cyril held up a hand. "Height?" he asked.

"What d'you want to know a' this crap for?"

"Just answer the question," Walker joined in.

"Five feet eight."

"Weight?" Cyril continued.

"Twelve an' a half stone."

"Shoe size?"

"Eight. But what's that got to do wi' anythin'?"

"Take off your shoes, please."

"Oh come on. This is unreal."

"Just remove them for me."

Hughie bent down and took off his trainers. Walker bent down, picked one of them up and examined it. A grin broke out on his face. "Struggling to break these in, Mr McKinley?" Walker said, passing the shoe to Cyril.

Cyril raised his eyebrows. "Might be a bit loose for you, Hughie, seeing as they're size nine."

"I bought them cheap. It was the nearest size they had."

"Was that the same place you got the suede jacket?" Walker added. "Looks a bit too big for you to me as well."

The man looked bamboozled.

Cyril leaned forward onto the table. "Look Hughie, we're not really interested in your second-hand clothing efforts ..."

Hughie rubbed his face.

"Whether you nicked it from another scumbag like Dougie Chalmers doesn't really interest us, for now. What we want to know is, where is Chalmers?"

"Look Mr Claydon, like we told the other detectives, we havenae seen him for weeks."

"I know it might be difficult for you to remember one day from the next but I really need you to think long and hard about when you last saw him." Cyril stood up. "For now, we'll give you time for that."

"But ..."

"We'll be back later."

With that, Cyril and Walker left the interview room and a uniformed constable stood in to keep an eye on McKinley.

Next door, Morag was sitting in a chair at exactly the same type of table Hughie was. "I could sue you fuckers," was her opening salvo. "Just what are we doin' in here anyway? We havnae done nuthin'."

"Morag, that's no way to address officers of the law," Cyril said, taking a seat opposite the woman in her forties with bleach blonde straggly hair. "We just need you to help us with our enquiries, that's all."

"Hmph!" She folded her arms and looked away.

Cyril waited for Walker to settle himself into the other chair before he began. "So what else did you take from Dougie Chalmers' room yesterday, Morag? Or maybe this morning."

"Nuthin'. I've taken nuthin'."

Cyril opened the manila folder he'd brought with him. "Oh, I find that hard to believe." He shuffled through some papers. "I mean, here for instance, shoplifting from Mothercare last year; Woolworths before that." He paused and waited for the woman to make eye contact. "Let's face it, if you're presented with a golden opportunity to help yourself to some goodies from a room you know to be unoccupied and the door is a little, shall we say, not as secure as it might have been, well … who could blame you?"

"I didnae take nuthin'. What would Chalmers have that I might want?"

"But you have been in the room? With Hughie, maybe?"

"Well, he said he needed some new shoes. Said he knew where he might be able to find somethin'. I didnae ken he was plannin' to break intae Chalmers' room."

"So this was all Hughie's idea? Nothing to do with you?"

"That's right."

"And just to be clear, if we searched your room right now, we wouldn't find anything else that belonged to Chalmers."

Morag coloured and looked away. "You'd need a search warrant," she mumbled.

Cyril looked to Walker. "I think that would be no problem, Bill, under the circumstances." He turned back to face the woman and leaned forward, both arms on the table. "Look Morag, we can waste everyone's time pursuing all this but what we're interested in right now is speaking to Mr Chalmers. If you have any idea where he might be, now's the time to tell me."

She looked straight at Cyril. "I havnae seen him for ages, Mr Claydon. That's the truth. We … well we used to keep our distance. He wasnae what you could call a good person to be around. Bloody psycho, if you ask me." She pointed a finger to her temple and made a face.

"Okay Morag, let's say I believe you. I need you to think hard; when was the last time you saw him?"

She puffed out her cheeks. "It's like I say, it must be aboot four or five weeks ago now."

"Come on Morag, you can do better than that,"

She screwed up her face, as if in pain then suddenly jolted, pointing a finger at Cyril. "The carnival. When was the carnival?"

Cyril looked to Walker and back to the woman then pulled out a diary from his jacket pocket. "The fifteenth," he announced.

"Right," Morag nodded. "It was before then but after the Bank Holiday."

Cyril sighed. "But the Bank Holiday was after that, on the thirtieth."

"No your one doon here, I'm talkin' aboot oors. The Scottish Bank Holiday's at the beginnin' o' August."

Another check of the diary. "That was the second."

"So it was a couple o' days after that. Maybe the Wednesday. That's when I saw him comin' back to his room."

"That would be Wednesday 4th August. Not Thursday, or the Friday?"

She snapped her fingers. "No. Definitely the Wednesday. I remember noo because that deaf old bugger in Room Seven had the telly on loud and *Coronation Street* was on."

"Okay Morag. We'll see what Hughie's been able to remember." Cyril stood to leave.

"Can I go now?"

"We've still got matters to look into."

She threw her head back as if in despair. "Aw come on. I've told ye all I know."

"But there's still more, I know there is."

She sounded desperate. "Would it help if I told you he wasn't alone?"

"Chalmers? He was with someone?"

"That's right, some other bloke."

"Who?"

"No idea but I could recognise him again."

"Was that the only time you'd seen him with this 'bloke' or had you seen them together at other times?"

"Only that last time."

"Okay, Morag, DC Walker here will bring you some mug shots to look through. Let's see if you can spot whoever it was."

53

While Bill Walker had the delightful task of taking Morag through the albums of photos of known offenders, Cyril made his way to DCI Sanderson's office. He looked through the half-glazed door and could see him on the phone. About to turn and walk away, Sanderson waved a hand to beckon him in.

"… okay, well you be aware of everything around you," Sanderson said into the handset. "And listen, steer clear of any dodgy clubs. You need to make the rendezvous tonight." He ended the call and rubbed his face with both hands.

"Close the door and sit down, Cyril," he said. "That was Dick. He managed to persuade some long-haired Dutch detective to let him call."

Door closed, Cyril took a seat opposite the DCI and grinned. "Is he keeping out of trouble?"

"As he said, so far so good." Sanderson leaned back in the chair. "I hear you've brought in a couple of ne'er-do-wells?"

"That's right, Hughie McKinley and Morag Watson."

Sanderson rolled his eyes. "Delightful."

Cyril proceeded to relate the morning's progress. "I've left Bill going through the mug shots with her," he concluded. "But I was thinking of checking on that key; the one we found on Jimmy Morgan."

"You reckon it might fit the door to the warehouse?"

"Only one way to find out."

Sanderson checked his watch. "Give me fifteen minutes and I'll come with you," he said.

"Perfect. I'll sign out the evidence bag." Cyril stood and left the DCI's office.

An hour later, Sanderson pulled his car onto the waste ground opposite the warehouse where Sam and Cyril had parked the day before. The building still looked deserted, the big vehicle doors firmly closed.

Overhead, some seagulls screeched as Cyril and Sanderson crossed the road and walked up to the building. Cyril took the bag from his jacket pocket and pulled out the Yale key that had been found in the lining of Jimmy Morgan's jacket. Forensics had been unable to retrieve anything useful from it by way of prints. He looked at the DCI and hesitated. Sanderson gave a slight nod and Cyril pushed the key into the lock of the pedestrian access door. As he thought, it turned. He held it over and gave the door a gentle push. It opened.

Quietly, both men stepped inside then paused. Cyril carefully closed the door behind them. For a second or two they stood and listened. All was silent apart from something rattling, somewhere higher up the building. The floor where the van had stood was empty, apart from a few old cardboard boxes and discarded newspaper pages.

"Okay then Cyril, show me what you found," Sanderson said in hushed tones.

Cyril led the way into the corner and up the wide timber staircase. At the next landing, they paused to listen again before stepping out onto the first floor. He indicated the footprints and scuff marks in the layer of dust on the floor as their footsteps echoed around the vast open area. They approached the bench.

Cyril pointed to the dark marks on its top surface. "These look like blood stains to me, Sir," he said. "And then there's this." He walked around the bench and looked down at the roll of plastic sheet lying in the same position as he'd seen it the day before.

Sanderson bent down and studied the stains on the bench before looking behind at the plastic. He took out a penknife, bent down and cut a small piece off the end. "I'll send this off to the lab when we get back; just in case this goes missing." He carefully placed the sample into a bag and put it in his pocket. "They'll be able to tell us if it's the same material that wrapped the bodies. But we'll need to get forensics in here as soon as."

A noise from the other side of the floor startled them. They held their breath and looked round, only to discover the source of the rattling from earlier. A window swung loosely in the shallow breeze.

"There's another floor, isn't there?" Sanderson asked.

"I think so, but I never had the chance to get beyond here," Cyril replied.

"Let's take a look." Sanderson strode over to the stairs and climbed up to the next level.

The top floor had a lower clear height than the first. It was mostly open revealing some magnificent Victorian timber trusses. There was less light up here – the windows were smaller than the floor below and some were covered over. Along the left-hand side a series of partitioned rooms kept that side of the floor in semi-darkness.

The floor was dusty but with signs of recent activity; footprints and scuff marks, like the lower floor. There were also discarded newspapers, cigarette packets and other items of detritus.

Sanderson made his way towards the row of rooms. He paused at the doorway to the first, Cyril at his shoulder. He pushed the door open to reveal an empty room with two windows, the glass grey with cobwebs, dust and rain marks. The DCI stepped in and walked over to one of them. It was obvious they'd never been opened in decades.

Cyril had meanwhile moved on to the second room. The door was closed but there was a key in the lock. He turned it, and slowly opened the door. The one window to this room had brown paper covering the glass. But there was enough light to see something that made him hesitate from entering. "Sir," he called out. "I think you should see this."

Sanderson joined him and looked past Cyril. "Shit," he said quietly.

A door banged from somewhere below and both men looked sharply at one another. They held their respective breaths and listened. Voices. Indistinguishable voices were speaking.

Cyril pulled the door to and turned the key. As silently as they could, they made their way back to the stairs. The voices were clearer here but still they couldn't make out what was being said.

'Ground floor,' Cyril mouthed.

Sanderson nodded and began to descend the stairs, one careful step at a time. By the time they reached the first floor landing, they could make out the conversation from the floor below.

"Do you need to see the rest of the building?" one asked.

"I don't think so, Mr Yardley," the other responded.

Cyril and Sanderson exchanged knowing glances.

"Unfortunately," the second man continued, "despite it being a magnificent Victorian structure, this will be worth more as a site than a building. You can just imagine the costs to bring it up to date with all that clients are looking for nowadays. Plus the maintenance costs on these old properties …"

"Okay thanks."

Footsteps sounded as the pair appeared to walk towards the stairs.

Cyril and Sanderson took a step onto the first floor.

"And you'll get back to me … when?" Yardley asked.

The sounds of a door opening.

"I should be able to have something for you …"

The door slammed shut and all was silent again.

Cyril walked over to the stain-encrusted window on the landing. He wiped a small section clear and could see Walter Yardley and another man in a suit carrying a clipboard walking across the open area of Yardley Electrical and back to their offices.

"Who did you say Yardley's bank with?" Sanderson asked.

"Williams & Glynn's on Head Street."

"I think we'd best pay them a visit, Cyril."

"So how are you getting along with DI Barton?"

"He's certainly unique," Cyril said.

DCI Sanderson was driving them into the centre of Colchester. They'd left the warehouse the same way they'd entered, Cyril making sure the door was as secure as when they'd found it.

"You mean he's difficult?"

"He has some good points, once you get past the exterior."

Sanderson smiled and nodded. "Here we are," he said, pulling the car to a halt kerbside outside the bank.

Their enquiry was finally met by a small bespectacled balding man in a pin-stripe suit leading them through several doors and along a corridor to a room announcing *'Mr C West, Manager'*. The man opened the door and sat down behind a large mahogany desk.

"Please gentlemen," he said, indicating two chairs opposite, "take a seat. How can I help you?"

"Mr West, we're making enquiries into the background of someone we believe to be one of your customers," Sanderson began.

The manager adjusted his glasses on the bridge of his nose before responding. "In what way can I help?"

"We were wondering what their financial status is."

"I'm not sure I have the authority to provide you with any confidential information, not without a warrant or permission from Head Office." West's tone was quiet, calm and measured. Cyril immediately thought of Richard Attenborough's portrayal of John Christie in the film, *10 Rillington Place*. He bore an uncanny resemblance too.

"We could go through the process of obtaining a warrant, having a word with your managers," Sanderson countered in equally measured tones. "But we are talking about a murder enquiry, Mr West."

The bank manager appeared to consider for a moment. "Which customer, may I ask?"

"We're interested in Yardley Electrical and Walter Yardley in particular."

West frowned. "Hmm."

He stood and walked over to a filing cabinet and pulled out a green folder. Returning to his desk he sat down, opened it and began to read. After a second, he paused and looked up at Sanderson. "Oh, excuse me, Chief Inspector, I've been rude. You and your colleague would like a drink? Tea or coffee?"

"We're fine at the ..." Sanderson said.

Cyril cut him off. "Actually, a cup of tea would be good, Mr West, thank you. He looked to Sanderson and nodded.

"Er, well, a coffee for me please," Sanderson joined in, realising what was happening.

"I'll just go and organise that for you gentlemen," West said. He stood and left them alone in his office, the green file open on his desk.

54

Barton replaced the telephone receiver on the detective's desk and stood up to leave. Before he could, 'Roger Daltrey' returned, two plastic cups of coffee in his hands.

"Here," he said. "I thought you could do with this."

Barton took the offered cup. "Thanks."

"You get through to the person you wanted?" the man asked.

"I did, thanks again."

The Dutchman sat down behind his desk. "I gather you came over on the ferry yesterday? A little unexpected, I believe."

Barton sipped more of his coffee. "You could say that, yes."

"But you're back on tonight's sailing?"

Barton was growing suspicious. He knew the man was a detective but he asked a lot of questions. And he knew the answers already. "Maybe. Just see how things go," he said, trying to knock the man off his stroke.

A slight smile played on Hendriks' face. "You are a little suspicious," he said. "Have you met Simon Holt, our London detective friend?"

Barton was surprised at the mention of the Met officer. "No."

"Nice man. We worked together on a couple of investigations in the past. I had a missing girl from a small town near here. Simon found her for me in London. Only fourteen."

Barton nodded sagely. "Anyway," he went on, "I'll let you get on. Thanks for the coffee. It's a bit better than we get in our station." He offered his hand.

Hendriks shook it. "You take care," he said.

Outside on the pavement, Barton found a street map on a noticeboard and studied his location and surroundings. He checked his watch and strode off, away from the railway station and towards the streets bordering the canals. First, he needed a change of underpants and maybe a fresh shirt. As he turned a corner, he got a pleasant surprise. There in front of him was a logo he instantly recognised; C & A.

He walked in and found menswear. Opting for the cheapest pack of three jockey shorts, he looked for a short-sleeved shirt. Finally, he settled on a cream cheesecloth one and paid for them. A quick check of his money revealed only about one hundred guilders left. That might just cover a couple of drinks, a snack and something for emergencies. In the first floor toilets he changed into his new purchases, put his old clothes in the bag and made for the exit.

Back out on the street, the sun was still blazing down. Time to find a quiet bar, have a drink and pass the time until he had to catch a train back to Haarlem.

Down a little side street he discovered a cosy looking establishment. The front was constructed in small Flemish brickwork incorporating a circular window and double doors. Above, a sign proclaimed it was *'Pippa's Bar'*.

He walked in from bright sunshine to a darkened interior. A few steps and he was at the bar. The barman asked what he'd like and he chose a bottle of Heineken. As he was waiting, his eyes began to grow accustomed to the light. That's when he noticed that all the customers were young attractive women. The one exception was a middle-aged man sitting at a table with a glamourous dark-haired woman in hot pants and a low cut top.

Oh shit, he thought, wondering how much his lager would cost and whether it would clean him out. Deciding not to be left with a shock, he insisted on paying when the barman placed it on the counter. At five guilders, he was pleasantly surprised and began to relax.

"Hello," said a sultry-sounding voice over his right shoulder.

He slowly turned to see the smiling face of a gorgeous blonde-haired woman of about twenty-five.

He hesitated. "Hi," he finally responded, turning to face her.

"Are you English?" she asked with a heavy Dutch accent.

"You've guessed right."

"On business here or holiday?"

He looked down to her cleavage then back to her face. Memories of the old TV series, *Rawhide* flashed through his mind. He could hear a cowboy character shout, 'Head 'em up, move 'em out.' He smiled, more at that thought than the woman.

"I suppose a bit of both," he said.

"Would you like to buy me a drink? We could sit down and have a nice time."

His smile developed into a grin. "I'd love to but I don't think I could afford it."

She pouted. "But you're a nice man, I can tell."

Barton nervously sipped his lager.

"I know," she continued, "you're married and you're worried she might find out?"

He shook his head and sipped some more.

"You know if I passed you on the street, I would not let on that I know you," she said, as if to allay his fears.

Finally, he gathered himself. "Look, you're a lovely looking woman but I'm just having this and I'm off." He drained his glass, placed it back on the bar and headed for the door. "See you," he said.

55

"So, it all bears out," Sanderson said.

They were on their way back to Clacton.

"They must be in some trouble if Walter Yardley has put his house in Frinton up as collateral," Cyril agreed. "No wonder he's looking to sell off some assets like that old warehouse."

"And it gives more credence to the rumours we've heard about him bringing in diamonds from Holland."

"You saw yourself he got off the ferry this morning."

"The question is," Sanderson pondered, "was he bringing something back with him, or just a genuine business trip?"

"He seemed nervous on board." Cyril turned in the front seat towards the DCI. "DI Barton is due back tomorrow. What's the plan? Do we organise a welcoming party at the warehouse or allow the porn shipment to pass on to London?"

"The Met would have liked things to have moved on to its conclusion in London but that can't happen now."

Cyril realised what was being said. "My fault, I know. I'm sorry about that."

"Don't worry, Cyril. We have our own crimes to solve here. The fact that it now appears to be entwined with their operations, well …" Sanderson braked and concentrated on manoeuvring around a roundabout before continuing. "At the moment, we'll have to strike when the van arrives." The DCI glanced towards Cyril. "But I think Dick might have something up his sleeve."

Back at the Clacton Station, Sanderson told Cyril to get off home. "You'll need a bit of recuperation time after your adventures," he said.

"I'll just check on Bill Walker first. I want to see where we are with Andy Stewart and Moira Anderson."

"Who? Oh, yes, very good." Sanderson smiled, making the connections. "I'll be calling a briefing for seven in the morning. The ferry doesn't dock until half past and by the time the van gets off the ship, that should give us time to action whatever we need to do. I'll see you then." The DCI strode off up the stairs.

Before he made his way to the CID office, Cyril had a quick look in the secretaries' room. He was disappointed there was no sign of Cathy. He checked his watch; just gone five.

Up in the CID room, Bill Walker spotted him arrive. "Ah, Sarge," he said, "I got a positive ID from Morag Watson."

Cyril walked over to Walker's desk where the DC turned a photo album the right way round for him to look at. "This one here," he said, pointing to a photo of a man who looked to be in his forties with dark receding hair, heavy jowls.

"Who's he?" Cyril asked.

Walker read from notes on a pad. "Tommy Marshall, forty-three, previous convictions for GBH, ABH, aggravated burglary and assault."

"Local?"

"No Sarge. London. But known associate of ..."

"The Robinsons," Cyril interrupted, nodding.

"Exactly."

Cyril half sat against an adjacent desk and folded his arms. "And what about McKinley? What did he have to say?"

"When I talked to him again, he was reluctant to say anything about the last time he'd seen Chalmers. I mentioned that Morag had already given us certain information. He wasn't best pleased and launched into a guttural attack on her. When he finally calmed down I asked him again about Chalmers. He seemed genuinely afraid. Eventually I got him to tell me that he'd seen Marshall twice. Once when he came into the Carlton Bar where Chalmers was drinking and once when he saw him leaving Chalmers room."

"Did he give any more details?"

"Only that he hadn't come into the pub to join Chalmers socially for a drink. In fact, he didn't have a drink. They just talked briefly, then Marshall left. He got the impression that it was more Marshall speaking to Chalmers rather than them having a conversation."

Cyril studied the photo more closely.

"And that last time, he only passed him on the stairs. McKinley was keen to keep his head down."

"All right, Bill, good work. Now if you haven't heard, the DCI is calling a briefing for seven in the morning, so don't be late."

"No, Sarge. I just want to follow something else up tonight before I clock off."

Cyril checked his desk for messages one last time before making for the door. As he did, he heard Walker on the phone.

"Can I speak to someone who could help me with medical records," he said, "going back possibly to 1946?"

Yes, Cyril thought, a conscientious lad, well worth encouraging.

56

It was just gone eight when Barton stepped off the train at Haarlem railway station. After the amusement of *Pippa's Bar*, he'd found himself somewhere quiet to eat at reasonable cost and meandered around Amsterdam's pavements for a while. He found the streets full of windows he'd heard so much about. It amazed him how there seemed to be every different taste catered for; all ages, some older than his grandmother; all sizes, thin to very fat; all nationalities. It also amused him to see the innovative use of lorry overtaking mirrors; bolted to the walls at the sides of the windows so the ladies could see who was approaching.

Back in Haarlem, early evening sun bathed the town in a warm light. It took him fifteen minutes to walk back to *Gert's Bar* where he nodded acknowledgement to the familiar barman and ordered himself a large draught lager.

He sat down at the same table as the night before, drawing no interest from the five men and two women who were seated at other tables.

Just before nine, the door opened and Freddie entered, dressed in jeans and trainers as he had been the previous night but with a different shirt. Barton watched as he approached the bar, ordered himself a bottle of lager then made his way over to sit down at his table.

"You have fun in Amsterdam, no?" Freddie asked, with a knowing smile.

"Interesting place," Barton responded.

"And the hotel, it was good, yes?"

"Comfortable." Barton looked around the room but no one was paying them any attention. "You have the van?"

"All ready for you, my friend," Freddie said. "You need to allow yourself a couple of hours to get to the ferry, so I'd advise you to leave in about half an hour. It's outside." He reached into his trouser pocket and brought out the keys, placing them on the table. "No need to look inside," he added.

"As long as Customs don't want to."

"They'll find nothing." Freddie produced an envelope. "You need this too. Paperwork for the export of flowers." He placed that on the table also.

Barton picked it up and had a cursory glance at the documents inside. Along with his return ticket and the paperwork DS Gray had given him, he should be able to board the ferry without any obstructions. He folded it up and tucked it into the inside pocket of Lennie King's leather jacket.

Freddie drained his lager bottle and stood. "Okay, I have to go now but see you next time perhaps?" He turned and casually walked out of the place.

"I doubt it," Barton said quietly to himself, playing with the set of keys to the van.

A short while later, he'd finished his lager and made his way out onto the street. It was getting dark, the sun had set and all seemed as quiet as before. The Holland Flower van was parked on the same side a short distance away, facing the direction he'd be going.

He didn't walk directly towards the van, deciding instead to walk away in the opposite direction for about a hundred yards, cross over and come back on the opposite side. All the while, he was keeping an eye out for anything unusual. He still didn't trust his situation. Was he (or Lennie for that matter) being set up? Eventually, having walked a circuit and seen nothing to arouse his suspicion, he sauntered up to the driver's door, unlocked it and climbed aboard. The chiller unit was humming away.

Twenty minutes into the journey, having kept a close lookout for any vehicles following, he pulled into a layby and waited. Nobody followed so he jumped down and walked to the back where he opened the doors. The van was chock full of cardboard boxes. Through holes in the sides he could see flowers. All appeared to be as it should. The important cargo would be behind the boxes and false front in the compartment where Cyril had concealed himself from the Robinsons back in Colchester.

Barton took a deep breath, closed the doors again, looked around him once more then climbed back into the cab and drove off towards the ferry terminal.

Traffic was steady until about ten miles from the port when red brake lights all came on ahead of him. Half a mile of slow progress eventually ground to a halt. Ten minutes of no movement looked permanent as drivers in the distance began to step out of their vehicles onto the road.

For the first time since he'd convinced Sanderson that he should pursue this strategy, panic began to set in. Shit, he thought. Shit, shit, shit! He'd never considered not being able to return on the sailing. What the Hell happens if he can't get the van back to Britain tomorrow for the rendezvous? How would anyone get word to Victor Robinson without revealing that he was under close scrutiny? And Lennie King; what if he was discharged from hospital and *made* the ferry and was spotted back in Essex without the shipment?

Barton leaned on the steering wheel and buried his head in his hands for a second. Tapping on the passenger window shocked him. Alarmed, he turned to see a man in police uniform with a motorcycle helmet on, visor up. He slid across onto the passenger seat and wound down the window.

The traffic cop had put his bike on its stand. "You're going to the ferry terminal, yes?" he asked.

Guardedly, Barton answered, "Yes."

"Follow me and stay close." The officer pulled his visor back down and climbed onto his motorcycle.

Barton was puzzled; and nervous. Why would a police motorcyclist stop and offer to help him? Was this a set-up? Truth be told, he wouldn't be able to tell a fake uniform from a genuine one.

The policeman had already switched on the bike's flashing lights.

One look up the line of stationary traffic convinced Barton he had no choice. The vehicles in front of him were already shuffling to the side, rear lamps blazing out looking like the parting of the Red Sea. He fired up the engine and gingerly followed his protector.

Slowly they made their way down the centre between the two lanes of traffic until they came to an exit which the motorcyclist cleared a way to. Barton followed onto a single carriageway unlit road for some distance. Finally, they came to an industrial estate, the road lined with warehouses and low-rise commercial units. At a junction controlled by traffic lights, the police rider turned left onto another poorly lit road.

Barton's heart rate increased. If he'd been duped and was about to be attacked, this would be the spot. He slowed and the motorcycle pulled away before it also slowed down. Now stationary, Barton checked that the cab doors were locked. With the van in gear ready for a getaway, he waited.

The policeman on the bike stopped, turned and looked back at him.

57

Cyril checked his fridge and found little with which to make a meal. Charlie, on the other hand, was pleased to eat the same food every day. Head down, ceramic bowl rattling on the tiles until he began to chase it round the kitchen, just to make sure he hadn't missed a morsel.

"You know what, lad," he said, "I think I'll get something from the chippy and take it down to the allotments. What d'you say?"

Charlie's tail wagged. As usual, he was just pleased to have company, and the prospect of a walk was a bonus, not to mention the possibility of a piece of batter from Cyril's fish.

Doris had looked after Charlie for two days now and Cyril felt uncomfortable that he had somehow been putting upon her quite a lot recently. She protested that she loved having the dog but he thought she deserved some time unhindered by him and his problems.

The aromas floating out into the street from the chip shop reminded Cyril just how hungry he was. He could imagine Maureen berating him for having neglected himself in recent days, but that was all down to circumstances beyond his control; well almost. Furthermore, she'd probably have a moan at him for eating greasy food. But when you're hungry and they smell as good as this, well …

"Ow's things, then Cyril?" Big Pete asked from behind the counter when he walked in. Pete was from Yorkshire and did the best fish and chips Cyril had tasted. And he was called Big Pete because he was only five feet five. "'Ere, what's happened to your …"

"Nothing, Pete." Cyril interrupted him, not wanting to have to explain his head injury again. "But I'm starving," he went on.

"Ah'll bet thee could eat Ghandi's loin cloth," Pete quipped in his strong Yorkshire accent then laughed like a drain.

Cyril couldn't help smiling. It was a line Pete had used many a time.

"Cod and chips please." He made an exaggerated gesture of looking round the empty shop. "This weather can't be doing much for your business though?"

"Could be better, but could be a lot worse. They've got standpipes in t'street back home," the man informed him.

Cyril was amused. Pete had been in Clacton since he was demobbed after the war but he still referred to Yorkshire as 'home'.

"Playing havoc with my leeks and as for the onions, they look like they might only be good for pickling this year. Here, maybe I could sell you some?"

"Supposed to be breaking soon, I heard." Pete shovelled chips into the wrapper on top of the battered fish. "Any bits?" he asked.

"No thanks, that's fine as it is."

"Salt and vinegar?"

"Just a little salt, please."

Food wrapped, Pete handed the package over. "Dining in then?"

"Not exactly." Cyril paid, took his supper and looked down at the dog. "Charlie and me are just heading down to the allotment to have these al fresco."

"You know how to live."

Cyril always felt cheered up when he spoke to Pete. He'd never heard him complain and he always had a quick retort; a half full sort of bloke.

Five minutes later, he sat down on the old bench he'd obtained years ago that looked out over his patch on the allotments and unwrapped his meal. The sun was just going down and the evening was still warm. There were three or four other gardeners walking up and down their

253

plots of land, watering cans in hand. Cyril hadn't heard any weather forecasts in recent days. Maybe Pete was right and this long dry spell was coming to an end. He broke off a chunk of batter and held it out to Charlie. The big dog licked his lips and gently took it from his fingers.

As he ate, Cyril's thoughts drifted to Cathy. He hadn't seen her since she blanked him in the corridor this morning. He couldn't blame her. He imagined her all ready for him to pick her up last night and he doesn't show. Anyone would be annoyed. But he had to see her; explain why. She'd understand, surely. There again, it was the second time he'd let her down. Perhaps it was Maureen's way of looking after him. Perhaps she didn't want him to become involved with anyone else. What the Hell was he thinking? He'd only spoken to the woman a few times. Yes he'd agreed to take her out but there was nothing to it. But there again, he recalled what Doris had told him of her conversations with Maureen. And when he was trapped in the van, what he heard then, Maureen talking to him; was that just his mind playing tricks?

Charlie rested his head on Cyril's knee, reminding him the best part of the fish supper was still in the paper.

"Go on then, but don't tell Doris," he said and held out a couple of chips.

Charlie took them from his hand softly, ate them, burped then lay down at Cyril's feet.

Cathy came into his mind once again. Now he knew where she lived, he'd thought about calling round to see her tonight but … it would be too late now. Morning then? Give her a lift into work? No, that wouldn't be possible. He had to be in at seven for the briefing.

That brought his thoughts round to Barton. He hoped he wasn't getting himself involved in anything stupid. He'd be like a kid in a sweetshop walking the streets of Amsterdam. There again, he was a detective, he should have some sense. Like all those getting tanked up after hours and expecting to be escorted home by uniform? Didn't quite work out for Danny Flynn though, one of the circumstances behind Cyril's involvement in this case in the first place.

It seemed a long time ago now since he had been sitting with Sam Woodbridge in the patrol car, looking forward to wrapping up the night-shift and spending some free time down here on the allotment. And then the crash; Jem Fletcher dead; Jimmy Morgan murdered; Adam Fletcher in debt and somehow pressured into involving his brother. A bent card school run by Dougie Chalmers was the catalyst. But where is Chalmers now? And who took over the debt? The Robinsons? Or this Tommy Marshall character running his own scam? Certainly Hughie McKinley was unnerved by him. Or are Chalmers and Marshall running some racket together? In any event, they still needed to track down Chalmers.

"Oh I don't know, lad," Cyril addressed Charlie, "there's still a lot we need to find out."

58

Eventually, the police motorcyclist approached the driver's side of the flower van and Barton wound the window down a touch.

The policeman pushed up his visor. "Something wrong?" he wondered.

"Just checking the map," Barton lied. "Are we far away?"

"Next turn to the right and there is a rear entrance to the ferry terminal in about a kilometre."

"Who sent you exactly?"

"You are suspicious, yes?" the policeman asked.

Barton said nothing.

"I was instructed to make sure you made the sailing by Inspecteur Lars Hendriks. Looks like your Roger Daltrey." The man grinned, replaced his visor and began to ride up the road.

Barton laughed to himself, lifted the clutch, released the handbrake and followed his guardian.

As he took the next right, the lights of the ferry terminal came into view. At the gates, the policeman turned the bike, waved a hand and rode off, leaving Barton to approach the barrier and begin the process of clearing the security procedures. Gray's documentation eased his passage through Immigration checks and, after a cursory inspection of the van's cargo by Customs, he drove onto the vehicle deck.

Safely on board the ferry, he wandered through the passenger lounges. They were a lot quieter than on the outward journey. He could do with something to eat before the boat sailed but the restaurant wouldn't open until after they'd moved off. It had been a long time since he'd eaten. Maybe a pint at the bar too. He had enough money left for that and hopefully some duty-free cigarettes. After all, never look a gift horse. A smile came to his face as he remembered the conversation he'd had in *Pippa's Bar*. Another time, maybe.

But first, he needed to ask a favour from the ship's wireless operator. As luck would have it, it was the same man on duty who had been in charge the day before. After tapping in some numbers, he handed Barton a telephone handset with a dialling tone buzzing from the earpiece.

He managed to catch Sanderson at home. He took him through the meet at *Gert's Bar* and the rendezvous a few hours ago. All seemed as it should as far as the flower cargo was concerned.

"Just give me a call from a callbox once you're off the ferry tomorrow morning. I'll be with the team for a briefing from seven," Sanderson said just before the call ended.

Barton thanked the wireless man and departed in search of some food.

Just before one o'clock, suitably fed and watered he settled down into a chair on the starboard lounge, wrapping Lennie King's leather jacket around him and cuddling his pack of 200 Peter Stuyvesant cigarettes. He closed his eyes and began to mull over what Sanderson had told him of events back in Clacton. Hugh McKinley and Morag Watson, the pair of pissheads had had some intriguing information. Tommy Marshall was not a name Barton was familiar with. But Cyril was on the case. He'd originally baulked at the idea of having him assist the CID team but he'd warmed to the man during this adventure. He'd begun to appreciate his qualities. God, he must be going soft.

He was on that slope down into deep sleep when a voice spoke to him.

"Glad to see you've looked after the leather jacket."

Barton opened his eyes to see Lennie King grinning at him before sitting down in the adjacent chair.

"I wondered if you'd make it." Barton struggled to open his eyes.

King laughed. "I told you I would."

Barton straightened himself up in the seat. "Well you had me fooled. I thought you were in a bad way. What happened at the hospital?"

"They reckoned I was okay. They couldn't find any evidence of the angina attack. Wanted to keep me in for forty-eight hours observation mind." King gestured with his hands. "So I discharged myself. No good sitting around in a foreign hospital."

"You certainly pulled the wool over the ship's doctor's eyes too."

"When you know the symptoms and the signs ..." King left the sentence unfinished. "Anyway, how did you get on in Haarlem?"

Barton gave a brief recount of the previous twenty-four hours. "But what was all that James Bond shit – code seven?" he concluded.

"It was a secure way to tell Holt that the operation had been compromised. That way he could make alternative plans for the shipment not making it to London." He paused for a second. "But there was something else he was concerned about. Hopefully, that should bear fruit."

"What's that?"

"The fewer people who know the better." King looked around before he spoke again. "But you'll need me to drive the van back to the warehouse."

"No fucking way," Barton exploded. It was his turn to glance around the lounge. There was no one within earshot. "I'm not letting you get behind the wheel."

King leaned in closer and lowered his voice. "So how do you think it'll look when you turn up with the shipment? I go off in the van and a copper drives it back."

"They won't know who I am. I'm just a mate of yours doing you a favour. You fell ill and you called me to stand in for you."

King threw his head back. "Are you serious? Of course they'll know you're job. Christ, they can smell you a mile off." He leaned forward once again. "Now I drove it away and, as far as they know, I've been to Haarlem and I'm driving it back to the warehouse."

Barton had to admit that that might give Sanderson a better option. He still didn't know for certain what was planned for their return. The Robinsons would know straight away something was wrong if King didn't reappear. And with their record for violence, that might not end well.

Barton wrestled with the problem as King watched him closely.

"I told you, I couldn't leave it unfinished. I owe Jimmy that," King added.

"What is it with you blokes and the war? Cyril's always going on about it."

King looked earnestly at the detective. "Cyril Claydon's a good bloke. Straight as they come. You're too young; you don't understand what our generation went through; the bonds that were formed. If it wasn't for ..."

"Okay, okay, I get the picture," Barton interrupted. "But tell me this, what do you know about Morgan's murder?"

"Know? I don't *know* anything for sure," King responded. "But I suspect."

"What do you suspect?"

"He was your grass, right?"

"What makes you ...?"

King stopped him. "Look, if you want me to be honest with you, the least you can be is honest with me."

Barton held up a hand. "All right," he sighed. "Yes, he used to come to me with snippets."

"And what was the last snippet he brought you?"

Barton stood up. "Let's get a drink. I think it might be a long night."

"Before you do," King looked straight at the DI. "Let's have my jacket back. It cost me an arm and a leg."

Barton couldn't help but grin, took off the jacket, handed it back to the man then headed for the cafeteria bar.

King opted for a mug of tea but Barton came back with a pint of lager for himself.

Back at the table, Barton explained that Morgan had told him about Walter Yardley's plans to bring diamonds into Britain illegally. He'd got no further details other than that; certainly not the expanded story of them picked off stolen items of jewellery from across Europe and no mention of Victor Robinson's involvement further down the line.

"I didn't know that until I spoke to him that last time," King explained, stirring sugar into his tea.

"And when was that?"

"It must have been … mid-August. Maybe a week or so before the plane crash. I met him for a pint."

Barton sipped his lager. "How did he seem?"

"Nervous." King caught Barton's expression. "Not from the flower runs. He'd done two of those already. He just had a feeling, you know?"

"I don't."

King leaned in closer. "Well, you know he was also doing some driving work for Yardley?"

Barton nodded.

"That was how he discovered Yardley's plans. He overheard a telephone conversation one night when he got back to the yard. I don't think Yardley expected anyone to hear."

"So did Yardley find out?"

"No." King took a drink of his tea. "At least at that point he didn't think so. But he was becoming suspicious of someone in the job."

"Like who?" Barton was indignant. "I hope you don't think it's me."

"It's a bit bloody late if I do, but no, he trusted you. I hope he wasn't wrong."

"Not with me. But in what way was he suspicious? Why?"

"He was beginning to wonder if someone was in the Robinsons' pocket. I must admit I'm a bit wary as well. But I got myself involved to try and find out who did for Jimmy."

"And just how did you manage that?"

"Jimmy had introduced me to Holt. I told you we were close. Jimmy told him I was interested in working with him inside the Robinson set up."

"Hold on," Barton said disbelievingly, "You couldn't have just walked in on the say so of Morgan."

King took a breath before he replied. "No, you're right. I knew Frank Robinson, the old man, during the war. We used to ... well, Jimmy too, later. In fact it was me who introduced Jimmy to Frank."

"But listen, are you saying it could be DCI Holt?"

King shook his head, "No, I don't think so. Why would he stitch us up to the Robinsons? He wanted us in there to find out what they did and how they did it." He drained his tea, looked down at the table for a second before focussing on Barton. "He thought it was someone in the local plod who was close to Yardley."

Barton leaned back and puffed out his cheeks. "Shit," he said quietly.

"Exactly. So how many know you've substituted for me? If word gets back to the Robinsons, I'll be the next stiff. Why should I trust you? How do I know for sure *you're* not in somebody's pocket?"

Barton mulled things over. "You don't," he finally said. "But I don't think you've got a choice."

King frowned and thought for a minute. "Okay, but I'm driving the van back to the warehouse."

59
Wednesday 8th September

It was six thirty when Cyril approached DCI Sanderson's office. He'd woken early, his mind lively. He'd glanced at the clock for the first time at four, unable to stop himself wondering how Barton was. If all was going to plan, he should be safely back on the ferry. If it wasn't - it didn't bear thinking about.

Sanderson saw him approach through the glazed partition and waved him in. "You couldn't sleep either?" he greeted.

Cyril shook his head. "Not with all this going on." He wasn't surprised to see the DCI dressed in a smart shirt and tie, and a suit jacket, even at this time of the day. "Have you heard from the DI?"

"He's on the ship with the van. He managed to call me last night at home."

"Everything okay?"

"As far as he could tell. Got a bit of help from a Dutch detective when the traffic snarled him up on the way to the port. I'm expecting him to call with a final update once he's off the vessel." He glanced at his watch. "They shouldn't be far off docking now."

"So what are your thoughts?" Cyril asked.

"Tell me again what you heard when DS Gray made that call on the ferry."

Cyril reprised what he'd overheard.

"And you've no idea who he was talking to?"

Cyril shook his head.

"His boss, Crimond maybe?"

"Might have been, but I couldn't say."

A grim expression formed on Sanderson's face. "Anything in his tone?"

262

"I've been turning it over in my head, but there's nothing really, except …"

"Except what?"

"I got the impression it was someone he knew well, as a friend maybe. That's not to say, it couldn't have been a work colleague."

"So it might have also been someone from the Met - Holt, or even one of the Robinsons."

"Sorry."

Both men were silent for a while before Cyril thought out loud, "Don't forget we had to tell Gray about Lennie King's participating informant status because he was present when DI Barton and I were discussing that someone should substitute for him."

"He seems to have been everywhere," Sanderson said, almost to himself.

Cyril could see the DCI was troubled. "Is there something else, Sir?"

Sanderson let out a deep breath, looked at him for a second before coming to a decision. "This is in strictest confidence, Cyril."

"Of course."

"I've been sifting through the events since Dick, I mean John, came to me with the information that Morgan had passed on to him about Walter Yardley's plans." Sanderson paused. "Well, the only one I can think of was …" He turned away and shook his head. "Oh, I can't believe I'm saying this."

"Go on," Cyril encouraged.

"Well it's the Chief Super."

"What, DCS Viney?" Cyril sounded incredulous. "Are you sure?"

Sanderson nodded. "Positive. I remembered I bumped into him in the corridor later that morning, after John had told me. He'd seen Morgan the night before. And when the Super asked me how things were going, I mentioned what I'd just been told."

"But he could have spoken about that to someone else; higher up maybe?"

"I considered that, but ..."

"Something else?"

"I seem to remember hearing that Yardley and he were close in the past. Socialise in the same circles. Mr Viney lives in Frinton too."

"Does he know about the DI's unplanned trip to Holland?"

Sanderson shook his head. "He's been on holiday, not back until tomorrow - golfing, I think. I didn't think I should try and get hold of him." A smile played on the DCI's lips.

"Because of your suspicions," Cyril completed.

Sanderson didn't react.

"So what are we doing, Sir?" Cyril asked.

The DCI hesitated for a second. "You've been in that warehouse," he said. "Do you think you can sketch out some plans before the rest turn up?"

"I should think so. So we're going in with the van then?"

"I'd like to keep my options open. Plan it that way but I'm hoping John will have something for me to work with. I don't have to make a definite decision until I know a bit more. In the meantime, use the blackboard in the CID office."

60

Barton's mind was humming. What King had said about someone in the local force made sense to him. But who? And who were they tipping off? Certainly the Robinson boys knew the raid was coming on their static. But Morgan came to him with information about Yardley. So did Yardley tell the Robinson brothers? After all, he's renting the warehouse to them. And he's hoping to fence his diamonds through them. But then, does he also know that Morgan and now King are working for the Met? If that's the case, King will be targeted when they get back to Colchester. But do the Robinsons also know about King's medical problem and the fact that he, Barton, had made the contact in Holland? He'd been convinced it wasn't DCI Sanderson. But was he duped? Could it be? Or is it, as Sanderson suggested, someone higher up?

King had explained all he suspected about Morgan's death and what he knew about the Met detective, DCI Holt. Somewhere along the line, he couldn't discount the possibility of someone on the payroll within Special Branch too.

Barton couldn't make any sense of it. His thoughts scrambled into one big mass like spaghetti. It turned out to be a long night. But somewhere around four in the morning, Barton and King had dropped off.

A few hours later, movement in the lounge brought Barton awake.

King stood up and stretched. "Just going for a pee and freshen up," he said and wandered off.

Barton returned to the cafeteria and bought two teas. As he did so, he scanned the other passengers for any faces he recognised, or any suspicious ones. Nothing.

Maybe he'd be followed once he left the ship. After all, the van was pretty distinctive.

King returned and welcomed the hot drink Barton had organised.

"So you travel through Customs and Immigration as a foot passenger with your passport and ticket," Barton instructed. "I'll take the van through and use the Special Branch pass DS Gray gave me."

"You're not going to piss off and leave me, are you?" King said. "That'll be a disaster for you."

"Trust me," Barton responded. "Make your way up to the roundabout and I'll pick you up there. But I'll need to make a phone call first."

As they finished their hot drinks, the crew made the announcement for all drivers to return to the vehicle decks and prepare to disembark.

Barton and King looked at one another. "Keep your eyes peeled for anything suspicious," Barton said. "Anybody following you, taking too much of an interest in you, anything at all. If in doubt, call the station in Clacton and speak to DCI Sanderson."

"But I'll see you up the road." King expressed it as a statement, rather than a question.

Barton nodded. "I'll be doing the same. But if I think someone is on to me, I'll abort the whole thing." Barton held out a hand. "Take care. See you later."

King shook it. "You too."

Barton made his way down to the vehicle deck via the toilets, staying alert for anything unusual. Back in the cab, he waited until the vehicles in front began to move. He fired up the engine and slowly made his way off the ferry.

61

By the time the room started to fill up, Cyril had drawn out the floor plans of the warehouse from memory onto the blackboard which stood on an easel.

"Morning, Skip," a familiar voice said.

Cyril turned to see Sam Woodbridge at his shoulder.

"I recognise that," he said, indicating Cyril's drawing. "Is that what all this is about?"

Cyril looked round and recognised the half dozen or so uniforms filtering into the room. He spoke quietly. "Looks like DCI Sanderson is preparing then. What have you been told?"

"Only to get in early this morning for a briefing. And to turn up in some scruffy clothes."

"Do me a favour Sam, don't let on to anyone you were with me in here the other day." Cyril tapped the blackboard.

"Sure." Sam turned and sat down with his colleagues.

Miller and Walker strolled in at that point, Miller especially looking bleary-eyed. A couple of other officers joined them before DCI Sanderson swept in to the room, walked to the blackboard and turned to face the gathering. The room hushed.

Cyril made to sit down with the others but the DCI put up a hand to stop him.

"Morning gentlemen," Sanderson began. "This morning, we will be carrying out an operation at a warehouse premises in The Hythe district of Colchester." He looked to Cyril. "DS Claydon will explain the layout, then I'll explain how our resources will be allocated."

Cyril proceeded to describe the location of the building in relation to its surroundings and the ground, first and second floor layouts before sitting down and handing over to the DCI.

Sanderson proposed there would be three teams. At Cyril's suggestion, one group would gain entry to the building and secrete themselves in the old ground floor toilets. Cyril and six uniforms would be stationed in a van parked up on waste ground over the road from the building. The third group would be liaising with Barton and the flower van on the outskirts of Colchester. Until he spoke to DI Barton, that was as much as he was prepared to say. "So take your refs now and be back here at 08:30," he concluded.

Cyril suspected that was because he hadn't yet formulated a firm plan.

As Sanderson left the room, he indicated for Cyril to follow.

Sam stood as he passed by. "What the Hell's going on, Skip?" he whispered.

"Just get the Transit prepared so we're all ready to go after the next briefing." Cyril rushed out of the room to catch up with the DCI.

*   *   *

Customs closely studied the documents Barton gave them. Finally, the officer moved to the rear of the van and opened the doors. He shuffled through a few boxes, gave up and closed the doors again. With a nod, he gave the paperwork back to Barton and moved onto the next vehicle.

Through Immigration with the aid of his warrant card, he set out on the road from the quayside. He made slow progress, checking his mirrors, imagining eyes on him from the offices above the terminal where Special Branch was based. Half a mile away, a lay-by came up on the near-side and he spotted the familiar figure of Lennie King, holdall at his feet, leaning against a phone box. Barton pulled in and drew to a halt alongside him.

Climbing down from the cab, Barton put the keys in his pocket and walked round the front to the phone box. "Didn't trust me?" he asked.

King ignored the question. "Everything okay?" he countered.

Barton nodded then pulled open the door of the phone box.

King opened the van's passenger door and climbed in.

From the box, Barton peered down the road towards the terminal and studied the vehicles driving past. None looked suspicious, so he turned, lifted the receiver and dialled the number for Clacton Police Station.

A minute later, the desk sergeant rang him back and immediately put him through to DCI Sanderson.

"Where are you?" Sanderson asked.

"Just got off the ferry, Sir."

"Everything okay?"

Another glance up and down the road before settling on the sight of Lennie King sitting in the passenger seat of the van. "Well there is one development ..."

*   *   *

Sanderson replaced the receiver slowly.

"Problems?" Cyril wondered having listened to one side of the conversation between Sanderson and Barton.

"Lennie King's showed up."

"I thought he might. So is he with the DI now?"

Sanderson nodded. "This could work in our favour. It'll give us a bit more time inside the warehouse before we spring the surprise. Just hope King is up to it."

"For what it's worth, I've known Lennie a long time. When I spoke to him on the ferry, he was determined to find out what had happened to his friend. He has his suspicions but he feels he owes Jimmy Morgan."

Sanderson looked at his watch and stood. "Right, let's brief them."

62

Sanderson's car was discreetly parked in an empty church hall car park, shielded from any prying eyes a couple of miles out of Colchester on the Ipswich Road. Miller sat in the front passenger seat, Walker and two uniforms sat in the back.

Miller checked his watch yet again. "Should be here by now, Sir."

Sanderson took a breath. "He's just taking his time, checking no one's following."

A minute later, the flower van rolled into the car park and pulled up alongside the car.

"Stay here a minute," Sanderson ordered, then got out.

Barton switched off the engine and opened the door.

Sanderson stood beside him. "Picked up a passenger, I see."

"Mr Sanderson," King greeted from the other side of the cab.

"Made a miraculous recovery then?"

"Just a little turn," King said, "I'm fine now."

Sanderson grew serious. "Anybody follow you, John?"

"Not that I can tell." Barton thumbed towards his passenger. "And Lennie's been looking out too."

King jumped down from the passenger side and walked round the front of the cab.

"This is a big risk, you know," Sanderson said to him.

"But it's an even bigger risk if I don't drive back."

Sanderson nodded. "I know." He looked back to his car. "Everything's in place down at the warehouse, so you know what to do, John?"

Barton stepped down from the driver's seat. "Yep. Who's with me?"

Sanderson waved at the car and the uniformed constables got out. "These two will be alongside you in the back." He walked to the rear. "Now, have we got to arrange some space for you?"

Barton opened the rear doors and shuffled some boxes around to give space for the three men to stand inside. "Bloody good job it's not for long," he said, "It's freezing in here."

"If Cyril managed it for a couple of hours, fifteen minutes should be a breeze for you lot. Anyway, Lennie can switch the chiller off for now."

With Barton and the two constables safely inside, King set off for the warehouse. Sanderson, with Miller and Walker followed at a safe distance.

*　*　*

The unmarked Ford Transit van drew to a halt on the patch of waste ground opposite the warehouse on The Hythe. Inside, six uniformed officers sat on side-facing bench seats. They hoped they wouldn't have to spend any considerable time in what was a tin box in the hot sun. But this morning had broken with widespread cloud cover. Was this the end of the long heatwave?

Up front, Sam Woodbridge, now dressed in a boiler suit, was sitting alongside Cyril who had driven. Cyril released the bonnet catch, got out and lifted the cover. If anyone paid any attention, it was just some unfortunate van driver with engine trouble.

Across the street, all was quiet at the warehouse. The vehicle doors were closed and the padlock was in place.

"Alpha one in position," Woodbridge said into the radio.

"Roger that," the answer came back. *"All clear here, no sign of the target as yet."*

Cyril checked his watch as he leaned in through the drivers' window. "Right Sam," he said. "You know what to do."

Woodbridge nodded and got out.

"You three with me." He indicated the officers sitting on the left hand side. "The rest of you wait until the van arrives."

About to leave, Cyril paused and had a quiet word with Sam.

Woodbridge nodded understanding then bent over with his head under the bonnet.

Cyril led the way across the road and up the right hand side of the building. "Right lads, radios on silent and follow me inside," he said. Two of his colleagues helped launch him up to the window sill and inside. The others followed.

63

A few spots of rain began to fall as the big grey Daimler rolled up outside the warehouse. A slightly-built man, in his sixties with thinning dark hair climbed from the drivers' seat and opened the rear passenger door. There was no mistaking the figure who stepped out from the front passenger side; Tommy Marshall. From the rear seats, Victor and David Robinson emerged into the overcast morning. All four glanced up and down the street, but paid no attention to the tall young lad dressed in overalls with his head in the engine compartment of the Ford Transit parked opposite.

Victor Robinson took out a key and opened the pedestrian door to the warehouse. His brother and Marshall followed suit, leaving the driver to stand outside, as if on sentry duty, watching approaching traffic.

Once inside, the Robinson brothers walked into the middle of the open space, Marshall remained by the doors.

"He'd better not be late," David said.

"Relax, will you. Everything's under control." Victor glanced at his watch. "The ferry docked on time and we arranged to meet up here by ten."

The noise of a lock being turned and the escape door at the rear of the building opening disturbed them. Through the door from the yard of the electrical factory came Walter Yardley. "Everything okay?" he asked.

"Everything's under control," Victor said.

Yardley looked anxious. "You're still on for the exchange?"

"Relax, Walter. All in good time." Victor approached the man. "You've got what you want to sell?"

Yardley tapped his pocket. "As we said. You have the money?"

Victor turned to his brother and smirked. "Anyone would think Mr Yardley here is desperate."

"I don't know why you want to get involved in that," David said dismissively.

"Just doing our friend a favour," Victor said.

"So when can we do it?" Yardley persisted.

"He is desperate," David commented.

Victor turned back to face Yardley, a strange smile on his face. "I want to sort out my business first, if that's all right with you."

Before anyone could say any more, the Daimler's driver put his head in through the pedestrian door. "Boss, he's here," he said, stepping inside and preparing to open the vehicle doors.

Marshall helped him. They could hear the noise of the van's engine as it stopped outside, waiting for the doors to open wide enough. Marshall and the driver stood either side and the van pulled in, Lennie King at the wheel.

Once inside, the doors were closed and Marshall and Robinsons' driver joined them by the drivers' side of the van.

King switched off the engine and opened his door.

"Everything go okay, Lennie?" Victor asked.

"Like clockwork, boss."

"Good man." Victor turned to Marshall and their driver. "Okay boys, let's check the load."

All four walked round to the rear of the van, leaving King to pick up his holdall from the passenger footwell. Marshall lifted the lever and opened the doors.

64

The van doors swung open to reveal DI Barton, hand outstretched holding his warrant card. Alongside him, two uniformed officers jumped out. "Police!" he shouted, stepping down. "Everyone stay where you are!"

Simultaneously, the three uniformed officers appeared from the toilet block by the side of the open area and spread out. Behind the surprised group, the sounds of a key turning in the pedestrian door announced the appearance of DCI Sanderson, DCs Miller and Walker and two more officers.

Lennie King sat still in the van seat. Marshall and the Robinsons' driver were startled and tensed as though they were about to make a run for it then relaxed, deciding not to. Initial surprised looks on Victor and David Robinson's faces melted into smirks.

"Well, well, well," Victor Robinson said. "DI Barton you're like a bad penny. And …?" He turned his attention to the group who had come in from the street.

"DCI Sanderson," he announced, displaying his warrant card.

"To what do we owe the pleasure this time?" David Robinson enquired.

"What's in the van?" Sanderson asked.

"I think you can see." Victor Robinson waved an arm in the direction of the van. "Flowers. And, if you don't mind, I need to get this into London this afternoon." He made to close the doors.

Barton stood in front of him. "We need to inspect this shipment."

Another smirk grew into a grin. Victor Robinson shrugged. "Okay. I don't know what you think you'll find

but we need to be on the road again, twelve at the latest."
He stood to the side next to his brother.

Sanderson gave a nod and DCs Miller and Walker,
along with the two uniformed officers who had emerged
from the back of the van, began to offload the boxes of
flowers.

Barton walked to the front of the van and approached
Yardley. "Mr Yardley," he said. "What involvement do you
have with this operation?"

A look of alarm spread over Yardley's face. "Nothing.
Nothing at all. I only rent the building to Mr Robinson and
I … I just came in to check on the place."

"Not involved in any deal then?"

A pile of boxes crashed from the van.

"Hey watch out! These are worth money," David
Robinson exclaimed, as a commotion broke out.

Yardley took advantage of the distraction and began
to edge towards the fire escape door.

"Just a minute," Barton said. "I'd like you to stay."

Yardley stepped forward and grabbed Barton around
the neck, turning him, back towards him and pointing a
gun to his head.

Barton was taken by surprise but was in no doubt
what was being held to his cheek. The cold, round,
unmistakable feel of a gun barrel.

One of the uniformed officers who'd emerged from the
toilets made to step forward but stiffened when Yardley
warned him. "Don't do anything stupid." Yardley adjusted
his grip. "Now, unless you want to have your colleague on
your consciences, I'd suggest you all back off."

Activity at the rear of the van died as everyone
became aware of what was happening.

There was no disguising the shocked look on Victor
Robinson's face. "Look, Walter, there's no need for this."

"What do you know," Yardley snarled. He began to
pull Barton backwards with him as he shuffled away from
the van towards the rear of the building.

Sanderson took a stride forward. "Put the gun down,
Mr Yardley. If that goes off, it's a whole new ball game.

As it stands, we can sort whatever it is without things getting too serious. But harming a police officer, well …"

Yardley paused. "You know nothing," he said. "Now, I'm leaving and you're not going to stop me." He started moving backwards once again.

From the shadows behind the staircase, Cyril moved slowly and silently towards Yardley and Barton. Shuffling in his pocket, he pulled out his pipe.

Yardley took another step towards the escape door in the rear wall then felt a shape prod into his back.

"That's far enough, Mr Yardley … Walter." Cyril had pressed the stem of his pipe into Yardley's back. "You don't want to do anything stupid."

Yardley froze but didn't ease his grip on Barton. "It's Sergeant Claydon, if I'm not mistaken."

"That's right. Now you don't want me to have to use this, do you? Why don't you let DI Barton go and, as Mr Sanderson said, we can sort this out?"

Yardley stiffened. "I can't do that. It's gone too far."

"Jimmy Morgan, you mean."

Again, a slight reaction in Yardley's posture. "He deceived me. You don't do that to people who've given you a chance. You should appreciate that. You were in the war."

"But we didn't kill our own. We dealt with it properly."

"I dealt with it properly," Yardley sneered. Then, with a thrust of the elbow of his gun hand, he swung round on Cyril, knocking the pipe from his grip. At the same time, Barton was thrown forward, stumbling to the floor.

Cyril went to grab Yardley's gun but wasn't quick enough. The butt of the revolver caught Cyril on the head, the same position as the wound sustained in the van a couple of days earlier. He dropped to his knees then sank to the floor unconscious.

Yardley made for the escape door and bundled his way through.

By the time Barton had recovered and made it to his feet, Yardley had disappeared. He took in the crumpled figure of Cyril lying on the ground, blood pouring from his head wound.

"Get after him!" Sanderson shouted.

Lennie King jumped down from the van and joined Barton who had knelt to tend to Cyril.

Several uniforms rushed for the exit door but it refused to open, despite their hammering on the release bolt.

"He's locked it from the other side," one of them said.

Cyril opened his eyes. "What's …?"

Sanderson turned to the group who'd followed him in through the pedestrian door. "Miller, take two others with you and get round to the front of Yardley's and grab him."

"Don't worry, Cyril," Barton said. "Yardley's gone through the fire escape. But we'll get him."

"Radio Sam," Cyril said quietly. "Tell him to get ready."

"Sam?"

"PC Woodbridge. Just radio him."

Barton switched on the radio and made the call.

* * *

Walter Yardley slammed the fire exit door behind him and slid the bolts across, top and bottom. For a second, eyes closed, he leaned against it. What the hell had he done? How had he gotten into this mess? He thrust the gun back into his jacket pocket.

Banging on the door focussed his thoughts. He had to get away. Hurrying across the yard, he burst in through the rear door to the offices.

"Mr Yardley, I need a signature …" a young woman sitting at the desk in the first office he came to said.

"Not now, Dawn. I'm in a bit of a rush."

"But …"

Yardley dashed through the office door and into a corridor. On past reception where a middle-aged woman looked up from answering the phone.

"I've got Mr …" she announced.

"Bit of a hurry."

Out through the main doors, he rushed down the steps and felt in his jacket pocket for his car keys. Distracted, he didn't notice the two figures approach him from either side of the entrance. Something tapped his heels and he lost his footing. Down onto the tarmac he fell. Hands grabbed his arms behind his back and handcuffs clicked shut.

"Walter Yardley, you're under arrest," Sam Woodbridge said.

* * *

"Come on Walker, get this unloaded," Sanderson instructed his officers by the rear of the van. "You lot, stay where you are," he addressed the Robinson brothers and their two sidekicks.

Dashing over to Cyril, he stood by Barton who was handing the DS a handkerchief to hold to his head.

"Take it easy, Cyril. We'll get some help," King said, easing him into a sitting position.

"How are you doing?" Sanderson asked.

"I'm getting a bit sick of this," Cyril said. "Always the same ruddy spot." He shuffled his position. Barton and King helped him to his feet. "Has he broken my pipe too? That was my favourite."

Barton looked to the floor where three pieces of pipe lay. "You mean you bluffed him with your pipe." The DI looked incredulous. "Christ he could have shot me."

"Desperate measures," Cyril said.

Sanderson listened to a radio transmission then said, "They've got him."

Cyril made his way to the back of the van, sat on an old upturned tea chest and watched as Walker and the other two uniforms piled boxes of flowers onto the concrete floor.

"Are you okay there?" Victor Robinson enquired. "That looks nasty."

"It looks worse than it is," Cyril responded.

"Look Mr Sanderson," David Robinson said, "We had no idea that idiot had a gun or was going to turn violent. It's got nothing to do with us."

"That's right. We only rent this place from him. Just a convenient stopping off point from the ferry," Victor added.

Cyril got to his feet and indicated for Barton to follow him down the side of the van away from the gaze of the Robinsons. "They're too self-assured," he whispered. "Did you check what was in the van?"

"How could I? The van was delivered back to me fully loaded." Barton looked worried. "But you're right. They've been smirking and cocky since we jumped out of the van."

As the two men walked back to the rear of the vehicle, loud drumming sounded as heavy rain fell on the roof above. Automatically, they glanced up to the upper floor before peering round to see inside the van. Only a few more rows of cardboard boxes to be removed and the false front of the inside would be revealed. No mistaking the confident body language of the brothers.

Finally, the last few boxes were cleared from the door to the false front. Walker slipped the catch and opened it. He looked inside then turned to Sanderson who was waiting expectantly. "Empty, Sir," he said.

"Are you sure?"

"Shit," Barton said.

The smirk re-appeared on Victor Robinson's face. "Oh dear. I don't know what you were expecting to find but we did say, all we had was flowers."

Barton stepped up inside the van and checked for himself. The space behind the false front was empty. He strode back down to the rear and looked at the Robinson brothers. "Think you're fucking smart, do you?"

The brothers looked at one another then Victor answered, "No idea what you're on about, Inspector."

Barton looked as if he was about to explode.

"Okay, John," Sanderson said looking at his DI. "We can keep this civil." He turned to Victor Robinson. "Have you ever been upstairs in this building, Mr Robinson?"

Victor shrugged and shook his head. "No need to."

Unnoticed, Marshall nudged the Robinsons' driver closer to the pedestrian door.

Sanderson looked from one Robinson brother to the other. "So we wouldn't find any evidence of either of you having been on the upper floors?"

"Of course not," David replied. "Now can we get these flowers back onto the van and on their way?"

Before anyone else could speak, Marshall and the driver dashed out of the door and into the street.

"Just a minute," Sanderson called.

Over the crescendo of rainfall, they could hear the noise of the Daimler's engine being started and the screech of tyres as it made a hurried departure.

"Christ's sake," Sanderson cursed. "John, Cyril, stay with this lot. They're going nowhere. You with me!" he bellowed to the last uniformed officer who'd come in with him and dashed out of the door.

"Why the Hell did those two dash off?" Barton queried.

"They've taken my bloody car too." Victor Robinson looked genuinely annoyed.

"Not a good day for you then," Barton said.

"Could say the same for you," David Robinson quipped.

"I've got an idea why," Cyril put to Barton.

*   *   *

Sanderson jumped into his car, gunned the engine and raced off in the direction of the town centre, the PC in the passenger seat.

"Radio in for back up." He leaned forward to see through the windscreen, the wipers struggling with the monsoon that appeared to be falling from the sky. "Tell control we're in pursuit of a grey Daimler being driven at speed up Hythe Hill in the direction of the town centre."

Sanderson wasn't keen to pursue them at high speed. As well as the heavy rain, this was a built-up area, the road was narrow with cars parked on either side. On top of that, it was a lorry route to the quayside. But when he got to the Town railway station, he was in for a surprise.

The Daimler had obviously made the mistake of attempting to cut up two army vehicles on their way from the barracks with numerous squaddies on board. Marshall and the driver were being hauled from the car and it looked like the soldiers were about to take matters into their own hands.

Sanderson skidded to a halt just as the rain eased. He and the uniformed constable jumped out. "Thank you gentlemen," he said, holding out his warrant card. "If you could just restrain yourselves and hold onto these two for us for a minute."

*　*　*

"What do you mean, Cyril?" Barton asked.

Once again Cyril walked down the side of the van away from the Robinsons' gaze. The three remaining PCs kept watch on the brothers. Lennie King stood by the van cab, hands in his pockets.

"Those old Jags, or Daimler in this case," Cyril began, "are favoured by villains for a number of reasons. One, is they're fast, but the other advantage is that they have voids behind the sills. Very useful place to keep a shotgun."

"Come on officers," Victor bleated. "Is there any chance we can get these flowers back onto the van? This is an expensive cargo."

Barton looked cheered up. "Not until all these boxes have been checked by forensics." He walked back to the rear of the van and surveyed the dozens of cardboard boxes strewn all over the concrete. "Who knows, you may be smuggling drugs in them."

David turned on his brother, "This is all your bloody fault," he scowled and paced the floor. "And as for that tosser you brought in to drive the van ..."

Barton pulled out his radio, stepped into the street and called Sanderson.

* * *

Sanderson concluded the radio conversation with Barton, walked over to his car, opened the glovebox and pulled out a pair of gloves. He approached the Daimler and crouched down on the driver's side. Feeling behind the sill, he could detect nothing untoward. As he walked round to the passenger side to do the same, he caught the concerned look on Marshall's face. This time, he detected the outline of something hidden behind. "Ah ha," he said. Dropping to both knees and using both hands, he gave the object a shake and a twist. Finally, something came loose. From beneath the vehicle, as if producing a rabbit from a hat, he stood up with a sawn-off shotgun in his hands.

"Well, well, well, Mr Marshall. Is this what you were expecting I might find?" Sanderson held up the gun.

"Never seen it before," Marshall said, none too convincingly.

A couple of the soldiers smirked as the DCI and the PC handcuffed Marshall and the driver, took them back to Sanderson's car and pushed them into the back seat. Sanderson then radioed for transport to take the prisoners.

65

Clacton Police Station was witnessing one of the busiest days in its history. Certainly not since the pitch battles through the town and on the beaches between the Mods and the Rockers back in '64 had the accommodation been so full.

The warehouse in Colchester had been sealed off as a crime scene and a team of forensics officers were working their way systematically through the building, some on the upper floors, others checking the van and its cargo.

Cyril had refused to leave until a patrol vehicle arrived to take the Robinson brothers and Lennie King separately, back to Clacton. He'd then taken Barton up to the first floor of the warehouse and shown him the workbench and the roll of industrial plastic. On up to the second floor, he told him about two of the rooms they suspected of being the site of the killings.

Barton finally persuaded Cyril to go to Clacton Hospital to have his head wound attended to. He and Walker stayed at the warehouse along with a couple of the uniforms until the forensics team arrived whilst Sam Woodbridge drove Cyril back to Clacton in the Transit van.

Victor and David Robinson were being held in separate interview rooms. Their solicitor had been called but had yet to arrive.

Walter Yardley was safely ensconced in another cell, dressed in a tracksuit, having given up his clothes for forensic analysis, the hand gun sealed in an evidence bag. Sanderson had no doubts it would be connected to the bullet they'd recovered from Jimmy Morgan.

The DCI had brought Marshall and the driver, a known villain by the name of Eddie Thompson, back to the station. They seemed relieved to have been rescued from the angry squaddies. They were in separate cells downstairs. The Daimler was being taken to a police garage in Colchester for forensic examination.

For appearances and possibly for his own protection, Lennie King was in another cell.

Up in the CID room, Sanderson was about to allocate who would conduct the various interviews when Detective Chief Superintendent Viney stormed in.

"Martin. A word now," Viney said, turned and left the room as quickly as he'd entered.

Sanderson followed him along the corridor to his office.

"What the Hell's going on?" Viney exploded as soon as the door was closed. "I have to hear about our big operation from some pompous arse in Colchester." Five feet eight with dark hair around a bald dome, he was two years away from his retirement age of fifty-five.

"I did try and contact you, Sir but I understood you were on the golf course," Sanderson replied calmly.

"But I wasn't on the golf course when Barton disappeared to Holland though, was I?" Viney was up close to Sanderson, staring hard.

"It was one of those fluid situations. We had to act quickly."

"And now I hear you've arrested Walter Yardley."

"That's correct Sir. He held a hand gun to DI Barton and assaulted Sgt Claydon. We also suspect he was involved in the murder of James Morgan, the corpse discovered in Yardley's crashed plane."

"You have evidence to support this?"

"Witnesses to the assault, including myself ..."

"I'm not talking about that, man. I mean the bloody murder."

"We're awaiting ballistic test results on his gun but I believe it will prove a match for the bullet we recovered from the body, Sir."

Viney seemed to deflate. "Christ, this is going to send shock waves. He was good friends with the ACC as well, you know."

Sanderson was encouraged. "What about yourself Sir? I mean you're practically neighbours in Frinton."

Viney's look hardened. "We may live in the same town and I believe he belongs to the tennis club, but we're not friends. There is no connection between us."

"Of course not, Sir."

Viney chose to ignore the last comment. "And you have the Robinson brothers in custody too?"

"We need to question them, yes."

Viney gave an ironic chuckle. "Have you formulated a strategy? Who's interviewing who?"

"I was just about to address the team on that, Sir."

"Best get on with it then. I'll have to speak with the ACC of course."

As Viney lifted the handset, Sanderson left the office and closed the door.

* * *

"Try and keep your head away from any more bumps, Mr Claydon," the doctor had said as he finished the dressing and removed his surgical gloves.

"Easier said than done, doctor."

Feeling obvious, with a white bandage protecting the doctor's fresh handiwork, Cyril returned to the waiting area. This was the second time in three days he'd had his head wound stitched.

A familiar figure stood up to greet him, a look of concern on her face.

"Hello," he said. "Are you here to see a doctor?"

She grinned. "No, you fool, I came to see how you were." Cathy Rogers studied his head. "That looks a neat job."

"They tell me it shouldn't scar ... well hopefully not."

She looked serious. "Sam told me what had happened. I'm sorry, Cyril. There's me giving you the cold shoulder and all the time …" she began to laugh.

He smiled. "What's so funny?"

"Sorry, it's just me, take no notice. It's just … well, Sam told me you were trapped in that van, with the chiller on, so you'd have had more than a cold shoulder in there." She held his gaze for a second before he also burst into laughter.

"So am I forgiven for not turning up when I said I would?"

She made a face. "Well … depends how you'll make it up to me."

There was an awkward pause before Cyril looked at his watch. "Look, I'll need to get back and find out what's been happening while I've been in here with my feet up."

"Of course," she said. "I need to get back too. I only nipped across on my break."

"I'll walk with you," he said and began to make his way out of the department.

She followed suit but began to talk. "I just need … I want to call in at a shop on the way. The others … they wanted …"

He stopped and faced her. "That's okay, Cathy. You do what you have to for your colleagues. I'll head back but look, when this has settled, do you still want to go to Dedham?"

She nodded and beamed at him. "If that's okay with you?"

"Of course it is." Another pause then, "I'll see you back there and … thanks for your concern." He smiled, turned away and disappeared through the doors.

* * *

Cyril walked back into the CID room just as Sanderson was resuming his briefing to the team. When the group saw him, a loud cheer broke out. He felt embarrassed.

Barton, who had returned just before him, came over. "What are you doing back," he said quietly. "You need to rest up."

"It's only a flesh wound." His hand went to the bandage.

"Come and sit down, Cyril," Sanderson said. "I was just bringing everyone up to speed with where we are and how we're going to take this forward."

Cyril spotted Sam and sat next to him.

"So," Sanderson continued. "Now you're back with us Cyril, you and DI Barton, I want you to interview Yardley. Myself and Miller will tackle the Robinsons." He paused to look round the room. "As for Marshall and Thompson, well, we'll let them stew for a while. The rest of you this will be your priorities ..." The DCI proceeded to allocate tasks to the assembled officers.

Woodbridge turned to Cyril and whispered, "Thanks for the tip with Yardley. It was a good collar for me." He was grinning.

"Just a hunch. I thought we'd best cover all the bases. Glad it worked."

Sam leaned in closer. "Did Cathy find you?"

He turned to his young colleague. "Yes, Sam. She did."

Sam smiled and faced the front once more. "Good," he said. "One good turn ..."

66

"So what are you going to do now, Lennie?" Cyril asked.

Barton, Cyril and King were standing in Barton's office. They'd brought him up from the cells before any of the other characters were to be questioned.

"I've got a sister in Nottingham," King replied. "I thought I'd go there."

"You'll need to keep your head down for a bit. The Robinsons will know you had something to do with that raid."

"I know." King thrust his hands deep in his trouser pockets. "But first, I need to see DCI Holt too. He'll want a statement from me before I disappear. I'll get my things together and catch the train this afternoon."

Barton offered a hand. "I admit I was suspicious of you at first."

King shook it.

"But Cyril here always had confidence."

King looked to the DS. "Thanks Mr Claydon."

"I'll see you out." Cyril led the way downstairs. He paused by the main doors. "Take care of yourself, Lennie," he said.

"You too," King replied, shook Cyril's offered hand and patted his arm.

Cyril returned to Barton's office and lit up a replacement pipe. He needed a smoke after all that had happened.

"How did you know to send Woodbridge and the other lad round to the front entrance of Yardley's offices?" Barton flicked ash from his cigarette into the Guinness ashtray on the desk, no doubt purloined from some drunken pub crawl.

"I just had a feeling Yardley might show up," he said. "And if he did, he might want to make a quick exit when we showed our hand. I knew he was in the offices when we arrived, I spotted his car outside. And the obvious escape route."

"You're wasted in uniform," Barton responded. He took a last draw on his cigarette before stubbing it out. Exhaling hard, he went on, "I'm going to let you take the lead on this."

Cyril said nothing, surprised at what sounded like praise from the DI who had once admitted, not that long ago, that he was 'an obnoxious arrogant twat'.

"I think you'll have more luck getting him to open up," Barton continued. "I heard what you were saying to him in the warehouse."

Walter Yardley cut a pathetic figure sitting on a chair, dressed in a borrowed tracksuit. He was hunched over the table as if to make himself as small as possible. He barely looked up as Cyril and Barton entered the interview room.

Barton gave a curt nod to the uniformed PC in attendance, who quietly left, closing the door behind him.

The detectives sat down opposite, Cyril placing a large brown envelope on the floor at his feet.

"Well, Mr Yardley," Cyril began. "This is a fine mess you've gotten yourself into."

Yardley merely grunted.

"Mr Yardley ... Walter," Cyril began in soft tones, "We need to talk."

Slowly Yardley raised his head. His eyes were red-rimmed and his face was ashen. He looked ten years older. "What do you want to know?" he said.

Cyril flicked open a notebook and began to take notes. "Earlier today, at the warehouse your company owns, you were in attendance when a van belonging to the Holland Flower Company entered the building. What can you tell me about that?"

Yardley shrugged. "Victor and David use that. They import flowers from Holland."

"But why were you there, Walter?"

"Just checking on things."

"So you weren't involved in the Robinsons' operations?"

"No."

Cyril bent down and rummaged in the envelope he'd brought with him, pulled out a small clear plastic bag and placed it on the table. "We found you in possession of these," he said. "We believe these to be diamonds that you brought into this country illegally."

Another shrug. "Then you know it all."

"You were about to sell these to Victor and David Robinson, weren't you?"

Again another shrug but no response.

Barton jumped up out of his seat. "Answer the fucking question!" he yelled.

Yardley jolted backwards, expecting Barton to reach across and grab him.

Cyril thought he might do too and put up a hand. "As DI Barton says, you do need to answer our questions," he continued calmly, casting a quick glance to the DI.

Barton subsided into his chair.

Yardley leaned back and rolled his eyes to the ceiling, tears forming. "It's all gone wrong," he said, rubbing his face. "All I was trying to do was keep the company afloat." With his head level once again, he looked directly at Cyril. "My father started that company in 1927. Next year and we'd have been celebrating fifty years. Ha." He gave an ironic laugh. "Except we won't make it."

"And you've put your house in Frinton up as collateral." Cyril pitched it as a statement rather than a question.

Yardley nodded.

"Where did these stones come from?"

"Old comrades. People I've known, in Holland, since the war."

"But not legitimate sources. Otherwise there would be no profit in them, would there?"

Yardley nodded.

"So you were fencing them to the Robinsons."

Again another nod.

"Tell me about Jimmy Morgan?" Cyril asked.

A brief surprised look swept over Yardley's face at the change of focus. "What about him?"

"He worked for you, didn't he?"

"Did a bit of casual driving. Local deliveries and such."

Cyril flicked back a few pages of his notebook. "This morning in the warehouse you said, 'He deceived me. You don't do that to people who've given you a chance'. What did you mean by that?"

"I'd given him a start ... a job. He came to me looking for work. Ex-army from the war, I thought I'd give him a break."

"But how did he deceive you?"

"He talked. About the diamond plan."

"How do you know that?"

Yardley looked down at his hands. "I just heard."

"And then you said ..." Cyril made a point of finding the exact quote he'd written. "'I dealt with it properly.' How did you deal with it, Walter?"

"I don't know."

"You don't know!" Barton stood up again, so violently, his chair tipped backwards across the floor. "You don't fucking know! You shot the poor bastard, didn't you?" He was leaning forward, both hands on the table, face about a foot away from Yardley's. "I'm not going to piss about like DS Claydon. You need to start telling us the truth. You're in deep shit here. The only chance you have is telling us what happened. And if ... if that fits with the forensic evidence, then we might be able to help you. Do you understand?"

In a quiet voice, Cyril added, "DI Barton's right, Walter. You see, from where we're sitting, the gun you hit me on the head with, and I'm a bit mad about that ..."

"I'm sorry, Mr Claydon."

"That gun will be tested at our ballistics lab. And I'm willing to bet that we can match it to the gun that fired the bullet we collected from Jimmy Morgan's skull."

This time, the tears flowed from Yardley. "Oh God," he said. "I didn't mean to. It's just … he made me mad … I was frightened he would spoil the plan."

"Just to be clear Mr Yardley," Cyril said in measured tones, "are you admitting shooting James Morgan?"

The formal use of Yardley's name wasn't lost on Barton.

"Yes," Yardley said, "But I didn't mean to do it. I just got angry."

"And for the record, Mr Yardley, where exactly did you murder James Morgan?"

"In the warehouse. Second floor. There are some rooms. I asked him to help me with something."

"You lured him?"

Yardley nodded. "I suppose."

Barton stood up once again but in a deliberate fashion this time. "Walter Yardley, I'm arresting you on suspicion of the murder of James Morgan." He then proceeded to issue the standard caution.

With the PC back in the room, Barton leaned against the wall of the corridor outside. "You did well in there, Cyril," he said.

"Good cop, bad cop," Cyril smiled. "I did think you were going to smack him at one point. And that wouldn't have helped."

Barton laughed. "It was tempting, I must admit, but you were getting through to him. I just thought I needed to focus his mind."

They began to walk down the corridor. "Come on," Barton said, "I think we need some refreshment."

67

Cyril and Barton sat in the canteen, both with mugs of tea, Barton with a plate of chips and Cyril with a ham sandwich. They were just finishing eating when Sanderson came in and walked over to them.

"Tea, Sir?" Barton offered.

"Thanks John, I need one." Sanderson sat in a vacant chair.

As Barton went off for the DCI's drink, Cyril drained his mug and leaned across. "How'd it go with the Robinson boys?"

Sanderson shook his head. "As you'd expect, denied any involvement in anything. They're running a legit business importing flowers and know nothing about any plans to buy diamonds from Yardley. Reckon he's a fantasist."

"And, of course, totally surprised we would even consider they were smuggling porn." Cyril took out his pipe and tobacco and began to fill it.

Barton returned with a drink for his DCI. Before he could ask for an update, the desk sergeant popped his head into the canteen and sought out Sanderson.

"Phone call for you, Sir," the sergeant announced.

A few minutes later, after Cyril had told Barton what Sanderson had said, the DCI returned and joined them at the table and took a swig of his tea.

With a serious look on his face, he addressed Cyril. "You told me when you were on the ferry coming back from Holland, you overheard DS Gray on the phone to someone."

"That's right," he said, puffing on his pipe and waving the smoke clear. "Is it important?"

"It might be," Sanderson said. "I'd like you to complete a statement form, and try to remember what you heard in as much detail as possible."

"Trouble?" Barton joined in.

"This DCI Holt from the Met is coming down to see us in the morning."

"Oh great," Barton sighed. "Will he be making sure his precious Robinson brothers walk away?"

"Actually John, you probably couldn't be more wrong. I told you of his suspicions during that first conversation we had when you were on the ferry."

"You did," Barton agreed.

"And thinking about things, I'd also like you to give as full an account as possible of your time on the ferry going over to Holland."

Barton looked from the DCI to Cyril and back again.

Cyril merely raised his eyebrows in acknowledgement.

* * *

"You know where this is going, don't you, Cyril?" Barton had paused in his writing to light up another cigarette.

Cyril had come into his office with his completed statement in his hand. The fact that Barton was now consulting him wasn't lost. No doubt about it, Barton's attitude towards him had mellowed. "I'm not exactly sure," he replied, "but I think there's a smell beginning to pervade all this."

"You mean the shit's about to hit the fan."

"Something like that." Cyril sat down opposite the DI. "Why do you think he wanted a statement from me about my overheard conversation on board?"

"Why do you think? I've concentrated on certain aspects of the journey myself."

"Times spent with DS Gray?"

Barton nodded. "He thinks he's bent."

DCI Sanderson gave a polite knock and swept into Barton's office. "All done?" he asked.

Cyril held up his statement.

"Just reading through mine Sir, then I'll sign it," Barton replied.

"Good." Sanderson remained standing. "Yardley has asked to see his wife, Edith. At the moment, I'm not prepared to do that. I'm just waiting on a warrant for his house in Frinton. I'd like to conduct a search there before we allow any contact."

"What about the Electrical Factory?" Cyril wondered.

"First thing in the morning." Sanderson studied them for a moment. "Look you two, get yourself off home and get some rest. You've put enough in today. Get in for seven and we'll sort out the searches when we get those warrants. Our guests can enjoy some hospitality in our luxury accommodation tonight and we can resume in the morning. By that time, we might have some initial findings from the forensics."

68

"Good God, Cyril, what have you done now." Doris fussed around when she opened her front door to him. "It looks worse than ever." She stared at his head.

"It looks worse than it is, Doris, that's what it does. Anyway, I'll be fine with a good night's sleep."

Charlie came lumbering up, wondering what all the fuss was about, only interested in getting some attention from his master.

Cyril rubbed the dog's head. He'd come to collect him and take him home; Doris had looked after him yet again.

"Come in. I'll cook you something," Doris persisted. "You need a good meal after all you've been through."

"I'll be fine. I've got something in," he lied.

"You had some greasy fish and chips last night, that's no good," Doris nagged. "Charlie told me." She chuckled as she saw Cyril's puzzled expression. "Okay, so Big Pete told me you were in. I saw him this morning."

"I will get something healthy tonight, I promise. And after a good night's rest. I'll be fine."

"You will, but you're coming in. I'll sort something for you." She held the door wide.

"It's okay, Doris. I'll …"

"No buts Cyril Claydon. I'm cooking you something decent to eat. You look too tired to do it yourself. And I don't trust that you will. What would Maureen say?"

Cyril held up both hands. "All right. I give in."

As she fussed around in the kitchen, Cyril sat in a comfortable armchair in Doris's front room, looking at, but not really watching the television.

Charlie was in the kitchen with her, munching his way through a bowl of dog biscuits.

Shortly afterwards, tantalising aromas were emerging from the kitchen.

"I hope you're not going to a load of trouble out there," he said.

"I can always knock up a meal. We didn't survive the war without being able to do that," she shouted back.

A smile grew on Cyril's face. After a long day with too much going on, it was pleasant to sit and relax and have someone else make a fuss. He just wanted to clear his mind of all the awful sights he'd witnessed over the past couple of weeks. The plane crash; both corpses, the workbench in the warehouse, then the rooms on the top floor.

He closed his eyes and put his hand to his head, gently touching the wound site.

"Leave that alone," she said.

He opened his eyes to see her standing in the doorway.

"Come and get this while it's hot."

As he stood up out of the chair and followed her to the kitchen, his legs felt stiff. The day's events had certainly taken their toll.

True to her word, Doris had cobbled together a tasty dish with vegetables and a tin of corned beef. Through the course of the meal, she never asked about the events of Cyril's day, concentrating conversation about her and Charlie, the weather finally breaking and some comments about the mess the politicians were making.

"You go and put your feet up now, Doris," Cyril said, collecting the plates to the sink. "I'll wash up."

"No you won't," she insisted with a fake temper. "You're my guest. Sit down next door and watch some telly."

"At least let me …"

"Go! Get out of my kitchen." Doris had a smile on her face.

Admitting defeat, not least because of the fatigue he was feeling, he returned to the living room and switched the TV back on. Another episode of the new series, *The*

Sweeney was starting. That reminded him of his meeting earlier with Jack Finnegan, the Butlin's chef who'd seen a big Daimler at the lane end to the airstrip on the morning of the crash. He tried to recall the scant descriptions he gave. He didn't think they matched the Robinson brothers, but could the two figures he saw sitting inside have been Marshall and Thompson?

The raised voices of John Thaw and Denis Waterman flooded over him and interrupted his thought patterns. God, he was tired. The last thing he could remember was Jack Regan announcing, *'You're nicked.'*

The Lancaster makes its catastrophic landing. The initial fireball rises into the early morning sky then clears. Cyril looks at Brian in the cockpit. The cover slides back and his friend, with arms on either side, pushes himself up from the confined space. But below his chest there is nothing. Brian looks straight at him, waves a hand in acknowledgement then fades from view.

Cyril tries to move his legs but his feet seem to be stuck fast. He looks down and sees water up to his knees. He looks round then sees a familiar floral dress and a pair of shapely legs.

He hears a voice, Maureen's voice, but he can't see her. "It's okay, Cyril. Time to move on. Go on, love. Go on."

* * *

Barton closed the flat door behind him and leaned against it for a second. He was tired. It had been a long day; a frustrating day. But not just physically. He was tired of this place. Tired of waking up with women he could hardly remember, like that old tart on Saturday morning.

He sniffed the air, then walked through to the kitchen. The smell was stronger in there. The bin. Shit, he meant to take it out on Monday but he'd forgotten. Missed the rubbish collection on Tuesday too. He bent down and opened the cupboard below the sink and pulled the bin out. He nearly gagged. Left over take-away from Friday night. Tying the bin liner up, he held his breath then took it outside and downstairs to the metal dustbin.

He was sorely tempted to go for a beer, but he knew what would happen. He'd have a few then migrate to a club and pull some bird and either go back to hers or bring her back here for another round of unsatisfactory sex. For a split second, he almost gave in. No, he decided, now he'd made a token start, why not see how long he could keep going and tidy the place up.

As he walked back up to his flat, he thought of Cyril. Funny old bugger. But straight as a die and with standards; surely no bad thing. And he'd taken one for him this afternoon in that warehouse. He smiled to himself as he thought of him sticking the end of his pipe in Yardley's ribs, pretending it was a gun; like some schoolboy game of cowboys and Indians.

Running hot water into the kitchen sink and piling in dirty dishes, he couldn't stop smiling to himself.

Cyril had done a competent job interviewing Yardley too. He'd have ended up grabbing hold of him but Cyril had achieved the required result with a gentle approach. He might try that himself at some point. Then again, maybe not.

He was surprised when an hour later he surveyed his accommodation and found it to be the tidiest he could remember in ages. Finally collapsing on the bed fully clothed, he drifted off within seconds.

* * *

Cyril turned over and tried to move his arm. He could feel nothing. Panic woke him from his sleep. He was confused. An orange glow from a streetlamp filtered in through unfamiliar curtains. Then he realised he was sitting in an armchair, a blanket over him. Of course, this was Doris's living room. A weird snorting and whistling noise came from somewhere near his feet. He looked down and made out Charlie's bulk, paws pounding over some dream-filled field, chasing rabbits no doubt.

The clock ticked on the mantelpiece and he squinted to see it showing a quarter past twelve. The rest of the house was quiet.

He stretched and stood up. Immediately, Charlie stirred, rolled over and struggled to his feet. "Come on, lad," Cyril said, "Let's get back to our own bed, eh?"

He quietly opened Doris's front door, let Charlie out then closed it behind them. Charlie turned left instead of right and waddled over to a lamp post. Cyril looked up at the light rain drifting past in the lamplight then decided to take him for a quick walk around the block before home.

69
Thursday 9th September

Sanderson held out a hand to the visitor. "DCI Holt, good to meet you at last," he said.

Holt looked to be in his mid-forties with curly dark hair and sideburns. "Simon, call me Simon." He smiled grimly and indicated the younger man with him. "And this is DS Morley."

His colleague standing slightly behind and holding a briefcase nodded a greeting then shook Sanderson's offered hand.

"Martin," Sanderson reciprocated. "My office is upstairs."

Door closed, all seated around the DCI's desk, Holt began. "As I indicated on the phone yesterday, this is a serious situation, Martin."

"We've been wondering about information leaking out for some time," Sanderson responded, "but ..."

"Did you obtain statements from your officers?"

Sanderson held out a sheaf of papers. "Got them here."

Holt took them and began to study the accounts Cyril and Barton had written the day before. As he read, he nodded at certain points. "This ties in with other evidence we've been gathering," he said once he'd finished.

Sanderson sighed deeply. "So what are your next moves?"

Holt glanced at his watch as he stood up. "Off to Harwich and make an arrest." He took the briefcase from Morley, placed the paperwork inside and handed it back to his DS.

Sanderson also got to his feet. "You don't want to interview the Robinson brothers?"

Holt shook his head. "No need. They'll be clean as a whistle. They knew all about your DI Barton taking the van to Holland and would have aborted that shipment. There'll be another time. Hopefully, sooner rather than later with this one off the field." He indicated the briefcase then held out his hand to Sanderson. "Thanks Martin," he said.

Sanderson shook it once more. "You will protect Lennie King, won't you? He asked. "My men couldn't have pulled this off without his help."

"Nor me," Holt agreed. "I'll do everything I possibly can."

Sanderson walked with the two Met officers back to the main entrance.

As they departed, Barton pulled in to the car park. Sanderson waited for him to approach.

"Is that who I think it is?" Barton asked, jettisoning his cigarette into a puddle.

"Holt, yes." Sanderson turned and led the way inside. "How did you get on?"

"As we thought, something fairly grisly happened on that upper floor." Barton had spent the first half of the morning at the Colchester warehouse. "The forensic boys are loving it; best they've had to deal with in ages." A broad smile on his face as they climbed the stairs.

"Come into the office and tell me what you know."

Barton sat down opposite his DCI and flicked open his notebook. "Okay," he began, "First off, the workbench on the first floor; confirmed as human blood there. They're running ABO blood grouping tests back in the lab." He flicked over some pages to the notes he'd taken during Morgan's post-mortem. "We know Morgan was A positive which is reasonably common, maybe about 30% of the population, but there were at least two other blood types present on that bench, so they told me."

Sanderson was thoughtful. "So there were at least three people who bled on there? Three victims?"

"Could be. We think Fletcher was on his third mission out to sea."

303

"What about the top floor?" Sanderson shuddered at the memory of what he and Cyril had seen when they'd visited two days before. "Cyril showed you, didn't he?"

"He did." A grim expression on his face, Barton reported, "Two rooms which showed evidence of violence. The third room along was the worst. Not only blood and brain matter on the brick wall but human hair and other fibres too. They're going to see if they can match any of that with what remains of our second corpse's head. They also recovered lead shot from the wall. That will be checked for shape and chemical composition."

"Any indication how long all this is going to take?"

"Weeks. Unless …"

"I'll see what we can do to speed things up." Sanderson reached out to pick up the telephone.

"So what's the deal with DCI Holt, Sir?" Barton asked.

Sanderson paused and pulled his hand away. "It's as you thought. They've gone off to Harwich to arrest DS Gray. Apparently, with yours and Cyril's evidence, combined with other things, it would appear that he's been on the Robinsons' payroll."

"The little shit. No wonder he was …" Barton thought back. "D'you remember when we first went into that office with Crimond? It was Gray who quickly pulled up the paperwork for the van."

Sanderson nodded knowingly. "And it was him who pointed out that the ferry had slipped its moorings."

"Not to mention making sure he was available to come with us."

Sanderson suddenly stood up. "Is Cyril in yet?" he wondered.

"Don't know, Sir." Barton got to his feet as well. "I came straight up with you."

"When you find him, I'd like the pair of you to interview Marshall then Thompson." He walked round the desk and opened the door. "Squeeze what you can out of the buggers. I'm off to see the Super. See if he can put some pressure on the lab to get some quicker results."

* * *

Cyril walked over to his desk and sifted through the messages that had been left there. As he did so, his attention was drawn to Walker who was talking on the phone.

Barton appeared at that moment. "Ah Cyril, I'd like to …" He stopped as Cyril put up a hand and nodded towards Walker. Both men remained silent as the young DC concluded his call.

"That's great," he said. "Well thanks for getting back to me. And if you could send that down to us … for my attention yes. Thank you very much." Walker replaced the receiver, a huge smile on his face. "Yes," he said punching the air.

"Good news then DC Walker," Barton said.

"You could say that, Sir."

"Tell us all about it then," he said making for his office.

"That was the records clerk at Glasgow Royal Infirmary," Walker began once all three were in Barton's office. "and you'll never guess who had their leg plated and set with that piece of metalwork?"

"I think I can guess," Cyril said.

"Go on," Barton encouraged.

"One Douglas Chalmers."

"Makes sense now you say it," Cyril added. "The guy hasn't been seen for four weeks; all his clothes left in his room and …" he rubbed his moustache in thought, "last seen in the company of our friend downstairs, Tommy Marshall."

Barton tensed. "Was he? I didn't know that." He turned his attention to Walker. "Listen Bill, that was good work. Thanks."

Walker seemed to colour. "Thank you, Sir," he said and returned to his desk.

"I'm impressed," Cyril said.

"No, I think he's showing signs," Barton nodded.

"Not him. I always knew he was bright. I mean you. That trip to Holland must have done you good."

Barton looked puzzled.

"When I first got involved here, you would never have given the lad any praise. What was it you called them, Bill and Ben, the Flowerpot Men."

Barton leaned forward on his desk. "Don't you bloody think I'm going soft. But listen, that piece of information is timely. We're going to interview that big bastard Marshall, and I want you with me." Barton stood, picked up a folder and walked round the desk. "But I'll be taking the lead this time."

Barton arranged for Marshall to be brought from his cell to one of the interview rooms before he and Cyril went to the canteen. "Let the bastard sweat a bit," he said. "Meanwhile, you can tell me what you found out this morning over in Frinton."

Cyril got the teas in as Barton claimed a table in a corner away from anyone else and slapped the folder down in front of him.

"So what did you find?" Barton asked as Cyril set down the drinks on the table.

"Well Mrs Yardley was extremely upset. I don't think she had any idea what Walter had been up to."

"Genuine?" Barton sipped his tea, then rummaged in a pocket for his cigarettes.

"I think so. She looks a bit older than him. I'll bet she's been the dutiful wife at home, running the domestics and he's had himself a free rein." Cyril took a drink, then followed Barton's lead by producing his pipe and tobacco pouch.

"Anything of interest in the house?"

"Oh, yes." He wiped his moustache then packed some tobacco into the bowl. "Good job he gave us the safe combination, we could have been there all day."

Barton inhaled sharply and blew out smoke. "What was in there?"

"Well," Cyril paused to light his pipe, puffed and exhaled. "We found another bag of sparklers and, interestingly, about a dozen rounds of ammunition for his handgun."

"All off to the lab?"

"Yep. And we've seized some files he had in his study. Huge house it is on Second Avenue."

Barton frowned. "And that slimy toad Viney lives on Third." He drained his tea and took one last drag of his cigarette before stubbing it out. "Come on then, let battle commence."

Cyril groaned, knocked out his pipe and followed Barton.

Tommy Marshall was sitting at the table in the interview room, arms folded, legs crossed at the ankles, looking as though he was just enjoying a rest.

Barton strode in purposefully, Cyril in his wake. A curt nod to the uniformed PC who had been keeping Marshall under scrutiny was the sign for him to leave. The DI pulled out a chair, placed the manila file on the table and sat down. Cyril, more slowly, eased himself into the seat on Barton's right hand side.

Cyril, attention focussed on Marshall, folded his arms whilst Barton opened the folder and leafed through a few pages, all the while clicking a pen. He could tell Marshall was becoming irritated.

Finally, the man leaned forward onto the table and stared at Barton. "Well," he said. "Are you going to keep me here all fucking day as well? Or are you beginning to realise you've got fuck all on me." A smirk crept over his face.

Eventually, Barton looked up from the paperwork. "How much are the Robinsons paying you?" His face was set in a neutral expression. "I hope it's worth it."

Marshall folded his arms once again. "What? For driving a van load of flowers up to Covent Garden? It passes my time," he replied.

Barton nodded.

From his peripheral vision, Cyril could see he was working hard to stay calm.

"Ever heard of a man by the name of Douglas Chalmers?" Barton asked.

Marshall shook his head instantly. "No, can't say I have. Why, what's he done?"

"How about James Morgan?"

A grin now appeared on Marshall's face. "Never heard of him. Are you just going through a register of old lags, or is there a point to all this?"

"So you reckon they're old lags? I'm not so sure that's how I would describe those men. How about you DS Claydon?"

Cyril's eyes never left Marshall as he gave a slight shake of the head. "No, not me."

Barton closed the folder. "Why did you leave the scene in the warehouse yesterday?"

"I was concerned for my safety, wasn't I? I mean, that nutter with the gun." He looked over for the first time towards Cyril. "I mean, you were lucky there. He only hit you with it. You're bloody lucky he didn't shoot you."

"But you didn't just get out of the building. You drove off in the Robinsons' Daimler."

"Ah, well, that wasn't me. I never drove anywhere. It was Eddie Thompson who drove off. I was only sitting in the passenger seat. I mean, I was trying to talk him into stopping. I told him it would end bad, but he wouldn't listen."

Barton shook his head and lifted the cover of the folder again. "That was bad luck then," he said, letting it close once more. "You just happening to be *sitting* in the passenger seat."

"Well it was raining ..."

Barton cut him off. "When you were stopped, and as I understand it, it was lucky for you we came along when we did, you'd upset a load of squaddies." Barton cast a quick glance to Cyril then back to Marshall. "What can you tell me about the shotgun we found hidden in the sill of that car?"

"Nothing to do with me. I've never seen it before. I don't have nothing to do with guns."

"So can you explain how your dabs are on the stock?"

No doubt, that knocked Marshall off his stride for a moment. "Ah, well, now let me think ..."

"In your own time," Barton sniped.

"Yeah, I remember now, Eddie asked me to hold it a minute while he got down on his knees. I had to hand it to him so he could fit it behind the sill."

Barton shook his head, a slight smile on his face. "Let me get this straight, you're now telling me that you, who 'don't have nothing to do with guns' has suddenly remembered you helped your friend hide it in the car we stopped you in?"

Marshall held up both hands in mock surrender. "I forgot."

"What a load of bollocks." Barton leaned back. After a second or two, he continued, "Have you ever been on the upper floors of that warehouse?"

Slowly shaking his head, Marshall eventually responded, "No, can't say as I have."

Barton turned to Cyril. "You see, I'm worried now that Mr Marshall's memory might not be too sound."

Marshall leaned forward once more, a sneer on his face. "You taking the piss?"

Barton snapped back at him, "You fucking started it!" He held his stare until Marshall finally looked away. "So we shouldn't find your prints anywhere in that building then?"

Marshall folded his arms once more. "I'm sayin' no more."

"And you still maintain you don't know Douglas, or would you know him better as Dougie Chalmers?"

"Shove it up your arse."

Finally, Barton snapped, jumped up and grabbed him by the lapels. "You piece of shit," he said, "you did for him and we'll prove it. That'll wipe that smug look from your face."

Cyril remained unmoved.

Barton released his grip, shoved the man back into the chair and picked up the file. "In the meantime, you're going nowhere." He turned and left the room, Cyril following and the uniform coming back in. "Take the prisoner back down," he said, "We're far from finished."

70

"I thought you were going to intervene," Barton said, reaching for the cigarette packet on his desk.

"Now why would I do that?" Cyril crossed his legs as he sat opposite.

"You're not so keen on giving a bit of stick in interviews." Barton lit up.

"There's a time and a place, and he was certainly asking for a slap. But you've got to know who to give a bit to. Not everybody will respond how you want." Cyril sat normally and leaned forward, making his point. "Yardley for instance, he's just a broken man. Now all this has surfaced, I can see him telling us all we want to know."

Barton drew on his cigarette, smiled and blew out smoke as he spoke. "You're a canny old bugger, aren't you?"

Cyril remained silent.

"I can see why Sanderson thought you were a good man to bring in."

Cyril shrugged. "You needed bodies and I was on hand. And I'd witnessed the crash."

"Ah, talking of which ..." Barton said looking through the glazed door.

Sanderson entered, looking serious. "I've had to release the Robinson brothers on bail. Their smarmy git lawyer turned up this morning. And basically, we've got nothing on them. Well not yet anyway."

"Bastards," Barton said, under his breath.

"Just hope forensics find something. In the meantime, their solicitor has had a word with Thompson and Marshall as well."

"And we've let him?" Barton blustered.

"I can't stop them seeing a solicitor, John. Anyway, he's gone now, he was driving Victor and David away a few minutes ago." Sanderson walked away.

Barton looked at his watch. "Okay," he said, "Let's get Thompson up from the cells in fifteen minutes and I think you should lead on his interview."

"Sure?"

Barton nodded. "I want to see what method you think will work with him."

Cyril stood. "I'll fetch his file and see you downstairs."

He'd studied the file of Edward Michael Thompson, Eddie as he was commonly known, and learned a bit about his background and criminal record. He was sixty-three and had been an associate of Frank Robinson since before the war. He'd managed to secure himself a reserved occupation as a dock worker during the hostilities; handy for Robinson and his scams but not exactly a holiday with the German bombing raids in London.

Cyril watched from along the corridor as Thompson was brought up to the interview room. He didn't think he looked a well man.

As he flicked through Thompson's file one more time, Cathy Rogers walked down the corridor towards him. Her face lit up in a smile when she saw him.

"How's the head?" she stopped to enquire.

"Better now after a good night's sleep."

"I hear you're all busy with yesterday's activities?"

He nodded, smiling. "Just about to interview another one."

She stood for a second and there was an awkward pause.

"Listen," he began to say, "I was wondering ..."

"Yes."

"Ready Cyril," Barton boomed as he rounded the corner and spotted him.

"Catch up with you later," Cyril said quietly.

"Okay," Cathy said, walking away as Barton approached, totally ignoring her.

"What have you learned?" Barton indicated the file in Cyril's hands. "Any weak points?"

"We'll see," he considered thoughtfully before opening the door to the interview room.

Cyril took the seat opposite Thompson this time, with Barton sitting alongside. The constable left them to it.

Cyril introduced himself and Barton before commencing the interview. "Mr Thompson, Eddie," he said, "why did you flee the scene yesterday?"

Thompson lifted his head, looked from Cyril to Barton and back again before answering. "Tommy wanted to get out." Head down once more.

"He got out. But that doesn't explain why you drove him away in the car."

"He told me to."

"And do you always do what Tommy Marshall tells you?"

Thompson gave a shrug. "Have you tried not to?" He looked up. "Sorry, of course not, you're police."

"So Thompson has a hold over you?"

"Put it this way, he's not the sort of man to argue with. It was just easier to drive."

"What do you know about a sawn-off shotgun found in the car you were driving yesterday?"

"Nothing much"

"So you didn't conceal it?"

"No."

"Who did? Victor Robinson? David Robinson? Maybe Tommy Marshall?"

"I don't know."

"Funny that, because Mr Marshall claims it was yours."

"He would."

"Come on Eddie, give us something to work with."

Finally, Thompson appeared to take things seriously. He leaned forward onto the table and looked straight at Cyril. "Whose prints did you find on the gun? I'll bet it wasn't mine. In fact, I'd hazard a guess that you found Tommy's."

313

Cyril leaned back, stroking his moustache. "And how would you know that?"

"Just a guess."

Cyril took a breath. "How many times have you been at that warehouse?"

"I've driven Victor and David there maybe five or six times."

"With Mr Marshall?"

"On two or three occasions."

"Ever been on the upper floors?"

A slight look of alarm passed over Thompson's face. "Can't say as I have," he answered after a brief pause.

"So we wouldn't find your fingerprints up there?"

"Well … maybe … I might have been upstairs once."

"Know a man by the name of James Morgan? Jimmy?"

"No … not sure."

"I'm surprised, because he drove the flower van back from Holland a couple of times. And if you'd taken the Robinson boys there to meet it, like you did today, you'd have met him."

Thompson gave an impression of a lightbulb going on in his brain. "Short bloke in his fifties, thinning fair hair. Was that him? I never knew his name."

Cyril looked to Barton then refocussed on the man in front of him. "So how about Douglas Chalmers?"

Again a flicker of something crossed his face but Thompson shook his head. "No idea."

Cyril left a pause and hoped Barton wouldn't jump in. Fortunately, he just sat back in his chair, relaxed.

Cyril opened the file. "How long have you worked for Frank Robinson?"

Thompson sucked in air. "Ooh, since about 1935."

"A long time then. Over forty years. All through the war, in fact."

"I had a reserved occupation."

Cyril nodded. "In the docks, I know. Handy for someone like Robinson."

"Don't know what you mean."

314

"So you'd feel a sense of great loyalty to Mr Robinson. I suppose you could say you helped his businesses develop?"

"What are you trying to say?"

"And you probably have that same sense of loyalty for his boys, Victor and David?"

"Watched them grow up."

"Looked out for them, probably?"

"Probably."

Cyril leaned in closer. "But I don't suppose you could ever feel that deep loyalty for Tommy Marshall?"

Thompson let out a gasp. "You must be joking."

"So why do you protect him, Eddie? A man who tells us that you owned that shotgun; it was you who secreted it in the car."

"No! No way."

"And it was you who was responsible for what happened to Jimmy Morgan and Dougie Chalmers."

"The lyin' bastard, it was nothing to do with me, it was all his ... hang on, he hasn't said that at all, has he?"

Cyril turned to Barton who, for the first time seemed to take an interest in the conversation. "It's true, Eddie. Marshall is hanging you out to dry," the DI confirmed.

Cyril watched closely as Thompson processed that information, then turned the screw even more, his voice growing louder. "But your reaction just now ... you know Morgan and Chalmers were murdered. You know it took place in the warehouse. You know, don't you Eddie?"

Thompson looked from Cyril to Barton, but he wasn't helping him, then back to Cyril. Nervously playing with his hands, head down, he started to mumble incoherently.

Cyril adopted a softer tone. "You're not a well man Eddie. I can see that. Your record - you've been involved in some scams for the Robinsons, carried the can for them too, I wouldn't wonder. Probably been well looked after. But this ..." Cyril glanced to Barton then leaned on the table again. "Look, are we right in thinking the Robinson lads weren't actually involved in the murders, not directly anyway?"

Finally, Thompson looked up, eyes moist. "Look Mr Claydon," he said, "I've got six months at most. Cancer. My mum's still alive and in a home in Shadwell. She's eighty-three. I'm all she has. I don't want to go to prison again. I haven't got the time. Can we do a deal?"

71

"He wants a deal?" Sanderson was standing looking out of the window in his office, hands in his pockets. The rain was siling down and he watched people scurrying past on the pavement, umbrellas and plastic macs being used for the first time in months.

"Cyril did a brilliant job, Sir," Barton said.

Sanderson turned and faced him, a surprised expression on his face. "So you rate him now, do you?"

Barton shrugged.

"And you two could work together?"

"He has qualities."

Sanderson decided to leave that line alone. "So what does he want?"

"He's terminally ill and he wants to have immunity from prison."

Sanderson shrugged. "Not sure we can guarantee that."

"But what have we got from forensics so far?" Barton wondered.

"They've lifted prints from door handles and door frames on the second floor as well as off the workbench and roll of plastic on the first floor. I've been on to the bureaux to get them to check against our suspects quickly."

"What about the other samples from those rooms?"

"At best a few days."

"Anything else?" Barton looked desperate.

"They've identified blood spots on the floor of the flower van. Again waiting on results." Sanderson sat down behind his desk. "Although that could be Cyril's. He took a head wound in there."

Barton snapped his fingers. "I've just remembered, the other thing the lab said they were looking at was fibres on the tape that bound the plastic on Morgan's body."

Sanderson's eyes widened. "I didn't know they'd found any."

"There was. They're comparing it to samples of the carpet in the boot of Robinson's Daimler."

"But doesn't Yardley have the same model?"

"A later model, and that has grey carpeting whereas Robinson's has black. And it was black we found on the tape."

"All right, I'll keep up the pressure on the lab. In the meantime, see what you can get from Thompson. Keep any talk of deals circumspect."

* * *

"Okay Eddie, we can't promise anything but, dependant on what you have to tell us, we will do everything we can to help you." Cyril spoke quietly to the man sitting opposite him. Barton was alongside, happy for him to resume his relationship with the Robinsons' driver.

"How do I know I can trust you?" Thompson asked.

"You have my word, as someone who served in the last war and who places great importance on doing things right," Cyril assured him. "But it's your decision."

Thompson hesitated for a second or two, looking at Cyril before leaning forward, placing both arms on the table. "All right, but I'm trusting that you'll keep me out of this as much as you can."

Cyril nodded and flipped open his notebook.

"The first bloke you mentioned, Morgan, we had nothing to do with him. That idiot Yardley who owned the building, he'd shot him. Marshall reckoned he could make him disappear."

"How was that?"

"Same way he got rid of the other two."

"Two?" Cyril paused writing, eyebrows raised.

"The other one you mentioned, Chalmers was it? I think he was one, then there was another before that, but I've no idea who." Thompson became defensive. "It's only what I heard."

"When did this happen exactly?" Cyril picked up his pencil.

Thompson puffed out his cheeks. "Not too sure on that. But this last one, Morgan, was a couple of days before the plane crashed. Marshall used a guy who'd fly the body out over the sea and dump it."

Cyril looked up at the man. "Okay Eddie, let's go back to the beginning of how you became involved with the Robinsons and Marshall."

Thompson began to tell how Frank Robinson, Victor and David's father, had given him work before the war and had looked out for him since. He'd been brought up in the same street in East London and his mother knew Frank's wife. Since the war, Thompson had driven for Frank and when his sons became involved in the 'business', Thompson would drive for them too. Mention of 'business' brought a snigger from Barton.

Thompson looked sharply at him but carried on undaunted. Robinson senior had had a caravan on the holiday park since the early sixties where he used to bring the family. The static the boys used was the third that Frank had owned in Clacton.

Barton interrupted. "Look, this trip down memory lane is all well and good ..."

"This is important background," Cyril said turning to Barton. "Let's just hear what Eddie has to tell us." He returned his attention to Thompson. "Perhaps we can concentrate on the events of this year though," he encouraged.

"As I said, I used to drive for Mr Robinson but Victor and David wanted me to drive them down here, sort of posing with the birds, if you know what I mean. Frank wanted me to keep an eye on them too."

"And where did you stay?"

"I'd get a B & B in Clacton."

"So when did Tommy Marshall come on the scene?"

"It was Victor who knew him. He said he was useful muscle. He began coming down with them at Easter. He'd stayed in the same B & B as me at first but then started finding his own. He used to go round the pubs and clubs and put himself about a bit. I suppose that's when it all started."

Thompson then went on to tell the story of how Marshall met a guy who was organising poker games. Marshall was a bit of a gambler and he got drawn in. It didn't take him long to realise the game was crooked. He wasn't standing for it and he got a bit heavy with this character. That was when Marshall learned about another punter who owed the man a sizeable sum but had a connection with access to light aircraft. That got Marshall's brain working. "I didn't trust him, but he mentioned to Victor that it could be useful and he had an idea how," Thompson said.

"So Victor Robinson became involved?" Cyril asked.

"No, no. Not so far as I know." Another defensive reaction from the man.

"Look, Thompson," Barton snapped. "Don't piss us about! Remember what we told you about being straight with us."

"I am, honest," Thompson responded. "The only definite times I knew of were these last two jobs and they were all Marshall's."

Cyril flicked over his notes. "This last job, the one that took place on the morning of the plane crash …"

Thompson nodded

"Did you help transport the body to the airstrip?"

"We used Victor's Daimler. He was down here for the week, him and David with a couple of tarts. So I knew I could have the use of it for a few days, unless he called me to drive them somewhere."

"Tell us about that."

"Tommy spoke to me the day before and said he had a job for me. I had to collect him about three in the morning and drive him to the warehouse. Yardley let us in. He opened the double doors. I had to back the car in and he closed them behind me. The flower van was sitting there, the chiller on. I drew up close to it and Yardley opened the back of the van. The two of them pulled out this bundle and loaded it into the boot. I had nothing to do with that. I'm not fit enough for any exertion."

"But you knew what it was?"

Thompson nodded. "Tommy told me."

"Then you drove to the airstrip?"

"We had to sit there for about twenty minutes until this other bloke in a van turns up to open the gate. We followed him up the track and Tommy and this other bloke gets the bundle out of the boot and takes it over to one of the planes."

"And you're telling me all this happened without Victor and David Robinson's knowledge?"

"No. Tommy said it was just a little job on the side."

Cyril looked over to Barton then back again. "You're honestly asking me to believe that?"

"That time of the day, the boys were bunked up with their lady friends. Tommy said we shouldn't say anything. He was doing it for a few quid from Yardley." Thompson began squirming in his chair. "Look Mr Claydon, can we stop for a minute? I really need a pee."

"No you bloody can't," Barton retorted.

"I can't help it, I've a weak bladder with all my treatment."

"I'll get the constable to take you Eddie," Cyril said. "I think we could all do with a break."

*　*　*

"I still think we should have made the little bastard suffer," Barton said.

They were in Sanderson's office reporting progress.

Cyril shook his head. "He's singing like a canary. It does no harm to give him a little bit of a break."

Barton turned to the DCI. "You said that the Robinson's solicitor had been to see him, didn't you Sir?"

"He did."

"Bloody obvious then," Barton went on, "He'll have told him to stick Marshall in the frame for the lot, leave precious Victor and David out of it and the old man'll look after him for however long he's got. But we'll still get the bastard on aiding and abetting though."

Sanderson was leaning back in his chair, right foot resting on his left knee. "Maybe so, but the problem is, we've got nothing that'll stand up against the Robinson boys."

"What have we actually got?" Barton despaired.

Sanderson sprang forward and shuffled through some papers on his desk. "I've been back onto the lab and tried to gee them up a bit." He pulled one sheet free and scanned it. "They now tell me there are three distinct blood groups from the workbench, two of which correspond with blood spatter in the upper floor rooms. We know Morgan was A positive and I'm waiting for word of what group Chalmers was, but that might only narrow down the possibilities."

"For what it's worth, I'm common as muck," Cyril said. "O positive."

"Okay, thanks, I'll let them know." Sanderson made a note. "But the other thing was they found two different blood groups in the flower van. Again, we'll see what actual group they can identify."

"All takes so bloody long though," Barton complained.

"But in the meantime, we get as much information from Thompson as we can. Hopefully, the forensics will bear out what he's telling us. And if Marshall is involved as much as we think, the case against him will strengthen." Sanderson stood up. "Also, we need to interview Adam Fletcher again; put some pressure on him to tell us everything."

"Will do." Barton headed for the door. "Come on then," he said to Cyril, "Let's get stuck in to Thompson.

* * *

"Now then Eddie, let's hear about the body *before* Jimmy Morgan," Cyril prompted once he and Barton were seated opposite Thompson in the interview room to resume questioning.

"I really don't know for sure who it was but that was a month ago and more now."

"We believe he was disposed of on Friday 6th August."

"Sounds about right."

"Now we also believe that was the body of Dougie Chalmers."

"If you say so."

"And that name meant something to you when we mentioned him earlier, didn't it?"

Thompson nodded. "He was the bloke that ran the poker games that Tommy got involved with."

"What happened with him then?"

"I don't know exactly. All I know is that Tommy tells me to pick him up early hours one morning and run him over to the warehouse. Only this time he had a key to get us in."

"Just the two of you on this occasion?"

"Yes."

"That means you'd have had to have helped, right?"

"No. Tommy disappeared upstairs. Next thing, he's struggling back down with this big package wrapped in black plastic over his shoulder in a sort of fireman's lift."

"But you knew it was a body though?"

Thompson nodded. "I guessed so. And then as he put it in the boot, it snagged on the boot lock. I could see the fingers of a hand. Tommy dashed back upstairs and came back with some tape to seal it up again."

"What happened next?"

"He got in and told me to drive to the airstrip."

"And the same pilot met you?"

"Yes, I think so."

"Again it was just the two of you in the car?"

"And the stiff, yeah."

"You mentioned there were two other corpses, apart from Morgan. What can you tell us about the first one?"

"Similar to that one I've just told you about - Chalmers."

Cyril looked over to Barton then back to Thompson. "Just you and Marshall? No help from Victor or David?"

"No."

"And Marshall brings the body down to the car from the upper floor in the warehouse?"

"Yeah."

"I think you're protecting someone else. Either Victor or David or another person you haven't told us about."

"No, why would I do that?"

"Loyalty Eddie. You see, although Tommy Marshall is quite a well-built man, I don't think he'd be capable of bringing a dead weight, because that's what a corpse is, down those stairs in that warehouse. Especially Dougie Chalmers who was a big man, probably sixteen stones. He'd have needed help."

"Well it wasn't me. I only drove the car."

"But there was someone else though?"

"Look, I've told you all I know. Marshall organised the disposal of those packages, on his own, and the Robinsons had no knowledge of any of it. And that's all I'm prepared to say." Purposefully, Thompson folded his arms over his chest.

72

"Well now Tommy," Barton began, "I was just wondering if your memory might have improved since we last spoke, not to mention your attitude."

Marshall shrugged. "What do you want to know?"

"The shotgun we found in the car. What can you tell me about it?"

"I'm looking after it for a mate."

"Which mate?"

"Can't remember."

"Not Victor or David Robinson?"

"No."

"But it was you who hid it behind the sills?"

Another shrug. "What of it?"

"Dougie Chalmers. I believe you do know him."

"Is that a question?"

Barton had reached tipping point. He stood up sharply and leaned close to Marshall over the table.

Marshall shied backwards.

Barton spoke, his voice rising with every word, "If you're going to persist in trying to take the piss, I'm going to send DS Claydon here from the room and I'll bring in a couple of PCs who play rugby regularly and like nothing better than taking their frustrations out on some obnoxious bastard who thinks he can waste my fucking time!"

Cyril stood alongside Barton. "I don't think the DI is joking, Mr Marshall."

Barton reached a crescendo, "Do I make myself clear? You useless piece of shit!"

Marshall looked away then down to the floor. He gave a nervous cough then responded, "Alright gents, no need to get carried away." He composed himself and finally answered the original question. "Dougie Chalmers made the mistake of trying to rob me blind in a card game. I wasn't having that; not from some thick bastard from north of Hadrian's Wall."

Barton slowly resumed his seat. "So you topped him."

"It was self-defence. He tried to attack me."

"Where?"

"At the warehouse."

"What was he doing there?"

"I told him it would be a good venue for a card game in Colchester. Quiet area after dark."

Barton had a smirk on his face. "A good venue for a card game. Let me guess – on the top floor; one of the rooms."

"That's right."

"And you just happened to have your sawn-off when he 'attacked' you."

"Yeah."

"What a load of old bollocks. You lured him there and blasted his fucking head off in that second room along. Tell me I'm wrong?"

Marshall said nothing, just looked down onto his lap.

"What did you do with the body?"

"You know what happened to it."

"I want you to tell me."

"I wrapped it in plastic then organised for it to be dumped at sea."

"All on your own?"

"Yeah … well no. I mean Eddie drove the body in the back of the Daimler, and that pilot organised the plane."

"The one who owed money to Chalmers?"

Marshall furrowed his brows. "No, that was his brother."

"The one you assaulted last week? The postman?"

"If you say so."

"And you were solely responsible for getting the body from the second floor in the warehouse down to the car on the ground?"

"Yep."

For the first time, Barton turned to Cyril. "How heavy was Mr Chalmers, do you think, DS Claydon?"

Cyril stroked his moustache. "Easily sixteen stones, I would think."

Barton focussed on Marshall. "And you could carry that dead weight on your own?"

The man grinned. "I'm strong," he said. "Used to box in my youth."

"And you managed to wrap it? All on your own too?"

"That's right."

"Tell me about the victim before Chalmers."

Marshall put on a puzzled expression. "No idea."

"We understand there was an earlier corpse you helped to get rid of."

He leaned forward onto the table. "Have you found one?"

Barton just held his stare.

"No, I didn't think so." Marshall relaxed back in the chair.

Cyril thought Barton was about to react but he just slowly stood up and told Marshall he would be charged with the murder of Douglas Chalmers and obstruction of justice with regards to the disposal of Chalmers' body and the attempted disposal of James Morgan.

73
Two Weeks Later
Friday 24th September

The endless hot summer days seemed a distant memory when Cyril and Barton sat in Sanderson's office discussing the latest developments of the warehouse cases.

"He was allowed out yesterday for his mum's funeral," Sanderson said. He was referring to Eddie Thompson who was being held on remand in Chelmsford. "DCI Holt managed to have a quiet word with him."

"Did he get anything out of him?" Barton asked.

"Only what we already suspected. The charming Robinsons were involved but there's no way Thompson would ever testify to that."

"What about the first victim, the one we have no trace of?" Cyril joined in.

"Some little low-life that irritated Robinson senior up in London," Sanderson reported. "He never knew who he was but there are a number of 'missing persons' it could be. Marshall was trying to ingratiate himself with Robinson senior by offering to dispose. Apparently bridge sites are becoming rarer these days in which to bury a corpse."

Barton snorted. "At least Marshall has pleaded guilty."

"But Frank Robinson's influences have spread far and wide," Sanderson mused. "He could make damn sure Marshall would get a rough ride inside if he tried to implicate his precious sons in all this. As it is, he'll probably be well looked after."

"He won't be bothering us for a long time," Cyril said. "And Adam Fletcher's statement helps too, so an aggravated assault charge to add to the mix."

"Well that and the forensic evidence," Barton added. "Fingerprints taken from the door frames on the top floor rooms and on the workbench matching Marshall; blood types AB positive which matches Morgan and only 3% of the population which was also picked up in the flower van, along with O positive, which is probably yours, Cyril. Then there were the fibre and hair samples from the wall up there which were a match for Chalmers clothes and the remains we found. All circumstantial in themselves but reinforcing what we were told."

"Any word from Lennie King?" Cyril asked.

"DCI Holt said he was up north somewhere, keeping his head down."

"Let's hope it's enough," Cyril said. "But I can't help feeling a bit for Yardley. He thinks he has good friends in Holland and they tuck him up with false diamonds."

Sanderson looked grim. "That was what Viney was saying this morning ..." He thought back to the conversation he'd had with the Chief Super an hour or so earlier.

Viney had laughed and said, 'So he was stitched up by his own so-called Dutch mates.'

Sanderson had nodded. 'And all this for nothing,' he'd said.

'Ironic really.'

'Ironic?' Sanderson's anger had risen. 'I tell you what's ironic. You tell Walter Yardley that Jimmy Morgan grassed on his operation and he dies. For what? A load of paste.'

Viney hadn't responded.

"... I don't mean about feeling sorry for him but the fact that he'd been duped."

The three were silent for a second before Sanderson snapped back to normal. "But listen Cyril, what are you going to do?" he asked.

"What about?" Cyril played dumb.

"Don't give me that. You were talking about retiring at the end of the year. You can't still be thinking you will?"

Cyril shrugged.

"Come on you old bugger," Barton joined in. "You know you've loved these past few weeks back in CID. Come and be my DS permanently?"

Cyril was surprised. "I'm sure your old mate Danny Flynn would be delighted."

"Danny'll be taken care of," Sanderson said, "Don't worry about him."

"I'll think about it," Cyril said.

"Don't leave it too long."

"Anyway," Barton put in. "Are you ever going to get round to taking that secretary out from downstairs?"

"How did …?"

The DI smirked. "Wouldn't be much of a detective if I hadn't noticed that."

"Well … tonight actually."

Barton held up a hand. "Too much information. Go get yourself ponced up ready then." A huge smile spread over his face.

"Go on, Cyril," Sanderson said. "Come back and see me on Monday morning."

74

The sun had come out for the first time in what seemed like ages, drying the road as Cyril drove them down the grade into the small town of Dedham. At long last he and Cathy had finally met up outside of work.

Cyril felt a mix of nervous excitement; a feeling he hadn't experienced in years. He'd picked her up from her house. He loved the dress she'd chosen, she looked beautiful.

He found a parking space outside the church in the main street and leapt out to open the door for her.

She laughed. "Why, thank you sir."

As he locked up she studied the tall tower of the parish church. "Have you ever been inside?" she asked.

"Yes. I love that building." Cyril moved beside her. "There are some interesting plaques on the walls."

"I know. One of my favourites is the lady who died after accidently swallowing a pin."

"And did you notice there were two years mentioned?"

She looked at him, puzzled. "I did, and I often wondered about that."

"They'd changed from the Julian to Gregorian calendars in 1742 and the years changed so you often find both dates given."

"See, I knew you'd be good on the pub quiz."

He smiled. "Sorry," he said. "Do you want to go in?"

"Let's walk down to the river. Make the most of the last of the sun for today."

They crossed over the road and turned down Mill Lane.

"I thought we might go in there later," Cyril said, indicating the Marlborough Head pub, a beautiful 17th Century building on the corner.

"Looks lovely."

About half a mile down the road they passed the old mill and were standing on the bridge over the River Stour. The river formed the boundary between Essex and Suffolk and they stared downstream over the fields in the direction of Flatford Mill.

"This is lovely," she said.

Before he could stop himself, Cyril had blurted out, "Maureen loved it here." He stopped, embarrassed by what he'd said. "Sorry, I didn't mean to …"

"It's okay Cyril. I know you were married for a long time. It's natural you want to remember."

"But here I am, the first time we've managed to make it out and I'm talking about …"

She put a hand on his arm. "Don't worry about it. I do understand."

After a few minutes, they turned back and made for the pub.

They sat on a bench seat at a table by a window looking out onto Mill Lane; Cyril with a pint of bitter and Cathy with a gin and tonic.

Cyril rubbed his face. "It's been a roller-coaster these past few weeks, Cathy," he said.

"I know. I'm processing the paperwork for when it all goes to court." She took a sip of her drink and paused before asking, "Well come on Mr Claydon, what are your plans now?"

"I must admit, when I started thinking about things, retirement wasn't particularly appealing. I suppose I was just drifting along towards it. It was only when young Sam mentioned it on the morning of the plane crash that I started to realise that I really wasn't ready for it."

Cathy sat back on the bench seat, saying nothing, allowing Cyril to talk.

"And over these past few weeks I've actually enjoyed using my brain, thinking on my feet and yes, the battles with Barton."

"Ignorant man," Cathy put in.

"I think a lot of his brusque ways are just for show. He needs a restraining hand now and then, but overall, he's a good detective."

"And are you that restraining hand?"

Cyril gave a laugh. "We've certainly had our ups and downs since Sanderson brought me into CID. But he did save my life, I'm sure. I don't think I'd have survived the journey in that van with the chiller on. And young Sam Woodbridge too." He looked at Cathy. "I suppose these past weeks have given me a purpose I felt I'd lost."

"So are you staying on?"

"Sanderson and Barton want me to."

"Dick Barton as well? Blimey."

"Don't sound so surprised."

"And are you? Staying on, I mean."

He smiled at her. "Never in any doubt."

She leaned over and kissed his cheek. "I'm glad. Have you told them?"

"Not yet," he said, taking her hand. "I'll tell them on Monday; make them sweat a bit."

THE END